Initially a Frercy changed careers to computer programming before the happy demands of marriage and motherhood. Very much a people person, and always interested in relationships, she finds the world of romance fiction a thrilling one, and the challenge of creating her own cast of characters very addictive.

CHAPTER ONE

'It's like a great big sail, Mama,' Theo said in awe, staring up at the most famous building in Dubai—Burj Al Arab, the only seven-star hotel in the world.

Tina Savalas smiled at her beautiful five-year-old son. 'Yes, it's meant to look like that.'

Built on a man-made island surrounded by the sea, the huge white glittering structure had all the glorious elegance of a sail billowed by the wind. Tina was looking forward to seeing as much of its interior as she could. Her sister, Cassandra, had declared it absolutely fabulous, a must-see on their two-day stopover before flying on to Athens.

Actually staying in the hotel was way too expensive—thousands of dollars a night—which was fine for the super-rich to whom the cost was totally irrelevant. People like Theo's father. No doubt *he* had occupied one of the luxury suites with butler on his way back to Greece from Australia, having put his *charming episode* with her behind him.

Tina shut down on the bitter thought. Being left pregnant by Ari Zavros was her own stupid fault. She'd been a completely blind naive fool to have believed he was as much in love with her as she was with him. Sheer fantasy land. Besides, how could she regret having Theo? He was the most adorable little boy, and from time to time, knowing Ari was missing out on his son gave her considerable secret satisfaction.

Their taxi stopped at the checkpoint gates which prevented anyone but paying guests from proceeding to the hotel. Her mother produced the necessary paperwork, showing confirmation that they had booked for the early afternoon tea session. Even that was costing them one hundred and seventy dollars each, but they had decided it was a once-in-a-lifetime experience they should indulge in.

The security man waved them on and the taxi drove slowly over the bridge which led to the hotel entrance, allowing them time to take in the whole amazing setting.

'Look, Mama, a camel!' Theo cried, delighted at recognising the animal standing on a side lawn.

'Yes, but not a real one, Theo. It's a statue.'

'Can I sit on it?'

'We'll ask if you can, but later, when we're leaving.'

'And take a photo of me on it so I can show my friends,' he pressed eagerly.

'I'm sure we'll have plenty of great photos to show from this trip,' Tina assured him.

They alighted from the taxi and were welcomed into the grand lobby of the hotel which was so incredibly opulent, photographs couldn't possibly capture all of its utter magnificence. They simply stood and stared upwards at the huge gold columns supporting the first few tiers of inner balconies of too many floors to count, the rows of their scalloped ceilings graduating from midnight-blue to aqua and green and gold at the top with lots of little spotlights embedded in them, twinkling like stars.

When they finally lowered their heads, right in front of them and dividing two sets of escalators, was a wonderful cascade of dancing fountains, each level repeating the same range of colours in the tower of ceilings. The escalators were flanked by side-walls which were gigantic aquariums where hosts of gorgeous tropical fish darted and glided around the underwater rocks and foliage.

'Oh, look at the fish, Mama!' Theo cried, instantly entranced by them.

'This truly is amazing,' Tina's mother murmured in awe. 'Your father always liked the architecture of the old world. He thought nothing could beat the palaces and the cathedrals that were built in the past, but this is absolutely splendid in its own way. I wish he was here to see it.'

He had died a year ago and her mother still wore black in mourning. Tina missed him, too. Despite his disappointment in her—getting pregnant to a man who was not interested in partnering her for life—he had given her the support she'd needed and been a marvellous grandfather to Theo, proud that she'd named her son after him.

It was a terrible shame that he hadn't lived long enough to see Cassandra married. Her older sister had done everything right; made a success of her modelling career without the slightest taint of scandal in her private life, fell in love with a Greek photographer—the *right* nationality—who wanted their wedding to take place on Santorini, the most romantic Greek island of all. He would have been bursting with pride, walking Cassandra down the aisle next week, his *good* girl.

But at least the *bad* girl had given him the pleasure of having a little boy in the family. Having only two daughters and no son had been another disappointment to her father. Tina told herself she had made up for her *mistake* with Theo. And she'd been on hand to take over the management of his restaurant, doing everything *his* way when he'd become too ill to do it all himself. He'd called her a *good girl* then.

Yet while Tina thought she had redeemed herself in her father's eyes, she didn't feel good inside. Not since Ari Zavros had taken all that she was and walked away from her as though she was nothing. The sense of being totally crushed had never gone away. Theo held her together. He made life worth living. And there were things to enjoy, like this hotel with all its splendours.

There was another glorious fountain at the top of the escalator. They were escorted down a corridor to the elevator which would whiz them up to the SkyView Bar on the twenty-seventh floor. They walked over a large circle of mosaic tiles, a blazing sun at its centre, over a carpet shaped like a fish in red and gold. Her mother pointed out vases of tightly clustered red roses, dozens of them in each perfect pompom-like arrangement. The doors of the elevator were patterned in blue and gold—everything unbelievably rich.

On arriving in the shimmering gold lobby of the bar, they were welcomed again and escorted into the dining area where the decor was a stunning blue and green, the ceiling designed like waves with white crests. They were seated in comfortable armchairs at a table by a window which gave a fantastic view of the city of Dubai and the man-made island of Palm Jumeirah where the very wealthy owned mansions with sand and sea frontage.

A whole world away from her life in every sense, Tina thought, but she was having a little taste of it today, smiling at the waiter who handed them a menu listing dozens of varieties of tea from which they could choose, as many different ones as they liked to try throughout the afternoon. He poured them glasses of champagne to go with their first course which was a mix of fresh berries with cream. Tina didn't know how she was going to get through all the marvellous food listed—probably not—but she was determined on enjoying all she could.

Her mother was smiling.

Theo was wide-eyed at the view.

This was a good day.

Ari Zavros was bored. It had been a mistake to invite Felicity Fullbright on this trip to Dubai with him, though it had certainly proved he couldn't bear to have her as a full-time partner. She had a habit of notching up experiences as though she had a bucket list that had to be filled. Like having to do afternoon tea at the Burj Al Arab hotel.

'I've done afternoon tea at The Ritz and The Dorchester in London, at the Waldorf Astoria in New York, and at The Empress on Vancouver Island. I can't miss out on this one, Ari,' she had insisted. 'The sheikhs are mostly educated in England, aren't they? They probably do it better than the English.'

No relaxing in between his business talks on the Palm Jumeirah development. They had to visit the indoor ski slope, Atlantis underwater, and of course the gold souks where she had clearly expected him to buy her whatever she fancied. She was not content with just his company and he was sick to death of hers.

The only bright side of Felicity Fullbright was she did shut up in bed where she used her mouth in many pleasurable ways. Which had swayed him into asking her to accompany him on this trip. However, the hope that she might be compatible with him on other grounds was now comprehensively smashed. The good did not balance out the bad and he'd be glad to be rid of her tomorrow.

Once they flew into Athens he would pack her off back to London. No way was he going to invite her to his cousin's wedding on Santorini. His father could rant and rave as much as he liked about its being time for Ari to shed his bachelor life. Marriage to the Fullbright heiress was not going to happen.

There had to be someone somewhere he could tolerate as his wife. He just had to keep looking and assessing whether a marriage would work well enough. His father was right. It *was* time to start his own family. He did want children, always enjoying the time he spent with his nephews. However, finding the right woman to partner him in parenthood was not proving easy.

Being head over heels in love like his cousin, George, was not a requirement. In fact, having been scorched by totally mindless passion in his youth, Ari had never wanted to feel so *possessed* by a woman again. He had a cast-iron shield up against being sucked into any blindly driven emotional involvement. A relationship either satisfied him on enough levels to be happily viable or it didn't—a matter of completely rational judgement.

His *dissatisfaction* with Felicity was growing by the minute. Right now she was testing his patience, taking millions of photographs of the inside of the hotel. It wasn't enough to simply look and enjoy, share the visual pleasure of it with him. Using the camera to the nth degree was more important, taking pictures that she would sift through endlessly and discard most of them. Another habit he hated. He liked to live in the moment.

Finally, *finally,* they got in the elevator and within minutes were being led to their window table in the SkyView Bar. But did Felicity sit down and enjoy the view? No, the situation wasn't perfect for her.

'Ari, I don't like this table,' she whispered, grasping his arm to stop him from sitting down.

'What's wrong with it?' he asked tersely, barely containing his exasperation with her constant self-centred demands.

She nodded and rolled her eyes, indicating the next

table along. 'I don't want to be next to a child. He'll probably play up and spoil our time here.'

Ari looked at the small family group that Felicity didn't like. A young boy—five or six years old—stood at the window, staring down at the wave-shaped Jumeirah Beach Hotel. Seated beside the child on one side was a very handsome woman—marvellous facial bones like Sophia Loren's—dark wavy hair unashamedly going grey, probably the boy's grandmother. On the other side with her back turned to him was another woman, black hair cropped short in a modern style, undoubtedly younger, a slimmer figure, and almost certainly the boy's mother.

'He won't spoil the food or the tea, Felicity, and if you haven't noticed, all the other tables are taken.'

They'd been late arriving, even later because of feeding her camera in the lobby. Having to wait for Felicity to be satisfied with whatever she wanted was testing his temper to an almost intolerable level.

She placed a pleading hand on his arm, her big blue eyes promising a reward if he indulged her. 'But I'm sure if you ask, something better could be arranged.'

'I won't put other people out,' he said, giving her a hard, quelling look. 'Just sit down, Felicity. Enjoy being here.'

She pouted, sighed, flicked her long blonde hair over her shoulder in annoyance, and finally sat.

The waiter poured them champagne, handed them menus, chatted briefly about what was on offer, then quickly left them before Felicity could kick up another fuss which would put him in a difficult position.

'Why do they have all those chairs on the beach set out in rows, Yiayia?'

The boy's voice was high and clear and carried, bringing an instant grimace to Felicity's pouty mouth. Ari recognised the accent as Australian, yet the boy had used the Greek word for grandmother, arousing his curiosity.

'The beach belongs to the hotel, Theo, and the chairs are set out for the guests so they will be comfortable,' the older woman answered, her English thick with a Greek accent.

'They don't do that at Bondi,' the boy remarked.

'No. That's because Bondi is a public beach for anyone to use and set up however they like on the sand.'

The boy turned to her, frowning at the explanation. 'Do you mean I couldn't go to that beach down there, Yiayia?'

He was a fine-looking boy, very pleasing features and fairish hair. Oddly enough he reminded Ari of himself as a child.

'Not unless you were staying in the hotel, Theo,' his grandmother replied.

'Then I think Bondi is better,' the boy said conclusively, turning back to the view.

An egalitarian Australian even at this tender age, Ari thought, remembering his own experiences of the people's attitudes in that country.

Felicity huffed and whined, 'We're going to have to listen to his prattle all afternoon. I don't know why people bring children to places like this. They should be left with nannies.'

'Don't you like children, Felicity?' Ari enquired, hoping she would say no, which would comprehensively wipe out any argument his father might give him over his rejection of this marital candidate.

'In their place,' she snapped back at him.

Out of sight, out of mind, was what she meant.

'I think family is important,' he drawled. 'And I have no objection to any family spending time together, any-where.'

Which shut her up, temporarily.

This was going to be a *long* afternoon.

Tina felt the nape of her neck prickling at the sound of the man's voice coming from the table next to theirs. The deep mellifluous tone was an electric reminder of another voice that had seduced her into believing all the sweet things it had said to her, believing they had meant she was more special than any other woman in the world.

It couldn't be Ari, could it?

She was torn by the temptation to look.

Which was utterly, utterly stupid, letting thoughts of him take over her mind when she should be enjoying this wonderfully decadent afternoon tea.

Ari Zavros was out of her life. Well and truly out of it. Six years ago he'd made the parting from her abso-lutely decisive, no coming back to Australia, no inter-est in some future contact. She had been relegated to *a fond memory,* and she certainly didn't want *the fond memory* revived here and now, if by some rotten coin-cidence it was Ari sitting behind her.

It wouldn't be him, anyway.

The odds against it were astronomical.

All the same, it was better not to look, better to keep her back turned to the man behind her. If it was Ari, if he caught her looking and recognised her…it was a stomach-curdling thought. No way was she prepared for a face-to-face meeting with him, especially not with her mother and Theo looking on, becoming involved.

This couldn't happen.

It wouldn't happen.

Her imagination was making mountains out of no more than a tone of voice. Ridiculous! The man was with a woman. She'd heard the plummy English voice complaining about Theo's presence—a really petty complaint because Theo was always well-behaved. She shouldn't waste any attention on them. Her mind fiercely dictated ignoring the couple and concentrating on the pleasure of being here.

She leaned forward, picked up her cup and sipped the wonderfully fragrant *Jasmin Pearls*. They had already eaten a marvellous slice of Beef Wellington served warm with a beetroot puree. On their table now was a stand shaped like the Burj, its four tiers presenting a yummy selection of food on colourful glass plates.

At the top were small sandwiches made with different types of bread—egg, smoked salmon, cream cheese with sun-dried tomatoes, cucumber and cream cheese. Other tiers offered seafood vol-au-vents with prawns, choux pastry chicken with seeded mustard, a beef sandwich, and basil, tomato and bocconcini cheese on squid ink bread. It was impossible to eat everything. Predictably,

Theo zeroed in on the chicken, her mother anything with cheese, and the seafood she loved was all hers.

A waiter came around with a tray offering replenishments but they shook their heads, knowing there was so much more to taste—fruit cake, scones with and without raisins and an assortment of spreads; strawberry and rose petal jam, clotted cream, a strawberry mousse and tangy passionfruit.

Tina refused to let the reminder of Ari Zavros ruin her appetite. There wasn't much conversation going on at the table behind her anyway. Mostly it was the woman talking, carrying on in a snobby way, comparing this afternoon tea to others she'd had in famous hotels. Only the occasional murmur of reply came from the man.

'I'm so glad we stopped in Dubai,' her mother remarked, gazing at the view. 'There's so much amazing, creative architecture in this city. That hotel shaped like a wave just below us, the stunning buildings we passed on the way here. And to think it's all happened in the space of what…thirty years?'

'Something like that,' Tina murmured.

'It shows what can be done in these modern times.'

'With the money to do it,' Tina dryly reminded her.

'Well, at least they have the money. They're not bankrupting the country like the aristocrats did in Europe for their grand palaces in the old days. And all this has to be a drawcard for tourists, bringing money into the country.'

'True.' Tina smiled. 'I'm glad we came here, too. It certainly is amazing.'

Her mother leaned forward and whispered, 'Seated at the next table is an incredibly handsome man. I think he must be a movie star. Take a look, Tina, and see if you recognise him.'

Her stomach instantly cramped. Ari Zavros was an incredibly handsome man. Her mother nodded encouragingly, expecting her to glance around. Hadn't she already decided it couldn't—wouldn't—be him? One quick look would clear this silly fear. *Just do it. Get it over with.*

One quick look...

The shock of seeing the man she'd never expected to see again hit her so hard she barely found wits enough to give her mother a reply.

'I've never seen him in a movie.'

And thank God the turning of her head towards him hadn't caught his attention!

Ari!—still a beautiful lion of a man with his thick mane of wavy honey-brown hair streaked through with golden strands, silky smooth olive skin, his strongly masculine face softened by a beautifully sculptured full-lipped mouth, and made compelling by thickly lashed amber eyes—eyes that Theo had inherited, and thank God her mother hadn't noticed that likeness!

'Well, he must be *someone,*' her mother said in bemusement. 'One of the beautiful people.'

'Don't keep staring at him, Mama,' Tina hissed, everything within her recoiling from any connection with him.

Her mother was totally unabashed. 'I'm just returning the curiosity. He keeps looking at us.'

Why??? screamed through Tina's mind.

Panicky thoughts followed.

Had the Australian accent reminded him of the three months he'd spent there?

He could not have identified her, not from a back view. Her hair had been long and curly when he'd known her.

Did he see a similarity to himself in Theo?

But surely he wouldn't be making a blood connection to himself personally, unless he was in the habit of leaving love-children around the world.

Tina pulled herself up on that dark thought. He had used condoms with her. It was unlikely he would think his safe sex had ever been unsafe. Whatever had drawn his interest…it presented a very real problem to her.

Since he and his companion had arrived late at this afternoon tea, it was almost inevitable that she and Theo and her mother would leave before them and they would have to pass his table on their way out. If he looked straight at her, face-to-face…

He might not remember her. It had been six years ago. She looked different with her hair short. And he'd surely had many women pass through his life in the meantime. But if he did recognise her and stopped her from making a quick escape, forcing a re-acquaintance, introductions…her mind reeled away from all the painful complications that might follow.

She did not want Ari Zavros directly touching her life again. That decision had been made before her pregnancy had to be revealed to her parents. It would have been unbearable to have him questioning an unwelcome paternity or sharing responsibility for Theo on some dutiful basis—constantly in and out of her life, always making her feel bad for having loved him so blindly.

It had been a wretched business, standing firm

against her father's questioning, refusing to track down a man who didn't want her any more, insisting that her child would be better off without any interference from him. Whether that decision had been right or wrong she had never regretted it.

Even recently when Theo had asked why he didn't have a father like his kindergarten friends, she had felt no guilt at telling him that some children only had mothers and that was the way it was for them. She was convinced that Ari could only be a horribly disruptive influence in their lives if, given the chance, he decided to be in them at all.

She didn't want to give him the chance.

It had taken so much determination and hard work to establish the life she and Theo now had, it was imperative to hold onto the status quo. This terrible trick of fate—putting Ari and herself in the same place at the same time with Theo and her mother present—could mess up their lives so badly.

A confrontation *had* to be avoided.

Tina pushed back the sickening waves of panic and fiercely told herself this shouldn't be too difficult. Ari had company. Surely it would be unreasonable of him to leave his tete-a-tete with one woman to re-connect with another. Besides, he might not recognise her anyway. If he did, if he tried to engage her in some awful memory-lane chat, she had to ensure that her mother had already taken herself and Theo out of this possible scenario.

She could manage that.

She had to.

CHAPTER TWO

The rest of afternoon tea took on a nightmarish quality for Tina. It was difficult to focus on the delicacies they were served, even more difficult to appreciate the marvellous range of tastes. Her mind was in a hopelessly scattered state. She felt like Alice in Wonderland at the mad hatter's tea party, with the red queen about to pounce and cut off her head.

Her mother demolished the fig tart and green-tea macaroon. Theo gobbled up the white chocolate cake. She forced herself to eat a caramel slice. They were then presented with another plate of wicked temptations: a strawberry dipped in white chocolate and decorated with a gold leaf, a meringue lemon tart, a passionfruit ball with an oozing liquid centre…more, more, more, and she had to pretend to enjoy it all while her stomach was in knots over Ari's presence behind her.

She smiled at Theo. She smiled at her mother. Her face ached with the effort to keep smiling. She silently cursed Ari Zavros for spoiling what should have been a special experience. The fear that he could spoil a lot more kept jogging through her mind. Finally her mother called enough and suggested they return to the grand lobby and take another leisurely look at everything before leaving.

'Yes, I want to see the fish again, Yiayia,' Theo agreed enthusiastically. 'And sit on the camel.'

Tina knew this was the moment when she had to take control. Every nerve in her body twanged at the vital importance of it. She had already planned what to say. It had to come out naturally, sound sensible. She forced her voice to deliver what was needed.

'I think a toilet visit first might be a good idea. Will you take Theo, Mama? I want to get a few photographs from different windows up here. I'll meet you at the elevator.'

'Of course I'll take him. Come, Theo.'

She stood up and took his hand and they went off happily together. Mission accomplished, Tina thought on a huge wave of relief. Now, if she could get past Ari without him taking any notice of her she was home free. If the worst happened and he chose to intercept her departure, she could deal with the situation on her own.

Having slung her travel bag over her shoulder, she picked up her camera, stood at the window, clicked off a few shots of the view, then, with her heart hammering, she turned, meaning to walk as quickly as she could past the danger table.

Ari Zavros was looking straight at her. She saw the jolt of recognition in his face, felt a jolt of shock run right through her, rooting her feet to the floor, leaving her standing like a mesmerised rabbit caught in headlights.

'Christina…' He spoke her name in a tone of pleasurable surprise, rising from his chair, obviously intent on renewing his *fond memory* of her.

No chance of escape from it. Her feet weren't receiving any messages from her brain which was totally jammed with all the misery this man had given her.

He excused himself from his companion who turned in her chair to give Tina a miffed look—long, silky, blonde hair, big blue eyes, peaches and cream complexion, definitely one of the beautiful people. Another *fond memory* for him, or something more serious this time?

It didn't matter. The only thing that mattered was getting this totally unwelcome encounter over and done with. Ari was approaching her, hands outstretched in charming appeal, his mouth tilting in a wry little smile.

'You've cut your beautiful hair,' he said as though that was a wicked shame.

Never mind the shame he'd left her in.

Her tongue leapt into life. 'I like it better short,' she said tersely, hating the reminder of how he'd enjoyed playing with the long curly tresses, winding it around his fingers, stroking it, kissing it, smelling it.

'What are you doing in Dubai?' he asked, his amber eyes twinkling with interest.

'Having a look at it. Why are you here?' she returned.

He shrugged. 'Business.'

'Mixed with pleasure,' she said dryly, with a nod at the blonde. 'Please…don't let me keep you from her, Ari. After all this time, what is there to say?'

'Only that it feels good to see you again. Even with

your cropped hair,' he replied with one of his megawatt smiles which had once melted her knees.

They stiffened in sheer rebellion. How dared he flirt with her when he was obviously connected to another woman? How dared he flirt with her at all when he'd used her up and left her behind him?

And she hated him saying it felt good to see her again when it made her feel so bad. He had no idea of what he'd done to her and she hated him for that, too. She wanted to smack that smile off his face, wanted to smack him down for having the arrogance to even approach her again with his smarmy charm, but the more dignified course, the *safer* course was simply to dismiss him.

'I'm a different person now to the one you knew,' she said oddly. 'If you'll excuse me, I'm with my mother who'll be waiting for me to catch up with her.'

Her feet obeyed the command to side-step, get moving To her intense frustration, Ari shot out a hand, clutching her arm, halting a swift escape from him. She glared at him, resentment burning deep from the touch of his fingers on her skin, from the power he still had to affect her physically. He was so close she could smell the cologne he used. It made her head swim with memories she didn't want to have.

The amber eyes quizzed hers, as though he didn't understand her cutting him off so abruptly. He wanted to know more. Never mind what she wanted.

'Your mother. And the boy…' he said slowly, obviously considering her family group and what it might mean. 'You're married now? He is your son?'

Tina seethed. That, of course, would be so nice and neat, dismissing the intimacy they had shared as nothing important in her life, just as it hadn't been important to him.

She should say *yes*, have done with it. Let him think she was married and there was no possible place for him in her life. He would shut the door on his *charming episode* with her and let her go. She would be free of him forever.

Do it, do it! her mind screamed.

But her heart was being ripped apart by a violent tumult of emotions.

Another voice in her head was yelling *smack him with the truth!*

This man was Theo's father. She could not bring herself to palm his fatherhood off on anyone else. *He* ought to be faced with it. A savage recklessness streaked through her, obliterating any caring over what might happen next.

'I'm not married,' she slung at him. 'And yes, Theo is my son.'

He frowned.

Single motherhood did not sit so well with him. She was free but not free, tied to a child.

No ties for Ari Zavros.

That thought enraged Tina further. She fired bitter truth straight at him.

'He's also your son.'

It stunned him.

Totally stunned him.

No seductive smile.

No twinkly interest.

Blank shock.

With a sense of fiercely primitive satisfaction, Tina got her feet moving and strode past him, heading for the elevator where she hoped her mother and Theo would be waiting for her. She didn't think Ari would follow her. Not only had she cut his feet out from under him, but he was with another woman and it was highly unlikely that he'd want to face her with the complication of an illegitimate son.

Though a fast getaway from this hotel was definitely needed. No loitering in the lobby. She'd tell her mother she didn't feel well—too much rich food. It was true enough anyway. Her stomach was churning and she felt like throwing up.

She shouldn't have told Ari he was Theo's father. She hadn't counted on how much he could still get to her—his eyes, his touch, the whole insidious charisma of his close presence. Hopefully telling his wouldn't make any difference. For a start, he wouldn't want to believe her. Men like him usually denied paternity claims. Not that she would ever make any official claim on him. All the same, it had been stupid of her to throw the truth in his face and give herself this panic attack, stupid and reckless to have opened a door for him into her life again when she wanted him out, out, out!

Please, God, let him not follow up on it.

Let him shrug it off as a put-down line.

Let him just go on with his life and leave her alone to go on with hers.

That boy…his son? *His* son?

Ari snapped out of the wave of shock rolling through

his mind, swung on his heel, and stared after the woman who had just declared herself the mother of his child. Christina Savalas wasn't waiting around to capitalise on her claim. Having delivered her bombshell she was fast making an exit from any fall-out.

Was it true?

He quickly calculated precisely *when* he had been in Australia. It was six years ago. The boy's age would approximately fit that time-frame. He needed to know the actual birth date to be sure if it was possible. That could be checked. The name was Theo. Theo Savalas. Who looked very like himself as a child!

A chill ran down Ari's spine. If Theo was his, it meant he had left Christina pregnant, abandoned a pregnant woman, left her to bring up his child alone. But how could that happen when he was always careful to sheath himself against such a consequence? Not once had he ever failed to use protection. Had there been a slip-up with her, one that he didn't remember?

He did remember she'd been an innocent. Unexpectedly and delightfully so. He hadn't felt guilty about taking her virginity. Desire had been mutual and he'd given her pleasure—a good start to her sexual life, which he'd reasoned would become quite active as time went by. Any man would see her as desirable and it was only natural that she would be attracted to some of them.

But if he had left her pregnant... That would have messed up her career, messed up her life—reason enough for those extremely expressive dark eyes of hers to shoot black bolts of hatred and contempt at him with her punishing exit line.

Impossible to ignore what she'd said. He had to check it out. If the boy was his son… Why hadn't Christina told him about his existence before this? Why go it alone all these years? Why hit him with it now? There was a hell of a lot of questions to be considered.

'Ari…'

His teeth automatically gritted. He hated that whiny tone in Felicity's voice.

'What are you standing there for? She's gone.'

Gone but not forgotten.

'I was remembering my time in Australia, which was where I'd met Christina,' he said, forcing himself to return to his chair and be reasonably civil to the woman he had invited to be his companion.

'What were you doing in Australia?'

'Checking out the wine industry there. Seeing if any improvements could be made to the Santorini operation.'

'Was this Christina connected to the wine industry?'

The tone had changed to a snipe.

He shrugged. 'Not really. She was part of an advertising drive for the Jacob's Creek label.'

One eyebrow arched in knowing mockery. 'A model.'

'She was then.'

'And you had fun with her.'

He grimaced at her dig, which he found extremely distasteful in the circumstances. 'Ancient history, Felicity. I was simply surprised to see her here in Dubai.'

'Well, she's loaded down with a child now,' she said with snide satisfaction. 'No fun at all.'

'I can't imagine it is much fun, being a single mother,' he said, barely containing a wave of anger at Felicity's opinion.

'Oh, I don't know. Quite a few movie stars have chosen that route and they seem to revel in it.'

Ari wanted this conversation finished. He heaved a sigh, then mockingly drawled, 'What do I know? I'm a man.'

Felicity laughed, leaned over and stroked his thigh. 'And a gorgeous one, darling. Which is why I don't like you straying, even for a minute.'

The urge to stray to Christina Savalas had been instant.

He'd had his surfeit of self-centred women like Felicity Fullbright and the flash of memory—a sweet, charming time—had compelled him out of his seat. But it wasn't the same Christina he'd known. How could it be, given the passage of years? A different person, she'd said. He would need to get to know her again if she was the mother of his child.

He would track her down in the very near future. Obviously she was on a tourist trip with her mother and would be on the move for a few weeks. Best to wait until she was back on home ground. In the meantime, he had to sever any further involvement with Felicity, attend his cousin's wedding, then free himself up to pursue the big question.

Was Theo Savalas his son?

If the answer was a definitive yes, changes to his life had to be made.

And Christina Savalas would have to come to some accommodation with him, whether she liked it or not.

A father had rights to his child, and Ari had no qualms about enforcing them.

Family was family.

CHAPTER THREE

TINA felt continually tense for the rest of their short stay in Dubai, knowing Ari Zavros was in the same city. Although she didn't think he would pursue the paternity issue, and a second accidental encounter with him was unlikely, she only felt safe on the red tour bus in between its stops at the various points of interest; the gold souks, the spice markets, the shopping centres. It was a huge relief to board their flight to Athens on the third day, not having had any further contact with him.

They were met at the airport by Uncle Dimitri, her father's older brother. After a brief stop to check in at their hotel, he took them on to his restaurant which was sited just below the Acropolis and where all their Greek relatives had gathered to welcome them home. It wasn't home to Tina or Theo, both of whom had been born in Australia, but it was interesting to meet her mother's and father's families and it was a very festive get-together.

Her mother revelled in the company and Theo was a hit—*such a beautiful grandchild*—but Tina couldn't help feeling like an outsider. The women tended to talk about her in the third person, as though she wasn't there at all.

'We must find a husband for your daughter, Helen.'

'Why did she cut her hair? Men like long hair.'

'She is obviously a good mother. That is important.'

'And if she is used to helping in a restaurant...'

Not helping, *managing,* Tina silently corrected, observing how Uncle Dimitri was managing his. He was constantly on watch, signalling waiters to wherever service was required. All the patrons were treated to a plate of sliced watermelon at the end of their meals—on the house—a nice touch for long hot evenings. People left happy, which meant return visits and good word-of-mouth. It was something she could copy at home.

Most of the tables were out on the sidewalk, under trees or umbrellas. Herbs were grown in pots, their aromas adding to the pleasant ambience. The food was relatively simple, the salads very good. She particularly liked the olive oil, honey and balsamic vinegar dressing—a combination she would use in future. It was easy to relax and have a taste of Athens.

There'd been a message from Cassandra at the hotel, saying she and her fiancé would join them at the restaurant, and Tina kept looking for their arrival, eager to meet up with her sister again. Cass had brought George home to Sydney with her six months ago, but had been working a heavy international schedule ever since. They had just flown in from London and were spending one night in Athens before moving on to the island of Patmos where George's family lived.

'Here they come!' her mother cried, seeing them first.

Tina looked.

And froze in horror.

There was her beautiful sister, her face aglow with happy excitement, looking every inch the supermodel she had become.

Hugging her to his side was George Carasso, grinning with pride in his bride-to-be.

Next to him strolled Ari Zavros.

Her mother turned to her. 'Tina, isn't that the man we saw...'

She heard the words but couldn't answer. Bad enough to find herself confronted by him again. It was much, much worse with him knowing about Theo!

People were on their feet, greeting, welcoming, hugging and kissing. Ari was introduced as George's cousin who was to be his best man at the wedding. *His best man!* And she was Cass's only bridesmaid! The nightmare she had made for herself was getting more torturous by the second and there was no end to it any time soon. It was going to be impossible to enjoy her sister's wedding. She would have to suffer through being Ari's partner at the ceremony and the reception.

If she hadn't opened her mouth in Dubai and let her secret out, she might have managed to skate over their past involvement. There was little hope of that now. No hope at all, given the look Ari Zavros had just turned her way, a dangerously simmering challenge in the riveting amber eyes.

'And this is your sister?' he prompted Cass, who immediately obliged with the formal introduction.

'Yes. Tina! Oh, it's so good to see you again!' she bubbled, dodging around the table to give her a hug. 'George and I are staying in Ari's apartment tonight and when we told him we were meeting up with you, he insisted on coming with us so you won't be strangers to each other at the wedding.'

Strangers!

He hadn't let the cat out of the bag.

Tina fiercely hoped it suited him not to.

Cass swooped on Theo, lifting him up in her arms and turning to show him off to Ari. 'And this is my nephew, Theo, who is going to be our page boy.'

Ari smiled at him. 'Your Aunty Cassandra told me it's your birthday this week.'

He'd been checking, Tina thought grimly.

Theo held up his hand with fingers and thumb spread. 'Five,' he announced proudly.

'It's my birthday this month, too,' Ari said. 'That makes us both Leos.'

'No. I'm Theo, not Leo.'

Everyone laughed at the correction.

'He didn't mean to get your name wrong, darling,' Cass explained. 'We're all born under star signs and the star sign for your birthday is Leo. Which means a lion. And you have amber eyes, just like a lion.'

Theo pointed to Ari. 'He's got the same colour eyes as me.'

Tina held her breath. Her heart was drumming in her ears. Her mind was screaming *please, please, please don't claim parentage now.* It was the wrong place, the wrong time, the wrong everything!

'There you are, then,' Ari said with an air of indulgence, taking Theo's outstretched hand and giving it a light shake. 'Both of us are lions and I'm very glad to meet you.' He turned to Tina. 'And your mother.'

Relief reduced her to jelly inside. He wasn't pushing his fatherhood yet. Maybe he never would. She should be saying *hello,* but she was so choked up with nervous tension it was impossible to get her voice to work.

'Tina?' He gave her a slightly quizzical smile as he offered his hand to her. 'Short for Christina?'

'Yes.' It was a husky whisper, all she could manage.

Then she was forced by the occasion to let his strong fingers close around hers. The jolting sensation of electric warmth was a searing reminder of the sexual chemistry that had seduced her in the past. It instantly stirred a fierce rebellion in her mind. No way was she going to let it get to her again, making her weak and foolish. If there was to be a fight over custody of Theo, she couldn't let Ari Zavros have any personal power over her. She wriggled her hand out of his as fast as she could.

Seating was quickly re-arranged so that Cass and George could sit beside her mother. Uncle Dimitri produced an extra chair for Ari at the end of the table, right next to her and Theo. It was impossible for Tina to protest this proximity, given they would be partners at the wedding and apparently Ari had already stated his intention to *make her acquaintance.*

The situation demanded polite conversation. Any

failure to follow that course would raise questions about her behaviour. As much as Tina hated having to do it, she adopted the pretence of being strangers, forcing herself to speak to George's *best* man with an air of natural enquiry.

'When did you meet my sister?'

It was a good question. She needed information and needed it fast to help her deal with Ari in the most sensible way. If it was possible to avoid a showdown with him over Theo, grasping that possibility was paramount.

'Only this evening,' he answered with a wry little smile. 'I knew of her, of course, because of her engagement to George, but within the family she was always referred to as simply Cassandra since she is famously known by that name in the supermodel world. I'd never actually heard her surname. I chanced to see it written on her luggage when she set it down in the apartment. Very opportune, given the circumstances.'

The fact that he'd immediately seized the opportunity for a face-to-face meeting with her gave no support to the wishful thought of avoiding an ultimate showdown.

'So you proceeded to draw her out about her family,' Tina said flatly, feeling as though a trap was closing around her.

'Very enlightening,' he drawled, his eyes mocking the secrecy which was no longer a secret to him.

Fear squeezed her heart. Sheer self-defence demanded she ignore his enlightenment. 'You live in Athens?'

'Not really. The apartment is for convenience. Anyone in the family can use it, which is why George felt free to bring Cassandra there for tonight. More private for her than a hotel.'

'Very considerate of him,' she dryly remarked. 'Where do you normally live then?'

All she'd previously known about him was he belonged to a wealthy Greek family with an involvement in the wine industry. During the time they'd spent together, Ari had been more interested in everything Australian than talking about himself.

He shrugged. 'Various business interests require quite a bit of travelling but my family home is on Santorini.'

'We're going to Santorini,' Theo piped up, looked at Ari as though he was fascinated by the man.

Ari smiled at him. 'Yes, I know. Perhaps we could do something special together on your birthday.'

Tina's stomach contracted. He was intent on moving in on her, getting closer to their son.

'Like what?' Theo asked eagerly.

'Let's wait and see what we might like to do, Theo,' Tina cut in firmly, inwardly panicking at spending any more time than she absolutely had to with Ari Zavros. She didn't know if it was curiosity driving him or he was dabbling with the idea of claiming Theo as his flesh and blood. She turned hard, quelling eyes to him. 'You said *family home*. Does that mean you're married with children?'

He shook his head and made an ironic grimace. 'Much to my father's vexation, I am still single. It's his home I was referring to.'

'Not exactly single, Ari,' she tersely reminded him.

He knew she'd seen him with a woman in Dubai. She didn't have to spell that out. If he thought he could start playing fast and loose with her again, cheating on the beautiful blonde, he was on an ego trip she would take great satisfaction in smashing.

'I assure you I am, Christina,' he replied without the blink of an eyelid.

Her teeth gnashed over the lilted use of her full name—a reminder of intimate moments that were long gone. She raked his steady gaze with blistering scepticism. The amber eyes burned straight back at her, denying the slightest shift in what he had just declared.

'Another *charming episode* over?' she sliced at him.

He frowned, probably having forgotten how he had described his relationship with her. Whether he recollected it or not, he shot her a look that was loaded with determined purpose. 'Not so charming. In fact, it convinced me I should free myself up to look for something else.'

His gaze moved to Theo, softening as he said, 'Perhaps I should become a father.'

Tina's spine crawled with apprehension. This was the last thing she wanted. The very last! Somehow she had to fight him, convince him that fatherhood would not suit him at all.

'I don't have a father,' Theo gravely informed him. 'I had a grandfather but he got sick and went to heaven.'

'I'm sorry to hear that,' Ari said sympathetically.

'I think people should be aware there's a very real and lasting responsibility about becoming a parent,'

Tina quickly stated, hoping to ward off any impulsive act that would end up badly.

'I agree with you,' Ari said blandly.

'Fly-by-night people shouldn't even consider it,' she persisted, desperately determined on pricking his conscience.

'What are fly-by-night people, Mama?' Theo asked curiously.

Ari leaned forward to answer him. 'They're people who come and go without staying around long enough to really be an important part of your life. They don't stick by you like your mother does. And your grandmother. And your friends. Do you have some friends, Theo?'

'I have lots of friends,' Theo boasted.

'Then I think you must be a happy boy.'

'Very happy,' Tina cut in, giving Ari a look that clearly telegraphed *without you*.

'Then you must be a very special mother, Christina,' he said in his soft, seductive voice. 'It could not have been easy for you, bringing him up alone.'

She bridled at the compliment. 'I wasn't alone. My parents supported me.'

'Family,' he murmured, nodding approvingly. 'So important. One should never turn one's back on family.'

The glittering challenge in his eyes spurred her into leaning over to privately mutter, 'You turned your back first, Ari.'

'I never have to any blood relative I knew about,' he shot back, leaning towards her and keeping his voice low enough for Theo not to hear his words. 'We can do this the easy way or the hard way, Christina.'

'Do what?'

'Fighting over him is not in our son's best interests.'

'Then don't fight. Let him be.'

'You expect me to ignore his existence?'

'Why not? You've ignored mine.'

'A mistake. Which I will correct.'

'Some mistakes can never be corrected.'

'We shall see.'

The fight was on!

No avoiding it.

The rush of blood to her head as she'd tried to argue him out of it drained away, leaving her dizzy and devastated by his resolute counter to everything she'd said.

He straightened up and smiled at Theo who was tucking into a slice of watermelon. 'Good?' he asked.

Theo nodded, his mouth too full to speak but his eyes twinkling a smile back at Ari. Tina seethed over his charming manner to her son. He'd been so very charming to her once. It meant *nothing!* But it was impossible to explain that to a five-year-old boy.

Ari turned his attention back to her. 'Cassandra told me you now manage a restaurant at Bondi Beach.'

'Yes. It was my father's. He trained me to take over when…when he could no longer do it himself.' Another bad time in her life but she had coped. The restaurant was still thriving.

'That surely means working long hours. It must be difficult, being a mother, too.'

She glared at him, fiercely resenting the suggestion

she might be neglecting her son. 'We live in an apartment above the restaurant. Theo attends a pre-school, which he loves, during the day. He can be with me or my mother at all other times. And the beach is his playground, which he also loves. As you remarked, he is a happy boy.'

And he doesn't need you. For anything.

'Mama and I build great sandcastles,' Theo informed him.

'There are lots of beaches on the Greek islands,' Ari said.

'Can anyone go on them?' Theo asked.

'There are public beaches which are for everyone.'

'Do they have chairs in rows like we saw in Dubai?'

'The private beaches do.'

'I don't like that.'

'There's one below where I live on Santorini that doesn't have chairs. You could build great sand-castles there.'

'Would you help me?'

Ari laughed, delighted he had won Theo over.

'I don't think we'll have time for that,' Tina said quickly.

'Nonsense!' Ari grinned triumphantly at her. 'Cassandra told me you're spending five days on Santorini, and Theo's birthday is two days before the wedding. It would be my pleasure to give Theo a wonderful time—a trip on the cable-car, a ride on a donkey…'

'A donkey!' Theo cried excitedly.

'…a boat-ride to the volcanic island…'

'A boat-ride!' Theo's eyes were as big as saucers.

'...and a trip to a beach where we can build the biggest sandcastle ever!'

'Can we, Mama? Can we?'

His voice was so high-pitched with excitement, it drew her mother's attention. 'Can you what, Theo?' she asked indulgently.

'Ride a donkey and go on a boat, Yiayia. For my birthday!'

'I said I would take him,' Ari swiftly slid in. 'Give him a birthday on Santorini he will always remember.'

'How kind of you!' Her mother beamed at him—the man gorgeous enough to be a movie star, giving his time to make her grandson's stay on Santorini so pleasurable!

The trap was shut. No way out. With both her mother and Theo onside with Ari, Tina knew she would just have to grit her teeth and go along with him. Being a spoilsport would necessitate explanations she didn't want to give. Not at this point. He might force her to make them in the very near future but she would keep it a private issue between them as long as she could.

Cass didn't deserve to have her wedding overshadowed by a situation that should never have arisen. With that one crazy urge to slap Ari with the truth in Dubai... but the damage was done and somehow Tina had to contain it. At least until after the wedding.

With the whole family's attention drawn to them, she forced herself to smile at Ari. 'Yes, very kind.'

'Cassandra mentioned you'll be staying at the El Greco resort,' he said, arrogantly confident of her agreement to the plan. 'I'll contact you there, make arrangements.'

'Fine! Thank you.'

With that settled, conversation picked up around the table again and Theo plied Ari with questions about Santorini, which were answered with obvious good humour.

Tina didn't have to say anything. She sat in brooding silence, hating Ari Zavros for his facile charm, hating herself for being such a stupid blabbermouth, gearing herself up to tolerate what had to be tolerated and savagely vowing that Ari would not get everything his own way.

Eventually Cass and George excused themselves from the party, saying they needed to catch up on some sleep. To Tina's huge relief, Ari stood up to take his leave, as well. She rose from her chair as he offered his hand which she had to be civil enough to take in front of company.

He actually had the gall to enclose her hand with both of his with a show of enthusiastic pleasure. 'Thank you for trusting me with Theo's birthday, Christina.'

'Oh, I'm sure I can trust you to give the best of yourself, Ari,' she answered sweetly, before softly adding with a touch of acid mockery, 'For a limited time.'

Which told him straight out how very little she trusted him.

He might have won Theo over—for a day—but he'd won nothing from her.

'We shall see,' he repeated with that same arrogant confidence.

General goodnights were exchanged and finally he was gone.

But he'd left his presence behind with her mother raving on about him and Theo equally delighted with the nice man.

No relief from the trap.

Tina had the wretched feeling there never would be.

CHAPTER FOUR

MAXIMUS Zavros sat under the vine-covered pergola at one end of the vast patio which overlooked the Aegean Sea. It was where he habitually had breakfast and where he expected his son to join him whenever Ari was home. Today was no exception. However he was taking no pleasure in his surroundings and none in his son, which was obvious from the dark glower of disapproval he directed at Ari the moment he emerged from the house.

'So, you come home without a woman to marry again!' He folded the newspaper he'd been reading and smacked it down on the table in exasperation. 'Your cousin, George, is two years younger than you. He does not have your engaging looks. He does not have your wealth. Yet he can win himself a wife who will grace the rest of his life.' He threw out a gesture of frustration. 'What is the problem with you?'

'Maybe I missed a boat I should have taken,' Ari tossed at his father as he pulled out a chair and sat down, facing him across the table.

'What is that supposed to mean?'

Ari poured himself a glass of orange juice. This was

going to be a long conversation and his throat was already dry. He took a long sip, then answered, 'It means I've met the woman I must marry but I let her go six years ago and somehow I have to win her again. Which is going to prove difficult because she's very hostile to me.'

'Hostile? Why hostile? You were taught to have more finesse than to leave any woman hostile. And why *must* you marry her? To saddle yourself with a sourpuss will not generate a happy life. I credited you with more good sense than that, Ari.'

'I left her pregnant. Unknowingly, I assure you. She gave birth to a son who is now five years old.'

'A son! A grandson!' The tirade was instantly diverted. His father ruminated over this totally unanticipated piece of news for several minutes before speaking again. 'You're sure he is yours?'

'No doubt. The boy not only has a strong resemblance to me but the birth date places the conception during the time I was with Christina.'

'Who is this Christina? Is it possible she could have been with another man?'

Ari shook his head. 'I can't even entertain that as a possibility. We were too intimately involved at the time. And she was a virgin, Papa. I met her when I was in Australia. She was at the start of a promising modelling career…young, beautiful, utterly captivating. When I concluded my business there I said goodbye to her. I had no plans for marriage at that point in my life and I thought her too young to be considering it, either. I thought her life was just starting to open up for her.'

'Australia…' His father frowned. 'How did you meet again? You haven't been back there.'

'George's wife-to-be, Cassandra…when they stayed overnight in the apartment at Athens, I discovered that she was Christina's sister. Christina is to be brides-maid at the wedding and her son, Theo—*my* son—is to be page boy. They were already in Athens en route to Santorini and I went to a family party to meet them.'

'Is it known to the family that you are the father?'

'No. They were obviously in ignorance of my in-volvement. But I cannot ignore it, Papa. Christina wants me to. She is appalled to find herself caught up in a sit-uation with me again.'

'She wants to keep the boy to herself.'

'Yes.'

'So… her mind-set against you has to be changed.'

It was a relief that his father had made a straight leap to this conclusion, although it had been fairly predict-able he would arrive at it, given the pull of a grandson.

'I intend to make a start on that tomorrow. It's Theo's fifth birthday and I managed to manipulate an agree-ment for the two of them to spend it with me.'

'She was not a willing party?'

'I made it unreasonable for her to refuse. The fact that she doesn't want to reveal to her family that I'm Theo's father gives me a lever into her life. At least until after the wedding. I suspect she doesn't want to take any focus off her sister at this time.'

'Caring for her family… I like that. Will she make you a good wife, Ari?'

He made an ironic grimace. 'At least she likes children which cannot be said for Felicity Fullbright. I still find Christina very attractive. What can I say, Papa? I've made my bed and I shall lie in it. When you meet the boy you'll know why.'

'When do they arrive on Santorini?'

'Today.'

'Staying where?'

'The El Greco resort.'

'I shall call the management personally. All expenses for their stay will be paid by me. Fresh fruit and flowers in their rooms. A selection of our best Santorini wines. Everything compliments of the Zavros family. They need to be acquainted with our wealth and power. It tends to bend people's minds in a positive manner.'

Ari kept his own counsel on this point. His father could be right. Generosity might have a benign influence. However, he was well enough acquainted with the Australian character to know they had a habit of cutting down tall poppies. However high people rose on their various totem poles, it did not make them better than anyone else. Apart from which, Christina had already demonstrated a strong independence. He doubted she could be bought.

'The mother might be favourably impressed,' he commented. 'Her name is Helen and she is a widow. It might help if you and Mama pay her some kind attention at the wedding.'

His father nodded. 'Naturally we will do so. As a grandparent she should be sympathetic to those who wish to be. I will make my feelings on the subject known.'

'She is Greek. So was her husband. The two daughters were born and brought up in Australia, but she would be familiar with the old ways...arranged marriages between families. If she understands it could be best for Christina and Theo to have the support and security our family can give them...'

'Leave it to me. I shall win over the mother. You win over the daughter and your son. It is intolerable that we be left out of the boy's life.'

That was the crux of it, Ari thought.

Whatever had to be done he would do to be a proper father to his son.

Ten hours was a long ferry ride from Athens to Santorini. Theo was fascinated by the wake of the boat so Tina spent most of the time on the outer rear deck with him while her mother relaxed inside with a book. They passed many islands, most of them looking quite barren and unattractive, and to Tina's mind, not the least bit alluring like the tropical islands back home. It was disappointing. She had expected more magic. However, these islands were obviously not the main tourist drawcards like Mykonos, Paros, Naxos, and most especially Santorini.

When the ferry finally entered the harbour of their destination, she easily understood the stunning attraction of the landscape created from the volcanic eruption that had devastated ancient civilisations. The water in what had been the crater was a gorgeous blue, the semicircle of high cliffs was dramatic, and perched on top of them the classic white Greek island townships glistened in the late afternoon sunshine.

She wished Ari Zavros did not live on this island. She had looked forward to enjoying it, wanted to enjoy it, and decided she would do so in spite of him. If he had any decency at all, he would let the paternity issue drop, realizing he didn't fit into the life she'd made for herself and Theo, and they were not about to fit into his with his obvious bent for a continual stream of *charming episodes.*

Transport was waiting for them at the ferry terminal. Theo was agog with how the mini-bus would negotiate the amazing zig-zag road which would take them from the bottom of the cliff to the top. As it turned out, the trip was not really hair-raising and the view from the bus-window was beautiful.

The El Greco resort faced the other side of the island, built in terraces down the hillside with rooms built around the swimming pools on each terrace. The buildings were all painted blue and white and the gardens looked very tropical with masses of colourful bougainvillea and hibiscus trees. The reception area was cool and spacious, elegantly furnished and with a view of the sea at the far end. A very attractive place, Tina thought. A place to relax. Except relaxation switched instantly to tension when they started to check in at the reception desk.

'Ah, Mrs Savalas, just a minute please!' the receptionist said quickly, beaming a rather unctuous smile at them. 'I must inform the manager of your arrival.' He ducked away to call through a doorway, 'The Savalas party has arrived.'

A suited man emerged from a back office, beaming a similar smile at them as he approached the desk.

'Is there a problem with our booking?' her mother asked anxiously.

'Not at all, Mrs Savalas. We have put you in rooms on the first terrace which is most convenient to the restaurant and the pool snack-bar. If there is anything that would make you more comfortable, you have only to ask and it will be done.'

'Well, that's very hospitable,' her mother said with an air of relief.

'I have had instructions from Mr Zavros to make you most welcome, Mrs Savalas. I understand you are here for a family wedding.'

'Yes, but…' She threw a puzzled look at Tina whose fists had instinctively clenched at the name that spelled danger all over this situation. 'It's very kind of Ari Zavros to…'

'No, no, it is Maximus Zavros who has given the orders,' the manager corrected her. 'It is his nephew marrying your daughter. Family is family and you are not to pay for anything during your stay at El Greco. All is to be charged to him, so put away your credit card, Mrs Savalas. You will not need it here.'

Her mother shook her head in stunned disbelief. 'I haven't even met this Maximus Zavros.'

It did not concern the manager one bit. 'No doubt you will at the wedding, Mrs Savalas.'

'I'm not sure I should accept this…this arrangement.'

'Oh, but you must!' The manager looked horrified at the thought of refusal. 'Mr Zavros is a very wealthy, powerful man. He owns much of the real estate on Santorini. He would be offended if you did not accept his hospitality and I would be at fault if I did not persuade you to do so. Please, Mrs Savalas… I beg you to enjoy. It is what he wishes.'

'Well…' Her mother looked confused and undecided until a helpful thought struck. She shot Tina a determined look. 'We can talk to Ari about this tomorrow.'

Tina nodded, struggling with the death of any hope that Ari might disappear from her life again. She couldn't believe this was simply a case of a rich powerful Greek extending hospitality. The words—*family is family*—had been like a punch in the stomach. She couldn't dismiss the sickening suspicion that Ari had blabbed to his father. It was the only thing that made sense of this extraordinary move.

'Let me show you to your rooms. A porter will bring your luggage.' The manager bustled out from behind the reception desk. 'I want to assure myself that all is as it should be for you.'

Their adjoining rooms were charming, each one with a walled outside area containing a table and chairs for enjoying the ambience of the resort. Complimentary platters of fresh fruit and a selection of wines were provided. The gorgeous floral arrangements were obvious extras, too. Her mother was delighted with everything. Tina viewed it all with jaundiced eyes and Theo was only interested in how soon he could get into the children's swimming pool.

Their luggage arrived. Tina left her mother in the room Cassandra would share with her the night before the wedding and took Theo into theirs. Within a few minutes she had found their swimsuits in her big suitcase, and feeling driven to get out of the Zavros-permeated room, she and Theo quickly changed their clothes and headed for the water.

She sat on the edge of the shallow pool while Theo dashed in and splashed around, full of happy laughter. Her mind was dark with a terrible sense of foreboding and it was difficult to force an occasional smile at her son. Ari's son. Maximus Zavros's grandson.

Did they intend to make an official claim on him?

People like them probably didn't care how much they disrupted others' lives. If something was desired, for whatever reason, they went after it. And got it. Like the rooms in this resort. Almost anything could be manipulated with wealth.

She couldn't help feeling afraid of the future. She was on this island—their island—for the next five days and it would be impossible to avoid meeting Ari's family at the wedding. Ironically, throwing his fatherhood in his face in Dubai was no longer such a hideous mistake. He would have figured it out at the wedding. There would have been no escape from his knowing. She'd been on a collision course with Ari Zavros from the moment Cassandra had agreed to marry his cousin.

The big question was…how to deal with him?

Should she tell her mother the truth now?

Her head ached from all the possible outcomes of revealing her secret before she absolutely had to. Better to wait, she decided, at least until after she'd spent tomorrow with Ari. Then she would have a better idea of what he intended where Theo was concerned and what she could or couldn't do about it.

Tomorrow… Theo's fifth birthday.

His first with his father.

Tina knew she was going to hate every minute of it.

CHAPTER FIVE

TINA and Theo were about to accompany her mother to breakfast in the nearby restaurant when a call from Ari came through to her room. She quickly pressed her mother to go ahead with Theo while she talked to *the nice man* about plans for the day. As soon as they were out of earshot she flew into attack mode, determined on knowing what she had to handle.

'You've told your father about Theo, haven't you?' she cried accusingly.

'Yes, I have,' he answered calmly. 'He had the right to know, just as I had the right to know. Which you denied me for the past five years, Christina.'

'You made it clear that you were finished with me, Ari.'

'You could have found me. My family is not unknown. A simple search on the Internet…'

'Oh, sure! I can just imagine how much you would have welcomed a cast-off woman running after you. Any contact from me via computer and you would have pressed the delete button.'

'Not if you'd told me you were pregnant.'

'Would you have believed me?' she challenged.

His hesitation gave her instant justification for keeping him in ignorance.

'I thought I had taken care of contraception, Christina,' he said, trying to justify himself. 'I would certainly have checked. However, we now have a different situation—a connection that demands continuation. It's best that you start getting used to that concept because I won't be cut out of my son's life any longer.'

The edge of hard ruthlessness in his tone told her without a doubt that he was intent on making a legal claim. A down to the wire fight over Theo was inevitable. What she needed to do now was buy time. Quelling the threatening rise of panic, she tried bargaining with him.

'You said in Athens we could do this the easy way or the hard way, Ari.'

'Yes. I meant it. Is there something you'd like to suggest?'

'You messed up my life once and I guess nothing is going to stop you from messing it up again. But please…don't make a mess of my sister's day in the sun as a bride. That would be absolutely rotten and selfish, which is typical of your behaviour, but… I'll make it easy for you to get to know your son over the next few days if you hold back on telling everyone else you're his father until after the wedding.'

The silence that followed her offer was nerve-wracking. Tina gritted her teeth and laid out *the hard way*. 'I'll fight you on every front if you don't agree, Ari.'

'When was I ever rotten or selfish to you in our relationship?' he demanded curtly, sounding as though his self-image was badly dented.

'You made me believe what wasn't true… for your own ends,' she stated bitingly. 'And may God damn you to hell if you do that to Theo.'

'Enough! I agree to your deal. I shall meet you at the resort in one hour. We will spend the day happily together for our son's pleasure.'

He cut the connection before Tina could say another word. Her hand was shaking as she returned the telephone receiver to its cradle. At least Cass's wedding wouldn't be spoiled, she told herself. As for the rest… the only thing she could do was deal with one day at a time.

It took Ari the full hour to get his head around Christina's offensive reading of his character. Anger and resentment kept boiling through him. He wasn't used to being so riled by any situation with a woman. It was because of Theo, he reasoned. It was only natural that his emotions were engaged where his son was concerned.

As for Christina, her hostility towards him was totally unreasonable. He remembered romancing her beautifully, showering her with gifts, saying all the sweet words that women liked to hear, wining and dining her, not stinting on anything that could give her pleasure. No one could have been a better first lover for her.

Was it his fault that the contraception he'd used had somehow failed to protect her from falling pregnant?

He had never, *never* intended to mess up her life. He would have dealt honourably with the situation had he known about it. She could have been living in luxury all these years, enjoying being part of a family unit instead of struggling along with single parenthood.

That was her decision, not his. She hadn't allowed him a decision. If there was any condemnation of character to be handed out on all of this, it should be placed at her door. It was *selfish* and *rotten* of her to have denied him the joys of fatherhood.

Yet…there was nothing selfish about not wanting anything to spoil her sister's wedding.

And he could not recall her ever making some selfish demand on him during the time they'd spent together. Not like Felicity Fullbright. Very, very different to Felicity Fullbright. A delight to be with in every sense.

Gradually he calmed down enough to give consideration to her most condemning words… *You made me believe what wasn't true…for your own ends.*

What had he made her believe?

The answer was glaringly simple when he thought about it. She'd been very young, inexperienced, and quite possibly she'd interpreted his whole seduction routine as genuine love for her. Which meant she'd been deeply hurt when he'd left her. So hurt, she probably couldn't bear to tell him about her pregnancy, couldn't bear to be faced with his presence again.

And she thought he might hurt Theo in the same way—apparently loving him, then leaving him.

He had to change her perception of him, make her

understand he would never abandon his child. He had to show her that Theo would be welcomed into his family and genuinely loved. As for winning her over to being his wife…trying to charm her into marrying him wasn't likely to work. Those blazing dark eyes of hers would shoot down every move he made in that direction. So what would work?

She had just offered him a deal.

Why not offer her one?

Make it a deal too attractive to refuse.

Ari worked on that idea as he drove to the El Greco resort.

'He looks just like a Greek God,' her mother remarked admiringly as Ari Zavros strode across the terrace to where they were still sitting in the open-air section of the restaurant, enjoying a last cup of coffee after breakfast.

Tina's stomach instantly cramped. She had thought that once—the golden Greek with his sun-streaked hair and sparkling amber eyes and skin that shone like bronze. And, of course, it was still true. The white shorts and sports shirt he wore this morning made him look even more striking, showing off his athletic physique, the masculine strength in his arms and legs, the broad manly chest. The man was totally charismatic.

This time, however, Tina wasn't about to melt at his feet. 'Bearing gifts, as well,' she said ironically, eyeing the package he was carrying under his arm.

'For me?' Theo cried excitedly.

Ari heard him, beaming a wide grin at his son as he

arrived at their table and presented him with the large
package. 'Yes, for you. Happy birthday, Theo.'

'Can I open it?' Theo asked, eagerly eyeing the wrapping paper.

'You should thank Ari first,' Tina prompted.

'Thank you very much,' he obeyed enthusiastically.

Ari laughed. 'Go right ahead. Something for you to
build when you have nothing else to do.'

It was a Lego train station, much to Theo's delight.

'He loves Lego,' her mother remarked, finding even
more favour with the Greek God.

'I thought he would,' Ari answered. 'My nephews
do. Their rooms are full of it.'

'Talking of family,' her mother quickly slid in. 'Your
father has apparently insisted on paying for all our accommodation here and...'

'It is his pleasure to do so, Mrs Savalas,' Ari broke in
with a smile to wipe out her concern. 'If you were staying on Patmos, George's family would see to it. Here,
on Santorini, my father is your host and he has asked
me to extend an invitation to all of you for dinner tonight at our family home. Then we will not be strangers at the wedding.'

Her mother instantly melted. 'Oh! How kind!'

Tina glared at Ari. Had he lied about keeping the
deal? And what of his parents? Had he warned them
not to reveal their relationship to Theo? He was pursuing his own agenda and she wasn't at all sure he would
respect hers. Far from melting at his *kindness,* every
nerve in her body stiffened with battle tension.

Ari kept smiling. 'I've told my mother it's your birthday, Theo. She's planning a special cake with five candles for you to blow out and make a wish. You've got all day to think about what to wish for.'

All day to worm his way into Theo's heart with his facile charm, Tina thought grimly. She knew only too well he could be *Mr Wonderful* for a while. It was the long haul that worried her—how *constant* Ari would be as a father.

'Are you coming with us today, Mrs Savalas?' he asked, apparently happy to have her mother's company, as well, probably wanting the opportunity to get her even more onside with him.

'No, no. It sounds too busy for me. I shall stroll into the township in my own time, take a look at the church where the wedding is to be held, do a little shopping, visit the museum.' She smiled at Tina, her eyes full of encouraging speculation. 'Much better for you young people to go off together.'

Tina barely stopped herself from rolling her own eyes at what was obviously some romantic delusion. Gorgeous man—unmarried daughter—Greek island in the sun.

'I shall look forward to the family dinner tonight,' her mother added, giving whole-hearted approval to Ari's plans for the whole day.

Tina smothered a groan.

No escape.

She had agreed to letting him into their lives in return for his silence until after the wedding, but if he or his parents let the cat out of the bag tonight, she would bite their heads off for putting their self-interest ahead of everything else.

After a brief return to their room to put the Lego gift on Theo's bed, refresh themselves, and collect hats and swimming costumes, they re-met Ari and set off for the five-minute walk into the main township of Fira. Tina deliberately placed Theo between them. He held her hand, and unknowingly, his father's. She wondered how she was going to explain this truth to him—another nail in her heart.

'Are your parents aware of our deal?' she asked Ari over Theo's head.

'They will be in good time,' he assured her.

She had to believe him…until his assurance proved false, like the words he had spoken to her in the past. Would he play fair with her this time? She could only hope so. This wasn't about him. Or her. It was about the life of their child.

The view from the path into town was spectacular, overlooking the fantastic sea-filled crater with its towering cliffs. Two splendid white cruise ships stood in the middle of the glittering blue harbour and Theo pointed to them excitedly.

'Are we going to ride in one of those boats?'

'No, they're far too big to move close to land,' Ari answered. 'See the smaller boats going out to them? They're to take the people off and bring them to the island. We'll be riding in a motor-launch that can take us wherever we want to go. You can even steer it for a while if you like.'

Theo was agog. 'Can I? Can I really?'

Ari laughed. 'You can sit on my lap and be the captain. I'll show you what to do.'

'Did you hear that, Mama? I'll be captain of the boat.'

'Your boat, Ari?' Tina asked, anxiously wondering what other goodies he had up his sleeve, ready to roll out for Theo's pleasure.

'A family boat. It will be waiting for us at the town wharf.'

His family. His very wealthy family. How could she stop the seduction of her son by these people? He was a total innocent, as she had been before meeting Ari. He was bound to be deeply impressed by them and the outcome might be a terrible tug-of-war for his love.

Tina suffered major heartburn as they strolled on into town. It was so easy for Ari to win Theo over. It had been easy for him to win her over. He had everything going for him. Even now, knowing how treacherous it was, she still had to fight the pull of his attraction. After him, no other man had interested her, not once in the years since he had left her behind. While he, no doubt, had had his pick of any number of beautiful women who had sparked his interest. Like the blonde in Dubai and probably dozens of others.

It was all terribly wrong. He had been the only man in her life and she'd meant nothing to him. She only meant something to him now because she was the mother of his child and he had to deal with her.

On the road up to the beautiful white church dominating the hillside, a statue of a donkey stood outside a tourist shop displaying many stands of postcards. The donkey was painted pink and it had a slot for letters in its mid-section. Over the slot was painted a red heart with the words POST OF LOVE printed on it.

'I didn't get to sit on the camel, Mama. Can I sit on this donkey?' Theo pleaded.

'You'll be sitting on a real donkey soon. Won't that be better?' Tina cajoled, mentally shying from anything connected with *love*.

Theo shook his head. 'It won't be pink. I'd like a photo of me on this one.'

'Then we must do it for the birthday boy,' Ari said, hoisting Theo up on the donkey and standing beside him to ensure he sat on it safely.

They both grinned at her, so much a picture of father and son it tore at Tina's heart as she viewed it through the camera and took the requested shot.

'Now if you'll stand by Theo, I'll take one of the two of you together,' Ari quickly suggested.

'Yes! Come on, Mama!' Theo backed him up.

She handed Ari her camera and swapped places with him.

'Smile!' he commanded.

She put a smile on her face. As soon as he'd used her camera he whipped a mobile phone out of his shirt pocket and clicked off another shot of them. To show his parents, Tina instantly thought. *This is the woman who is Theo's mother and this is your grandson.* It would probably answer some fleeting curiosity about her, but they would zero straight in on Theo, seeing Ari in him—a Zavros, not a Savalas.

'You have a beautiful smile, Christina,' Ari said

warmly as he returned her camera and lifted Theo off the donkey.

'Stop it!' she muttered, glaring a hostile rejection at him. She couldn't bear him buttering her up when he probably had some killing blow in mind to gain custody of his son.

He returned a puzzled frown. 'Stop what?'

Theo was distracted by a basket of soft toys set out beside the postcard stands, giving her space enough to warn Ari off the totally unwelcome sweet-talking.

'I don't want any more of your compliments.'

His gesture denied any harm in them. 'I was only speaking the truth.'

'They remind me of what a fool I was with you. I won't be fooled again, Ari.'

He grimaced. 'I'm sorry you read more into our previous relationship than was meant, Christina.'

'Oh! What exactly did you mean when you said I was special?' she sliced back at him, her eyes flashing outright scepticism.

He gave her a look that sent a wave of heat through her, right down to her toes. 'You were special. Very special. I just wasn't ready to take on a long-term relationship at the time. But I am now. I want to marry you, Christina.'

Her heart stopped. She stared at him in total shock. No way had she expected this. It was Theo, her stunned mind started to reason. Ari thought it was the best way—the easiest way—to get Theo. Who *she* was, and what *she* wanted was irrelevant.

'Forget it!' she said tersely. 'I'm not about to change my life for your convenience.'

'I could make it convenient for you, too,' he quickly countered.

Her eyes mocked his assertion. 'How do you figure that?'

'A life of ease. No fighting over Theo. We bring him up together. You'll have ample opportunity to do whatever you want within reason.'

'Marriage to you is no guarantee of that. You can dangle as many carrots as you like in front of me, Ari. I'm not biting.'

'What if I give you a guarantee? I'll have a prenuptial agreement drawn up that would assure you and Theo of financial security for the rest of your lives.' His mouth took on an ironic twist. 'Think of it as fair payment for the pain I've given you.'

'I'm perfectly capable of supporting Theo.'

'Not to the extent of giving him every advantage that wealth can provide.'

'Money isn't everything. Besides, I don't want to be your wife. That would simply be asking for more pain.'

He frowned. 'I remember the pleasure we both took in making love. It can be that way again, Christina.'

She flushed at the reminder of how slavishly she had adored him. 'You think a seductive honeymoon makes a marriage, Ari? Taking me as your wife is just a cynical exercise in legality. It gives you full access to our son. Once you have that, I won't matter to you. You'll meet other women who will be happy to provide you with a *special* experience. Can you honestly say you'll pass that up?'

'If I have you willing to share my bed, and the family I hope we'll have together, I shall be a faithful husband like my father,' he said with every appearance of sincerity.

'How can I believe that?' she cried, sure that his sincerity couldn't be genuine.

'Tonight you will meet my parents. Their marriage was arranged but they made it work. It was bonded in family and they are completely devoted to each other. I see no reason why we cannot achieve that same happiness, given enough goodwill between us. Goodwill for the sake of our son, Christina.'

'Except I don't trust you,' she flashed back at him. 'I have no reason to trust you.'

'Then we can have it written into the prenuptial agreement that should you file for divorce because of my proven infidelity, you will get full custody of our children, as well as a financial settlement that will cover every possible need.'

Tina was stunned again. 'You'd go that far?'

'Yes. That is the deal I'm offering you, Christina.' As Theo moved back to claim their attention, Ari shot her one last purposeful look and muttered, 'Think about it!'

CHAPTER SIX

ARI was deeply vexed with himself. Christina *had* pushed him too far. He should have stuck to the financial deal and not let her mocking mistrust goad him into offering full custody if he didn't remain faithful to their marriage. It was impossible to backtrack on it now. If she remained cold and hard towards him, he'd just condemned himself to a bed he certainly wouldn't want to lie in for long.

The will to win was in his blood but usually his mind warned him when the price to be paid was becoming unacceptable. Why hadn't he weighed it up this time? It was as though he was mesmerised by the fierce challenge emanating from her, the dark blaze of energy fighting him with all her might, making him want to win regardless of the cost.

The stakes were high. He wanted his son full-time, living in his home, not on the other side of the world with visits parcelled out by a family law-court. But something very strong in him wanted to win Christina over, too. Maybe it was instinct telling him she could make him the kind of wife he'd be happy to live with—

better than any of the other women he knew. She'd proved herself a good mother—a deeply caring mother. As for the sharing his bed part, surely it wouldn't prove too difficult to establish some workable accord there.

She'd been putty in his hands once, a beautiful rosebud of a girl whose petals he had gradually unfurled, bringing her to full glorious bloom. She was made of much stronger stuff now. The power of her passion excited him. It was negative passion towards him at the moment, but if he could turn it around, push it into a positive flow...

She did have a beautiful smile. He wanted to make it light up for him. And he wanted to see her magnificent dark eyes sparkling with pleasure—pleasure in him. The marriage bed need not be cold. If he could press the right buttons...he had to or he'd just proposed the worst deal of his life.

He took stock of this different Christina as they wandered through the alleys of shops leading up to the summit of the town. The short hair did suit her, giving more emphasis to her striking cheekbones and her lovely long neck. Her full-lipped mouth was very sexy—bee-stung lips like Angelina Jolie's, though not quite as pronounced. She wasn't quite as tall as her sister, nor as slim. She was, in fact, very sweetly curved, her breasts fuller than when she was younger, her waist not as tiny—probably because of childbirth—but still provocatively feminine in the flow to her neatly rounded hips.

Today she was wearing a pretty lemon and white striped top that was cut into clever angles that spelled designer wear—possibly a gift from Cassandra. She'd teamed it with white Capri pants and she certainly had the legs to wear them with distinction—legs that Ari wanted wound around him in urgent need. She could make him a fine wife, one he would be proud to own, one he wouldn't stray from if she let herself respond to him.

He would make it happen.

One way or another he had to make it happen.

Marriage! Never in her wildest imagination had Tina thought it might be a possibility with Ari Zavros, not since he'd left Australia, putting a decisive end to any such romantic notion. But this wasn't romance. It was a coldly calculated deal to get what he wanted and he probably thought he could fool her on the fidelity front.

How on earth could she believe he wouldn't stray in the future? Even as they strolled along the alleys filled with fascinating shops women stared at him, gobbling him up with their eyes. When she stopped to buy a pretty scarf, the saleswoman kept looking at him, barely glancing at Tina as she paid for it.

The man was a sex magnet. Despite how he'd left her flat, she wasn't immune to the vibrations, either, which made it doubly dangerous to get involved with him on any intimate level. He'd only hurt her again. To marry him would be masochistic madness. But it was probably best to pretend to be thinking about *his* deal until after Cass's wedding to ensure he kept *her* deal.

Then the truth could come out without it being such a distracting bombshell and visitation rights could be discussed. She wouldn't deny him time with his son since he seemed so intent on embracing fatherhood, but he would have to come to Australia for it. Greece was not Theo's home and she wasn't about to let that be changed.

They reached the summit of the town where a cable-car ran down to the old port. Alternatively one could take a donkey-ride along a zig-zag path from top to bottom. Tina would have much preferred to take the cable-car. Ari, however, was bent on making good his promise to Theo, and she made no protest as he selected three donkeys for them to ride—the smallest one for their son, the biggest one for himself and an average-sized one for her.

Theo was beside himself with excitement as Ari lifted him onto the one chosen for him. Tina quickly refused any need for his help, using a stool to mount her donkey. She didn't want to feel Ari's hands on her, nor have him so close that he would have a disturbing physical effect on her. She'd been unsettled enough by his ridiculous offer of marriage.

He grinned at her as he mounted his own donkey, probably arrogantly confident of getting his own way, just as he was getting his own way about Theo's birthday. She gave him a *beautiful* smile back, letting him think whatever he liked, knowing in her heart she would do what *she* considered best for her child, and being a miserable mother in a miserable marriage was definitely not best.

'I'll ride beside Theo,' he said. 'If you keep your

donkey walking behind his, I'll be able to control both of them.'

'Are they likely to get out of control?' she asked apprehensively.

'They're fed at the bottom and some of them have a tendency to bolt when they near the end of the path.'

'Oh, great!'

He flashed another confident grin. 'Don't worry. I'll take care of you both. That's a promise, Christina.'

His eyes telegraphed it was meant for the future, too.

He could work overtime on his deal, making it as attractive as he could, but she wasn't having any of it, Tina thought grimly. However, she did have to concede he kept their donkeys at a controlled pace when others started to rush past them. And he cheerfully answered Theo's constant questions with all the patience of an indulgent father.

Her son was laughing with delight and giving Ari an impulsive hug as he was lifted off the donkey. For Tina, it was a relief to get her feet back on solid ground. She'd been far too tense to enjoy her ride.

'We'll take the cable-car back up when we return,' Ari said soothingly, aware of her unease.

She nodded, muttering, 'That would be good.'

'Which boat is ours?' Theo asked, eagerly looking forward to the next treat.

Ari pointed. 'This one coming into the wharf now.'

'Looks like you already have a captain,' Tina remarked.

'Oh, Jason will be happy to turn the wheel over to Theo while he's preparing lunch for us. It will be an easy day for him. When the boat is not in family use, he takes out charters, up to eight people at a time. Today he only has three to look after.'

The good-humoured reply left her nothing to say. Besides, she was sure everything on board would run perfectly for Theo's pleasure. Ari would not fail in his mission to have his son thinking the *nice* man was absolutely wonderful. He'd been wonderful to her for three whole months without one slip for any doubt about him to enter her head.

The white motor launch was in pristine condition. A blue and white striped canopy shaded the rear deck which had bench seats softened by blue and white striped cushions. Tina was invited to sit down and relax while Jason got the boat under way again and Ari took Theo to fetch drinks and give him a tour of the galley.

She sat and tried to concentrate on enjoying the marvellous view, let the day flow past without drawing attention to herself. Tonight's family dinner would test her nerves to the limit, but at least her mother would be there, helping to keep normal conversation rolling along. And despite the stress this meeting with Ari's parents would inevitably cause, Tina told herself she did need to see the Zavros home environment, check that it would be a good place for Theo to be if visits to Santorini had to be arranged.

She smiled as she heard Theo say, 'I'm not allowed to have Coca-Cola. Mama says it's not good for me. I can have water or milk or fruit-juice.'

Welcome to the world of parenting, Ari. It isn't all fun and games. Making healthy choices for your child is an important part of it. Would he bother to take that kind of care or would he hire a nanny to do the real business of parenting?

Tina mentally ticked that off as an item to be discussed before agreeing to visits.

'Okay, what would you like?' he asked, not questioning her drinks ruling.

'Orange juice.'

'And what does your Mama like?'

'Water. She drinks lots of water.'

'No wine?'

Not since you put intoxicating bubbles in my brain.

'No. It's water or coffee or tea for Mama,' Theo said decisively.

'Well, after our hot walk, I guess iced water would be the best choice.'

'Yes,' Theo agreed.

He carried out jugs of orange juice and iced water, setting them on the fixed table which served the bench seats. Theo brought a stack of plastic glasses, carefully separating them out as Ari returned to the galley, emerging again with a platter containing a selection of cheeses and crackers, nuts, olives and grapes.

'There we are! Help yourselves,' he invited, though he did pour out the drinks for them—water for him, too.

'I love olives,' Theo declared, quickly biting into one.

'Ah! A true Greek,' Ari said proudly.

Tina instantly bridled. 'Theo is an Australian.'

'But Yia Yia is Greek, Mama,' Theo piped up.

'Definitely some Greek blood there,' Ari declared,

a glittering blast from his golden eyes defying Tina's claim.

'True,' she agreed, deciding the point that needed to be made could be driven home when Theo was not present. Australia was their home country. Theo was an Australian citizen. And the family court in Australia would come down on Tina's side. At least she had that in her favour.

Ari chatted away to their son who positively basked in his father's attention. He explained about the volcano as they sailed towards what was left of it, telling the story of what had happened in the far distant past, how the volcano had erupted and destroyed everything. Theo lapped it up, fascinated by the huge disaster, and eager to walk up to the crater when they disembarked there.

Then it was on to the islet of Palea Kameni for a swim in the hot springs—another new exciting experience for Theo. Tina didn't really want to change into her bikini, being far too physically conscious of Ari looking at her to feel comfortable in it, but she liked the idea of letting Theo go alone with him even less. He was *her son* and she was afraid of giving Ari free rein with him without her supervision.

Unfortunately Ari in a brief black swimming costume reduced her comfort zone to nil. His almost naked perfectly proportioned male body brought memories of their previous intimacy flooding back. She'd loved being with him in bed; loved touching him, feeling him, looking at him, loved the intense pleasure he'd given her in so many ways. It had been the best time of her life. It hurt, even now, that it had only been *a charming episode* for him. It hurt even more that she couldn't control the treacherous desire to have him again.

She could if she married him. She probably could anyhow. He'd lusted after her before without marriage in mind. But having sex with him again wouldn't feel the same. She wouldn't be able to give herself to him whole-heartedly, knowing she wasn't the love of his life. There would be too many shadows in any bed they shared.

It was easier to push the memories aside when they were back on the boat and properly dressed again. Ari in clothes was not quite so mesmerising. He and Theo took over the wheel, playing at being captain together, steering the boat towards the village of Oia on the far point of Santorini while Jason was busy in the galley.

They had a delicious lunch of freshly cooked fish and salad. After all the activity and with his stomach full, Theo curled up on the bench seat, his head on Tina's lap and went to sleep. Jason was instructed to keep the boat cruising around until the boy woke. If there was still time to visit Oia, he could then take them into the small port.

'We don't want him too tired to enjoy his birthday party tonight,' Ari remarked to Tina.

'No. I think we should head home when he wakes. We've done all you promised him, Ari. He should have some quiet time, building the Lego train station before more excitement tonight,' Tina said, needing some quiet time for herself, as well. It was stressful being constantly in the company of the man who was intent on breaking into her life again.

'Okay.' He gave her an admiring look. 'You've done a good job with him, Christina. He's a delightful child.'

She gritted her teeth, determined not to be seduced by his compliments, deliberately moving her gaze to the black cliffs ahead of them. 'I think it's important to instill good principles in a child as early as possible,' she said, a sudden wave of resentment towards him making her add, 'I don't want him to grow up like you.'

His silence tore at her nerves but she refused to look at him.

Eventually he asked, 'What particular fault of mine are you referring to?'

'Thinking women are your toys to be picked up and played with as you please,' she answered, wishing he could be honest about himself and honest to her. 'I want Theo to give consideration to how he touches others' lives. I hope when he connects with people he will always leave them feeling good.'

Another long silence.

Out of the corner of her eye she saw Ari lean forward, resting his forearms on his thighs. 'If you had not fallen pregnant, Christina,' he said softly, 'wouldn't I have left you with good memories of our relationship?'

'You left me shattered, Ari,' she answered bluntly. 'My parents had brought me up to be a good girl believing that sex should only be part of a loving relationship. I truly believed that with you and it wasn't so. Then when I realised I was pregnant, it made everything so much worse. I had to bear their disappointment in me, as well as knowing I'd simply been your sex toy for a while.'

In some ways it was a relief to blurt out the truth to him, though whether it meant anything to him or not was unknowable. Maybe it might make him treat her with more respect. She was not a pawn to be moved around at his will. She was a person who had to be dealt with as a person who had the right to determine her own life and this time she would do it according to her principles.

Ari shook his head. He was in a hard place here. He wasn't used to feeling guilty about his actions or the decisions he'd made. It was not a feeling he liked. Christina had just given a perspective on their previous relationship that he'd never considered and quite clearly it had to be considered if he was to turn this situation around.

She was staring into space—a space that only she occupied, shutting him out. Yet her hand was idly stroking the hair of their sleeping son. He was the connection between them—the only connection Ari could count on right now. He was no longer sure he could reach her sexually, though he would still give it a damned good try. In the meantime he had to start redeeming himself in her eyes or she would never allow herself to be vulnerable to the physical attraction which he knew was not completely dead.

He'd felt her gaze on him at the hot springs, saw it quickly flick away whenever he looked at her. She kept shoring up defences against him by reliving how he'd wronged her in the past. Would she ever let that go or would he be paying for his sins against her far into the future?

'I'm sorry,' he said quietly. 'It was wrong of me to take you. I think it was your innocence that made you so entrancing, so different, so special, and the way you looked at me then… I found it irresistible, Christina. If it means anything to you, there hasn't been a woman since whose company has given me more pleasure.'

As he spoke the words which were designed to be persuasive, there was a slight kick in Ari's mind—a jolting realization that he was actually stating the truth. When he'd moved on, he'd mentally set her aside—too young, not the right time for a serious relationship—but the moment he'd recognised her in Dubai, he'd wanted to experience the sweetness of her all over again, especially when he'd just been suffering the sour taste of Felicity Fullbright.

Christina shook her head. She didn't believe him.

'It's true,' he insisted.

She turned to look at him, dark intense eyes scouring his for insincerity. He held her testing gaze, everything within him tuned to convincing her they could make another start, forge a new understanding between them.

'You didn't come back to me, Ari,' she stated simply. 'You forgot me.'

'No. I put you away from me for reasons that I thought were valid at the time but I didn't forget you, Christina. The moment I recognised you in Dubai, the urge to pick up with you again was instant. And that was before you told me about Theo.'

She frowned, hopefully realising the impulse had been there before she had spoken of their son. 'You were with another woman,' she muttered as though that urge was tarnished, too.

'I was already wishing that I wasn't before I saw you. Please…at least believe this of me. It's true.'

For the first time he saw a hint of uncertainty in her eyes. She lowered her long thick lashes, hiding her thoughts. 'Tell me what your valid reasons were.'

'To my mind, we both still had a lot to achieve on our own without ties holding us back from making choices we would have made by ourselves. You'd barely started your modelling career, Christina, and it was obvious you had the promise of making it big on the international scene. As your sister has done.'

Her mouth twisted into a wry grimace as she looked down at their sleeping son. 'If you didn't forget me, Ari, did you ever wonder why I never broke into the international scene?'

'I did expect you to. I thought you had chosen to stay in Australia. Some people don't like leaving everything that is familiar to them.'

'I wasn't worth coming back to,' she murmured, heaving a sigh that made him feel she had just shed whatever progress he had made with her.

'I was caught up dealing with family business these past six years, Christina,' he swiftly argued. 'It's only now…meeting you again and being faced with my own son that my priorities are undergoing an abrupt change.'

'Give it time, Ari,' she said dryly. 'They might change again.'

'No. I won't be taking my marriage proposal off the table. I want you to consider it very seriously.'

She slid him a measuring look that promised nothing. 'I'll think about it. Don't ask any more of me now.' She nodded down at Theo. 'I'm tired, too. Please ask Jason to head back to Fira.'

'As you wish,' he said, rising from the bench seat to do her bidding.

Trying to push her further would not accomplish any more than he had already accomplished today. She didn't trust him yet but at least she was listening to him. Tonight would give him the chance to show her the family environment he wanted to move her and Theo into. He had to make it as attractive as he could.

CHAPTER SEVEN

WHILE Theo was occupied fitting the pieces of the Lego train station together, Tina tried to imagine what her life might have been like if she hadn't fallen pregnant. Would she have picked herself up from the deeply wounding disillusionment of her love for Ari and channelled all her energy into forging a successful modelling career?

Almost certainly.

She had been very young—only eighteen at the time—and having been rejected by him she would have wanted to *show* him she really was special—so special he would regret not holding onto her.

Cassandra would have helped her to get a foot in on the international scene. Given the chance, she would have tried to make it to the top, delivering whatever was required to keep herself in demand and in the public eye; fashion shows, magazine covers, celebrity turn-outs that would give her even more publicity. Ambition would have been all fired up to make Ari have second thoughts about his decision, make him want to meet her again.

When and if he did she would have played it very cool. No melting on the spot. She would have made him chase her, earn her, and she wouldn't have given in to him until he'd declared himself helplessly in love with her and couldn't live without her. He would have had to propose marriage.

Which he'd done today.

Except the circumstances were very different to what might have been if Theo had never been conceived. That completely changed the plot, making the marriage proposal worth nothing to her.

Though Ari's face had lit up with pleasure at seeing her in Dubai.

But that was only a *fond memory* rekindled.

She wasn't the same naive, stars-in-her-eyes girl and never would be again, so it was impossible for him to recapture the pleasure he'd had in her company in the past. Surely he had to realise that. Empty words, meaning nothing.

She shouldn't let herself be affected by anything he said. Or by his mega sex appeal which was an unsettling distraction, pulling her into wanting to believe he was sincere when he was probably intent on conducting a softening-up process so she would bend to his will. It was important to keep her head straight tonight. He had rights where Theo was concerned. He had none over her.

It was still very hot outside their room when it came time to dress for the birthday party. Her mother, of course, was wearing black—a smart tunic and skirt with an array of gold jewellery to make it look festive.

Tina chose a red and white sundress for herself, team-
ing it with white sandals and dangly earrings made of
little white shells.

She put Theo in navy shorts, navy sandals, and a
navy and white top with red stripes across the chest. He
insisted on having the big red birthday badge with the
smiley face and the number 5 pinned onto it. Ari had
bought it for him this morning on their stroll around
the shops and Theo wore it proudly.

'See!' he cried, pointing to his badge when Ari came
to pick them up.

Ari laughed, lifted him up high, whirled him around,
then held him against his shoulder, grinning at him as
he said, 'It's a grand thing to be five, Theo.'

There was little doubt in Tina's mind that Theo
would love to have Ari as his Papa. Her heart sank at
the thought of how much would have to change when
the truth had to be admitted. Ari's parents already knew.
She could only hope they would handle this meeting
with care and discretion.

To her immense relief, Ari seated her mother beside
him on the drive to his home on the other end of the island. It was near the Santo winery, he said. Which reminded Tina that he had come to Australia on a tour
of the wine industry there. As they passed terraces of
grapevines, it was fascinating to see the vines spread
across the ground instead of trained to stand in upright
rows. To protect the grapes from the strong winds, Ari
explained to her mother who happily chatted to him the
whole way.

Eventually they arrived at the Zavros home. The

semicircular driveway was dominated by a fountain with three mermaids as its centrepiece, which instantly fascinated Theo. The home itself appeared to be three Mediterranean-style villas linked by colonnades. Naturally it was white, like most of the buildings on Santorini. Ari led them to the central building which was larger than the other two. It all shrieked of great wealth. Intimidating wealth to Tina.

'We're dining on the terrace,' he informed them, shepherding them along a high spacious hallway that clearly bisected this villa.

The floor was magnificently tiled in a pattern of waves and seashells. They emerged onto a huge terrace overlooking the sea. In front of them was a sparkling blue swimming pool. To the left was a long vine-covered pergola and Tina's heart instantly kicked into a faster beat as she saw what had to be Ari's parents, seated at a table underneath it.

They rose from their chairs to extend a welcome to their guests. Tension whipped along Tina's nerves as both of them looked at Theo first. However their attention on him didn't last too long. They greeted her mother very graciously and waited for her to introduce her daughter and grandson.

Maximus Zavros was an older version of Ari in looks. His wife, Sophie, was still quite a striking woman with a lovely head of soft wavy hair, warm brown eyes and a slightly plump, very curvaceous figure. Although they smiled at her as she was introduced, Tina was acutely conscious of their scrutiny—sizing her up as the mother of their grandson. It was a relief when they finally turned their gaze to Theo again.

'And this is the birthday boy,' Sophie Zavros said indulgently.

'Five!' Theo said proudly, pointing to his badge. Then he gave Ari's father a curious look. 'Your name is Maximus?'

'Yes, it is. If it is easier for you, tonight you can call me Max,' he invited, smiling benevolently.

'Oh, no! I *like* Maximus,' Theo said with a broad smile back. 'Mama took me to a movie about a girl with very long hair. What was her name, Mama?'

'Rapunzel,' Tina supplied, barely stopping herself from rolling her eyes at what was bound to come next.

'Rapunzel,' he repeated. 'But the best part of the movie was the horse. His name was Maximus and he was a great horse!'

'I'm glad he was a great horse,' Ari's father said, amused by the connection.

'He was so good at everything!' Theo assured him. 'And he saved them in the end, didn't he, Mama?'

'Yes, he did.'

Ari's father crouched down to Theo's eye level. 'I think I must get hold of this movie. Maybe you and I could watch it together sometime. Would you like to see it again?'

Theo nodded happily.

'Well, I'm not a horse but I can give you a ride over to the table.'

He swept his grandson up in his arms and trotted him to the table, making Theo bubble with laughter. It startled Tina that such a powerful man would be so play-ful. Her mother and Sophie were laughing, too—any awkwardness at meeting strangers completely broken. She glanced at Ari who was also looking on in amuse-ment.

He quickly moved closer to her, murmuring, 'Relax, Christina. We just want to make this a special night for Theo.'

'Have you told them of your plan to marry me?' she asked quickly, wanting to know if she was being sized up as a possible daughter-in-law.

'Yes, but there will be no pressure for you to agree tonight. This is a different beginning for us, Christina, with our families involved, because it is about family this time.'

His eyes burned serious conviction into hers.

It rattled her deep-seated prejudice against believ-ing anything he said. She sucked in a deep breath and tried to let her inner angst go. This *was* a different sce-nario between them with their families involved. She decided to judge the night on its merits, see how she felt about it afterwards. To begin with she told herself to be glad that Ari's parents were the kind of people Theo could take to because there was no avoiding the fact they would feature in his future.

Maximus Zavros had seated Theo in the chair on the left of his own at the head of the table. Sophie ush-ered Tina's mother to the chair next to Theo's and to the right of her own chair at the foot of the table. Ari guided Tina to the chair opposite Theo's, putting her next to his father before sitting beside her.

As soon as they were all seated a man-servant appeared, bringing two platters of hors d'oeuvres. Another followed, bringing jugs of iced water and orange juice.

Ari's father turned to her, pleasantly asking, 'Can I persuade you to try one of our local wines?'

She shook her head. 'No, thank you. I prefer water.'

He looked at her mother. 'Helen?'

'I'm happy to try whatever you suggest, Maximus. I've tasted two of the wines that were sent to my room and they were quite splendid.'

'Ah, I'm glad they pleased your palate.' He signalled to the servant to pour the chosen wine into glasses while he himself filled Tina's glass with water and Theo's with orange juice. He beamed a smile at his grandson. 'Ari tells me you can swim like a fish.'

'I love swimming,' was his enthusiastic reply.

'Did your Mama teach you?'

Theo looked at Tina, unsure of the answer. 'Did you, Mama?'

'No. I took you to tadpole classes when you were only nine months old. You've always loved being in water and you learnt to swim very young.' She turned to Maximus. 'It's important for any child to be able to swim in Australia. There are so many backyard pools and every year there are cases of young children drowning. Also, we live near Bondi Beach, so I particularly wanted Theo to be safe in the water.'

'Very sensible,' Maximus approved, nodding to the pool beyond the pergola. 'There will be no danger for him here, either.'

That was just the start of many subtle and not so

subtle points made to her throughout the evening, by both of Ari's parents. They were clearly intent on welcoming their grandson into their life, assuring her he would be well taken care of and greatly loved. And not once was there any hint of criticism of her for keeping them in ignorance of him until now.

She fielded a few testing questions from Maximus about her own life, but for the most part Ari's parents set out to charm and Tina noticed her mother having a lovely time with Sophie, discussing the forthcoming wedding and marriage in general.

After the hors d'oeuvres, they were served souvlaki and salad which Theo had informed Ari on the boat was his favourite meal. Then came the birthday cake and Ari reminded Theo to make a wish as he blew out the candles—all five of them in one big burst. Everyone clapped and cheered at his success.

The cake was cut and slices of it were served around the table. It was a rich, many layered chocolate cake, moist and delicious, and Theo gobbled his piece up, the first to finish.

'Will I get my wish?' he asked Ari.

'I hope so, Theo. Although if you were wishing for a horse like Maximus, that might be asking for too much.'

'Is wishing for a Papa too much?'

Tina's hands clenched in her lap. Her lungs seized up. The silence around the table felt loaded with emotional dynamite.

'No, that's not asking for too much,' Ari answered decisively.

Her mother leaned over and pulled Theo onto her

lap, giving him a cuddle. 'You miss your Papou, don't you, darling?' She gave Sophie a rueful smile. 'My husband died a year ago. He adored Theo. We didn't have sons, you see, and having a grandson was like a beautiful gift.'

'Yes. A very beautiful gift,' Sophie repeated huskily, her gaze lingering on Theo for a moment before shooting a look of heart-tugging appeal at Tina.

'I think with Ari giving him such a wonderful time today...' her mother rattled on.

'Ari is very good with children,' Sophie broke in. 'His nephews love being with him. He will make a wonderful father.'

Ostensibly she was speaking to her mother but Tina knew the words were for her. Maybe they were true. He might very well be a wonderful father, but being a wonderful husband was something else.

'Maximus and I very much want to see him settled down with his own family,' Sophie carried on.

'Mama, don't push,' Ari gently chided.

She heaved a sigh which drew Tina's mother into a string of sympathetic comments about young people taking their time about getting married these days.

Tina sat in frozen silence until Ari's father leaned towards her and asked, 'Who is managing your family restaurant while you are away, Christina?'

She had to swallow hard to moisten her throat before answering, 'The head chef and the head waiter.'

'You trust them to do it well?'

'Yes. My father set it up before he died that both men

get a percentage of the profits. It's in their best interests to keep it running successfully.'

'Ah! A man of foresight, your father,' he said with satisfaction.

Tina *knew* he was thinking the restaurant could keep running successfully without her. 'It needs an overall manager and my father entrusted me with that job,' she said with defiant pride.

'Which is a measure of his respect for your abilities, Christina. But as a Greek father myself, I know it was not what he wanted for you.'

His amber eyes burned that certain knowledge into her heart. There was no denying it. Her father had not been against his daughters having a career of their choice but he had believed a woman was only truly fulfilled with the love of a good husband and the love of their children.

It hurt, being reminded of her failure to live up to his expectations of her, but the big word in her father's beliefs was love, and Ari did not love her. She faced his father with her own burning determination. 'I have the right to choose what I do with my life. My father respected that, as well.'

'I don't think the choice is so unequivocal when you are a mother, Christina,' he shot back at her. 'The rights of your child have to be considered.'

'Papa…' Ari said in a low warning voice.

'She must understand this, Ari,' was the quick riposte.

'I do,' Tina told him flatly. 'And I am considering them.' She lowered her voice so as not to be overheard at the other end of the table as she fiercely added, 'I hope you do, too, because I *am* Theo's mother and I always will be.'

She would not allow them to take over her son. She would concede visits but knew she would hate every minute Theo was away from her. Not all their wealth and caring would make any difference to the hole that would leave in her life until he returned to her. Tears pricked her eyes. Her head was swimming with all the difficulties that lay ahead.

'Please, forgive me my trespasses,' Ari's father said gruffly. 'You're a fine mother, Christina. And that will always be respected by our family. The boy is a credit to you. How can I put it? I want very much to enjoy more of him.'

A warm hand slid over one of her clenched fists and gently squeezed. 'It's all right, Christina,' Ari murmured, 'You're amongst friends, not enemies.'

She stared down at his hand, biting her lips as she tried to fight back the tears. He'd offered his hand in marriage, which was the easiest way out of the custody issue, but how could she take it when she felt so vulnerable to what he could do to her—twisting up her life all over again?

She swallowed hard to ease the choking sensation in her throat and without looking at either man, said, 'I want to go back to the resort now, Ari. It's been a long day.'

'Of course.' Another gentle squeeze of her hand. 'It's been good of you to let us spend this time together.'

'Yes. A wonderful evening,' his father chimed in. 'Thank you, Christina.'

She nodded, not wanting to be drawn into another stressful conversation. She felt painfully pressured as it was. Her gaze lifted to check Theo who was now nodding off on her mother's lap.

Ari rose from his chair. 'Helen, Mama… Christina is tired and it looks like Theo is ready for bed, as well. It's time to call it a night. I'll carry him out to the car, Helen.'

Ari's parents accompanied them out to the car, walking beside her mother who thanked them profusely for their hospitality. All three expressed pleasure in meeting up again at the wedding. Both Maximus and Sophie dropped goodnight kisses on Theo's forehead before Ari passed him over to Tina in the back seat. She thanked them for the birthday party and the car door was finally closed on it, relieving some of the tension in her chest.

Theo slept all the way back to the resort and the conversation between Ari and her mother in the front seats was conducted in low murmurs. Tina sat in silence, hugging her child, feeling intensely possessive of him and already grieving over how much she would have to part from him.

Having arrived at El Greco, Ari once again lifted Theo into his arms and insisted on carrying him to their accommodation. Tina did not protest, knowing that to her mother this was the natural thing for a man to do. The problem came when she unlocked her door and instead of passing Theo to her, Ari carried him straight into her room.

'Which bed?' he asked.

She dashed past him to turn back the covers on Theo's bed and Ari gently laid him down and tucked him in, dropping a kiss on his forehead before straightening up and smiling down at his sleeping son, making Tina's heart contract at the memory of Theo's wish for a Papa. He had one. And very soon he had to know it.

Ari turned to her and she instantly felt a flood of electricity tingling through her entire body. He was too close to her, dangerously close, exuding the sexual magnetism that she should be immune to but wasn't. Being in a bedroom with Ari Zavros, virtually alone with him, was a bad place to be. She quickly backed off, hurrying to the door, waving for him to leave.

He followed but paused beside her, causing inner havoc again. He raised a hand to touch her cheek and she flinched away from the contact. 'Just go, Ari,' she said harshly. 'You've had your day.'

He frowned at her unfriendliness. 'I only wanted to thank you, Christina.'

She forced her voice to a reasonable tone. 'Okay, but you can do that without touching me.'

'Is my touch so repellent to you?'

Panic tore through her at how vulnerable she might be to it. She stared hard at him, desperate not to show him any weakness. 'Don't push it, Ari. I've had enough, today.'

He nodded. 'I'll call you in the morning.'

'No! Tomorrow is *my* family day,' she said firmly. 'Cassandra will be joining us and so will all our relatives from the mainland. We'll meet again at the wedding.'

For one nerve-wracking moment she thought he would challenge her decision. It surprised her when he smiled and said, 'Then I'll look forward to the wedding. Goodnight, Christina.'

'Goodnight,' she repeated automatically, watching him in a daze of confusion as he walked away from her.

He hadn't done anything *wrong* all day. For the most part, he'd been perfectly charming. And she still *wanted* him, despite the grief he'd given her. There had never been any other man who made her feel what he did. But he probably made every woman feel the same way. It meant nothing. It would be foolish to let it cloud her judgement.

When Theo was told that Ari was his Papa, he would want them to be all together, living happily ever after.

But that was a fairy-tale and this story didn't have the right ingredients. The prince did not love the princess, so how could there be a happy ever after?

Tina fiercely told herself she must not lose sight of that, no matter what!

CHAPTER EIGHT

ARI stood beside George in the church, impatient for the marriage service to be over, his mind working through what had to be accomplished with Christina. Theo was not a problem. His son had grinned broadly at him as he had carried the cushion with the wedding rings up the aisle. He would want his Papa. But Christina had only smiled at George, keeping her gaze averted from him.

She looked absolutely stunning in a dark red satin gown. Desire had kicked in so hard and fast Ari had struggled to control the instinctive physical response to instantly wanting her in his bed again. 'She is magnificent, is she not?' George had murmured, meaning his bride, and she was, but Cassandra stirred nothing in him.

There were many beautiful women in the world. Ari had connected to quite a few of them, but none had twisted his heart as it was being twisted right now. He had to have Christina again. Perhaps she touched something deep in him because she was the mother of his child. Or perhaps it was because he had taken her innocence and she made him feel very strongly about righting the wrong he had done her. The reasons didn't matter. Somehow he had to persuade her to be his wife.

His parents certainly approved of the marriage and not only because of Theo.

'She's lovely, Ari, and I could be good friends with Helen,' his mother had remarked.

His father had been more decisive in his opinion. 'Beautiful, intelligent, and with a fighting spirit I admire. She's a good match for you, Ari. Don't let her get away from you. The two of you should have many interesting children together.'

Easier said than done, Ari thought grimly.

She didn't want him to touch her.

Today, she didn't want to look at him.

Was she frightened of the attraction she still felt with him, frightened of giving in to it? She would *have* to look at him at the wedding reception *and* suffer his touch during the bridal waltz. Not just a touch, either. Full body contact. He would make the waltz one of the most intimate dances she'd ever had, force the sexual chemistry between them to the surface so she couldn't hide from it, couldn't ignore it, couldn't deny it.

She was not going to get away from him.

Tina listened to the marriage service as she stood beside her sister. These same words could be spoken to her soon if she said *yes* to Ari's proposal. Would he take the vows seriously, or were they just mumbo-jumbo to him—the means to an end?

He *had* offered the fidelity clause in a prenuptial agreement. She would get full custody of Theo and any

other children they might have together if he faltered
on that front. Could she be happy with him if he kept
faith with his marriage deal?

It was a risk she probably shouldn't be considering.
Cass's wedding was getting to her, stirring up feelings
that could land her in a terrible mess. Plus all the marriage talk amongst her Greek relatives yesterday had
kept Ari's offer pounding through her mind—no relief
at all from the connection with him.

Her mother had raved on about how kind he'd been—
taking Tina and Theo out for the day, the birthday party
at his parents' home—which had reminded the relatives
of how attentive he'd been to Tina at the family party
in Athens. Comments on how eligible he was followed,
with speculative looks that clearly said Helen's daughter
might have a chance with him. Being a single mother
was…*so unfortunate.*

Little did they know that Theo was the drawcard, not
her. They would all be watching her with Ari today—
watching, hoping, encouraging. She would have to look
at him soon, take his arm as they followed Cass and
George out of the church, be seated next to him at the
wedding reception, dance with him. The whole thing
was a nightmare with no escape, and it would be worse
when the truth was told.

Her mother would want her to marry Ari.

Her relatives would think her mad if she didn't.

Only Cass might take her side, asking what *she*
wanted, but Cass wouldn't be there. She and George
would be off on their honeymoon. Besides, what Tina
wanted was impossible—utterly impossible to go back

to the time when she had loved Ari with all her heart and believed he loved her. How could she ever believe that now?

She felt a sharp stab of envy as George promised to love Cass for the rest of his life. There was no doubting the fervour in his voice, no doubting Cass, either, as she promised her love in return. A huge welling of emotion brought tears to Tina's eyes as the two of them were declared husband and wife. She wished them all the happiness in the world. This was how it should be between a man and a woman, starting out on a life together.

She was still blinking away the wetness in her eyes when she had to link up with Ari for the walk out of the church. He wound her arm around his and hugged her close, instantly causing an eruption of agitation inside Tina.

'Why do women always weep at weddings?' he murmured, obviously wanting her to focus on him.

She didn't. She swept her gaze around the gathered guests, swallowed hard to unblock her voice and answered, 'Because change is scary and you hope with all your heart that everything will work out right.'

'What is right in your mind, Christina?' he persisted.

Christina...he invariably used her full name because it was what she had called herself for the modelling career that had been cut short after he had left her pregnant. During the months they'd spent together she'd loved how that name had rolled off his tongue in a caressing tone. She wished he wouldn't keep using the same tone now, that he'd call her Tina like everyone else. Then she wouldn't be constantly reminded of the girl she had been and how much she had once loved him.

She wasn't that girl any more.

She'd moved on.

Except Ari could still twist her heart and shoot treacherous excitement through her veins.

It was wrong for him to have that power. *Wrong!* And the pain of her disillusionment with him lent a vehement conviction to her voice as she answered him. 'It's right if they keep loving each other for the rest of their lives, no matter what happens along the way.' She looked at him then, meeting the quizzical amber eyes with as much hard directness as she could muster. 'We don't have that basis for marriage, do we?'

'I don't believe that love is the glue that keeps a marriage together,' he shot back at her. 'It's a madness that's blind to any sensible judgement and it quickly burns out when people's expectations of it aren't met. Absolute commitment is what I'm offering you, Christina. You can trust that more than love.'

His cynical view of love was deeply offensive to her, yet she felt the strength of his will encompassing her, battering at her resistance to what he wanted. 'I'd rather have what Cass and George have than what you're offering,' she muttered, resenting the implication that her sister's happiness with her marriage wouldn't last.

'I understand that change must be scary to you, Christina,' he murmured in her ear. 'I promise you I'll do all I can to make the transition easy for both you and Theo.'

The transition! He expected her to give up her life in Australia—all she'd known, all she'd worked for—to be with him. It wouldn't work the other way around. She knew that wouldn't even be considered. She was supposed to see marriage to him as more desirable than anything else, and she would have seen it that way once, *if he'd loved her.*

That was the sticking point.

Tina couldn't push herself past it.

The hurt that he didn't wouldn't go away.

Outside the church they had to pose for photographs. Tina pasted a smile on her face. Her facial muscles ached from keeping it there. Ari lifted Theo up to perch against his shoulder for some shots and everywhere she looked people seemed to be smiling and nodding benevolently at the grouping of the three of them—not as bridesmaid, best man and page boy, but as wife, husband and son. Ari's parents stood next to her mother and Uncle Dimitri. They would all be allied against her if she decided to reject the marriage proposal.

She ached all over from the tension inside her. At least the drive to the reception spared her any active pressure from Ari. Theo rode in their car, sitting between them on the back seat, chatting happily to the man he would soon know as his father. Tina was grateful not have to say anything but she was acutely aware of Theo's pleasure in Ari and Ari's pleasure in his son. How could she explain to a five-year-old boy why they couldn't all be together with the Papa he had wished for?

They arrived at the Santo winery. Its reception centre was perched on top of a cliff overlooking the sea. To the side of the dining section was a large open area shaded by pergolas and normally used for wine-tasting. Guests gathered here while the bridal party posed for more photographs. Waiters offered drinks and canapés. A festive mood was very quickly in full swing.

Tina thought she might escape from Ari's side for a while after the photographer was satisfied but that proved impossible. He led her straight over to George's family who were all in high spirits, delighted to meet their new daughter-in-law's sister and press invitations to be their guest on Patmos at any time.

Then he insisted on introducing her to his sisters and their husbands—beautiful women, handsome men, bright beautiful people who welcomed Tina into their group, making friendly chat about the wedding. Their children, Ari's nephews, all four of them around Theo's age, quickly drew him off with them to play boy games. Which left Tina very much the centre of attention and as pleasant as the conversation was, she knew they were measuring her up as wife material for Ari.

After a reasonable interval she excused herself, saying she should check if Cass needed her for anything.

It didn't provide much of an escape.

'I'll come with you,' Ari instantly said. 'George might require something from me.'

As soon as they were out of earshot, Tina muttered, 'You told them, didn't you?'

'Not the children. Theo won't hear it from them. Keeping it from your family until after the wedding will be respected, Christina. I simply wanted my sisters to understand where you are with me.'

'I'm not anywhere with you,' she snapped defensively, giving him a reproachful glare.

He held her gaze with a blaze of resolute purpose. 'You're my intended wife and I told them so.'

'Why are you rushing into this?' she cried in exasperation. 'We can make reasonable arrangements about sharing Theo. Other people do it all the time. You don't have to *marry* me!'

'I *want* to marry you.'

'Only because of Theo and that's not right, Ari.'

'You're wrong. I want you, too, Christina.'

She shook her head in anguished denial, instantly shying away from letting herself believe him. Cass and George were chatting to a group of their modelling-world friends and Tina gestured to the gorgeous women amongst them. 'Look at what you could have. I'm not in their class. And I bet they'd lap up your attention.'

'You're in a class of your own and I don't want their attention. I want yours.'

'Today you do, but what about the rest of your future, Ari?'

'I'll make my future with you if you'll give it a chance.'

Again she shook her head. There was no point in arguing with him. He had his mind set on a course of action and nothing she said was going to shift him from it.

'It's worth a chance, isn't it, Christina?' he pressed. 'We were both happy when we were intimately involved. It can be that way again. You can't really want to be separated from Theo during the time he spends with me if you insist he has to bounce between us.'

She would hate it.

But she was also hating the way Cass's girlfriends were gobbling Ari up with their eyes, watching him approach the bride and groom. Not that she could blame them for doing it. He was even more of a sex magnet today, dressed in a formal dinner suit which enhanced his perfect male physique, highlighting how stunningly handsome he was. *A Greek God.* Tina had no doubt they were thinking that. And envying her for having him at her side.

Could she stand a lifetime of that with Ari?

Would he always *stay* at her side?

She felt sick from all the churning inside her. Any distraction from it was intensely welcome. Hopefully Cass would provide it for a while. She and Ari joined the celebrity group and were quickly introduced around. One of George's friends, another photographer, took the opportunity to give Tina his business card.

'Come to me and I'll turn you into a model as famous as your sister. No disrespect to you, Cass, but this girl has quite a unique look that I'd love to capture.'

Cass laughed and turned a beaming smile to Tina. 'I've always said you don't have to be a homebody.'

'But I like being a homebody.' She tried to hand the card back, embarrassed by the spotlight being turned on her. 'Thank you, but no.'

'Keep it,' he insisted. 'I mean it. I would love to work

with that wonderful long neck and those marvellous cheekbones. Your short hair sets them off to perfection.'

'No, please, I don't want it. I have nowhere to put your card anyway.'

'I'll keep it for you. You might have second thoughts,' Ari said, taking the card and sliding it into his breast pocket. He smiled around at the group. 'No disrespect to any of you lovely ladies, but I also think Christina is unique. And very special.'

Which was virtually a public declaration of his interest in her, putting off the interest that any of the lovely ladies might want to show in him.

Tina's *marvellous cheekbones* were instantly illuminated by heat.

Cass leaned over to whisper in her ear. 'Mama is right. Ari is very taken by you. Give him a chance, Tina. He's rather special, too.'

A chance!

Even Cass was on Ari's side.

Tina felt the whole world was conspiring to make her take the step she was frightened of taking.

'I think I need some cool air,' she muttered.

Ari heard her. He took her arm. 'Please excuse us, everyone. We're off to catch the sea breeze for a breather.'

He drew her over to the stone wall along the cliff edge. Tina didn't protest the move. It was useless. She was trapped into being Ari's companion at this wedding and he was not about to release her.

'Why did you take that card?' she demanded crossly.

'Because it was my fault that you didn't continue the modelling career you might have had. It's not too

late to try again, Christina. You actually have a more
individual beauty now. If you'd like to pursue that path
you'd have my full support.'

She frowned at him. 'I'm a mother, Ari. That comes
first. And isn't it what you want from me, to be the
mother of your children?'

'Yes, but there are models who are also mothers. It
can be done, Christina.' He lifted his hand and gently stroked her hot cheek, his eyes burning with what
seemed like absolute sincerity. 'I destroyed two of your
dreams. At least I can give one of them back to you.
Maybe the other…with enough time together. '

She choked up.

It was all too much.

Her mind was in a total jumble. She wanted to believe him, yet he couldn't give her back what he had
taken. Whatever they had in the future would be different. And was he just saying these things to win her
over? She'd trusted him with her heart and soul once
and here she was being vulnerable to his seduction
again. How could she believe him? Or trust him? She
desperately needed to clear her head.

She stepped back from the tingling touch on her
cheek and forced herself to speak. 'I'd like a glass of
water, Ari.'

He held her gaze for several moments, his eyes
searching for what he wanted to see in hers—a softening towards him, cracks in her resistance. Tina silently
pleaded for him to go, give her some space, some relief
from the constant pressure to give in and take what he
was offering.

Finally he nodded. 'I'll fetch you one.'

She stared out to sea, gulping in fresh air, needing a blast of oxygen to cool her mind of its feverish thoughts.

It didn't really work.

Despite her past experience with Ari Zavros, or maybe because of it, one mind-bending thought kept pounding away at her, undermining her resistance to the course he was pressing her to take.

Give it a chance.

Give it a chance.

Give it a chance.

CHAPTER NINE

THE bridal waltz…

Tina took a deep breath and rose to her feet as Ari held back her chair. He'd been the perfect gentleman all evening. The speech he'd made preceding his toast to the bride and groom had contained all the right touches, charming the guests into smiling and feeling really good about this marriage. An excellent Best Man.

Maybe he was the best man for her, given that she'd not felt attracted to anyone else in the past six years. If she never connected with some other man… did she want to live the rest of her life totally barren of the sexual pleasure she had known with Ari?

Give it a chance…

As he steered her towards the dance floor, the warmth of his hand on the pit of her back spread a flow of heat to her lower body. The band played 'Moon River,' a slow jazz waltz that Cass and George obviously revelled in, executing it with great panache; gliding, twirling, dipping, making it look both romantic and very, very sexy.

Little quivers started running down Tina's legs as

she and Ari waited for their cue to join in. It had been so long since he had held her close. Would she feel the same wild surge of excitement when she connected to his strong masculinity? It was impossible to quell the electric buzz of anticipation when their cue came and he swept her onto the dance floor, yet she stiffened when he drew her against him, instinctively fighting his power to affect her so *physically*.

'Relax, Christina,' he murmured. 'Let your body respond to the rhythm of the music. I know it can.'

Of course, he knew. There was very little he didn't know about her body and how it responded. And she had to find out what it might be like with him now, didn't she? *If she was to give it a chance.*

She forced herself to relax and go with the flow of the dance. He held her very close; her breasts pressed to his chest, her stomach in fluttering contact with his groin area, her thighs brushing his with every move he made. Her heart was pounding much faster than the beat of the music. Her female hormones were stirred into a lustful frenzy. She was in the arms of a Greek God who was hers for the taking and the temptation to take whatever she could of him was roaring through her.

Ari made the most of Christina's surrender to the dance, hoping the sexual chemistry sizzling through him was being transmitted through every sensual contact point. She felt good in his arms. She was the right height for him, tall enough for their bodies to fit in a very satisfying way as he moved her around the dance floor. The sway of her hips, the fullness of her breasts impacting with their lush femininity, the scent of her skin and hair…everything about her was firing up his desire to have her surrender to him.

The waltz ended. She didn't exactly push out of his embrace but eased herself back enough to put a little distance between them. Her cheeks were flushed and she kept her eyes lowered, their thick black lashes hiding any vulnerable feelings. He was sure she had been physically affected by the intimacy of the dance but whether that was enough to sway her his way he didn't know.

The Master of Ceremonies invited all the guests to dance to the next song which had been especially requested by the bride. Ari instantly understood its significance when the band started playing the tune. He and Christina had heard Stevie Wonder's version of it on the car radio on one of their trips together.

'You are the sunshine of my life,' he said, recalling how he had applied the words to her. 'It's your father's favourite song.'

'Yes,' she said huskily. 'Cass misses him, too. He would have been very proud of her today.' Her lashes lifted and she gave him a wry little smile. 'I'm surprised you remembered.'

'Special songs can be very evocative. You *were* the sunshine of my life while we were together, Christina.'

The smile twisted into a grimace. 'There's been a long night since then, Ari. Though I'm sure you found plenty of sunshine elsewhere.'

'Not of the same quality.'

Her gaze slid away from his. 'We have to dance,' she muttered.

She allowed him to hold her close again without any initial resistance. It was *some* progress, he thought, though he savagely wished she wouldn't keep harping on the other women who'd been in his life. The past was the past—impossible to change it. If she'd just set her sights on the future, that was the progress he needed.

He bent his head closer to hers and murmured, 'What you and I can have *now* is what matters, Christina.'

She didn't answer.

Hopefully she was thinking about it.

Tina fiercely wished she could forget everything else but *now,* pretend she was meeting Ari for the first time, feeling all that he made her feel, her whole body brilliantly alive to exciting sensations. She wouldn't care about the other women if this was her first experience with him. She'd be blissfully thinking that he was the man who could make her life complete.

Maybe he would if she set the pain he'd given her aside. He'd said he wanted to give her back the dreams he'd destroyed. Yet it was a terribly risky step, trusting his word. If he didn't keep it, she would hate herself for being a fool, hate him for his deceit, and end up a totally embittered woman.

But she could make him pay for it.

He would lose Theo and any other children they might have if he broke his promise of fidelity. She wouldn't have to worry over the custody issue. All rights would be hers. In which case, it was worth taking the chance, wasn't it?

Her father's favourite song came to an end. She saw Cass go over to her mother who had danced with Uncle Dimitri and give her a hug and a kiss. It caused a painful drag on Tina's heart. She knew her father would have wanted her to marry Ari. It might have made him proud of her if she did.

She looked up at the man who was her son's father, and the seductive amber eyes instantly locked onto hers, simmering with the promise of all the pleasure they'd once had together. Her heart quivered over the decision she had made but it *was* made and she wasn't going to fret over it any longer.

'Let's go where we can talk privately,' she said firmly.

He nodded, quickly obliging her by steering her off the dance floor, then taking her arm and walking her out to the large open patio where they'd been before the reception dinner.

'Would you like to sit down?' he asked, waving to the wooden tables under the pergola.

'Yes.' Her legs were feeling wobbly. Besides, sitting across from him at a table would be more comfortable for laying out the deal she would accept.

They sat. Ari spread his hands in an open gesture, inviting her confidence. 'What do you want to say, Christina?'

Her hands were tightly clenched in her lap. This was it—the moment when her life would begin to take a totally different direction. A wave of trepidation mangled her vocal chords. She looked hard at him, forcing her imagination to see him as a caring and committed father and husband. If she could believe it, maybe the marriage would work out right. She desperately wanted it to.

The first step was to say the words.

Say them.

Just do it and have done with the whole nerve-wracking dilemma.

'I... I...'

'Yes?' Ari encouraged, leaning forward, giving her his concentrated attention.

A surge of panic had made her hesitate. Her mind was screaming *wait! Don't commit yet!* But what would she be waiting for? The situation wasn't going to change. This man was Theo's father and she had loved him with all her heart once. If he was serious about forging a good relationship with her, shouldn't she give it a chance?

'I'll marry you,' she blurted out, sealing the decision.

His face broke into a happy grin. His eyes sparkled with pleasure. Or was it triumph, having won what he wanted? 'That's great, Christina!' he enthused. 'I'm glad you've decided it's the best course because it is.'

He was *so* positive it instantly raised doubts in Tina's mind. Was she a fool for giving in? She had to put a high value on the marriage so he would treat her as he should.

'Give me your hand,' he pressed, reaching across the table to take it.

She shook her head, keeping both hands tightly in her lap. 'I haven't finished what I want to say.'

He frowned at her reluctance to meet his offered hand. He spread his fingers in open appeal. 'Tell me what you need from me.'

'I need you to sign the prenuptial agreement you offered me,' she threw back at him, determined that those terms be kept. It was her safeguard against being used to give Ari a stronger paternal position than he had now.

He drew back, his mouth twisting into an ironic grimace. A sharp wariness wiped the sparkle from his eyes. Tina's stomach cramped with tension. If he retracted the offer, she could not go ahead with the marriage, regardless of any pressure from any source. It was risking too much. He might walk away from her again and take Theo with him.

She waited for his reply.

Waited…and waited…her nerves stretching tighter with every second that passed.

Ari's mind was swiftly sifting through Christina's possible motivations. She didn't trust his word. He understood where she was coming from on that score. What concerned him most was if she had a vengeful nature.

The prenuptial agreement he'd offered gave her everything if he didn't remain a faithful husband. What if she planned to be such a cold, shrewish wife, he would be driven to find some pleasure in other company? If she was secretly determined not to be responsive to him, he'd be condemning himself to a hellish marriage. He needed more than her public compliance to a couple of dances to feel secure about winning her over in bed.

Out here alone together, she wouldn't even give him her hand.

What was in her mind?

What was in her heart?

A totally selfish revenge on him…or hope that they could make a happy future together?

He was risking a lot.

He decided she had to meet him halfway before he tied a knot which could not be undone.

'I am prepared to sign it, Christina,' he said, his eyes burning a very direct challenge at her as he added, 'If you're prepared to spend one night with me before I do.'

She stared at him, startled by the provision he was laying down. 'Why? You'll have all the nights you want with me after we're married.'

'I want to be sure that I will want them. I won't sign away my right to my son to a woman who'll turn her back on me. I need you to show me that won't happen, Christina. Right now your attitude towards me is hardly encouraging. You won't even give me your hand.'

Heat surged up her neck and scorched her cheeks. Her eyes glittered a challenge right back at him. 'I think it's a good idea for us to spend a night together before either of us commit ourselves to anything. Maybe you're not as good a lover as you used to be, Ari.'

Relief swept through him at her ready acceptance of a sex-test. He smiled. 'And maybe you'll warm to me once I prove that I am.'

Again her lashes swept down, veiling her feelings. She heaved a sigh, probably relieving tension. 'We're scheduled to leave Santorini the day after tomorrow,' she muttered.

'That can easily be changed.'

She shook her head. 'I'll spend tomorrow night with you.' Her lashes lifted and there was resolute fire in her eyes. 'That can be the decider for both of us.'

She would bolt if he didn't satisfy her. Ari was confident that he could if she was willing to let it happen.

'Agreed,' he said. 'However, our other deal ends tonight, Christina. Tomorrow you tell your mother and Theo that I am his father. Whatever happens between us, this has to be openly acknowledged.'

She nodded. 'I'll do it in the morning.'

'Make sure your mother understands the circumstances, that I was not told you had my child until we met in Dubai. I would have come back to you had I known, Christina.'

She made a wry grimace. 'Since I've decided I might marry you, naturally I'll put you in as good a light as possible to my mother.'

'It's the truth,' he rammed home as hard as he could, wanting her to believe at least that much of him.

'And my truth is you left me and I didn't want you back,' she shot out, her eyes glittering with angry pride. 'Don't you start harassing me, Ari. I'll do what I have to do to smooth the path to a workable future.'

His father's words about Christina were instantly replayed in his mind...*beautiful, intelligent, and with a fighting spirit I admire.* If she shared his own strong desire for everything to turn out well, there was no need to concern himself about her presentation of the past to her mother.

'I'd like to be there when you tell Theo I'm his father,' he said softly, needing to remove the anger he'd unwittingly triggered. 'I've missed so much—not being there when he was born, his first words, his first step, learning to swim, his first day at kindergarten. I want to see the expression in his eyes when he realises I am the Papa he wished for. Will you give me that, Christina?'

Her eyes went blank, probably focussing inward on the memories she hadn't shared with him. He willed her to be more generous now. Yet when she did speak, her whole expression was one of deep anxiety.

'I hope you really mean to be a good father to him, Ari. Please don't lead him on and then drop him, pursuing other interests.'

He knew she felt he had done that to her.

It had been wrong of him, letting temptation overrule good sense. She had been too young, too impressionable. Theo was much more so and she was frightened for him. Her fear evoked a powerful surge of emotion in him. He wanted to say he'd look after them both for the rest of his life. He hated seeing the fretful doubts in her eyes. But laying them to rest would take time.

'Give me your hand, Christina,' he gently commanded, his eyes pleading for her acquiescence.

Very slowly she lifted it from her lap and held it out to him.

He enclosed it with his. 'I promise you I'll do everything I can to win Theo's love and keep it,' he said fervently. 'He's my son.'

Tears welled into her eyes. She nodded, unable to speak. He stroked her palm with his thumb, wanting to give comfort and reassurance, wishing he could sweep her into his embrace but cautious about rushing her where she might not be ready to go.

'If it's okay with you, I'll come to the El Greco resort tomorrow afternoon. We can spend some time with Theo before having our night together,' he quietly suggested.

She nodded again, sucked in a deep breath and blurted out, 'I'm sorry. It was mean of me…leaving you out of Theo's life.'

'You had your reasons,' he murmured sympathetically. 'It's how we take it from here that will count most to Theo.'

'Yes,' she agreed huskily, taking another deep breath before adding, 'He usually takes a nap after lunch. If you come at four o'clock, we'll tell him then.'

'Thank you.'

She gave him a wobbly smile. 'If that's everything settled, we should go back to the wedding reception. We'll be missed. It is Cass's night and I want to be there for her.'

'And I for George.'

Their first deal was still in place. He had to wait until tomorrow before taking what he wanted with Christina, yet her hand was still in his and as he rose from the table, the temptation to draw her up from her seat and straight into his embrace was irresistible. She didn't try to break free but her free hand fluttered in agitation

against his chest and there was a heart-piercing vulnerability in the eyes that met his.

He hated her fear. It made him feel even more wrong
about what he'd taken from her in the past. He pressed
a soft kiss on her forehead and murmured, 'I'll make it
right, Christina. For you and for Theo.'

He gave her what he hoped was a reassuring smile
as he released her, only retaining her hand, keeping that
physical link for the walk back to the wedding reception, wanting her to feel secure with him.

Tonight belonged to Cassandra and George.

Tomorrow was his.

He could wait.

CHAPTER TEN

Tina waited until after their Greek relatives departed for the mainland so she could have a private chat to her mother about her connection to Ari. Everyone had still been revelling in Cass's wedding—such a wonderful family celebration. Amongst the happy comments were a few arch remarks about Ari's interest in her.

'He didn't have eyes for anyone else.'

'Never left your side all evening.'

'Such a charming man!'

'And so handsome!'

Tina had shrugged off the curiosity, discouraging it by refocussing the conversation on her sister's life. However, she saw the same curiosity in her mother's eyes, and when they were finally alone together, relaxing on the lounges by the swimming pool, watching Theo practice diving into it, she didn't have to think about how to lead into revealing the truth. Her mother did it for her.

'Are you seeing Ari again today, Tina?'

'Yes. And there's something I have to tell you, Mama.' She took a deep breath to calm her jumpy nerves and started at the beginning. 'Ari Zavros and I were not meeting for the first time in Athens. Six years ago he was in Australia on a three-month tour of the wineries in our country. I met him on a modelling assignment and fell in love with him.'

Her mother instantly leapt to the truth, understanding of Ari's behaviour towards them flashing straight into her eyes. 'He's Theo's father.'

'Yes. I didn't expect to ever see him again. It was a shock when he was presented to us as George's best man. I asked him to wait until after the wedding before revealing that my son was also his because it would have been a major distraction from Cass and that wasn't fair, but today we have to deal with it, Mama.'

'Oh, my dear!' Her mother swung her legs off the lounge to face her directly with a look of anxious concern. 'These past few days must have been very difficult for you.'

Tina had to fight back tears. She hadn't expected such a rush of sympathy from her mother. Shock and perhaps criticism for her silence, worry over the situation, fretting over the choices to be made… she'd geared herself to cope with all this but not the caring for her feelings and the quick understanding of the distress she had been hiding.

'I thought…he was gone from my life, Mama,' she choked out. 'But he's not and he never will be again. He's made that very clear.'

'Yes…very clear,' her mother repeated, nodding as she recollected how Ari had inserted himself and his family into their time on Santorini. 'I don't think that's going to change, Tina. He's definitely intent on making a claim on his son.'

'And he has the wealth and power to back it up. There's no point in trying to resist his claim, Mama. I have to give way.'

'Has he said how he wants to deal with the situation?'

Tina's mouth instantly twisted into an ironic grimace. 'He wants me to marry him.'

'Ah!'

There was no real shock in that *Ah!*—more a realisation of the bigger claim being made—one that would completely change her daughter's life, as well as her grandson's.

After a few moments' thought, her mother asked, 'His family knows all this?'

'He told them after our meeting in Athens. He had no doubt that Theo was his child. His age…his eyes…'

'Yes…now I see.' Her mother nodded a few times. 'They have been extending a welcome to join their family because of Theo.'

'He is the main attraction,' Tina said dryly.

'But they have been very gracious to us, as well, Tina. Which shows they are prepared to accept you as Ari's wife. How do you feel about it?'

She shook her head. 'I don't know. He said he would have come back to me had I told him he'd left me pregnant. I didn't tell him because he didn't love me. I was only a…a charming episode…that he could walk away from.'

'But you loved him.'

'Yes. Totally.'

'And now?'

'I doubt there will ever be anyone else for me, Mama, but it's Theo he wants. I can't fool myself that I'm suddenly the woman he loves above all others.'

'Perhaps you are more special to him now because you are the mother of his child. It's a very Greek way of thinking, Tina. And sometimes love grows from sharing the most precious things to both of you.'

Tina choked up, remembering Ari listing how much he had missed of Theo because she had denied him knowledge of his son.

Her mother heaved a sigh. 'It's not for me to say what you should do, my darling. What do you think is best for you?'

'Oh, probably to marry him,' Tina said in a rush, relieved in a way to finally have it out in the open. 'I think he will be a good father. He's asked me to wait until he comes here this afternoon for us to tell Theo together that he does have a Papa. And after that—well, Ari and I need some time alone to…to see how we feel about each other, Mama. He wants to take me somewhere. Will you look after Theo, have him in your room tonight?'

'Oh, dear!' Her mother shook her head in dismay at realising what the all-night arrangement most probably meant. 'There's so much to take in. I wish your father was here.'

'Don't worry, Mama. I have to make a decision and I think this is the best way to do it.'

'Well, of course I will look after Theo, but…do be careful, Tina,' she said anxiously. 'If you decide not to marry Ari...I remember how you were when you were pregnant with Theo.'

'That won't happen again, Mama,' Tina assured her. It didn't matter this time if Ari used a contraceptive or not. She knew she was in a safe period of her cycle. She reached across and took her mother's hand. 'Thank you taking all this so well. I hate being a problem to you.'

'Not a problem, dear. Just... I do so want you to have a happy life and I wish with all my heart that everything turns out well with Ari.'

The fairy-tale happy ending.

Maybe if she could believe in it enough, it might happen. She'd have a better idea of how the future would run after tonight. Right now she couldn't trust Ari's word that he would remain a faithful husband. Even if they did find sexual pleasure with each other, that was no guarantee he would always be satisfied with her. She might begin to believe they really could forge a good marriage together after he signed the prenuptial agreement.

If he did.

Ari spent an extremely vexatious morning with his lawyer who was dead against signing away paternal rights under any circumstances. A financial settlement was fine in the case of divorce but giving up one's children was utter madness, especially since Ari was marrying to have his son.

'I'm not here for your advice,' Ari had finally said. 'Just draw up the agreement I've spelled out to you. It's an issue of showing good faith and I *will* show it.'

'Show it by all means,' his lawyer shot back at it him, 'but don't sign it.'

He hadn't...yet.

He'd done many deals in his life but none as risky as the one he'd proposed to Christina. The money didn't worry him. He would never begrudge financial support for her and their children. But if the response he needed from her was not forthcoming tonight, marrying her might be too much of a gamble.

His head told him this.

Yet his heart was already set on having Christina Savalas as his wife.

She touched him in ways no other woman had. He had been her first lover, almost certainly her only one, which made her his in a very primal sense. Plus the fact she had carried his child made her uniquely special. Besides, his wealth was not a big attraction to her or she would have gone after a slice of it to support their son rather than taking complete responsibility for him. She was only concerned about the kind of person he was. Looks, money...none of that counted. If he didn't measure up as a man she wanted in her life, he'd be out of it.

He'd never been challenged like this. Who he was on the surface of it had always been enough. Christina was hitting him at deeper levels and he felt totally driven to prove he did measure up—driven to remove all fear from her eyes. Winning her over had somehow become more important than anything else in his life.

The compelling tug of having Theo was a big part of it, but she was part of Theo, too. Ari couldn't separate them in his mind. Didn't want to separate them. The three of them made a family. *His* family. He had to make it so by any means possible because he couldn't tolerate the idea of Christina taking their son back to Australia and shutting him out of their lives as much as she legally could.

He lunched with his parents who were eager for another visit with their grandson. 'Tomorrow,' Ari promised them. 'I'll bring Christina and Theo and Helen back here tomorrow to sort out what is to be done.'

He had to stop them leaving Santorini on schedule. Even if Christina rejected his offer of marriage, she had to see reason about discussing future arrangements for their son. If she accepted his proposal, they would have a wedding to plan. More than a wedding. There would be many decisions to be made on setting up a life together—tying up ends in Australia, where best to make their home.

Ari was tense with determination as he drove to the El Greco resort. He told himself the meeting with Theo was relatively uncomplicated. There was no need to be uptight about his son's response. He had wished for a Papa. Revealing who that Papa was would certainly be a pleasure. What happened afterwards with Christina was the critical time. He fiercely hoped that was going to be a pleasure, too. If it wasn't... He instantly clicked his mind off any negative train of thought. This had to work.

Tina and her mother and Theo were sitting at one of the snack bar tables having afternoon tea when Ari arrived. He came striding down the ramp to the pool patio, a hard purposeful expression on his face, and headed straight towards where their rooms were located.

'We're here!' Tina called out, rising from her chair to catch his attention, her heartbeat instantly accelerating at what his arrival meant for both her and Theo.

His head jerked around and his expression immediately lightened on seeing them. Theo jumped off his chair and ran to meet him. Ari scooped him up in his arms and perched him against his shoulder, smiling broadly at his son's eagerness to welcome him.

'I finished the train station. You must come and see it, Ari,' Theo prattled happily.

'As soon as I say hello to your mother and grandmother,' he promised.

He shot a sharp look of enquiry at Tina as he approached their table. She nodded, assuring him her mother had been told. He smiled at both of them but the smile didn't quite reach his eyes. It made Tina wonder how tense he was over the situation. Marriage was a big step and it might not be the best course for them to take. Was he having second thoughts about his proposal?

He addressed her mother directly, speaking in a quiet tone that carried an impressive intensity of purpose. 'Helen, I want you to know I will look after your daughter with much more care than I did in the past. Please trust me on that.'

'Tina and Theo are very precious to me, Ari,' her mother answered. 'I hope your caring will be as deep as mine.'

He nodded and turned his gaze to Tina. 'Theo wants me to see his train station.'

'I'll take you to our room. He did a great job putting all the Lego together.' She smiled at her son. 'It was very tricky, wasn't it, darling?'

'Very tricky,' he echoed, then grinned triumphantly at Ari. 'But I did it!'

'I knew you were a clever boy,' he warmly approved.

'Will you wait here, Mama?' Tina asked.

'Yes, dear. Go on now.'

Theo was full of questions about Ari's nephews whom he'd spent most of his time with at the wedding reception. Tina didn't have to say anything on their walk to her room. She was acutely conscious of the easy bond Ari had already established with their son and felt fairly sure there would be no trauma attached to revealing the truth. If she made it like a fairy-tale to Theo, he might accept it unquestioningly. On the other hand, there could be a host of questions both of them would have to answer.

Her chest ached with tension as she opened the door to her room and stood aside for Ari to carry Theo inside. He paused a moment, giving her a burning look of command as he said, *'I'll tell him.'*

She felt an instant wave of resentment at his arbitrary taking over from her, yet it did relieve her of the responsibility of explaining the situation to Theo. *Let him get it right for their son,* she thought, closing the door behind them, then parking herself on the chair at the writing desk while Ari duly admired the Lego train station.

'Does your Mama tell you bed-time stories, Theo?' he asked, sitting down on the bed beside the fully constructed station.

'Yes. She points to the words in the book and I can read some of them now,' he answered proudly.

'I think you must be very quick at learning things. If I tell you a story, I wonder if you could guess the ending,' Ari said with a teasing smile.

'Tell me! Tell me!' Theo cried eagerly, sitting cross-legged on the floor in front of Ari, his little body bent forward attentively.

Ari bent forwards, too, his forearms resting on his knees, his gaze locked on the amber eyes shining up at him. 'Once upon a time a prince from a faraway country travelled to a land on the other side of the world.'

Tina was totally stunned that Ari had chosen to use a fairy story to convey the truth, yet how much of the truth would he tell? The tension inside her screwed up several notches.

'There he met a beautiful princess and she was like no one else he'd ever met. He wanted to be with her all the time and she wanted to be with him so they were together while he was in her country. But eventually he had to leave to carry out business for his kingdom back home. It hurt the princess very much when he said goodbye to her and when she found out that she was going to have a baby she decided not to send any message to the prince about it. She didn't want him to come back, then leave her again because it would hurt too much. So she kept the baby a secret from him.'

'Was the baby a boy or a girl?' Theo asked.

'It was a boy. And he was very much loved by her family. This made the princess think he didn't need a Papa because he already had enough people to love him. She didn't know that the boy secretly wished for a Papa.'

'Like me,' Theo popped in. 'But I didn't wish for one until I went to school. It was because my friends there have fathers.'

'It is only natural for you to want one,' Ari assured him.

'Does the boy in the story get his?'

'Let me tell you how it happened. After a few years the sister of the princess was to marry a man who came from the same country as the prince, so her family had to travel halfway around the world to attend the wedding. The princess didn't know that this man was a cousin of the prince and she would meet him again. It was a shock to her when she did, and when the prince saw her son, he knew the boy was his son, too. They had the same eyes.'

'Like you and me,' Theo said, instantly grasping the point.

'Yes. Exactly like that. But the princess asked the prince to keep her secret until after her sister's wedding because she didn't want to take people's attention away from the bride. The prince understood this but he wanted to spend as much time as he could with his son. And he also wanted the princess to know that being a father meant a lot to him. It made him very sad that he had missed out on so much of his son's life and he wanted to be there for him in the future.'

'Can I guess now?' Theo asked.

Ari nodded.

Theo cocked his head to the side, not quite sure he had it right, but wanting to know. 'Are you my Papa, Ari?'

'Yes, Theo. I am,' he answered simply.

Tina held her breath until she saw a happy grin break out on Theo's face. The same grin spread across Ari's. Neither of them looked at her. This was their moment— five years in the waiting—and she couldn't resent being excluded from it. It was her fault they had been kept apart all this time. Ari had been fair in his story-telling and she now had to be fair to the bond she had denied both of them.

'I'm glad you're my Papa,' Theo said fervently, rising to his feet. 'After my birthday party I dreamed that you were.'

Ari lifted him onto his knee, hugging him close. 'We'll always celebrate your birthday together,' he promised huskily.

'But I don't want you to hurt Mama again.'

Tears pricked Tina's eyes, her heart swelling at the love and loyalty in Theo's plea to his father.

'I am trying very hard not to,' Ari said seriously. 'I kept her secret until today, and now your Mama and I are going to work out how best we can be together for the rest of our lives. Will you be happy to be with your grandmother while we do that?'

'Does Yiayia know you're my Papa?'

'Yes. Your Mama told her this morning. And now that you know, too, you can talk about it to your grandmother. Tomorrow, if it's okay with your Mama, I'll take you to visit your other grandparents whom you met at your birthday party.'

Theo's eyes rounded in wonderment. 'Is Maximus my Papou?'

'Yes, and he very much wants to see you again. So does my mother. You will have a much bigger family. The boys you played with at the wedding are your cousins.'

'Will they be there tomorrow?'

'Yes.' Ari rose to his feet, hoisting Theo up in his arms. 'Let's go back to your grandmother because your Mama and I need to have some time to talk about all this.'

The face Theo turned to Tina was full of excitement. 'Is it okay with you, Mama?' he asked eagerly.

'Yes,' she said, not yet ready to commit to a mass family involvement until after her night with Ari, but smiling at her son to remove any worry from his mind.

It was enough for Theo.

He was content to be left with her mother, happy to share the news that his birthday wish had come true and ask a million questions about what might happen next. He waved goodbye to Tina and Ari without a qualm.

All the qualms were in Tina's stomach.

She was about to face a new beginning with Ari Zavros or an end to the idea of marrying him.

CHAPTER ELEVEN

ARI took her hand as they walked up the ramp to the courtyard in front of the reception building. The physical link flooded her mind with thoughts of the intimacy to come. For him it was probably just another night of sex—the performance of an act that had been commonplace in his life, varied only by the different women he'd taken to bed with him.

For her...a little shiver ran down her spine...it had been so long, and she wasn't dazzled by him this time.

Could she really shut off her disillusionment with the love she'd believed he'd shared and take pleasure in what he could give her? He'd said he'd try very hard not to hurt her. There was no need to be frightened of him, but she was frightened of the feelings he might evoke in her. This was not a time to be weak or confused. There was too much at stake to blindly follow instincts that had led her astray in the past.

Though she had to concede that Ari had been very good with Theo. He'd also saved her from the dilemma of how to explain the truth to their son. At least that was done with, and done well, which was only fair to acknowledge.

'I liked your fairy story,' she said, slanting him an appreciative little smile.

He flashed a hopeful smile back. 'We have yet to give it a happy ending.'

'To dream the impossible dream…' tripped straight off her tongue.

'Not impossible, Christina. Open your mind to it.'

They reached his car and he opened the passenger door for her. She paused, looking directly at him before stepping in. 'I don't know *your* mind, Ari. That's the problem.'

Intensity of purpose glittered in his amber eyes as he answered, 'Then I hope you'll know it better by tomorrow morning.'

'I hope I do, too.' She gestured to the car. 'Where are you taking me?'

'To Oia, the northern village of Santorini, the best place for watching the sunset. I've arranged for a suite in a boutique hotel which will give us the perfect view. I thought you would like it.'

'That's…very romantic.'

'With you I want to be romantic,' he replied, his whole expression softening with a look of rueful tenderness that twisted her heart.

She tore her gaze from his and quickly settled herself in the passenger seat, silently and furiously chastising herself for the craven wish to be romanced out of all her mistrust of his fairy-tale happy ending. He was going to make it all too easy to surrender to his charm and there was a huge vulnerable part of her that wanted to believe she was special to him this time and there would be no turning away from her ever again.

But it was his child he really wanted. She was the package deal. And she had no idea how long the package would stay attractive to him. Even if Ari romanced her beautifully tonight, she had to keep her head on straight and insist on the prenuptial agreement he'd offered. It was her insurance against making another big mistake with him.

He chatted to her about the various features of the island they passed on their way to Oia, intent on establishing a companionable mood. Tina did her best to relax and respond in an interested fashion. She remembered how interested he had been in Australia, always asking her questions about it whenever they were driving somewhere together.

'Where would you want us to live if I marry you, Ari?' she asked, needing to know what he had in mind.

He hesitated, then bluntly answered, 'Australia is too far away from my family's business interests, Christina. We could base ourselves anywhere in Europe. Athens if you would like to be near your relatives. Perhaps Helen would like to return there. She would see more of Cassandra and George in the future if she did, and put her closer to us, as well.'

It meant completely uprooting herself. And Theo. Though Ari had made a good point about her mother. So much change…she would end up leading an international life like Cass. Her sister had acclimatised herself to it. Loved it. Perhaps she would learn to love it, too.

'It's also a matter of choosing what might be best for our children's education,' Ari added, shooting her a quick smile.

Our children... It was a very seductive phrase. She adored having Theo. She'd love to have a little girl, as well. If she didn't marry Ari, it was highly unlikely that she would have any more children. But if she had them with Ari, she didn't want to lose them to him.

'Are you okay with that, Christina?' he asked, frowning at her silence.

'I'm opening my mind to it,' she tossed at him.

He laughed, delighted that it wasn't a negative answer.

They had to leave the car on the outskirts of the village and continue on foot through the narrow alleys to the hotel. Both of them had brought light backpacks with essentials for an overnight stay. It only took a minute to load them onto their shoulders and Ari once again took possession of Tina's hand for the walk into the village. It felt more comfortable now, especially as they navigated past the steady stream of tourists that thronged the alleys lined with fascinating shops.

Again she was acutely aware of women looking Ari over but the handhold meant he belonged to her, and she firmly reminded herself that not even Cass's beautiful model friends had turned his head last night. If she could just feel more confident that he could be content with only having her, the female attention he invariably drew might not worry her so much. It hadn't worried her in the past. She had been totally confident that he was hers. Until he wasn't hers any more.

But marriage was different to a *charming episode*.

A wedding ring on Ari's finger would make him legally hers.

Very publicly hers.

That should give her some sense of security with him.

In fact, being the wife of Ari Zavros would empower her quite a bit on many levels.

If she could make herself hard-headed enough to set aside any possible hurt from him in the future and simply go through with the marriage, dealing with each day as it came, her life could become far more colourful than she would ever manage on her own. Besides which if it ended in divorce, the financial settlement would give her the means to do whatever she chose. Wanting Ari to love her…well, that was probably wishing for the moon, but who knew? Even that might come to pass if her mother was right about sharing what was precious to both of them.

All the buildings in Oia were crammed up against each other, using every available bit of space. The entrance to the hotel opened straight onto an alley with pot-plants on either side of the door its only adornment. It was certainly boutique size. The man at the reception desk greeted Ari enthusiastically and escorted them to a suite on what proved to be the top level of three built down the hillside facing the sea. The bathroom, bedroom and balcony were all small but perfectly adequate and the view from the balcony was spectacular.

'Sunset is at eight o'clock,' their escort informed them before departing.

Almost three hours before then, Tina thought, dumping her backpack on a chair and gravitating straight to the balcony, suddenly too nervous to face Ari in the bedroom. A spiral staircase ran down the side of the hotel, linked by landings to each balcony, giving guests easy access to the small swimming pool which took up half the courtyard that extended from the hotel's lowest level. A few people were lounging on deck chairs beside it. She stared down at them, wondering where they had come from and what had brought them here. Probably nothing as complicated as her own situation.

Behind her she heard the pop of a champagne cork. A few moments later Ari was at her side carrying two glasses fizzing with the bubbly wine.

'You used to drink this with me. Will you try it again, Christina? It might relax you,' he said kindly.

She heaved a sigh to ease the tightness in her chest and took the glass he offered. 'Thank you. It's been six years since I was in an intimate situation with a man,' she said with a rueful smile. 'This might take the edge off.'

'I guess having Theo made it difficult for you to form relationships,' he remarked sympathetically.

Not Theo. You. But telling him so would let him know she was stuck on him and it was better that he didn't know. She didn't want him taking anything for granted where she was concerned.

'Don't worry that I'll make you pregnant tonight. I'll be very careful,' he assured her.

She shook her head. 'You won't anyway. This is a safe week for me.'

'Ah!' He grinned, the amber eyes twinkling with pleasure. 'Then we may be totally carefree which will be much better.' He clinked her glass with his. 'To a night of re-discovery, Christina.'

She took a quick sip of the champagne, hoping to settle the flock of butterflies in her stomach. Ari's arm slid around her waist, his hand resting warmly on the curve of her hip, bringing his body closer to hers, stirring memories of how well they had fitted together in the past and triggering the desire to re-discover every sweet nuance of her sexuality.

'I don't want to wait until tonight,' she said decisively, setting her glass down on the top of the balcony wall and turning to face him, a wave of reckless belligerence seizing her and pouring into urgent words. 'Let's just do it, Ari. I don't want to be romanced or seduced or…or treated to any other lover routine you've got. This is a need to know thing, isn't it?'

He set his glass down next to hers and scooped her hard against him, his freed hand lifting to her chin, tilting it up, his eyes blazing a heart-kicking challenge right at her. 'A great many needs to be answered on both sides and I don't want to wait, either.'

His mouth came down on hers so hard she jerked her head back, afraid of what she had just invited. He'd been a tender lover to her, never rough. Panic kicked into her heart. What did she know of him now? If he had no real feeling for her…

'Damn!' he muttered, his chest heaving as he sucked in breath, a glint of anguish in the eyes that bored into hers. 'I *will* control myself. Let me start again, Christina.'

He didn't wait for a reply. His lips brushed lightly over hers, back and forth, back and forth, making them tingle to the point where she welcomed the running of his tongue-tip over them. *Yes,* she thought dizzily, the stiffness melting from her body, panic washed away by a soothing flood of warmth. She lifted her arms and wound them around his neck as she gave herself up to a kiss that was more familiar to her, a loving kind of kiss.

She didn't mind opening her mouth to the gentle probe of his tongue, liking the intimate sensation of tangling her own with it, the slow gathering of excitement. It was easy to close her eyes and forget the years of nothing, remembering only the girl she had been in this man's arms, experiencing sexual pleasure for the first time.

His hand slid down over her bottom, pressing her closer to him, and the hardness of his erection filled her mind with giddy elation. He couldn't fake that. He really did want her. She was still desirable to him so it was okay to desire him, too. And she did, quite fiercely, given the confidence that this wasn't just a cynical seduction to weaken her stance against him.

A wild ripple of exultation shot through her when his kissing took on a more passionate intensity, his tongue driving deep, challenging her to meet its thrust, revel in the explosion of need behind it. Her hands slid into his hair, fingers digging in hard to hold his head to hers, the desire to take possession of him and keep him forever running rampant through her mind.

He couldn't walk away from this.

Not ever again.

She wouldn't let him.

He wrenched his head from her tight grasp, lifting it back from her mouth enough to gasp, 'Must move from here. Come.'

He scooped her off the balcony and into the bedroom, striding for the bed with her firmly tucked to his side. Tina's heart was pounding with both fear and excitement. This was the moment to undress. She would see him again fully naked. But he would see her, too. How did she measure up against the other women who'd been in his life... the blonde in Dubai whose breasts had been more voluptuous?

But he *was* aroused, so maybe the *idea* of her made physical factors irrelevant. And although she was carrying more flesh than when he had been with her before, her body was still okay—no looseness from having the baby. It was silly to fret over it. He wanted sex with her. He was up and ready for it and it was going to happen.

He stopped close to the bed and swung her to face him, his hands curling around her shoulders, his eyes sweeping hers for any hint of last-minute rejection. She stared back steadily, determined not to baulk at this point.

'You move me as no other woman ever has, Christina,' he murmured, and planted a soft warm kiss on her forehead.

Her heart contracted at those words. Whether they

were true or not, the wish to believe them was too strong to fight. She closed her eyes wanting to privately hug the strong impression of sincerity in his, and he gently kissed her eyelids, sealing the positive flow of feeling he had evoked.

She felt his thumbs hook under the straps of the green sundress she'd worn and slowly slide them down her upper arms. He kissed her bared shoulders as he unzipped the back of her bodice. Tina kept her eyes shut, fiercely focussing on her other senses, loving the soft brush of his lips against her skin and the gentle caress of his fingers along her spine as it, too, was bared. She breathed in the slightly spicy scent of his cologne. It was the same as when they were together before. He hadn't changed it. And the thrill of his touch was the same, too.

Her dress slithered down to the floor. The style of it hadn't required a bra so now her breasts were naked. Her only remaining garment was her green bikini pants, but he didn't set about removing this last piece of clothing. His hands cupped her breasts, stroking them with a kind of reverence that she found emotionally confusing until he asked, 'Did you breast-feed Theo, Christina?'

He was thinking of his son. He was not looking at her as a woman but as the mother of his child.

'Yes,' she answered huskily, telling herself it was okay for him to see her in this light. It made her different to the other women who'd been in his life. More special. Her body had carried his child, had nurtured his child.

'He must have been a very happy baby,' he murmured, and his mouth enclosed one of her nipples, his tongue swirling around it before he sucked on it.

Tina gasped at the arc of piercing pleasure that hit her stomach and shot past it to the apex of her thighs. Her hands flew up and grasped his shoulders, fingers digging into his muscles, needing something strong to hold onto as quivers ran through her entire body. He moved his mouth to her other breast, increasing the sweet turbulence inside her. For her it had been a physical pleasure breast-feeding Theo but it hadn't generated this acute level of sexual excitement. Tina was so wound up in it, she didn't know if it was a relief or a disappointment when he lifted his head away.

Almost immediately he was whipping down her bikini pants and her feet automatically stepped out of them. Any concern about how she looked to him had completely disappeared. He scooped her into such a crushing embrace she could feel his heart thumping against his chest-wall and then he was kissing her again; hard, hungry kisses that sparked an overwhelming hunger for him. She wanted this man. She'd never stopped wanting him.

He lifted her off her feet and laid her on the bed. The sudden loss of contact with him instantly opened her eyes. He was discarding his clothes with such haste Tina was in no doubt of his eagerness to join her, and it was thrilling to watch his nakedness emerge. He was a truly beautiful man with a perfect male body. His olive skin gleamed over well-defined muscles. His smooth hairless chest was sculpted for touching, for gliding hands over it. He had the lean hips and powerful thighs of a top athlete. And there was certainly no doubt about his desire for her, his magnificent manhood flagrantly erect.

Yet when he came to her he ignored any urgency for instant sexual satisfaction. He lay beside her, one arm sliding under her shoulders to draw her into full body contact with him, his free hand stroking long, lovely caresses as his mouth claimed hers again, more in a slow seductive tasting than greedy passion. It gave her the freedom to touch him, to revel in feeling his strong masculinity against her softer femininity, the whole wonderfully sensual intimacy of flesh against flesh.

His hand dipped into the crevice between her thighs, his fingers moving gently, back and forth, intent on building excitement until she felt the exquisite urgency he had always made her feel in the past. Tina lifted her leg over his, giving him easier access to her, refusing to let any inhibitions deny her the pleasure she remembered. He changed the nature of his kissing, his tongue thrusting and withdrawing, mimicking the rhythm of what was to come, accelerating the need to have him there.

But still he didn't hurry. He moved down the bed, trailing kisses to the hollow of her throat, then sucking briefly on her breasts, heightening their sensitivity before sliding his mouth to her stomach, running his tongue around her navel.

'Was it a difficult labour with Theo, Christina?' he asked in a deeply caring tone.

She'd been so focussed on feeling, it took a concentrated effort to find her voice. 'Some…some hard hours,' she answered, savagely wishing he wasn't thinking of their son. Yet that was why he was here, with her, doing what he was doing, and she wouldn't be having this if she hadn't had his child.

'I should have been there,' he murmured, pressing his mouth to her stomach as though yearning for that lost time. 'I would have been there. And I will be for the rest of our children,' he said more fiercely before lifting himself further down to kiss her where his son had emerged from her womb.

I'm not going to think of why, Tina decided with wild determination. *I want this. I want him inside me again.*

The tension building in her body obliterated any further thought. Need was screaming through every nerve. It reached the point where she jack-knifed up to pluck at his shoulders, crying out, 'Enough! Enough!' She couldn't bear another second of waiting for him.

To her intense relief he responded instantly, surging up to fit himself between her legs which were already lifting to curl around his hips in a compulsive urging for the action she frantically craved. Her inner muscles were convulsing as he finally entered her and just one deep plunge drove her to an explosive climax, the exquisite torture peaking then melting into wave after wave of ecstatic pleasure as Ari continued the wonderfully intimate stroking.

It was incredibly satisfying, feeling him filling her again and again. Her body writhed exultantly around him. Her hands dragged up and down his back, urging on the rhythm of mutual possession. The sheer elation of it was so marvellously sweet nothing else existed for Tina, not the why or the where or the how.

When Ari cried out at his own climax, it sounded like a triumphant trumpet of joy to her ears. *She* had brought him to this. He shared the same heights of sensation he had led her to. And she revelled in that sense of intense togetherness as all his mighty strength collapsed on her and she hugged him with all her strength. He rolled onto his side, clutching her tightly against him, holding onto the deep connection, clearly wanting it to last as long as possible.

He didn't speak for quite a long time and Tina didn't want to break the silence. She lay with her head tucked under his chin, listening to his pulse-rate slowing to a normal beat. It was the first time today she actually felt totally relaxed. The sex-test was over. He had certainly satisfied her as a lover and if he was satisfied that she wouldn't turn her back on him, maybe they could move towards a commitment to each other.

It might even have a chance of sticking.

If she kept on having his children.

Was that the key to having him come to love her?

If only she could be sure he would in the end...truly love her for herself...and never want any other woman.

Marrying Ari was a terrible gamble.

But having had him again, she didn't want to let him go.

CHAPTER TWELVE

ARI felt happy. Usually after sex he felt satisfied, content, relaxed. Happiness was something more and it made him wonder if it was a temporary thing or whether having Christina would always give him this exultant sense of joy. Maybe it was simply a case of having risen to the challenge and won the response he wanted from her.

It had been damnably difficult to rein himself in to begin with. Having been forced to exercise control on the physical front for the past few days and suddenly being presented with the green light to go ahead, all the bottled-up desire he'd felt had blown his mind. And almost blown his chance with her.

But she wasn't pulling away from him now. He wished she still had long hair. He remembered how much he'd enjoyed running his fingers through it when she'd lain with him like this in the past. Though it didn't really matter. It was so good just having her content to stay where she was—no barriers between them. No *physical* barriers. He hoped the mental resistance she'd had to him had been stripped away, too.

He knew he'd given her intense sexual pleasure. Was it enough to sway her into marrying him? She had to be considering what Theo wanted in his life, too, and there was no doubt he wanted his father. What more could be done to clinch a future together?

He probably should be talking to her, finding out what was in her mind, yet he was reluctant to break the intimate silence. They had all night, plenty of time for talking. It was great being able to revel in the certainty that she would not be cold to him in the marriage bed.

She stirred, lifting her head. 'I need to go to the bathroom, Ari.'

He released her and she instantly rolled away and onto her feet on the other side of the bed, only giving him a back view of her as she walked swiftly to the bathroom, no glimpse of the expression on her face. However, he couldn't help smiling at the lovely curve of her spine, the perkiness of her sexy bottom and the perfect shape of her long legs.

There was nothing unattractive about Christina Savalas. No one would be surprised at his choice of wife. Not that he cared about what anyone else thought but it would make it easier for Christina to be readily accepted as his partner in life. Women could be quite bitchy if they perceived any other woman as not measuring up to what they expected. Felicity Fulbright had sniped about quite a few while in his company.

Of course he would be on guard to protect Christina from any nastiness but there were always female get-togethers when he wouldn't be present. On the other hand, the fighting spirit his father admired in her was undoubtedly a force to be reckoned with in any kind of critical situation. She would have no qualms about setting people straight as she saw it. She'd done it to him repeatedly in the past few days.

All in all, Ari was quite looking forward to a future with Christina now that the sexual question was answered. However, his satisfaction took a slight knock when she re-emerged from the bathroom, wearing a white cotton kimono which covered her from neck to ankle. It signalled that she wasn't about to jump back into bed with him.

'I found this hanging on a peg behind the bathroom door,' she said, putting a firm knot in the tie-belt and not quite meeting his gaze as she added, 'There's another one for you if you want to wear it after your shower. Easier than re-dressing for sitting on the balcony to watch the sunset.'

And easier for undressing afterwards, Ari thought, accepting her plan of action without argument. It was obvious that she had already showered—no invitation for him to join her—so she was putting an end to their intimacy for a while, which raised questions about how eager she was to continue it. An intriguing combination—hot in bed, cool out of it—another challenge that he had to come to grips with.

She wasn't won yet.

'Have a look at the menu on the desk while I shower,' he said invitingly. 'See what you'd like for dinner. We can order it in.'

It stopped her stroll towards the balcony. She paused at the desk to pick up the menu and began to study it, not even glancing at him as he rose from the bed and moved towards the bathroom. Was she embarrassed by her body's response to his love-making? Was she always going to close up on him afterwards? How much was she truly willing to share with him?

Ari mused over these questions while taking a shower. In every one of his relationships with women there had always been mutual desire and mutual liking, at least at the beginning. It had certainly been so with Christina six years ago. In fact, looking back, that had been the only relationship he'd been reluctant to end. Nothing had soured it. Christina had not deceived him in any way, nor done anything to turn him off. The timing had been wrong, nothing else.

He was still sure his reasons for limiting it to his time in Australia were valid, yet his decision then kept coming between them now and he was no longer sure that good sex was the answer to reaching the kind of relationship he wanted with his wife.

Though it still made the marriage viable.

The mutual desire was right.

He just had to work on getting the mutual liking right again.

Having picked up their clothes from the floor and hung them over a chair, Tina took the menu out to the balcony and sat down at the small table for two. She was hungry, having only had a very light lunch, too full of nervous tension to enjoy food. Now that she felt less uptight about spending the night with Ari, a sunset dinner was very appealing.

She studied the list of dishes with interest, thinking this was the first meal she would spend alone with Ari since meeting him again. It was an opportunity to extend her knowledge of his lifestyle, which was an important preparation for being his wife. There was more to marriage than good sex and she wasn't about to let Ari think that was all he had to give her.

Though it was a very powerful drawcard, completely meddling with Tina's common sense when he strolled out to the balcony. His white kimono barely reached his knees and left a deep V of gleaming olive-skinned chest, causing her to catch her breath. He was so overwhelmingly male and so vitally handsome, all her female hormones were zinging as though caught in an electrical storm. Chemistry still humming from the sex they'd just shared, Tina told herself, but the desire for more of it could not be denied.

'Found what you'd like?' he asked, gesturing towards the menu.

'Yes.' She rattled off a starter, a main dish, and sweets, as well.

He grinned approval at her. 'I've worked up an appetite, too. Give me the menu and I'll call in an order now.' He nodded at the lowering sun. 'It will be pleasant to dine as we watch the sunset.'

Both the sky and the sea were already changing colour. Ari tucked the menu under his arm, picked up the half-empty champagne glasses from the balcony wall and returned to the bedroom to make the call. Tina watched the shimmering waves with their shifting shades of light, trying to calm herself enough to conduct a normal conversation without being continually distracted by lustful thoughts.

Ari brought back two clean wine glasses and an ice-bucket containing a bottle of light white wine which he said would go well with their starters. Tina decided she might as well give up her alcohol ban. Wine was part and parcel of Ari's life and it was more appropriate for his wife to partake of some of it.

He was standing by the balcony wall, opening the bottle of wine when he was hailed from below.

'Ari... Ari... It is you, isn't it?'

Tina's nerves instantly twanged. It was a female voice with a very British accent, like that of the woman who'd been with him in Dubai.

He looked down, his shoulders stiffening as he recognised the person. He raised a hand in acknowledgement but made no vocal reply, quickly turning back to the task of filling their glasses. His mouth had thinned into a line of vexation. His eyes were hooded.

Clearly this was an unwelcome intrusion and Tina felt impelled to ask, 'Who is it?' Facing other women who'd been in his life would have to be done sooner or later and it was probably better that she had a taste of it now, know whether or not she could deal with it.

He grimaced. 'Stephanie Gilchrist. A London socialite.'

'Not a fond memory?' she queried archly, pretending it wasn't important.

His eyes blazed annoyance. 'An acquaintance. No more. I see she's here with her current playmate, Hans

Vogel, a German model who's always strutting his stuff. I had no idea they were booked into this hotel.'

Just two people he didn't want to mix with tonight, Tina thought with considerable relief. She didn't really want to be faced with a woman who had shared his bed, not when the intimacies they had just shared were so fresh in her mind, not when her body was still reacting to them. This new beginning would not feel so good. Later on, when she felt more confident about being Ari's partner—when he made her feel more confident—it might not matter at all.

'Ari!' Stephanie called more demandingly.

'Damned nuisance!' he muttered savagely as he swung around to deal with the problem.

Having regained his attention, Stephanie bluntly asked, 'What are you doing here? I thought you had a home on Santorini. I'm sure Felicity told me...'

'This hotel has a better view of the sunset,' Ari swiftly cut in. 'Why don't you and Hans just lie back on your lounges and enjoy it?'

He waved his hand dismissively but Stephanie apparently had some personal axe to grind with him. 'I'm coming up,' she announced belligerently.

Ari cursed under his breath. He turned sharply to Tina, his brow creased with concern, the amber eyes glittering with intense urgency. 'I'm sorry. I can't stop her. The spiral staircase is open to all guests. I will get rid of her as fast as I can.'

Tina shrugged. 'I can be polite to one of your acquaintances for a few minutes,' she said, eyeing him warily, wondering if he had lied to her about the less than intimate connection to this woman.

Ari swiftly rattled out information. 'She's a close friend of Felicity Fullbright. Felicity was the woman you saw me with in Dubai. Since Stephanie is here, I don't know if she's been told I've ended the relationship with her friend. Anything she says… it's irrelevant to us, Christina. Don't let it worry you.'

It worried him.

Here's where I learn if I'm a fool to even consider marrying him, Tina thought, putting a steel guard around her vulnerability to this man.

Her heart started a painful pounding. 'How long were you with Felicity, Ari?' she asked, needing to know more.

'Six weeks. It was enough to decide she didn't suit me,' he answered tersely.

'You haven't been with me for a week yet,' she pointed out just as tersely.

The clip-clop of sandals was getting closer.

Ari frowned, shaking his head at her assertion. 'It's different with you, Christina.'

Because of Theo. But if they married, he would have to live with her, too, and how long would that suit him? They had had a harmonious relationship for three months but still he'd left her. It hadn't been enough to keep him at her side.

Stephanie's arrival on the staircase landing adjacent to their balcony put a halt to any further private conversation. She was a very curvy blonde with a mass of long, crinkly hair, and wearing a minute blue bikini that left little to the imagination. Her very light, almost aquamarine eyes instantly targeted Tina.

'Well, well, off with the old and on with the new,' she drawled. Her gaze shifted to Ari. 'That must be a quick-change record even for you. I ran into Felicity at Heathrow just a few days ago. She was flying in from Athens and Hans and I were on our way here. She said you'd split but she sure didn't know you had a replacement lined up.'

No waiting for an introduction.

No courtesy at all.

Tina sat tight, watching Ari handle the situation.

'You're assuming too much, Stephanie,' he said blandly, gesturing towards Tina. 'This is Christina Savalas whom I met in Australia quite a few years ago. She happens to be Cassandra's sister who married my cousin, George, yesterday. The wedding gave us the opportunity to catch up again, which has been amazingly good.' He smiled at Tina. 'Wouldn't you say?'

'Amazing,' she echoed, following his lead and smiling back at him.

Stephanie arched her eyebrows. 'Australia? Are you heading back there now that the wedding is over?'

Tina shrugged. 'I shall have to go sometime.'

'Not in any hurry since you've snagged Ari again,' came the mocking comment.

The woman's sheer rudeness goaded Tina into a very cold retort. 'I'm not into snagging men. In fact…'

'I'm the one doing all the running,' Ari cut in. 'And having found out what you wanted to know, why don't

you run along back to Hans, Stephanie? You're not exactly endearing yourself to a woman I care about.'

'Really care?' She gave Ari a derisive sneer. 'It's not
just a dose of the charm you used to bowl over Felicity?
You didn't care about her one bit, did you?'

'Not after she displayed a dislike for children, no,'
he answered bitingly.

'Oh!' With her spite somewhat deflated, she turned
to Tina for a last jeer. 'Well, I've just done you a favour.
You'd better show a liking for children or he'll throw
you over as fast as he caught up with you. Good luck!'

With a toss of her hair she flounced off their balcony.

Tina stared out to sea as Stephanie's sandals clattered
down the spiral staircase. She wondered if it was good
luck or bad that had brought her back into Ari's life.
Whatever…luck had little to do with making a marriage
work. At least, a liking for children was one thing they
definitely shared. Ari wouldn't be throwing her over on
that issue. But Stephanie had implied he had a quick
turnover of women in his life, which meant he wasn't
in the habit of holding onto a relationship. What if she
didn't *suit* him after a while?

'You hardly know me, Ari,' she said, suddenly frightened that her suitability might be very limited.

'I know enough to want you as my wife,' he whipped
out, an emphatic intensity in his voice. 'And not only
because you've given me a son. There's nothing I don't
like about you, Christina.'

She sliced him a wary look. 'What do you actively
like?'

He sat down at the table, pushing one of the glasses

of wine over to her, obviously playing for time to think. 'Take a sip. It doesn't have a sour taste like Stephanie,' he assured her.

She picked up the glass and sipped, eyeing him over its rim.

The expression on his face softened, the amber eyes telegraphing appreciation. 'I like how much you care for your family. I like the way you consider others. I like your good manners. I think you have courage and grit and intelligence—all qualities that I like. They make up the kind of character that I want in a partner.'

He wasn't talking love. He was ticking off boxes. She could tick off the same boxes about him. A matchmaking agency would probably place them as a likely couple, especially since there was no lack of sexual chemistry between them. But there was one big factor missing.

Tina heaved a sigh as she remembered how Cass and George had acted towards each other yesterday. It hurt that she would never have that wonderful emotional security with Ari. What if she married him and he was bowled over by some other woman further down the track? It could happen. She had to be prepared for it, safeguard herself against it, be practical about what she could expect from him and what she couldn't.

'Tell me about your life, Ari,' she said, needing to feel more informed about what a future with him would entail. 'What are the business interests that take you travelling? I only know of your connection to the wine industry.'

He visibly relaxed, happy to have the Stephanie can of worms closed.

Tina listened carefully to the list of property investments the Zavros family had made in many countries as far apart as Spain and Dubai where Ari had so recently been checking up on an estate development. Mostly they were connected to the tourist industry—resorts and theme parks and specialty shops. They had also tapped into the food industry with olives, cheeses and wine.

'You're in charge of all this?' she enquired.

He shook his head. 'My father runs the ship. I report and advise. The decisions are ultimately his. Most of the family is involved in one capacity or another.'

It was big business—far more complex than managing a restaurant. Tina continued to question him about it over dinner which was as tasty as it had promised to be. The sunset was gorgeous, spreading a rosy hue over all the white buildings on the hillside that faced it. For real lovers this had to be a very romantic place, Tina thought, but she couldn't feel it with Ari. As charming as he was, as good a lover as he was, no way could she bring herself to believe she was the light of his life.

Her own experience prompted her to ask, 'Have you ever been in love, Ari? So in love that person mattered more than anything else? Wildly, passionately, out of your mind...*in love?*'

As she'd been with him.

He frowned, obviously not liking the question. His jaw tightened as he swung his gaze away from hers, staring out to sea. She saw the corner of his mouth turn down into a grimace. He had experienced it, she thought, but not with her. A lead weight settled on her heart. He might very well experience it again with someone else.

CHAPTER THIRTEEN

IN LOVE...

Ari hated that memory. It was the one and only time he'd completely lost his head over a woman. He'd been her fool, slavishly besotted with her while she had only been amusing herself with him.

He wished Christina hadn't asked the question. Yet if he wasn't honest with her she would probably sense it and that would be a black mark against him in her mind. Besides, he was a different person to the boy he was then. He just didn't like dragging up that long-buried piece of the past and laying it out but he had to now. He'd left Christina too long without a reply.

He turned to her, the cynicism he'd learnt from that experience burning in his eyes and drawling through his voice. 'Wildly, passionately in love...yes, that happened to me when I was eighteen. She was very beautiful, exotically glamorous, and incredibly erotic. I would have done anything for her and did do everything she asked.'

'How long did it last?'

'A month.'

Christina raised her eyebrows. 'What made you fall out of love?'

'Being faced with reality.'

'Something you didn't like?'

'I hadn't understood what I was to her. I knew she was years older than me. It didn't matter. Nothing mattered but being with her. I thought she felt the same about me. It was so intense. But she was simply enjoying the intensity, revelling in her power to make me do whatever she wanted.'

'How did you come to realise that?'

'Because I was her Greek toy-boy, a last fling before she married her much more mature American millionaire. *It's been fun,* she said as she kissed me goodbye. *Fun...*'

He snarled the word and immediately cursed himself for letting it get to him after all these years.

'You were badly hurt,' Christina murmured sympathetically.

He shrugged. 'I'm not likely to fall in love again, if that's what you're worried about, Christina. Being someone's fool does not appeal to me.'

'You think your head will always rule your heart?'

'It has since I was eighteen.'

Except with her and Theo. His heart was very much engaged with his son and according to his lawyer, he'd completely lost his head in proposing the prenuptial agreement to induce Christina to marry him, ensuring that Theo would be a constant in his life. But he did feel the fidelity clause was not so much of a risk now. And he did like and admire Christina. He would make the marriage work. They would have more children... a family...

'I was eighteen when I fell in love with you.'

The quietly spoken words jolted Ari out of his confident mood and sent an instant chill down his spine. Her dark eyes were flat, expressionless, steadily watching whether he understood the parallel of what had been done to him—not only the hurt, the rejection of any lasting value in the love offered, but also the shadow it cast over any deep trust in a relationship. Giving oneself completely to another was not on. He'd never done it again.

Was this how Christina felt about him? Had he just ruined every bit of progress he'd made with her, bringing the past back instead of focussing her mind on the future they could have? Was this why he couldn't reach what he wanted to reach in her? He had to fix this. It was intolerable that she cast him in the same mould as the woman who'd taken him for a ride.

Before he could find the words to defend himself she spoke again, cocking her head to one side, her eyes alert to weighing up his reply. 'Did you think it was *fun* at the time?'

'Not like that!' he denied vehemently. He leaned towards her, gesturing an appeal for fairness. 'There was no one else in my life, Christina. I wasn't having a fling with you, cheating on a woman I intended to marry. The thought of having a little fun with you never crossed my mind. That was not part of it, I swear. I was enchanted by you.'

'For a while.' Her mouth twisted with irony. 'I can

imagine an older woman being enchanted by you when you were eighteen, Ari. You would have been absolutely beautiful. But her head ruled her heart, just as yours did with me. Too young…wasn't that how you explained leaving me behind?'

'You're not too young now.' The urgent need to stop this treacherous trawling through the past pushed Ari to his feet. He took Christina's hands, pulling her out of her chair and into his embrace, speaking with a violence of feeling that exploded off his tongue. 'I wanted you beyond any common sense then. And God knows I've lost any common sense since I've met you again. I want you so much it's been burning me up from the moment I saw you in Dubai. So forget everything else, Christina. Forget everything but this.'

He forgot about being gentle with her. The fierce emotion welling up in him demanded that he obliterate any bad thoughts from her mind and fill it with the same all-consuming desire he felt. He kissed her hard, storming her mouth with intense passion. A wild exultation ran through him as she responded with her own fierce drive to take what he was doing and give it right back.

No hesitation.

No holding back.

Frenzied kisses.

Frenzied touching.

Mutual desire riding high, her body pressed yearningly to his, making him even more on fire for her. Primitive instincts kicked in. He needed, wanted, had to have total possession of this woman. He swept her off her feet, crushed her to his chest as he strode to the bed. Even as he laid her down she was pushing her kimono apart, opening her legs wide for him, not wanting to wait, eagerly inviting instant intimacy.

He tore his own robe off, hating the thought of it getting in the way. Then he was with her, swiftly positioning himself. She was slick and hot, exciting him even further with her readiness. Her legs locked around him, heels digging into his buttocks, urging him on. He pushed in hard and fast and barely stopped himself from climaxing at the very first thrust, just like a teenage boy experiencing the ultimate sex fit.

He sucked in a quick breath, savagely telling himself to maintain control. He tried to set up a slow, voluptuous rhythm with his hips but she wouldn't have it, her body rocking his to go faster, faster. He felt her flesh clenching and unclenching around his and her throat emitted an incredibly sexy groan.

His head was spinning, excitement at an intense level. Her fingers dug into the nape of his neck. Her back arched from the bed. He felt the first spasm of her coming and was unable to hold off his own release any longer. He cried out as it burst from him in violent shudders, and the flood of heat from both of them was so ecstatically satisfying he was totally dazed by the depth of feeling.

He'd collapsed on top of her. She held him in a tightly possessive hug. Was she feeling the same? He had to know. Had to know if all the bad stuff from the past had been wiped out of her mind. He levered himself up on his elbows to see her face. Her eyes were closed, her head thrown back, her lips slightly apart, sucking in air and slowly releasing it.

'Look at me, Christina,' he gruffly commanded.

Her long lashes flicked up. Her eyes were dilated, out of focus. A thrill of triumph ran riot through Ari's mind. She was still feeling him inside her, revelling in the sheer depth of sensation. It gave him a surge of confidence that she wouldn't walk away from this— what they could have together. The glazed look slowly cleared. Her tongue slid out and licked her lips. He was tempted to flick his own tongue over them, but that would start them kissing again and this moment would be swallowed up and he wouldn't know what it meant to her.

'This is now, Christina,' he said with passionate fervour. 'The past is gone. This is now and you're feeling good with me. Tell me that you are.'

'Yes.' The word hissed out on a long sigh. She half-smiled as she added, 'I'm feeling good.'

He nodded. 'So am I. And I truly believe we can always make each other feel good if the will is there to do it.' He lifted a hand to stroke the soft black bangs of hair away from her forehead, his eyes boring into hers to enforce direct mental contact with her. 'We can be great partners in every sense there is, starting now, Christina. We look ahead, not back. Okay?'

There was no instant response but her eyes didn't disengage from his. Their focus sharpened and he had the feeling she was trying to search his soul. He had nothing to hide, yet he was acutely conscious of tension building inside him as he waited for her answer.

He'd hurt her in the past and she'd nursed that hurt for years. It had erupted in his face tonight and he was asking her to let it go, leave it behind them. It was a big ask. He recalled the look of heart-piercing vulnerability he'd seen after they'd made the sex-deal last night. But he'd just proved she had nothing to fear from an intimate connection with him. She'd conceded he'd made her feel good.

He willed her to grasp what could be grasped and take it into the future with them. It was best for their son, best for their lives, too. Surely she could see that.

'Have you had the prenuptial agreement you offered me drawn up, Ari?'

It wasn't what he wanted to hear from her. It meant that it didn't matter what he said or did, she still had a basic mistrust of how he would deal with her in the future. He could pleasure her all night but that verbal kick in the gut told him it would make no difference.

'Yes. It's in my backpack,' he said flatly.

'Have you signed it?'

'Not yet.'

'Will you do so in the morning if…if you're still feeling good with me?'

'Yes,' he said unequivocally, though hating the fact it was still necessary in her mind.

She hadn't faked her response to him. There was nothing fake about Christina Savalas and it was clear that she needed a guarantee that if there was anything fake about him, she would not lose her son by marrying him.

She reached up and gently stroked his cheek. 'I'm

sorry I can't feel more secure with you, Ari. I promise you to do my best to be a partner to you in every sense. If I fail and you end up finding someone else who suits you better, I won't deny you a fair share of Theo. I just need protection against your taking him from me.'

'I'd never do that,' he protested vehemently. 'You're his mother. He loves you.'

She heaved a deep sigh as though that claim meant little in the bigger scheme of things. 'It's impossible to know how things will turn out along the track,' she said in a fatalistic tone. 'As sincere as your commitment might be to me now, as sincere as mine is to you, it's in our minds, Ari, not our hearts, and you might not think so now, but hearts can over-rule minds. I know. It's why I never told you about Theo when I should have. My heart wouldn't let me.'

There was sadness in her eyes—the sadness of betrayed innocence—and Ari knew he'd done that to her. Determination welled up in him to replace it with joy—joy in him and the children they would have together.

'Our marriage will be fine, Christina,' he promised her. 'I don't mind signing the prenuptial agreement. I want you to feel secure, not frightened of anything. And given more time, I hope you'll come to trust me, knowing without a doubt that I mean you well and want you to be happy with me.'

It brought a smile back to her face. 'That would be good, Ari.' Her hand slid up and curled around his head. 'I could do with some more of feeling good.'

He laughed and kissed her.

The night was still young. They proceeded to a more

languorous love-making for a while, pleasuring each other with kisses and caresses. It delighted Ari that Christina had no inhibitions about her sexuality and no hesitation in exploring his. He hoped it would always be like this, no holding back on anything.

The commitment was made now.

Ari felt right about it—more right than he'd ever felt about anything else in his life. And he'd make it right for Christina, too. It would take more than a night to do it. It might take quite a long while. But he was now assured of all the time he would need to wipe out her doubts and win her trust. When that day came—he smiled to himself—all of life would be good.

CHAPTER FOURTEEN

TINA was determined not to regret marrying Ari Zavros but to view her time with him—regardless of what happened in the end—as an experience worth having. In any event, she would not lose Theo or any other children they might have. The signed prenuptial agreement was in her keeping.

Everyone was happy that a wedding would soon take place. The Zavros family seemed particularly pleased to welcome her into their clan and Theo was over the moon at belonging to so many more people. Plans were quickly made. Her mother had no hesitation in deciding that Athens would be the best place for her to live— much closer to her daughters—and Maximus immediately offered to find the best property for her while they dealt with winding up their lives in Australia.

Ari accompanied them back to Sydney. He organised the sale of the restaurant to the head chef and the head waiter. Tina suspected he financed the deal. Everything in their apartment was packed up by professionals— also organised by Ari—and stored in a container which would be shipped to Athens. He was a whirlwind of activity, determined on moving them out with the least amount of stress. Her mother thought he was wonderful.

Tina couldn't fault him, either. He was attentive to their needs, carried out their wishes, and to Tina's surprise, even purchased an extremely expensive three-bedroom apartment overlooking Bondi Beach.

'To Theo it's the best beach in the world,' he explained. 'He might get homesick for it. You, too, Christina. We can always take time out to come back here for a while.'

His caring for their son was so evident, so constant, it continually bolstered her decision to marry him. Theo adored him. Her reservations about his constancy where she was concerned remained in her mind but were slowly being whittled away in her heart. He was so good to her, showing consideration for whatever she wanted in every respect.

Within a month they were back on Santorini. Her mother was to be a guest in the Zavros villa until her furniture arrived for her new apartment in Athens. Maximus, of course, had found the perfect place for her. She quickly became fast friends with Ari's mother who had been organising the wedding in their absence. It was almost the end of the tourist season when most places closed down on the island. They only had a week to finalise arrangements—a week before Tina's life began as Ari's wife.

Cass had been informed of the situation via email and was delighted that everything seemed to be working out well. She insisted on buying Tina's wedding dress and kept sending photographs of glorious gowns until Tina chose one. She let Cass select her own bridesmaid dress. George was to be best man—a reversal of their previous roles.

The same church was to be used for the marriage service and the same reception centre. Both places had also been chosen for the weddings of Ari's sisters. Apparently it was customary for the Zavros family and Tina didn't raise any objection although privately she would have preferred not to be following in her sister's footsteps, being reminded of the real love Cass and George had declared for each other.

She didn't feel like a bride. She looked like one on the day. And despite the lateness of the season, the sun was shining. It made her wonder if Ari had arranged that, too, everything right for the Golden Greek. It was a weird feeling, walking down the aisle to him—more like a dream than reality. Everything had happened so fast. But her feet didn't falter and she gave him her hand at the end of the walk, accepting there was no turning back from this moment.

Her ears were acutely tuned to the tone of Ari's voice as he spoke his marriage vows. It was clear and firm, as though he meant them very seriously. Which Tina found comforting. She had to swallow hard to get her own voice working at all, and the words came out in jerky fashion which she couldn't control. But they were said. It was done. They were declared man and wife.

To Tina, the reception was a blur of happy faces congratulating her and Ari and wishing them well. Everyone from both families was there, along with Ari's close business connections and friends. Tina couldn't remember all their names. She just kept smiling, as a bride should. Ari carried off the evening with great panache and he carried her along with him—his wife.

He took her to Odessa for a honeymoon. It was a beautiful city, called The Pearl of The Black Sea, and for the first time since her future with Ari had been decided, Tina could really relax and enjoy herself. There was nothing that had to be done. Theo was undoubtedly having a great time with his doting grandparents. She was free of all responsibility. And Ari was intent on filling their days—and nights—with pleasure.

The weather was still hot and they lazed away mornings on the beach, had lunch in coffee shops or restaurants beside lovely parks, browsed around the shops that featured crafts of the region—marvellous cashmere shawls, beautifully embroidered blouses, and very different costume jewellery.

They went to a ballet performance at the incredibly opulent opera house—totally different architecture and interior decoration to the amazing hotel in Dubai but just as mind-boggling in its richness.

When she commented on this to Ari he laughed and said, 'Europe is full of such marvels, Christina, and I shall enjoy showing them to you. When we go to Paris, I'll take you to Versailles. You'll be totally stunned by it.'

He was as good as his word. In the first six months of their marriage, she accompanied him on many trips around Europe—Spain, Italy, England, France, Germany. All of them were related to business but Ari made time to play tourist with her. He was the perfect companion, so knowledgeable about everything and apparently happy to spend his free time with her.

There were business dinners they had to attend, and parties they were invited to which invariably made Tina nervous, but Ari never strayed from her side whenever they were socialising. He bought her beautiful clothes so that she always felt confident of her appearance on these occasions and he constantly told her she was beautiful, which eased her anxiety about other women.

They had decided on Athens as their home base. Tina wanted to be close to her mother and it was easier for Theo to be enrolled in the same private English-speaking school as his cousins. He accompanied them on trips which didn't interfere with his schooling but at other times he was happy to stay with family while they were away.

However, when Tina fell pregnant, as happy as she was about having a baby, the morning sickness in the first trimester was so bad she couldn't face travelling anywhere and she couldn't help fretting when Ari had to leave her behind to attend to business. Each time he returned she searched for signs that he was growing tired of her, finding her less attractive, but he always seemed pleased to be home again and eager to take her to bed.

She expected his desire for her to wane as her body lost its shape but it didn't. He displayed a continual fascination with every aspect of her pregnancy, reading up on what should be happening with the child growing inside her, lovingly caressing her lump, even talking to it in a besotted manner and grinning with delight whenever he felt a ripple of movement. He always smiled when he saw her naked, his eyes gloating over her as though she presented an incredibly beautiful image to him, pregnant with his child.

Tina reasoned that obviously having children meant a lot to Ari. He had married her because of Theo and being the mother of his children did make her uniquely special to him. If he never fell in love with anyone else, maybe their marriage would become very solid and lasting. She fiercely hoped so because she couldn't guard against the love that she hadn't wanted to feel with him.

It sat in her heart, heavy with the need to keep it hidden. Pride wouldn't let her express it. Sometimes she let herself imagine that he loved her, but he never said it. Their marriage was based on family. That had to be enough.

She was eight months pregnant and looking forward to the birth of the baby when fate took a hand in ending her happy anticipation. She'd been shopping with her mother, buying a few extra decorations for the newly furnished nursery at home; a gorgeous mobile of butterflies to hang over the cot, a music box with a carousel on top, a kaleidoscope to sit on the windowsill.

They planned to finish off their outing with a visit to a hairdressing salon which was located a few blocks away from the department store where they had purchased these items. Tina felt too tired and cumbersome to walk that far, so they took a taxi for the short trip. It was crossing an intersection when a truck hurtled across the road from the hilly street on their right, clearly out of control, its driver blaring the horn of the truck in warning, his face contorted in anguish at being unable to avoid an accident.

It was the last thing Tina saw—his face. And the last thing she thought was *the baby!* Her arms clutched the mound of the life inside her. It was the last thing she did before the impact robbed her of consciousness.

Ari had never felt so useless in his life. There was nothing he could do to fix this. He had to leave it up to the doctors—their knowledge, their skill. He was so distressed he could barely think. He sat in the hospital waiting room and *waited.*

Theo was taken care of. His parents had flown over from Santorini to collect him from school and take him back home with them. He was to be told that Mama and Papa had been called away on another trip. There was no point in upsetting him with traumatic news. When the truth had to be told—whatever it turned out to be— Ari would do it. He would be there for his son.

His sisters had wanted to rush to the hospital, giving their caring support but he'd told them not to. He didn't want their comforting gestures. He was beyond comfort. Besides, it would be a distraction from willing Christina to get through this. She had to. He couldn't bear the thought of life without her.

Cassandra was flying in from Rome to be with her mother. He didn't have to worry about Helen—just bruises, a broken arm, and concussion. Her relatives were sitting with her and she would be allowed out of hospital tomorrow. She was frantically worried about

Christina. They all were, but he didn't want to listen to any weeping and wailing. He needed to be alone with this until the doctors came back to him.

Head injuries, smashed clavicle, broken ribs, collapsed lung, ripped heart, and damage to the uterus, but the baby's heart was still beating when they'd brought Christina into the emergency ward. A drug-induced coma was apparently the best state for her to be in while undergoing treatment for her injuries and it had been deemed advisable to perform a Caesarian section. It wasn't how Christina had wanted the baby delivered but he'd been told there was no choice in these circumstances.

Their second child…

A brother or sister for Theo…

They'd been so looking forward to its birth, sharing it together. Now it felt like some abstract event…in the hands of the doctors. No mutual joy in it. A baby without a mother unless Christina survived this.

She had to, not only for their children, but for him.

She was his woman, the heart of his life, and his heart would be ripped out if she died. Just thinking about it put one hell of a pain in his chest.

One of the doctors he'd spoken to entered the waiting room, accompanied by a nurse. Ari rose to his feet, his hands instinctively clenching although there was nothing to fight except the fear gripping his stomach.

'Ah, Mr Zavros. The Caesarian went well. You're the father of a healthy baby girl.'

The announcement hit the surface of his mind but didn't engage it. 'And Christina?' he pressed.

'Your wife will be in the operating theatre for some hours yet. The baby has been taken to an intensive care ward and placed in a humidicrib. We thought…'

'Why?' Ari cut in, fear for the life of their child welling up to join his fear for Christina. 'You said she was healthy.'

'Purely a precautionary measure, Mr Zavros. She is very small, a month premature. It is best that she be monitored for a while.'

'Yes…yes…' he muttered distractedly, his mind jagging back to Christina. 'The injuries to my wife…it *is* possible that she can recover from them?'

'One cannot predict with certainty but there is a good chance, yes. The surgeons are confident of success. If there are no complications…' He shrugged. 'Your wife is young and healthy. That is in her favour.'

Please, God, let there be no complications, Ari fiercely prayed.

'If you would like to see your daughter now…?'

His daughter. Their daughter. Seeing her without Christina at his side. It felt wrong. There was a terrible hollowness in his heart. It should have been filled with excitement. And that was wrong, too. Their baby girl should be welcomed into this world, at least by her father.

'Yes… please…' he replied gruffly.

He was escorted to the maternity ward and led to where his daughter lay in a humidicrib attached to monitoring wires. She looked so little, helpless, and again Ari was assaulted by a wretched sense of powerlessness. Right now he couldn't take care of Christina or their child. He had to leave them both in the hands of others.

A smile tugged at his lips as he stared down at the shock of black hair framing the tiny face. Christina's hair. Her lips were perfectly formed, too, just like her mother's.

'Would you like to touch her?' the nurse beside him asked.

'Yes.'

She lifted the lid of the humidicrib. He reached out and gently stroked the super-soft skin of a tiny hand. It startled and delighted him when it curled tightly around one of his fingers. Her eyes opened—dark chocolate eyes—and seemed to lock onto his.

'I'm your Papa,' he told her.

Her little chest lifted and a sigh whispered from her lips as though the bond she needed was in place. She closed her eyes. The grip on his finger slowly eased.

'Be at peace, little one. I'm here for you,' Ari murmured.

But she would need her mother, too.

He needed Christina, though he wasn't sure how much that would mean to her. She had accepted him as her husband. He saw the love she openly showered on their son, but whatever was in her heart for him had always been closely guarded.

So he willed her to live for their children.

That was the stronger pull on her.

Her son and her daughter.

CHAPTER FIFTEEN

SIX weeks… They'd been the longest six weeks of Ari's life. The doctors had explained it was best that Christina remain in a coma until the swelling of her brain had gone down and her injuries had healed. They had also warned him she would initially feel lost and confused when they brought her out of it and would need constant reassurance of where she was, why, and what had happened to her.

Most probably any dreams she may have had during this time would be more real to her than reality and it would require patient understanding from him to deal with her responses to the situation. Ari didn't care how much patient understanding he had to give as long as Christina came back to him. Yet as mentally prepared as he was to deal with anything, it hit him hard when she woke and stared at him without any sign of recognition.

Tears welled into her eyes.

He squeezed her hand gently and quickly said, 'It's okay, Christina. Everything's okay.'

'I lost the baby.'

'No, you didn't,' he vehemently assured her. 'We have a beautiful little baby girl. She's healthy and happy and Theo adores her. We've named her Maria—your favourite name for a girl—and she looks very like you.'

The tears didn't stop. They trickled down her cheeks.

Ari told her about the accident and the need for a Caesarian birth and how their daughter was thriving now. She kept staring at him but he didn't think she was registering anything he said. The look of heart-breaking sadness didn't leave her face. After a while she closed her eyes and slid back into sleep.

He took Theo and Maria with him on his next visit, determined to set Christina's mind at rest.

Again she woke and murmured the mournful words, 'I lost the baby.'

'No, you didn't,' he assured her. 'Look, here she is.'

He laid Maria in her arms and she stared at the baby wonderingly as he explained again about the accident and their daughter's birth. Then Theo, super-excited at having his mother finally awake from her long sleep, chattered non-stop, telling her everything about his new sister. She smiled at him and was actually smiling at the baby as her eyes closed. Ari hoped her sleep would be less fretful now.

Yet from day to day she seemed to forget what had been said and he would have to remind her. He started to worry that she might never fully recover from her head injuries. The doctors explained that it could take a while for the drugs to wash out of her system. Until she completely emerged from her dream-state, it was impossible to gauge if there was some negative side-effect that would have to be treated.

Mostly he just sat by her side and prayed for her to be whole again.

It felt like a miracle when one day she woke up and looked at him with instant recognition. 'Ari,' she said in a pleased tone.

His heart kicked with excitement, then dropped like a stone when her expression changed to the darkly grieving one that had accompanied her other awakenings. But her words were slightly different.

'I'm sorry. I lost the baby.'

'No!'

Encouraged by the certainty that she was actually talking to him this time, he explained the situation again. There was an alertness in her eyes that hadn't been there before. He was sure she was listening, taking in all the information he gave, sifting through it, understanding. A smile started to tug at her mouth.

'A daughter,' she said in a tone of pleasure. 'How lovely!'

Elation soared through him. 'She's beautiful. Just like you, Christina,' he said, smiling back.

A frown of concern puckered her brow. 'And Theo? I've been here…how long?'

'Two months. Theo is fine. Missing his Mama but happily distracted by having a baby sister. I'll bring both of them in for you to see as soon as I can.'

'Maria…' She smiled again, a look of blissful relief on her face. 'Oh, I'm so glad I didn't lose her, Ari.'

'And I'm so glad I didn't lose you,' he said fervently.

Her eyes focussed sharply on him for several moments before her gaze slid away to where her fingers started plucking at the bed-sheet. 'I guess that would have been...inconvenient for you.'

Inconvenient!

Shock rattled Ari's mind. It took him several moments to realise she had no idea how much she meant to him. He'd never told her. He reached out and enclosed the plucking fingers with his, holding them still.

'Look at me, Christina,' he quietly commanded.

She did so, but not with open windows to her soul. Her guard was up, as it had been from the day she had agreed to marry him. He had never worn it down. He should have felt grateful for this return to normality, but the need to break through it was too strong for patience in laying out what was very real to him—had been real for a long time although he hadn't recognised it until faced with losing her from his life.

'Do you remember asking me about falling in love and I told you about the American woman I'd met when I was eighteen?' he asked.

She slowly nodded.

'It was nothing but blind infatuation, Christina,' he said vehemently, his eyes burning into hers to make her believe he spoke the truth. 'I didn't love her. I didn't know her enough to love the person she was. Being with you this past year...I've learnt what it is to really love a woman. I love you.'

Her eyes widened but still they searched his warily.

'If you'd died from this accident, it would have left a hole in my life that no one else could ever fill. It wouldn't have been an inconvenience. Christina. It would have been...' He shook his head, unable to express the terrible emptiness that had loomed while he'd waited for the miracle of her return to him. 'I love you,' he repeated helplessly. 'And please, please, don't ever leave me again.'

'Leave you?' she echoed incredulously. 'I've always been afraid of you leaving me.'

'Never! Never! And after this, let me tell you, I'm going to be nervous about letting you out of my sight.'

She gave him a rueful little smile. 'That's how I felt... nervous when you were away from me. Women always look at you, Ari.'

'They don't make me feel what I do for you, Christina. You're my woman, the best in the world. Believe me.'

Tina wanted to. Somehow it was too much...waking up from the dreadful nightmare of loss and being handed a lovely dream. She lifted her free hand to rub her forehead, get her mind absolutely clear.

'My hair! It's gone!'

'It's growing back,' Ari instantly assured her. 'They had to shave it for the operation.'

Tears spurted into her eyes as she gingerly felt the ultra-short mat of hair covering her scalp. Ari had liked it long so she had let it grow after their wedding. She remembered taking the taxi to the hairdressing salon...

'My mother!'

'She's fine. Minor injuries. She was only in hospital for one day. Everything's fine, Christina. Nothing for you to worry about.'

'Who is looking after the children?'

'The housekeeper, the nanny for Maria, your mother, my mother, my sisters, your aunts...our home is like a railway station for relatives wanting to help.'

The sudden rush of fear receded, replaced by a weird feeling of jealousy that a nanny was replacing her for Maria. 'I need to go home, Ari,' she pleaded.

'As soon as the doctors permit it,' he promised.

'I need to see my children.'

He squeezed her hand. 'You rest quietly now and I'll go and get them, bring them here for you to see. Okay?'

'Yes.'

He rose from the chair beside her bed and gently kissed her forehead. 'Your hair doesn't matter, Christina,' he murmured. 'Only you getting well again matters.'

The deep caring in his voice washed through her, soothing the tumult of emotions that had erupted. Everything was all right. Ari always made perfect arrangements. And he'd said he loved her.

She didn't rest quietly. No sooner had Ari gone than doctors came, asking questions, taking her blood pressure, checking tubes and wires, removing some of them. She had questions for them, too. By the time they left she knew precisely what she had been through and how devoted her husband had been, visiting her every day, doing his best to console her whenever she'd shared her nightmare with him.

The doctors had no doubt that Ari loved her.

Tina started to believe it.

Theo came running into the hospital room, his face

lighting up with joy at seeing her awake and smiling for him. 'Mama! Mama! Can I hug you?'

She laughed and made room on the bed for him to climb up beside her. 'I want to hug you, too.' Her beautiful little son. Hers and Ari's. It was wonderful to cuddle him again.

'And here is my sister,' he declared proudly as Ari carried their baby into the room, grinning delightedly at the two of them together.

Theo quickly shuffled aside to let Ari lay the baby in her arms. Tina felt a huge welling of love as her gaze roved over her daughter, taking in the amazing perfection of her.

'Maria's got more hair than you, Mama,' Theo said, and she could laugh about it, no longer caring about the loss of her long, glossy locks.

'She has your mother's hair, and her eyes and her mouth,' Ari said, as though he was totally besotted by the likeness to her.

Tina couldn't help smiling at him. He smiled back and the words simply spilled out of the fullness of her heart. 'I love you, too, Ari.'

His eyes glowed a warm gold. He leaned over and kissed her on the mouth. 'I will thank God forever that you've come back to us, Christina,' he murmured against her lips, leaving them warm and tingling, making her feel brilliantly alive.

A new life, she thought. Not only for the baby in her arms, but for her and Ari and Theo, too.

A family bonded in love.

It was what her father had wanted for her.

No more disappointment.

She had it all.

It was summer on Santorini again and both families had gathered in force to attend Maria's christening. The same church, the same reception centre, but for Tina, this was a much happier occasion than her wedding. Although Ari's family had welcomed her into it before, she really felt a part of it now, and she also felt much closer to her own family, no longer having the sense of being an outsider who had broken the rules.

It was a truly joyous celebration of life and love. The sun shone. There were no shadows between her and Ari. She saw desire for her simmering in his eyes all day and her own desire for him was zinging through her blood. No sooner was the party over and the children finally asleep in their part of the Zavros villa, than they headed off to their own bedroom, eager to make love. But before they did, there was one thing Tina wanted to do.

She'd put the prenuptial agreement in the top drawer of the bedside table and she went straight to it, took it out and handed it to Ari. 'I want you to tear this up.'

He frowned. 'I don't mind you having it, Christina. I want you to feel secure.'

'No. It's wrong. It's part of a bad time that's gone, Ari. If you were asking me to marry you now, I wouldn't insist on a prenuptial agreement. I trust you. I believe what we have is forever. It is, isn't it?'

He smiled. 'Yes, it is.'

He tore it up.

She smiled and opened her arms to him, opened her

heart to him. 'I love you. I love our family. We're going to have a brilliant life together, aren't we?'

He laughed, lifted her off her feet, twirled her around and dumped her on the bed, falling on top of her, although levering his weight up on his elbows as he grinned down at her. 'Brilliant and beautiful and bountiful, because I have you, my love.'

She reached up and touched his cheek, her eyes shining with all he made her feel.

'And I have you.'

* * * * *

ONE NIGHT IN HIS BED

BY
CHRISTINA HOLLIS

Christina Hollis was born in Somerset, and now lives in the idyllic Wye Valley. She was born reading, and her childhood dream was to become a writer. This was realised when she became a successful journalist and lecturer in organic horticulture. Then she gave it all up to become a full-time mother of two and to run half an acre of productive country garden. Writing Mills & Boon romances is another ambition realised. It fills most of her time, between complicated rural school runs. The rest of her life is divided between garden and kitchen, either growing fruit and vegetables or cooking with them. Her daughter's cat always closely supervises everything she does around the home, from typing to picking strawberries!

To Jenny, whose enthusiasm really keeps me going!

CHAPTER ONE

'SUPERSTITIOUS old Enrica saw a black cat this morning. She told me it means there are pirates in town. You had better put on something sexier than that black shroud and try to catch yourself a rich one, Sienna!' Imelda Basso jeered out of an upstairs window. Down in the courtyard, her stepdaughter Sienna gritted her teeth and smiled. She said nothing. Sometimes, silence was her only weapon against Imelda.

Sienna loaded a last box into the local Co-operative's van and escaped to market. Working on the stall got her out of the house, but freedom was a mixed blessing. It made her feel like a hen released from a broody coop. The noise and dazzling colour of Portofino always came as a shock to her. It was such a contrast with her daily life that all Sienna wanted to do when she got there was to retreat back into herself, to concentrate on her knitting and take up as little space as possible. But that was no good. Nobody would buy from a mouse. The Piccia Co-operative needed sales. Its members relied on this stall. They intended to increase their contribution to local charities this year, too. That meant everyone had to do their bit—Sienna included. She had to push herself.

She was developing a coping strategy. She kept her head down, and made sure she always looked busy. It was the perfect way to avoid having to talk to anybody until the exact moment they were ready to buy.

Sienna recognised a lot of familiar faces around the market, although she had never been brave enough to strike up a conversation with any of them. Yet today was different. Someone new caught her eye—and held it. A tall stranger was moving through the chaos of deliveries and conversations on the other side of the square. Sienna had to look away, fast. He was so different from the market men that her stomach contracted. A single glance was enough to tell her that this was someone special. He was really well dressed, and the quiet confidence of his movements set him apart from the brash, swaggering pitchers around him. Sienna risked a couple of direct looks at the stranger, as well as more covert glances from beneath her lashes. She reassured herself that no one would suspect a shy widow of anything more than curiosity.

The new arrival was certainly worth examining. His determined attitude, coupled with that neat dark hair and the clean, strong lines of his jaw, marked him out as someone very special indeed. He moved from stall to stall with all the style of a Roman emperor on a tour of inspection. Sienna wondered what it was like to be so self-assured. This man obviously expected to go anywhere and do anything. She watched as he sampled olives, tasted walnuts, or accepted a spoonful of goats' cheese spread on a biscuit. He did not stop anywhere long enough to buy, but moved on in a restless search for the next novelty. Sienna would never have dared to try something at a stall and then leave without purchasing. She wondered how he could have the nerve. His easy manner showed it was not a problem for him.

Hypnotised by watching him idle along from place to place, she suddenly realised it was almost time for her stall to come under his scrutiny. Her mind dissolved in horror. What would she say? Here was a gorgeous man—with plenty of money to spend, judging by his appearance. He would be an ideal customer. If only she could succeed in getting him to buy where everyone else in the market had failed…

With difficulty, she kept her gaze away from the approaching stranger. If she didn't look at him directly, he might pass on by. She screwed her hands into balls of nerves. Why did this have to happen when she was working alone? Anna Maria or any one of the other co-op members would have leapt forward and made a sale. All Sienna could do was blush and shrink and turn aside, hoping that the handsome newcomer would pass straight by.

She counted the change in the pouch at her waist. Then she switched her attention back to her table, making sure the goods were still neatly displayed, touching everything as though for luck. She repeated her little rituals until she was sure he must have passed by. Even so, it was quite a while before she felt brave enough to glance around the market again.

There was no sign of the stranger. With a huge sigh of relief Sienna relaxed. It was all too much for her. She hadn't wanted to be seen blushing, as she knew she would have done if she'd spoken to the handsome stranger. In Piccia, where she lived, good reputations took a lifetime to forge. And people expected to see a certain standard of behaviour from a widow. One word or action out of place could destroy her reputation in an instant. Sienna thought of the local woman whose husband had divorced her in order to marry his mistress. The wife had been the innocent party, but looks and whispers had followed her everywhere. Eventually she had been hounded out of her birthplace.

Sienna could not bear to think of being the subject of gossip. Her stepmother, Imelda, would never forgive her. And her anger frightened Sienna. Just the thought of Imelda's displeasure was enough to keep Sienna on the straight and narrow—but then virtue was an easy path in Piccia. There was no temptation. All the boys left as soon as they could. Only men with private incomes or those too old to escape lived in Piccia now.

Sienna sighed. She liked the quiet village life, but it came at a huge price. Imelda was determined to marry her off to a rich man again as soon as it was decent. Sienna's late husband had had only one blood relative, a distant cousin called Claudio di Imperia, and Imelda had him in mind as Sienna's next suitor. One look at Claudio's pinched, pale face had told Sienna that 'fun' was not a word with any meaning for him. If I have to be married, why can't *I* choose who it's going to be? she thought angrily.

The good-looking stranger was now bending over a stand on the far side of the market. He was concentrating on a display of everything imaginable that could be made from chestnuts. While he was busy, Sienna took the chance to study him again—but only while the other stallholders weren't looking.

The visitor was dressed in Armani, she noticed, and his thick dark hair was neatly trimmed. What a contrast he made with her unwanted future husband. Claudio wore his frayed cuffs and bad haircut like medals for economy. But Imelda always said it didn't matter what a man looked like as long as he had plenty of money in the bank. In Sienna's house, Imelda Basso's word was law. The only thing *that* woman feared was public opinion—which was why Sienna was determined to wear black for as long as possible. It was protection. No one in the village would forgive Imelda if she tried to marry off her stepdaughter when the 'poor girl' was still in mourning.

Snared away from her thoughts, Sienna realised in a panic that he was coming in her direction again. She looked down quickly, already worrying about what to say if he spoke to her. Then she remembered her stepmother's mocking laughter. *Who is going to be interested in Piccia's homespun rubbish?*

Sienna's shoulders sagged. Was there no escape from the echo of that woman's voice? It was even invading her daydreams.

Was Imelda right? Would anybody as rich as him be interested in her stall? The gorgeous stranger would probably buy some of those dark handmade chocolates wrapped in crackling cellophane and ribbon for his equally shrink-wrapped and sophisticated girlfriend. He's bound to have one, Sienna thought, and I'll bet *she* never wears black.

'Excuse me, miss—I wonder if you could direct me to the Church of San Gregorio?'

A loud, cultured voice made her flush with confusion. She looked up—but it was not the person she had hoped it would be. Instead of her dashing hero, she found herself staring at the expectant faces of a couple of tourists.

All Sienna's tension dissolved in a self-conscious giggle. She gave the directions, and even managed to exchange a few cheerful words. Then a cloud blotted out her relief. While she had been busy chatting, a presence had arrived beside her. That was the only way she could describe it. The tall, well-dressed stranger had materialised at her elbow.

All her worries flooded back, stifling her voice as soon as the tourists said goodbye. She was alone with him. Sienna had no option but to look up and smile. Straight away she made sure she could not be accused of flirting. It didn't matter that she was twenty kilometres from home, Sienna knew that the moment she showed the slightest interest in any male over the age of ten, the news would reach her stepmother before you could say 'torrid affair'.

The vision smiled back. Sienna gazed at him, at a loss. And then he spoke.

'I heard you speaking English to that couple.' He came straight to the point in a distinctive accent. It matched his frank, typically American expression. 'I wonder—could you please direct me to the best restaurant around here?'

Was that all he needed? Sienna wanted to feel relief rush through her, but it didn't happen. His steady gaze was too intense for that. His dark brown eyes mesmerised her, in the split second she allowed herself to look up into his face. Quickly, she looked down again. The very *best* place to eat was about twenty kilometres away, up in the hills. No one in Piccia could afford to eat in Il Pettirosso, where Anna Maria's husband Angelo worked, but it was the restaurant Sienna always visited in her daydreams. As all the staff were local, and this visitor had chosen her for her ability to speak English, it might not be for him. But his confident yet relaxed stance told Sienna that this man would fit in anywhere. And *he is exactly the sort who might try and turn my simplest reply into a conversation,* she thought nervously.

Conversation was a risk Sienna could not take. She had enough grief in her life already, and didn't want any more. *This would never have happened if the man had bought something when he'd first walked into the market,* she reflected. The other stallholders always spoke English when a customer showed real signs of spending money. She glanced sideways at the walnut-faced market men squinting through smoke from their roll-ups, and the *nonnas* sitting in judgement like black toads.

'There are lots of good restaurants down by the sea, *signor*. Many of them have menus printed in French or English,' she added helpfully.

'I've heard that some places on the coast take advantage of the tourist dollar, and as I can actually speak a little Italian, *signorina*, the language won't necessarily be a problem for me.'

He smiled, and Sienna could believe it.

'In which case, the best place is twenty or thirty minutes' drive out of town. And it's quite a walk to the cab rank from here.'

Especially in shoes like those, she thought, her gaze firmly fixed on his Guccis.

'That won't necessarily matter. I was going to hire a car and invite some old friends out for lunch while I'm in their neighbourhood.'

The urge to look up at him grew too strong, so Sienna

gave in. A change had come over his expression. It was as though a cloud had passed in front of the sun, and she realised he disliked giving out information about himself.

Sienna nervously passed the tip of her tongue over her lips. 'The only thing is…the restaurant I recommended really needs somebody in your party who has an ear for the local dialect. Perhaps your friends are fluent, *signor*? Il Pettirosso is remote, and very much a haunt of those "in the know", as I think the saying goes. Are you sure you wouldn't be better off going to one of the fashionable places down by the sea after all? They get so much business from tourists that it's accepted all their staff will speak English. All sorts of famous people go there,' she finished lamely, in case he was famous, too, and she simply hadn't recognised him. With those expectant eyes and resolute mouth, he looked as though he should have an international fan club.

'I loathe watching money being thrown around solely in the hope of making an impression,' he announced. 'I prefer good food and service in excellent company. In which of your suggested places would *you* choose to eat?'

'If I could go anywhere?' Sienna could hardly imagine such luxury.

'Go anywhere, spend anything—I don't care what it costs as long as it's value for money.'

'Oh, then that's easy!' Sienna warmed with the thought of it. 'Il Pettirosso—even if it means buying a phrasebook to help with the ordering. It's a wonderful place with smoked glass windows so passers-by can't see inside. They specialise in local dishes, and everything is freshly prepared from the finest ingredients. Regional food is cooked there to the highest possible standard.'

His smile returned. 'That sounds just my sort of place. Authentic cuisine and an authentic name!'

'It's actually a sort of bird, *signor*. They live in the woodlands, and I shouldn't think you would ever see one inside Il Pettirosso. Unless they have pictures of them on the menu, of course.'

Putting his head on one side, he looked at her acutely. 'Are you telling me you've never actually eaten there?'

Sienna shook her head. The thought of trying to get her late husband Aldo over the threshold of a place like that made her smile.

The stranger reached inside his jacket and pulled out a small mobile phone. Flipping it open, he handed it to Sienna. She looked at him in bewilderment.

'Go on, then—the choice is made. Would you mind booking it for me, please, *signorina*? I might have a problem making myself understood if I can't give them some visual clues. I'll need a table for four at midday. That will give me plenty of time to make all the other arrangements.'

'I shall need a name, *signor*.'

'Oh, just tell them it is for Garett Lazlo,' he said, as though giving her the answer to everything.

Sienna's eyes widened at this, but she rang the restaurant as instructed. To her amazement, the booking was accepted straight away. Within seconds the formalities were complete. Next moment, the receptionist at Il Pettirosso was thanking her for the call with a warm goodbye. For a few precious seconds Sienna could fool herself that she was his glamorous personal assistant, making an official business call.

The phone was warmed by a faint fragrance of handsome Mr Lazlo. Sienna savoured it for as long as she could, until she had to hand it back.

'And now, *signorina*—can you achieve a double triumph, and point me in the direction of a decent car?'

Garett Lazlo tucked the phone back inside his jacket, all set to go. The part of Sienna that was not still under the influence of his masculine aroma almost managed to feel relieved.

'If you go straight through the market, then turn right and carry on across town, there is a prestige hire firm within a kilometre. Keep your back to the harbour and you can't miss it,' she said quickly.

'Thank you.'

It sounded as though there was a smile in his voice, but Sienna did not trust herself to check. When she eventually raised her head her visitor was strolling away, his jacket slung over one shoulder. With an unfamiliar pang of excitement she realised she could stare at him openly now, because everyone else in the market was doing exactly the same thing. Among that gallery, one more person admiring the tall, slim stranger would go unnoticed. Even if that person was 'poor, downtrodden Sienna', as everyone called her when they thought she could not hear.

She dared herself to take in his appearance for a few more minutes. There were always plenty of foreigners in Portofino, but this one was definitely something special. As she watched him walk away, Sienna was reliving every word he had spoken to her. Their conversation ran through her mind on an endless loop—his self-confidence, and her hesitancy. Butterflies were dancing in her stomach, although he had probably forgotten her almost instantly. He was looking over the other stalls again, and with genuine interest. The morning sunlight glowed against the dazzling white of his shirt. In contrast, his hair was gypsy-dark. Only a slight natural curl softened the depths of its carelessly expensive cut. Sienna found herself wondering what it would be like to trail her fingers through its luxuriance. The thought alarmed her, and she tried to look away. But it was hopeless. She had no choice but to watch him furtively until he was right out of sight, around the corner.

He never looked back. In contrast, Sienna spent the next hour glancing around for him.

It was still early in the day, and the season had barely started. Although there were a lot of visitors to Portofino, business was quiet. Sienna tried to keep her mind off the handsome American, but it was difficult. He had stirred a strange yearning in her. She made work for herself—arranging and rearranging the items on the co-op's table. Handmade lace produced in her village was always popular, and now that Molly Bradley was learning to make it as well, there would be no shortage of things to sell.

Kane and Molly Bradley were new arrivals in Piccia—polite, and not at all pushy. Sienna had first met them in the local store, where their 'teach yourself' Italian had earned them nothing but mutinous stares from the staff. Once Sienna had sorted everything out, the Bradleys had slowly but surely worked their way towards acceptance by the villagers.

The best sort of incomers were like that. They felt they had to work twice as hard as the locals to be thought half as good. Sienna did not mind newcomers, as long as they were like Kane and Molly. At least *they* weren't keeping holiday homes empty for most of the year, or playing at farming on the hills.

* * *

Sienna was wondering whether to pour herself a cup of coffee when someone spoke, making her jump guiltily.

'Hello again, *signorina*—I'd like to thank you for your directions. They were perfect.'

There was no mistaking that voice. It was like mountain honey. With dread in her heart, but hope in her eyes, Sienna straightened up to be confronted by all her dreams and nightmares rolled into one handsome package. That old woman back at home had been right when she'd said pirates had landed today, Sienna thought, as the fluttering feeling rose up from her stomach and turned all her sensible thoughts into butterflies.

She did not dare acknowledge the stranger with anything more than a nod. He took no notice of her nervous silence. Leaning forward, he planted his hands firmly on the edge of the table. He made it instantly obvious that, whatever he had come for, it was not souvenirs.

'Don't mention it,' Sienna said, turning hot pink as she felt the eyes of all the other stallholders fastening on her. She was already thinking of this stranger as 'The Pirate' so the thrust behind his next words should have come as no surprise—but it did.

'I've got the hire-car, and as none of the phrasebooks on sale in town included detailed directions to Il Pettirosso, I'm here to collect *you*.' He homed in on her with a devastating smile.

'Me?' Sienna stared around, flustered. Everyone was looking. She was the centre of attention, which she hated, but at least they were all smiling.

'It's the perfect solution, *signorina*. You'll be able to

make sure I get there on time, in one piece, and by the most direct route.'

Distracted, Sienna plucked at her skirt. If Garett Lazlo had been one of the regular guys who cruised the stalls on the lookout for lone girls that would have been easily fixed. She had no hesitation in telling strangers where to go. But this man was different. He was serious, formal, and truly stunning—and for the moment at least he seemed to have eyes only for her.

Sienna began to panic. She ached to break free from her boring life and do something different, but her reputation was on the line. She imagined all the elderly Ligurian matrons in their doorways and loggias, on their stalls and balconies, shaking their heads and sucking their remaining teeth in disapproval. She could almost feel their eyes boring into her. One wrong move, one word out of place, and Sienna was sure her honour would be gone for ever. She had not felt so totally alone since her wedding day.

Garett Lazlo smiled again. Sienna did not need to look up and see it. Her heightened senses were already filling in the details of his irresistible face and those tempting dark eyes…

If only she was free. She wished with all her heart that the world would go away and let her be herself for once. But who *am* I? she thought helplessly. It's been years since I've been allowed to give it any thought. So now I'm nothing but a girl who is too scared to say yes. Even to a once-in-a-lifetime offer like this!

'Don't tell me you're going to resist coming along for the ride?' he said silkily. 'I've picked up *such* a car. It's beautiful—sleek and shiny—and it is exactly the same shade of Mediterranean blue as your eyes.'

'How do you know, *signor*?'

Despite her nerves, this man aroused strange, conflicting feelings inside her, and she felt she had to challenge him.

'My attention to detail is said to be legendary. But allow me to check—'

Before Sienna knew what was happening, cool, strong fingers had slipped beneath her chin and tilted up her head. In the last hour she had agonised over Garett Lazlo's approach, and then been struck dumb by his presence. But such intimacy from this stranger cleared her mind in a flash. She jumped back, cannoning into her stall. As she did so her vacuum flask overbalanced, bounced off the corner of the table and landed with a shuddering thump in her open lunchbox. Coffee and sparkling shards of glass spilled out over the focaccia and salad she had been about to eat.

For one second everyone looked at the scene in shocked silence. Then Sienna drew in a great breath and rounded on the American. 'Oh, *look* what you've done!'

Garett spread his hands in an artless gesture. 'What can I say? I am sorry—but I didn't expect you to act like a frightened rabbit. All I did was make a perfectly reasonable request for you to accompany me to an appointment as my guide and interpreter. I may have backed it up with a little harmless flirtation, but if you aren't in the market for that—well, it's fine by me.' He shrugged one shoulder, unconcerned by what he deemed to be her overreaction.

Sienna had to concentrate hard to stop her eyes filling with tears. She was hungry, and she didn't have any cash on her.

'My food is ruined,' she said in a small voice.

The way she spoke provoked a slightly amused expression.

'Problem solved—you're lunching with me.'

'He's got you there. You can't argue with that!' One of the *nonnas* nodded with satisfaction.

Sienna had been scared of the elderly ladies who manned the other market stalls. Now she turned to stare at this one with open amazement. The old woman grinned back at her.

'He's ruined your lunch. A girl must eat—so the least he can do is feed you!'

'Thank you, *signora*,' Garett replied to the bystander, whose intonation worked in any language. He looked back at Sienna in obvious triumph. 'The fact is, *signorina*, you need a lunchtime break and some refreshment. I need directions and a translator. If I take you to lunch now, that will solve all our problems—yours and mine. Therefore I am your perfect lunch companion, and you are mine.'

'No, I'm not! I don't know… I can't…' Sienna struggled, wishing she could say yes but knowing she would never allow herself to do so.

Garett Lazlo met all her excuses with amusement, which gave her no help at all.

'Il Pettirosso has a strict dress code…it is that sort of place. I couldn't possibly walk in there dressed like this!' She flipped her fingers over the plain black of her clothes. This expanded his smile still further.

'I don't see why not. Black is always in fashion.' His gaze travelled slowly down from her face in cool appraisal. 'It's true that your clothes are a little austere, *signorina*, but as far as I am concerned less is more in that department. Especially when it can be dressed up so easily.' He threw his glance across the handicrafts on her table and it stopped when he saw a beautiful angora wrap. It was as blue as an angel's eyes and as insubstantial as gossamer. Picking it up, he swept it in a misty billow around her shoulders, arranging it gently against her neck.

For those few precious seconds Sienna was enveloped in his clean, masculine fragrance once again. Intoxicated now, as well as astonished, she watched him in silence. He was casting a connoisseur's eye over the delicate jewellery she had brought to sell. When he lifted a fine filigree of silver from her display, and held it up to catch the dancing sunlight, she knew there would be no resisting his next suggestion—whatever it was.

'Now, all you need is this lapis necklace and matching bracelet and there will be no one at Il Pettirosso—no matter how sophisticated the place might be—who can raise a candle to you, *signorina*,' he said calmly, handing it to her.

Thank goodness he didn't try to put it on me, Sienna thought, almost deafened by the sound of her heart hammering against her ribs. She hesitated at the sight of the beautiful necklace in her hands. It glittered and tempted her like cool water in a drought.

'Yes...but I really cannot let you do this, *signor*!' She shook her head and turned away, thinking of the craftsmen and women back in Piccia. They were depending on her to make them some money. 'All these things are for sale. They aren't here to act as a dressing up box for me. I can't possibly use them! And what would I tell the co-opera-tive—that I just danced off for lunch when I should have been taking care of business here?'

She put one hand up to her neck, touching the place where the beautiful necklace would have lain against her skin. She ached, and hoped it was because she wanted to feel the kiss of its metal there, rather than Garett Lazlo's lips. That did not bear thinking about.

As her fingers fluttered over the smooth lines of her collarbone a shaft of sun streaked over the golden band on her wedding finger. Garett leaned back. It was only a slight movement, but it released Sienna from his shadow. Glancing up, she waited to feel relief that he no longer seemed about to force his presence on her. But when it came, the feeling was tinged with the faintest trace of disappointment.

'I have a duty to the people who sent me here, *signor*,' she said quietly.

'Your loyalty does you credit, *signora*. But you have overlooked one simple fact. I'm not asking you to do anything immoral. Accompany me to lunch now, and I shall pay for all the things you are borrowing from your stall. When we return you will give me an estimate of the money you might reasonably have expected to make in the length of time you have been away. What could be fairer than that?'

'Nothing!' one of the stallholders called out.

Sienna looked around at the *nonnas* and market men. The thought that they were waiting for her to step out of line had been terrifying her for weeks. It was true that they were all watching her today, but it was with interest and genuine amusement. None of them looked in the least bit disapproving.

'I'd go with him like a shot if I was fifty years younger!' a nearby stallholder suggested. She was a tiny, bird-like woman, grinning up from her knitting.

'Do you think it would be all right, *signora*?' Sienna asked doubtfully.

The old lady rested the lacy beginnings of a matinee jacket in her lap. Loosening another length of baby-pink wool from the skein in her enormous carpetbag, she looked up with a mischevious twinkle.

'My long life has taught me that you should grab opportunity with both hands whenever it shows up. And especially if it looks like him!' She gestured with one long, fine knitting needle. Everyone within earshot laughed out loud.

Garett Lazlo studied them all as though his face was carved in stone. 'Did I understand that correctly, *signora*?'

'N-no. Probably not.' She hoped.

'I certainly hope you did, *signor*!' The *nonna* chuckled with delight, speaking in heavily accented English this time. 'Take her away with a clear conscience, *signor*, and for as long as you like. I shall look after her stall.'

'Thank you.' Garett inclined his head graciously and took a firm hold on Sienna's elbow.

'She speaks English?' he queried, drawing Sienna quickly across the marketplace before she had time to think up any more delaying tactics.

'We all do. If the price is right.' But as she said the words she worried that he would take them the wrong way. Had she just wrecked her own reputation?

CHAPTER TWO

THEY were leaving the busy market behind. He was drawing her away from the crowds. If she were forced to call for help, then soon there would be no one to hear her. Panic began to bubble up, foaming into real fear. Garett Lazlo was so much bigger than she was. Fighting him off, if worse came to the worst, would not be an option.

Sienna did the only thing she could. Stopping abruptly, she caught him off balance.

'Wait—I wasn't expecting you to take me to lunch, Mr Lazlo, much less anything else. I'm not looking to make anything out of this at all—honestly! If you are going to regret dressing me up like this, then you should know that I made this wrap, and my friend designed and made the jewellery. I can pay her back for that, and at least no one but me will be any the poorer if my wrap has to be given away, rather than sold. It won't cost you a thing. I can easily make the co-operative another one.'

'You made this?'

She nodded, on firm ground for once. 'I keep rabbits for meat. It is easy to hide a few Angoras in their shed as well.' Sienna warmed with the thought of that tiny triumph, which she had managed in the face of Imelda and Aldo. Neither of them would have recognised a rabbit outside of a casserole dish.

Intrigued, he lifted the trailing edge of the cornflower-blue shrug and inspected the fine stitches. 'It's exquisite. And you look ravishing in it, by the way,' he added disarmingly. 'But I find dedication and skill like this in one so young slightly worrying. A beautiful woman like you really should get out more, *signora*.'

'I'm not allowed—that is, I don't get the chance. I have to keep house for my stepmother on top of everything else,' Sienna corrected herself quickly. Imelda might treat her like Cinderella, but she did not want this real-life Prince Charming to think she was a push-over—especially if they were about to enter a secluded alleyway together. 'That doesn't leave me the time or the energy for anything else,' she finished primly.

'I see.'

Her message must have been clear enough, for his grip on her elbow eased slightly. To Sienna's relief, he let go completely as they entered the warren of streets leading out of town.

She thought it was because he respected the line she had drawn between them, but Garett's mind was actually elsewhere. He was uneasy. His escape from Manhattan had been so sudden, and it meant travelling without the comfort of a schedule. His working days used to run like clockwork, but that was behind him for the moment. The alphabet soup of PAs, PDAs and GPS which made sure he got from A to B and back again in the shortest possible time was nothing but a memory. He patted his jacket, feeling the reassuring bulge made by his passport. With that, and his unlimited funds, Garett could do what he liked and go where he wanted. The world should be his oyster. But he was finding freedom unexpectedly hard work.

This thought carved furrows in his brow. He had more money to burn than most people made in a lifetime, and yet it was no longer enough. Why not? Something—some basic truth obvious to everyone else—still evaded him. From the age of six he had worked continuously—because when he stopped the restlessness returned. A vital element was missing from his life. He had discovered a disturbing new side to himself earlier that week. It had made him realise he *must* find out what he lacked—immediately— but how? Work was clearly part of the problem. The only way he could think to avoid its siren song was to put a few thousands miles and complete radio silence between him and his headquarters. The moment he tried to log in to the office computer system his staff would be on his case like kids mobbing a tomcat. He needed space, and time to think.

Garett put one hand in his pocket. It was only the third time he had checked for the hire-car keys since they'd been handed to him. He must be slowing down. As he thought that, he noticed another change in himself. Strolling through these airless city passageways with a nervous stranger should have been hell—a horrible reminder of what he had escaped. Instead, he found himself actually enjoying the sensation of not being expected to make conversation. What was happening to him?

Without realising it, he slowed his walk still further. It gave him the chance to look around for once. Lifting his gaze from the pavement, he sent it up to where the

tenement canyons showed a strip of sky. The silhouette of
a woman with bulky breasts and a wayward home perm
loomed out of an upstairs window. She was holding a big
juice container. With a shout of cheerful warning she
poured water from it into her flower boxes. A noisy cascade
of liquid ran out from beneath her billowing scarlet
geraniums, darkening the front of the apartment block
before dripping down to the flagstones.

A trickle ran towards the feet of Garett's unwilling
companion. She was lost in thought and had not noticed
the gardener overhead. Now she looked up and frowned at
the clear, cloudless sky above.

'An April shower?' Garett spoke his thoughts aloud.
Then he smiled, realising that for the first time in decades
he was thinking about something other than work.

It might not be the whole answer to his problems.

But it was a start.

The car was every bit as beautiful as he'd said it would be.
Sienna slid into the passenger seat with a sigh of real longing.

'Good, isn't it?' He smiled, slipping behind the wheel
with similar satisfaction.

Sienna nodded, but did not speak. She was determined
to keep her head down. Garett Lazlo had not laid a finger
on her since letting go of her arm. Whatever her secret
feelings about that, she knew she must not encourage him
in way. But modesty was not the only reason for her
silence. On the way to the restaurant they would be passing
within a few kilometres of Piccia. She could only hope and
pray that none of the villagers saw her being driven along
in a car like this.

Although I'm the last person anyone would expect to see in a Lamborghini. She smiled to herself. They'd probably write it off as a hallucination, brought on by too much sun.

'You're the first girl who's ever smiled at my driving. They usually squeal and grab at something.' Garett glanced at her as he pulled away from the kerb. 'What's the joke?'

'N-nothing,' she said nervously, 'except that…travelling along like this reminds me of that old song: "If My Friends Could See Me Now". I was wondering what my stepmother would say if she caught sight of me in this!' She ran her hand lovingly over the passenger seat. It was made from softest glove-leather, and had the fragrance of money well spent.

His face cleared, and his eyes narrowed with devilment.

'Let's call in on her and find out, shall we?'

Sienna was horrified. 'No! Please don't! She would kill me! Respectable women aren't seen in fast cars with strange men.'

'Why not? Better that, surely, than being spotted in a strange car with a fast man? Are we going to pass your house?'

'No—thank goodness,' Sienna said with real feeling. 'It's too far from here to take a detour without making you late for your table reservation, *signor*.'

'I get the message—you're keeping me safely at arm's length. But that's no reason to be so formal. You can call me Garett.'

Sienna's lips flickered briefly into a smile. Then it was gone and she looked out of her window again. This was not what he had come to expect from women.

'Don't you have a given name, *signora*?' he prompted her.

'Of course, but perhaps we should keep this formal.' Sienna pursed her lips.

'I call all the ladies of my acquaintance by their first names, so why not give me yours?'

Sienna took this as an order. She was used to those, but it didn't make carrying them out any easier. Besides, this was a total stranger. She had to make a stand somehow, and insist on keeping him at a distance. Resisting would overturn everything she had been taught about obedience—but the idea excited her. She had already done one astonishing thing today, by coming this far with him. Why not another?

'My name is Signora di Imperia.' She looked at Garett boldly, daring him to challenge her for more information.

One hand on the steering wheel, he watched her with interested eyes. Sienna returned his look. And then, almost imperceptibly, he smiled. Then he transferred his gaze to the road ahead. As he did so, he gave the same small, formal bow of his head he had given the respectable matron back in the market place.

Sienna knew now why the old woman had giggled like a teenager. Garett Lazlo's talent for melting women with his smallest gesture was at work on her, too. Oh, if only they could exchange more than pleasantries…

After Garett pulled his car into Il Pettirosso's car park and killed the ignition, he drew out his mobile and made a quick call before getting out.

'First they're engaged. Now they've switched their damned answering machine on!' he announced.

Sienna flashed a look at him. His lips were a taut line. A pulse was beating visibly at his temple. But when he finally spoke into the phone his confident tone was in total contrast with his strained features.

'It's me,' he said, without bothering to explain who 'me' was. 'The time is eleven fifty-nine a.m., Tuesday. I'm sitting in Il Pettirosso with my credit card in my hand just waiting to entertain you. So if you want to make the most of this outrageous offer, you'll get down here for lunch ASAP!'

He ended the call, and then clicked his tongue in disappointment. Shoving the phone back into his pocket, he slammed the door of his hire-car with a report that echoed across the nearby valley like a gunshot. Sienna gulped. As they walked the few metres from his car to the smoked glass door of the restaurant she hoped he would not need her to do much translating for him. If he was cross already, he might not take kindly to having the menu deciphered for him as though he was illiterate.

She need not have worried. They followed in the restaurant manager's highly polished footsteps to a discreetly placed table for four. Sienna was gazing around in awe at the clean, modern lines of the restaurant, but Garett had his eyes on something much more down to earth.

'Ah—so that's what a *pettirosso* is!' He pointed to the beautifully painted European robin on the front of his menu. 'Do you know, there's a duke in England who has one of these living in the grounds of his historic house that will actually hop onto his hand to be fed?'

Sienna watched him for a minute to see if he was joking. But his smile seemed quite genuine, and she decided to probe further.

'How do you know?'

'He does it as a kind of party trick to impress visitors.

I think the poor old guy's lonely. He valued me as much as someone to talk to as a business advisor.'

Sienna raised her eyebrows and lowered her head to study the menu. She did not want Garett to see her amazement at what he had said. A man who talked to dukes was sitting opposite her in the restaurant of her dreams! She tried to concentrate on the list of dishes before her, but that made her feel still more nervous. Il Pettirosso offered everything from asparagus to zucchini. She had no idea what to select, nor—more importantly—how much of his money Garett would be willing to spend on her.

'Choose what you like, Signora di Imperia.' he announced, as though reading her thoughts. 'If a place is good value for money, I don't bother with budgeting. Just order, and I'll see to the rest. For myself, I've been living off chateaubriand and fries for days, so I think I'll make it something vegetarian for my main course. I fancy a change today.' He lifted one shoulder in an easy gesture.

Vegetarian—that sounded reassuringly cheap. Sienna decided to order the same thing he did, but went on pretending to study the menu. This was partly to give his friends time to arrive, but also because it was a rare luxury. Sienna had not been out to lunch for years, and certainly never to a bewitching place like this. The experience ought to be played out for as long as she could manage.

Poring over the deckle-edged, beautifully inscribed menu, she waited until, despite his obvious good manners, Garett showed signs of becoming a little restless. Eventually she looked up shyly. He smiled and summoned the waiter.

'What have you chosen, Signora di Imperia?'

Sienna stopped smiling. 'Oh…er…actually, it all

looks so good I was hoping you could give me some suggestions…Garett…'

'I think we need a few more moments to decide, *signor*.' Garett nodded to their waiter. The moment the man stalked away, Sienna's host leaned forward with the look of someone who was about to reveal a great secret.

'You were right, *signora*, this place might have been beyond me if I had come here on my own. I thought to follow *your* selection! I can recognise all the general words, for things like soup and pasta, but some of these regional names are beyond me. Could we perhaps puzzle them out between us?'

Laughing, they went through the choices together, and came up with *cacciucco* for their starter, with *pansôti al preboggion* to follow. Sienna stayed with her idea of choosing the same things he did. It made ordering easier, and gave her a few extra seconds to gaze around in awe at her surroundings—and, more secretively, at her host.

The headwaiter materialised beside Garett the moment they were ready. Sienna looked up and smiled a little apprehensively as the man flourished his silver fountain pen over a small leatherbound notepad.

'Don't worry. I'll do the ordering,' Garett said smoothly, before she could open her mouth.

She held her breath, waiting to see what would happen.

His pronunciation was faultless. Before Sienna could congratulate him, a telephone call from his mobile burst in between them.

'Darn—it seems like we're going to be lunching on our own after all, *signora*. My friends can't make it,' he said when he had taken the call. He clicked his tongue, and then smiled at her reaction. 'What's the matter? Anyone would think you weren't looking forward to eating here in your dream restaurant.'

'It isn't that.' Sienna watched him switch off his phone and tuck it away. Suddenly it was as though the shrinking market girl had returned, trying to take up as little room as possible at his table. 'I had not expected to be dining alone with you.'

He narrowed his eyes in a way that made her smile, despite her nerves. 'That cuts both ways, you know, *signora*. But I suppose we're both going to have to buckle down and endure it.' He sighed theatrically, making Sienna giggle.

As her laughter died away, the sophisticated silence of the restaurant closed in. Garett was completely at ease. He sat back and studied his surroundings openly. Sienna could not manage to look anywhere directly, taking small swift glances around the room when she thought no one else was looking. Her mind was as active as her eyes, although it was not doing her much good. She desperately wanted to start up a witty, sparkling conversation. Only two things stopped her. Not being able to look at him without blushing was bad enough, but the second reason was still more of an obstacle.

She could not think of a single sensible thing to say. But then she was rescued by the most unlikely of sources. A butterfly flitted in through an open window of the restaurant.

'Oh, look—an orange tip!'

'You know about butterflies, *signora*?' He quirked a brow, suitably impressed.

'Not really, but they've increased at home since the place

has been allowed to run wild. They like the purple flowers that have seeded themselves all the way through the old terrace walls. The name is one I like, too—easy and obvious.'

Sienna almost felt she might be about to relax, but the arrival of their wine and first course put a stop to that. Her stomach contracted to the size of a split pea again. As usual, Garett took the attentions of the staff in his stride. Even before they swept away he leaned over his dish and inhaled appreciatively.

'Ah—so *cacciucco* must be fish soup, Signora di Imperia?'

'That's right. I don't know how much you picked up from the menu, but it said all the restaurant's raw materials are brought in fresh each morning. They come from a few kilometres away at the coast, or from local farms and smallholdings.'

He paused while breaking his bread, and leaned towards her with an enigmatic look on his face.

'I saw that. It made me realise that the ordinary people around here have to make things, as you do, or wrestle produce out of their surroundings. The menu really brought it home to me.' He paused again, considering what a strange word 'home' was in his circumstances. He tried to laugh again, but it came out as a harsh, dry sound. 'I ate nothing but junk until I managed to make a better life for myself. The chance to eat fresh local food in a place like this is a luxury.'

Sipping at a spoonful of her soup, Sienna regarded him. His mouth was a grim line now, and his eyes were hard as he stared past her into space.

'Perhaps it is all this home-grown fresh food in Liguria that keeps us so good-tempered?' she risked, testing his mood.

That broke Garett's trance. A puzzled frown flickered across his features, and he looked down at his clenched hand as though it belonged to someone else. Sienna noticed that it took him a conscious effort to relax his fingers. She went on watching him from beneath her lashes, and as she did so he began to lose the hunched tension that made him look like a prizefighter. He picked up his spoon, but to Sienna's relief did not actually attack his meal. He skimmed the *cacciucco* with graceful, economical movements.

Relieved, she concentrated on her own lunch. Even so, he had completely finished before she dared to speak again.

'I wish I had more of the killer instinct,' she said, almost making it sound casual. 'It would make an event like this less of an ordeal for me.' She tried to laugh, but it did not work.

'Fine dining is supposed to be a pleasurable experience.' Tipping his bowl away from him, he finished the last of his soup. Then he laid down the spoon. His every movement seemed measured to Sienna, as though he was unable to relax for a moment.

'Do you enjoy it, *signor*?'

'In the right company, yes.'

'Then it is a shame your friends are not here.'

'Oh, I'm doing fine, *signora*.'

He smiled, and the richness of his tone made Sienna wonder if he was only talking about lunch…

CHAPTER THREE

FOR once in his life, seduction was not on Garett's agenda. He was visiting Europe for a rest, not more of the same. He glanced across at her, the smile still teasing his lips. Seduction might be too much hassle at the moment, but fantasies…they were another thing altogether. He would find time for those instead.

As though reading his mind, the girl blushed and lowered her head. Amused, Garett went back to his meal. He did not anticipate any trouble from a casual lunch guest like this. She was intended as nothing more than visual entertainment for him. He liked to furnish his world with beautiful things, but, while he looked on works of art as investments to be studied as well as displayed, his women were different. They were like butterflies. They flitted into his life through one window of opportunity and out through the next. This one would be no different. If anything, she would make less impact on him than his usual pick-ups. Signora di Imperia was safe from everything but his active imagination—although he intended to let that run as free as it liked.

Garett went on watching her covertly. He was savouring the idea of stripping away her inhibitions one by one, as her shock and confusion melted into desire. It awakened in him a feeling that he thought would be hard to better—and then something happened that improved on it. She looked up as their main course arrived, and in a reflex action her tongue darted out to moisten her lips. Her anticipation fired Garett's—but for something far more pleasurable than mere food. He imagined her using that neat little pink tip to caress him all the way to paradise. As the waiter moved to his side of the table, Garett had to pull his chair in closer to the table to hide the most obvious sign of his arousal. Trying to distract himself, he stared down into the white porcelain dish of ravioli that had been placed before him. It was still bubbling, as hot as his thoughts.

A squeak from the other side of the table made him jerk his head up again. An eruption of sauce had splashed out and burned Signora di Imperia's hand. As he watched, she sucked her finger to cool the heat. But it did nothing to quell Garett's desire.

Then her gaze flew to his. Her blue eyes opened wide. Instantly she withdrew her finger and hid it in her lap.

'Oh—I am so sorry, *signor*! What can I say? It's just that…I'm so nervous. Coming to a place like this is such a novelty for me—I've never been anywhere so wonderful—'

'Don't mention it,' he murmured, his mind on something else entirely.

'Be careful—the dish is very hot. I hope you like it.'

'I'm sure I shall.' He smiled with complete conviction.

While waiting for his food to cool a little, Garett took a sip of wine and congratulated himself on his choice.

This Moscato was a light, yet aromatic example of its type. It perfectly complemented both their soup and now their main course. He counted himself lucky to be able to experience it. No, I've earned the right to do this, he corrected himself quickly. Garett was a strong believer in making his own luck. *Anybody* could do what he had done if they wanted success badly enough. When would people learn that all it took was hard work?

Then Garett realised his companion was dissecting her dish of pasta pillows in their velvety sauce in a particular way. It was a delaying tactic he recognised from his life on the streets. She had already told him that dining like this was out of her league. Now he sensed she was trying to make the experience last for as long as possible.

He could only hope there was not another, darker reason for her time-wasting. Watching her slender wrists and delicate hands as she toyed with her food, he wondered when she would next see a decent meal. An unlikely interest in some people's habits was another legacy of his deprived childhood.

Garett's frown of concern was enough to bring their waiter scurrying to his side.

'I wonder, could you bring me some more of this, please? And another serving of garlic bread?'

Sienna was so amazed, words burst from her before she could stop them.

'But you haven't touched what is in front of you yet, *signor!*'

'Good grief—that isn't the sort of reaction I'm used to from my dinner guests.' He laughed.

Sienna paused, and then shot a glance across at him.

He had turned on a particularly winning smile, aimed at the restaurant staff scurrying up with his additional order.

'It's all for you, *signora*,' he whispered. 'Enjoy!'

Plates were juggled and the table rearranged to make space for the extra dishes. Sienna was speechless, but at least the shock gave her time to consider her reply.

'This is very kind of you, Signor Lazlo,' she murmured as soon as all the waiters were out of earshot, 'but I'm sure I shall never manage all this. What made you think my own meal wasn't big enough?'

He shrugged. 'You're as thin as a rail, and white as paper. Eat up. The servings here may not be American-sized, but they'll still put some roses in your cheeks.'

'So…does that mean your own meal is too small?'

He began making great inroads into his own ravioli, with evident satisfaction.

'Not at all. I can never stand to see good food go to waste, so I always eat everything that is put in front of me.'

'It seems to do you good.'

The words were out before Sienna could stop them. She gasped, desperate to take them back, but Garett had heard too many empty compliments in his life to take much notice of hers. And he chuckled at her innocent remark.

'What I meant was…I mean, you look perfectly—that is…'

He let her flounder about, watching with amusement as she got more and more flustered, and more and more embarrassed. It pleased him to see a woman struggling over compliments. The girls who slinked up to him at parties all read from the same script. They had their patter worked out. This Signora di Imperia was anything but practised.

She was obviously attracted to him, but trying not to show it. This made a refreshing change for Garett. Though of course he would never respond to any come-on from a mousy little innocent like her! It was all he could do not to laugh out loud at the idea of it. What sort of attraction could she possibly hold for him?

The lure of the forbidden: the most powerful one in the world, his body told him suddenly, with an alarming jolt.

Disturbed, he looked up from his meal. Their eyes met across the table and he found himself looking temptation straight in the face. Suddenly the innocence in her large, clear eyes began to inflame rather than quell his feelings. The urge to stir those Mediterranean depths with desire— desire for him and him alone—was almost overwhelming…

But he wouldn't let that distract him now. He smiled lazily in her direction. 'Forget it, *signora*—I already have. Now, let's enjoy our delicious lunch!'

His unruly libido was not so easily distracted.

Their pudding was a wonderful shared confection of cream, chocolate mousse and chestnut puree.

'It's such a shame your friends weren't able to enjoy this lovely meal.' Sienna slumped in her seat with a sigh of satisfaction as coffee was served. Garett had been so charming over lunch that she was almost tempted to forget her suspicions about his motives. Then she thought of what Aldo would have said at such terrible backsliding, and sat up again smartly.

'I shouldn't waste too much sympathy on them, *signora*. We all eat like this far too often for our own good. It's the executive's plague.'

Sienna believed him, but could tell instinctively that this wasn't a man who overindulged too often. He liked to be in control. She suddenly had a delicious vision of him working his body in his private gym...

'I wish I could eat like this all the time.' She sighed with longing, dabbing her lips with her starched white napkin. Even that was luxury. The damask was so thick and perfect. She folded it neatly and dropped it beside her plate as her host summoned the waiter.

'But you can if you want to, *signora*,' Garett said softly as he paid the bill.

She looked up at him. Was this the moment he closed in on her? What would she say? What could she do? Resistance would be useless—but how could she possibly square it with her conscience, or keep it a secret, or—?

'All you have to do is get yourself a dream, then go all-out to seize it with both hands,' he went on smoothly.

Sienna might have been relieved—if she hadn't been so disappointed.

'That's easy for you to say, *signor*. Dreaming isn't going to pay my bills or put food on our table, is it?' She spoke quickly, trying to cover her confusion.

'It's worked OK for me.'

'Yes, but I live in the real world, *signor*.'

'So do I.'

He stood up to take possession of Sienna's wrap and draped it around her shoulders. As he did so, he half-turned to thank their waiter for his service. The movement threw her against Garett—their bodies touching and her lips only inches from his.

What happened next was almost too much for Sienna

to bear. With a gentle smile he lifted his hand and caressed it softly against her hair. This was the moment. The moment she had wished for, daydreamed about in the marketplace. For a heartbeat Sienna was paralysed with fear. She had been terrified that this might happen. She didn't know what to do or how to react. Instinctively she leapt away from him and ran like a frightened rabbit.

Garett watched her go, stunned. What was all *that* about?

'Well, that's a first!' he joked to their equally astonished waiter. 'I've never been abandoned by a girl before.'

'Don't take it personally, *signor*,' the man confided. 'Women don't like insects. It was just a reaction to feeling that butterfly on her head, that is all. She will return.'

But she didn't.

A few hours later, Garett was revelling in the amusement the tale of his lunchtime adventure was giving his hosts.

'I tell you, Kane, it was such a pity you couldn't make lunch today. You should have been there. All through the meal that girl looked at me as though I was trying to buy her soul. I had no intention whatsoever of coming on to her, but watching her wondering how on earth she was going to say no to me was priceless. And then I just moved to brush that butterfly away from her, and she vanished.'

'And when did any woman last say no to you, Garett?' Kane Bradley nudged his guest confidentially.

'I don't remember.'

'That's because it's never happened.' Kane's wife Molly chuckled indulgently, then stood up. 'But if you two are going to start talking dirty, I'm off to check on dinner.' She moved smoothly to the dining room door.

The moment she was out in the hall, she called for her butler.

'Is Sienna here yet, Luigi?'

'*Sì, signora*—I showed her straight upstairs to your dressing room.'

'Good. Did she manage to smuggle a decent dress from home to change into, do you know? Or will she be borrowing one of mine?'

Molly did not need an answer. The sight of her second dinner guest appearing on the first-floor landing silenced all her questions.

Sienna looked stunning in a perfectly plain black evening dress. Its plunging neckline and sleek, stark lines were accentuated by a glitter of diamonds at her neck and a worried look in her eyes.

'You look absolutely wonderful!' Molly rushed forward to brush a kiss against Sienna's cheek as she reached the bottom of the stairs. Slipping an arm around her friend's narrow waist, the hostess led her across the hall. 'Now, don't forget—your job is to bring a little local colour into the life of one of Kane's oldest friends. We're worried about him. There's something wrong, but he's not a guy who makes a lot of fuss. He won't tell, and we know better than to pry. At least we've managed to persuade him to stay here with us for a while. His original idea was to work his way around the Med, but it's clear he needs more than that. You'll see it as soon as you look at him. And, as we don't speak Italian fluently yet, I thought you would be the perfect bridge between him and the locals while he's here.'

Sienna allowed herself to be drawn along to the dining room. She was fretting about everything—from the excuses she had made at home to the unfamiliar make-up she had applied so hurriedly in the borrowed dressing room. 'You know I'd do anything to help you, Molly, but if my stepmother finds out about this—'

'For goodness' sake, girl! You're twenty-six years of age. The mistress of your own house and estate. You don't need anybody's say-so!'

'Yes…but I'm still not sure…'

'Then the least you can do is come in and enjoy a good dinner with us while you make up your mind.' Molly gave her reluctant guest a gentle shake, and put her hand to the dining room door.

Garett was trying to let the future take care of itself for once, but one thing still bothered him. For some reason he had been unable to shake off the memory of Signora di Imperia. Until now, no woman had ever lingered long in his memory. They passed through and vanished with all the speed of happy thoughts. But images of the girl from Portofino would not let him go. Speaking about her to Kane and Molly had been his way of exorcising her image, but it had not worked. It was beginning to irritate him. He could not forget the woman, and it was no longer funny.

He tapped the rim of his cocktail glass, unable to concentrate on the conversation in hand. As his host talked, Garett's mind wandered far away. What was she doing right now? He had waited for her, and he had worried—two notable firsts for Garett. Learning that she had got a lift back to Portofino market with one of the restaurant's cleaners had not really satisfied him. He needed to know that she had returned safely. Thoughts of what might have happened to her had been distracting him all day. It was proving impossible to pull his thoughts away from that girl. Especially when the alternative was listening to Kane's tale about some old dame living in the villa next door.

Garett took another drink, and tried to concentrate on what his friend was telling him. As a favoured guest, it was the least he could do. Relaxation was impossible for him, but the Bradleys were old friends, and they were trying so hard. He owed it to them to make an effort—right down to discreetly investigating the financial situation of the respectable widow who would be joining them for dinner that evening. He accepted another vermouth from Kane, and nodded as his host droned on about their worries for this Sienna.

The open fire crackling in the hearth had warmed Garett from the moment he'd first walked in. Whether it could thaw the ice at his core was another matter. He went on letting his mind wander. It was supposed to head away from trouble, but it kept on veering towards the unattainable girl he had picked up in the market. Her quiet beauty had attracted him from right across the square, like a panther drawn to a fawn. But his recent escape from routine had stopped him following his usual well-worn path from banter to bedroom. He sighed. Sleeping with her would definitely have prevented her gaining such a hold over his mind. Giving in to instinct there and then would have stopped her image working its way under his skin so successfully.

On the surface, Garett seemed to be the perfect guest. He made small talk and nodded in all the right places as his host chatted. Yet behind this polite façade his mind was working. There was only one way to rid himself of his beautiful distraction. He would find that girl again. Whatever it took. He began to work out a plan of campaign. A suite in the Hotel Splendido would do it. If Il Pettirosso had impressed her, then a visit to that peach of a place would guarantee her fall. And Garett would be there to catch her in his arms.

All he had to do now was track her down again.

That might take time. He already knew that separate markets were held on different days. For any other man, there would be no guarantee she could be found. But success for Garett was a mere formality. He was already drawing up details of where to go and who to see in the search for his shy interpreter when something momentous happened. It was something that had him mentally screwing up all his plans and kicking them into touch.

He wouldn't have to bother going all the way to Portofino—visiting markets and asking around— because his mystery girl was walking straight into the room to meet him.

CHAPTER FOUR

GARETT considered himself to be the complete master of his emotions. People only saw what he wanted them to see. So when the shimmering vision of Sienna di Imperia was formally introduced to him, Garett's calming, confident smile was already in place.

'It's my beautiful lunch guest—with a beautiful name to match. Well, I can certainly vouch for her honour, Kane, if not for mine.'

'Then you've met before?' Molly Bradley's eyes were twinkling. 'You never told us, Sienna.'

'I didn't realise your guest was going to be Mr Lazlo.' Sienna tried to remain cool, but her temperature was already rising.

'This makes it two prestige meals in one day for us, Molly. It's a pleasure to see you again Signora di Imperia.' Garett stepped forward and took Sienna's hand. Raising it to his lips he brushed it with the lightest of formal kisses— but his eyes were alight with devilment.

'This is the first time we have been formally introduced,' Sienna said with as much dignity as she could manage in the face of the surrounding smiles.

All she wanted to do was run and hide, but she had promised to make Molly's guest feel welcome. She had to follow through, however alarmed she felt.

'I told Mr Lazlo he might need an interpreter for his lunch at Il Pettirosso. When he asked me to act for him, he was not expecting to eat alone,' she added meaningfully.

'But I'll bet he soon made up for our absence. That's our Garett!' Kane rocked back on his heels, laughing. 'He never lets a pretty girl slip through his fingers. Molly must have encouraged you to get all dressed up this evening. She's incorrigible.'

'No.' Sienna's blush deepened.

Spending her lunch hour being tempted by the presence of Garett Lazlo had been bad enough. Now, good manners had cornered her in a far worse situation. She had already lied to her stepmother that evening, and said she was going out for a walk. That was hardly innocent, but now she was being drawn deeper and deeper into a web of deception—and it was all Molly's fault.

'Actually, Molly is such a perfect hostess that she was probably worried that three for dinner was an awkward number. I live just down the lane, so it was convenient to invite me. I'm afraid I must have been the only person available, Mr Lazlo.'

'Don't do yourself down, Signora di Imperia.' He smiled. 'I prefer to look on it as Molly's unfailing good taste. She's picked out the one girl I would have chosen myself. This is obviously my lucky night.' Garett made an expansive gesture towards her with his glass.

Sienna's colour deepened to Tuscany velvet. Inside, she was crumpled up with embarrassment, but he was clearly revelling in the situation. All his easy amusement triggered a reaction in her, making her want to stand her ground for once.

'I don't think so, Mr Lazlo,' she said with shy formality. 'My husband has only been dead for three months.'

Sienna's remark left a heavy silence in the air.

Garett drew his glass in towards him again, but took his time before taking a sip. Then he concealed his other hand in his pocket before replying.

'I offer you my condolences, Signora di Imperia,' he said at last.

Sienna nodded in acknowledgement. She had learned long ago that silence was the best defence when it came to her marriage. Even those who were most curious about her relationship with Aldo never pried beyond the distant, sad smile she spent ages perfecting in front of her dressing room mirror.

'Hey—I've just had a thought. Garett here works to help the aristocracy maximise their profits all the time, Sienna. He'd be just the man to cast an eye over your estate.'

'Kane!' His wife was horrified at such a tactless approach.

'Oh, I'm sure Mr Lazlo has far too many other calls on his time,' Sienna said as the Bradleys' butler called them in to dinner.

'Actually, I'm on a self-imposed sabbatical from my city office at the moment. So in theory I could be all yours, *signora*.'

Before Sienna could put a decent distance between them, Garett took her arm and escorted her into the dining room, along with their hosts.

'Then if you are on holiday, Mr Lazlo, I'm quite sure

the last thing you want to do is work.' Sienna smiled. It was an expression she had less practice in using, but the smile dazzled nonetheless.

'Don't be too sure.' He laughed, and then paused, 'I'm just a workaholic, I guess.' He laughed and patted her hand, but it wasn't only the gesture that set Sienna's nerves on edge. There had been a slight hesitation in Garett Lazlo's voice. He had thought twice about his words, and chosen them more carefully the second time. His reaction had been quicksilver, but not fast enough to fool Sienna. In that instant she realised Molly was right. However good a friend this Garett Lazlo was to them, he was hiding something.

Sienna felt curiosity glittering within her.

She would find out his secret. It was the least she could do for her friends Molly and Kane, she thought, with only a *tiny* shred of guilt.

They were to eat in the Bradleys' summer dining room. Lit by candles, the room basked in the warmth of the flickering light. The butler pulled out a chair as Sienna reached the table. While she was busy smoothing down her gown and unfolding her napkin, Garett took the seat next to hers.

She automatically shrank back as he moved in.

'I'm only straightening my jacket, *signora*,' he murmured. 'You should know by now that I am *almost* civilised.'

There was a twinkle in his watchful dark eyes that fanned the sparks of Sienna's interest. Warmth began to trickle through her veins. It suffused her cheeks and increased the power of the applewood fire glowing in the grate.

'Are you all right, *signora*? You seem rather flushed.' Garett raised an eyebrow quizzically. His eyes did not soften the gesture, and she realised that running away from him after lunch had raised an invisible barrier between them. Trying to convince herself that this was a good thing, she flicked the briefest of smiles in his general direction.

'I am fine, thank you, Mr Lazlo. It is just that I am not used to such lovely warmth when dining at home, that is all.'

'Then your house is cold, *signora*?'

Sienna looked away quickly. 'With only the two of us living there now, myself and my stepmother, there isn't any point in lighting a fire when summer is only a few weeks away.'

'It can still get chilly in the evenings. Would you like to borrow my jacket, *signora*?'

'Garett! You'll embarrass the poor girl!' Molly chortled with laughter as their smoked salmon starter arrived. 'Don't worry, Sienna—your recipe for *tagliata* is coming up next. Good red meat will satisfy the animal in him.'

Garett gave Sienna a look that warned her not to be too sure about that. She wondered what his real reaction would be to their main course. At lunch, he had implied he was sick of steak. Dining out in such luxury must be nothing but a tiresome chore for a man like this, she thought wryly and that made her remember how different her life was from his.

'We've got Sienna to thank for more than her way with beef this evening.' Molly smiled at Garett as the staff fussed around them. 'When we first moved here, the shopkeepers made out they couldn't understand us. Apparently, when our boys visited this place during the Second World War, some of them forgot to settle their debts. Memories are long in these parts, Garett. In the interests of international relations, Sienna suggested that Kane and I should suddenly remember a whole heap of relatives. By happy coincidence a lot of them were GIs who'd come over here in forty-four. And guess what? All their names matched up with the ones on those unpaid bills posted behind the counter. One fistful of euros later and, thanks to Sienna, all the shopkeepers for miles around now greet us like best buddies.'

'Hmm. You don't want them thinking you're a soft touch, Molly,' Garett warned, although he was looking at Sienna with intrigue in his eyes.

'They would certainly never make that mistake about you, Mr Lazlo.'

'I shall take that as a compliment, Signora di Imperia.'

Sienna wanted to say that was not how she had intended it, but something happened. Between thinking the words and saying them, she looked too directly into his eyes. That did it. Her heart flipped. It knocked all the air from her lungs and every sensible thought from her head. He was irresistible—and he was looking straight at her. A dangerous echo rang in her ears. Imelda had told her to catch herself a rich pirate. By accepting Molly's simple invitation to dine, Sienna was laying herself wide open to being used like that all over again.

But if Garett Lazlo really tried directing all his charm onto her, how could she possibly resist him?

Garett was never off duty. He knew exactly what was expected of him. Nothing would make the Bradleys happier than to see Garett focus his full power on Signora Sienna di Imperia that evening. Minutes earlier, the

Bradleys' guest of honour would have been only too happy to oblige. Now he was equally determined to resist. The last thing he needed now was a widow. He was trying to leave stress behind. This was not the time to shoulder someone else's emotional baggage, as well as his own heap of troubles.

At least the Widow di Imperia's scruples seemed almost equal to his own. His mind slipped back to the time they had spent over lunch. Her nervous restraint had been spiced with a flash of spirit when she ran away from him. Her frosty resistance tonight showed that core of steel again. She was sitting beside him as though her spine was a subway rail. Now she was within his reach, Garett could have purged her from his mind in an instant if he had chosen. A few moments of flirtation and she would be his. Once he got her into bed that would be it. All the magic she held for him would evaporate. It had happened to him so often in the past. Her hold over his subconscious would be broken. He would be free.

There was only one problem. He was not going to allow himself to do it. Sienna di Imperia was struggling to keep back the tide of financial disaster after the death of her husband. He knew that much from the Bradleys. He certainly didn't need any further hassle in his life. His solution would be to act his usual delightful self over dinner—while resolutely refusing to take any romantic bait laid for him either by his hosts or the lovely Sienna.

Resisting the impulse to seduce her was going to be torture. Garett smiled to himself. He loved a challenge. For him to pass up any pretty woman might be thought impossible. He knew better. As a businessman, he was invincible.

It was surely only a matter of applying cold, calculated best practice to the problem of Sienna di Imperia. He would concentrate his charm on Molly and Kane instead. The beautiful butterfly pinioned beside him would be treated to nothing more than the fallout from his brilliance.

A glass of champagne with the salmon underscored Garett's recent discovery that being entertained without strings felt good. The Bradleys never normally did this kind of thing because they wanted something from him. Tonight was an exception. They usually entertained him just because they liked him. As he considered this fact, the ghost of a frown crossed his face. Perhaps he *should* make room for a life outside of work. The problem was that Garett found it difficult to think of the way he earned a living as 'work'. It involved hours of conference calls, meetings, deadlines, travelling, jet lag and smiling until his jaws ached. The only time he realised how hard an act it was to maintain was when he stopped. That was why he *never* stopped. Real life only gave him the opportunity to think about things that were best left buried.

Garett Lazlo was famous as the man who outlawed holidays. He and his staff worked in shifts around the clock and around the year—with the exception of Christmas Day. He used that to catch up on his sleep and rediscover the trouble-free delight of carry-outs: dim sum, or brisket with latkes.

The event that had so recently driven him out of Manhattan was supposed to have changed his outlook. But it hadn't happened. He moved restlessly in his chair. It was too late for change, he told himself. Relaxation didn't fit easily with his image. Without constant mental and physical stimulation he felt uneasy. He knew for a fact that if you didn't keep on pushing, you slipped back. Growing up on the streets had taught him that. From his earliest days, Garett had heard all the people around him wishing their lives were different. It had made him realise he was unusual. Everyone else had that one single thing in common—they *wished*, but they didn't *do* anything to make their dreams come true. Garett had never been content with that. From the moment he'd learned how to sneak in and out unnoticed from his bunk at the children's home, he had set about carving out a better life for himself. The irony was, now that he had that better life, there wasn't any time left to enjoy it.

Garett had never wanted to give himself that time—until tonight. Now something had happened. All the screwed-up elements of his life must have tangled themselves to a standstill at last. The tensions of his past and present were meshed together in a standing wave, enabling him to find something strangely soothing about dining by candlelight. The meal was tolerable, and the company was unbeatable. Of course, it helped that he was sitting next to the most beautiful girl in the world—even if she was pretending to ignore him. That only made her all the more intriguing.

He might not allow anything to happen between them, but he could certainly admire and take his time over it. There was plenty to appreciate: the fragility of her, and the delicacy of her movements. Old Aldo di Imperia had been a lucky man. His young widow was beautiful, graceful, and intelligent company. They were precious qualities in themselves, but to find them combined in one woman was truly remarkable. Fortunately, Garett assured

himself, his dining companion was as loyal as she was
stunning. Her mouth, which was made for kissing, could
have been carved from coral. She might smile, but it
was never at him. Her glamorous black evening dress
accentuated the beautiful sweep of her spine, but she sat
in her seat as rigidly as an ice statue. The glory of her
auburn hair was piled high on her head, and at one point a
wayward curl escaped to coil against the creamy skin of
her neck. With any other woman, at any other time, Garett
would have made a great show of twining it back into its
pins for her. After what had happened at Il Pettirosso, it was
impossible to imagine doing such a thing to Signora Sienna
di Imperia. Even if he had been tempted…

'Molly tells me you live right next door to this place,
signora?' Garett picked up a crystal decanter of red wine
and filled a glass for her while the beef was being served.
'That must be convenient for visiting.'

'My house is actually about eight hundred metres away,
but we share a boundary fence, yes.'

She looked at him directly then, and he caught his lower
lip between his teeth to stop himself smiling at the sight.
It did not do full justice to her eyes to simply call them blue.
They were a colour in which a man could lose himself. A
susceptible man, he reminded himself. Dancing firelight
added a halo of gold dust around her large pupils. He gazed
into them, expecting the delicious shyness she had shown
at the market to lower those dark lashes again. He had a
long wait. Gradually it occurred to him that she wasn't
merely looking at him tonight. She was challenging him
now, in a way that other women never did. And that was
the reason Garett decided then and there to help her. She

had spirit, and that impressed him. And it was no hardship that that spirit came wrapped in a beautiful package!

Sienna smiled as she watched their hosts. The Bradleys were an ideal couple. As she looked at them, Kane speared a particularly succulent piece of steak on his fork and laughed, offering it to Molly. She accepted his donation, parting her scarlet lips with a full-throated giggle. Sienna looked away—and her gaze instantly locked with Garett's.

A tremor thrilled through her body—had he watched that touching little scene being acted out before them? How would it feel to have him indulge her like that, presenting her with food like a gift of love? Suddenly, her skin tingled with anticipation. A fine ecstasy of perspiration broke out all over her body. Flustered, she reached for her wine to break the moment—exactly as the butler moved forward to offer her a refill. In the confusion, her glass tumbled to the table. The last few drops of Barolo twinkled onto the tablecloth, glowing like blood against the luminous white. Despite their hosts' cries that it didn't matter, and the butler's practised efficiency, Sienna leapt into action, moving aside plates, cutlery, glasses and napkins to limit the damage.

'Don't let them embarrass you with all their happy-ever-after play-acting. The ties of love aren't as tight between them as you might think,' Garett murmured to her, under the guise of helping to mop up the wine.

Sienna stopped and stared at him. What on earth had prompted that? His easy smile had changed, she noticed. It was as though he might resent Kane and Molly's display of togetherness. This man wore charm like a mask.

Underneath it, he might be as cutthroat as any pirate, for all she knew.

When the panic was over, Sienna sank back into her seat. She had a lot to think about. It sounded as though all four of them gathered around the table might have something to hide. She wondered all through dessert. Her friend Molly was desperate to know what Garett was concealing. Sienna was curious about him, too. If this international troubleshooter could be persuaded to audit her estate, it might do them both some good. While he checked her land and holdings, she would have a golden opportunity to find out his secrets by observing him.

Which she would do—with very great care.

It was still dark when Sienna woke next morning. She lay in bed, listening to owls calling in the wood as they made their way to bed. She loved this shadowy margin between night and day. Sleep left her refreshed, but there was still time to linger before the busy day crowded in. She stretched, wondering what Kane and Molly's visitor was doing now.

In order to change and still get home at a reasonable time for someone who had just been 'out for a walk' Sienna had left the dinner party straight after dessert. She remembered her last sight of Garett Lazlo with a pang. Her memory combined passion and panic, and she ran her hands over her naked skin as though she could still feel the sear of his gaze. He had stood up when she left, like a true gentleman, although the look in his eyes had been anything but good-mannered. I'll bet he only pretends to like me, Sienna thought. Whenever Kane had tried to press him into helping untangle her affairs, Garett had become lukewarm about the whole thing. His behaviour should have made Sienna glad that, if he did not accept the challenge to look over her estate she might never meet him again. Instead it left her feeling cheated, as though there was unfinished business between them.

Sienna knew this was a one-sided sensation. Garett Lazlo did not strike her as a man who would waste a single second worrying about *her*. As soon as the door had closed behind her last night he would have sunk straight back into his comfortable club chair beside the fire. Sienna idly imagined what might have happened next. No doubt Garett and Kane would have sampled the Bradleys' collection of fine wines until late into the night. Then Garett would have made his way up the villa's long marble staircase, perhaps stripping off that smart black silk tie as he went. He might even have been given the same guest suite Sienna had used when the Bradleys gave her refuge immediately after Aldo's death. She closed her eyes, remembering the comforting luxury of slipping between those crisp, freshly ironed cotton sheets. Now that tall American with the mysterious eyes was stretched out there instead. She wondered what he was wearing now—or what any single man wore in bed, for that matter.

Sienna had only ever slept with her husband.

The memory of Aldo made her shiver, and she turned over, burrowing down beneath the duvet in search of a warmth that was missing from her life. Aldo would never have moved as quickly as Garett had done to help her blot the spilled wine from Molly's tablecloth. Aldo would never have moved at all. In fact, he would have withered Sienna with a look if she had done anything to help the butler clean up. Silent rage would have radiated from him, spoiling the rest of the dinner party.

Presumably Garett Lazlo hid his true feelings in front of his friends. He had been light, easy company the night before. But there had been a few moments when she'd seen beneath the surface. She smiled, filling the shadowy dawn. Garett was obviously someone who liked being the centre of attention and totally in control. For a few glorious minutes she fantasised about him taking charge of her life. He would brush away all the petty worries and major concerns that loomed over her every waking moment. Sweeping her up in his arms, he would crush her tightly against his broad chest, kiss her until she lost her mind, and then—

And then the alarm burst into life, and Sienna had to drag on the harness of duty all over again.

The first thing she did was to inspect her evening dress as it hung on the front of her wardrobe. She would sponge it later. In the old days it would have been whisked away as soon as she'd stepped out of it. Sienna would not have concerned herself with trivial day-to-day matters like getting the gown all the way to the dry-cleaners in town and then fetching it again a few days later.

But these were not the old days, despite her stepmother's grand plans and secret schemes. Aldo was gone, and with him most of the money. Only Sienna's careful housekeeping managed to keep the bailiffs from the doors nowadays.

She thought over her most pressing problems as she showered and got ready for the day. This house, which some might say was her greatest financial asset, was also the biggest drain on her resources. It held no emotional pull for Sienna. She would have sold it in an instant, and gladly gone back to live in the little house where she had been born, but Imelda was convinced that no one would look at them twice if they left the villa.

Sienna sighed, brushing her long auburn hair in front of the bathroom mirror. It felt ungrateful to worry, somehow. Many people would kill to have problems like hers. Her father had worked hard to secure himself a respected position in the village. Signor Basso had owned the local mill and bakery, which at one time had brought in a good living. Unfortunately, after the death of Sienna's mother, her father had spent all his time on his business. He had never found any opportunity to benefit from his money. When his health had broken, Sienna had blackmailed him into taking a holiday on the Riviera dei Fiori to recover. While she had worked to keep his business going, her father had fallen prey to one of the women who haunted the coastal resorts looking for prosperous husbands. He had returned with Imelda as his wife, and an overdraft.

Signor Basso had started going downhill after that. He had died from overwork. Now his bakery and mill were empty and desolate. Imelda wanted the buildings sold, but Sienna kept trying to dodge the issue. They had been her home, and she loved them. She avoided her stepmother as much as possible. This was easy, as Imelda Basso spent virtually all her time in her self-contained suite of rooms on the villa's top floor. After engineering Sienna's marriage to the oldest euro millionaire in the province, Imelda was not going to give up the benefits of her new life easily.

As she left her own high-ceilinged rooms and walked out onto the upper landing, Sienna began to see her stepmother's point. This was a beautiful house, fading gracefully into old age. The cornices and chandeliers that had echoed with grand balls between the two World Wars were now dusty and dull. Such a house did not deserve to sink into its foundations, but restoring it was beyond Sienna. She walked downstairs and through to the kitchens, despairing all the way that the marble floors would never again ring to the clatter of footsteps or resonate with children's laughter. This old place deserved more. It wanted someone with enough money to treat it properly—like an aristocratic old lady with nothing to prove.

Sienna gave a sad smile as she reached for her apron. It hung on one of a row of curled brass hooks, left behind from the days when the house had employed dozens of staff. Even the servants' working quarters here were on an impressive scale. The parts that nobody of quality would dream of visiting had soaring ceilings and carved plasterwork. It was a shame those times were gone, but their passing gave Sienna one small freedom. She could at least work in her own kitchens. She much preferred keeping busy. She took pride in her cooking, as she did with her knitting. Making things with her own hands gave her a real sense of satisfaction.

Today would be a baking day, she decided. As well as bread and cakes, she would make enough pasta to last the week.

Starting before sunrise gave her a head start, but it was not all work. Each time she needed to use the sink, she paused to watch the sky over the nearest ridge of hills. First the pearly shades of morning became suffused with rose-pink, aqua, and finally the purest shade of Madonna blue.

It was a sight that warmed her heart. No matter how busy she was, Sienna always made time to marvel and dream.

Today was slightly different. From the start, she tried to keep her fantasies to a minimum, because they kept being hijacked by thoughts of Garett Lazlo. Each time she took her mind off the task in hand it wandered back to the previous day—and night. He had disrupted her work at the market, and then distracted her over dinner. She could not afford to let him wreck another day. Turning back to the big marble slab she used for working dough, she scooped great measures of flour onto its grey-veined surface. Hollowing out its peak, she broke egg after egg into the Vesuvius-like caldera. Completely absorbed, she did not hear footsteps approaching the open kitchen door.

'Good morning.'

Sienna turned, amazed. Her darkest, most private thoughts had sprung to life in the very real and very dashing form of Garett Lazlo. He had one palm resting against the doorframe, while his other hand was hooked into the belt of his well-cut jeans. All her feverish ideas of him languishing in bed vanished in an instant. He definitely did not look like a man who had been drinking late into the night. His white short-sleeved polo shirt showed off muscular arms and a temptation of chest hair at its open neck. The thoroughly civilised tuxedo he had worn for dinner the night before had aroused Sienna without hinting at any of the wonders it was hiding. Now she was faced with 'Garett Casual', it took her some seconds to find her voice.

'Mr Lazlo…I never expected to see you again so soon…' She managed eventually.

'Likewise—but I never could resist anything that Molly asked of me, and she's determined to get you sorted out. So, against my better judgement, I've come over to make you a proposition.'

He strolled into the kitchen, gazing up at its high ceilings.

Sienna did not need to copy him. She knew what he was looking at, and it hit her like a physical pain.

'Don't—please don't…' she pleaded. 'I haven't had a chance to get the cobwebs down for ages…'

He lowered his gaze to hers.

'Surely your staff worry about all that, not you?'

'I—I don't have any proper staff. I have to do most of the work myself…although, as you can see, an awful lot of it has to stay undone. Like cleaning the ceilings,' she finished miserably.

He grimaced, and turned his attention to the dough she was working on. Its clinging strands had such a good hold on Sienna that she had no hope of a quick escape from her visitor's scrutiny.

'Don't bother dusting on my account, *signora*. It's too late for that. You'll only get bits in your cooking. What are you making?'

'I've got several things in progress at the moment. There was a nice fresh batch of candied peel in Piccia market the other day. When I saw it, and remembered how long it was since I last tasted *pandolce*, I just had to buy some,' she said breathlessly, nodding towards the kitchen dresser.

Garett went over to it. For once he was in no particular hurry to get down to business, so this was a good diversion. Hollow shells of lemon, orange and citron peel crusted with sugar lay on a lake of crinkled cellophane. He bent down and considered them like an expert.

'When I was little, I always used to wonder about sugar-plums whenever some do-gooder read us the poem that starts "'Twas the night before Christmas…" but none of us kids had ever seen one. Are they like this, *signora*?'

'I have no idea.'

He broke off a fragment of sweet orange rind and popped it into his mouth.

'That,' he said with relish, 'is even better than I imagined it would be.'

'They always say that forbidden fruits taste sweetest.'

It was then that he saw the look on Sienna's face.

'You tipped your head toward them,' he said, in his own defence. 'So I thought you were giving me the go-ahead, since you were up to your elbows over there. No matter— I'll replace it when I next take you out to lunch.'

Sienna stopped kneading. A trickle of egg breached the defence of flour between her hands. She didn't notice.

'Lunch again? With you? Me?'

'Yes,' he said confidently, as though there might be some problem with the translation.

'But…Mr Lazlo—you don't know what you're saying! Whatever has come over you? I can't be seen in public with a lone man a second time. Especially not the *same* lone man. It's bad enough that you have invited yourself into my kitchen this morning. What will everybody think? What will my stepmother say?'

'Why should *you* care about that?' he chuckled.

Sienna could not believe what she was hearing. The single meander of reckless egg that had escaped from her dough split into a delta and dribbled across the tabletop, heading for the floor. Cooking was the last thing on her mind now. Incredulous, she stared at him. 'Because—because…'

He waited. Garett was not normally a patient man, but he was almost enjoying this.

'Mmm?'

Sienna stopped trying to find the words everyone else wanted her to say, and went back to the wreckage of her dough. The soggy mountain of its remains was like her life. It was formless, hopeless, and a bit wet. Hot with indignation, she began furiously recapturing the escaped egg by sweeping flour around the heap to enfold it all again.

He watched her for some time before speaking.

'Suit yourself, *signora*—although lunch is nothing compared to what else I might have on offer. I've come to you with a business proposition.'

Long practice had taught Garett Lazlo exactly how to deal with women. Lowering his chin and raising his dark brows, he coaxed a response from her with an expression full of promise. It worked instantly.

'Go on, *signor*,' she said, with a nervousness in her voice that she tried to disguise.

He leant casually against the worktop. 'I think a lot of the Bradleys, and they're worried about you. They want me to help you. Last night I told them over and over again, in words of one syllable, that I've come here for a holiday, not to work. But nothing I could do would stop them nagging, so in the end I had to override my better judgement and give in.' He smiled in a way that he knew no woman was able to resist. 'So here's my offer: I will bring all my expertise to your house and estate, but for a very limited period only. This place is going to be put straight in the shortest possible time. Then I'm out of here. What you do with it then is up to you. I told you yesterday that you should grab every opportunity to make your dreams come true. So when I've finished you can sell everything and go wild with the cash, or carry my business plan forward, or simply leave all my good works to crumble into dust. It will be entirely up to you.'

He spoke in a low, persuasive whisper. It was charming, it was warm, and when Sienna shivered it wasn't his clinical businessman's brain that was affecting her.

'But a successful man like you isn't running a charity.' she said uncertainly. 'What is all this going to cost me?'

'Genius has its price, of course, but it won't be anything that you can't afford.'

'Which is?'

His lips parted. Sienna caught sight of the gleam of his perfect white teeth.

One way or another, this meant trouble.

CHAPTER FIVE

'Is THERE somewhere we can talk frankly, Signora di Imperia, without the risk of being disturbed? Or coated in flour.' He looked down at her hands meaningfully.

'Of course—give me a few minutes to settle my step-mother. I shall tell her Molly has arrived here for another lace-making lesson. That will keep her well out of the way. Then I will make us both some coffee—'

'No—don't bother to do that, *signora*. I've brought something with me that will take its place. And I'll sort everything out down here.'

Sienna washed her hands, and then ran upstairs. It took her a few minutes and a lot of half-truths to settle Imelda. Struggling with her conscience would take Sienna much longer. By the time she reached the kitchen again she was pink with guilt. Her colour deepened when she found that Garett had been roaming around the ground floor unsupervised. He was waiting for her in the only place fit for visitors. She dreaded to think what he might have come across before he found it.

Her guest stood in the drawing room, beside its central table. The salon was large, and flooded with natural sunlight. With his back to one of the tall windows he made a forbidding silhouette. When he turned to face her Sienna realised he was in the midst of opening a bottle of champagne. The cork was released with a sigh, and he poured out two crystal flutes before placing the bottle down on a silver tray. The room was so quiet as he picked up one of the glasses and walked towards Sienna that she could hear its foam of bubbles bursting at the brim.

'Don't bother saying it's too early for this until you've heard everything I have to say,' he murmured.

She tried to refuse, but he stood his ground.

'One glass of bubbles *signora*. Allow yourself a little luxury,' he said mildly, offering her the glass.

She eyed it warily. 'I have told you how difficult things are in Piccia, *signor*. If anyone saw you coming in here with that bottle, or if they discovered that I have been alone in this salon with you…' She wavered, and his face immediately became strained.

'Signora di Imperia—Sienna—you can't go on tying yourself up in other people's morals. If you don't have the spirit to act in your own best interests, then you might as well simply hand the keys of this place to the nearest bank manager and save yourself, Molly and Kane a lot of—'

'I *do* have spirit.' Sienna tilted her chin. She had cut him off in mid-flow, and his eyes flashed a warning. She took no notice—but she did take the champagne.

'It is simply that I must respect the wishes of my stepmother, *signor*,' Sienna said with regret. 'She is not strong. The dignity of my father's name and my late husband's house are the only things she has left in life. I must respect that, and be respected in return.'

'I heard less favourable comments about Imelda from Molly.'

Sienna took a sip of champagne before replying. Lowering the glass, she gave him a frank, open look.

'You will never hear them from my lips, Mr Lazlo. And that is why warning my stepmother that Molly is visiting makes sure she stays up in her suite. Molly and Imelda have met on several occasions.'

'Crossed swords, you mean?'

Sienna took another sip of champagne.

'I've never tasted anything like this before. I want to enjoy it.'

'You can.' A girl like you should, he thought, moving in to refill her glass. 'There's plenty more where this came from. My business has been running on it for more than twenty years.'

Sienna accepted a top-up, but on her own terms. 'I must warn you, Mr Lazlo. I have no intention of getting drunk so that you can take advantage of me.'

He met her stare with interest, and tried his hardest to conceal a smile. 'I'm shocked that you should think so little of me, *signora*. I don't need alcohol to help me seduce a woman. Good grief—what sort of men have you been used to?'

None except Aldo, Sienna thought. And he was certainly *nothing* like you, Garett Lazlo.

She took another small sample of the champagne—her courage increasing.

'The only men I deal with are those who can be useful to me.'

She heard herself marking out terms, and hoped her

amazement did not show in her face. I sounded almost snappy, she thought. Where did *that* come from? Champagne at this time in the morning obviously has its uses.

'Then we speak the same language, Signora di Imperia.' He inclined his head graciously. 'That is exactly my offer. I can be everything you need.'

His expression was impenetrable. Sienna waited for him to explain, growing uneasier by the second. Finally, her resistance crumbled.

'Please come to the point, Mr Lazlo.'

'Only when we become Garett and Sienna again. You were happy enough with that informality last night.'

'I'd rather keep things formal while we're alone. Please—if you don't mind.'

Sienna netted the fingers of both her hands around her champagne flute to give her courage. 'Look, Signor Lazlo—Garett—it won't be long before my stepmother is calling for her lunch tray…'

'Then she must learn that her beautiful, attentive nurse has a life of her own, *signora*.'

His eyes temporarily lost their direct, piercing look. Now his expression was softer—but probably more dangerous, Sienna realised.

She was right. Reaching out, he took the glass from her fingers. As her hands dropped to her sides he caught one and drew her closer to the table. His fingers fastened firmly on her wrist, expecting resistance. When she allowed herself to be led in silence, he smiled appreciatively. This was more like it. In the hours since she'd left the Bradleys' dinner party Garett had spent a long time savouring all the feelings she aroused in him. They did not affect his determination to resist her. In fact they strengthened his resolve. Fantasies were so much easier to manipulate than real life. All his affairs with rich, powerful women had been turbulent and irritating. A stress-free, hands-off approach would make a pleasant change.

Sienna might have a thread of steel, but it was deeply buried. The nervousness shadowing her eyes proved that. Garett wondered how long he could extend the pleasure of imagining that pliant little beauty submitting to him. The fantasy was a long way removed from reality, of course. Her nervousness and his determination to resist would see to that.

His smile darkened. Anticipation was the greatest aphrodisiac, and it was working its magic on him right now.

'What is the matter, Mr Lazlo?'

She was pulling away from him. He let her go—but slowly, enjoying the sensation of dragging his fingers lightly over her skin.

Sienna enjoyed it, too, which was why she did not retreat too quickly. Decency was not what filled her mind now. He was touching her. His hand was warm and welcoming, a world away from Aldo's cold desiccation. What would it feel like to abandon all her principles and surrender to that slow-burning passion in his eyes?

'I'm afraid you aren't going to like what I have to say.' He sighed.

If only that was true, Sienna thought, slowly lowering her lashes. It was a gesture that disappointed them both. She wanted to go on looking at him; he wanted her to.

'It might be better if you got out of this place right now, *signora*. Turn your back and walk away while you still have everything going for you. With youth on your side you can go anywhere, do anything, be anyone. If you stay chained to life in this place as it is, it will be your financial death sentence.'

The quiet confidence behind his words was powerful. If she was being honest with herself, Sienna had suspected the truth behind his words all along. But this was a man who had everything: all the calm assurance and determination she lacked. It was all very well for *him* to suggest that she should tear her life up by the roots and transplant it somewhere else on a whim...

She steeled herself to challenge him. 'What proof do you have for saying that?'

A shadow passed across his expression. Sienna had managed to surprise him. It gave her an unexpected shot of pleasure.

He shook his head gravely. 'I was up before first light to check out what the Bradleys were letting me in for. Unfortunately, what little I've seen of your estate has already opened my eyes to the difficulties of living around here. Unless you can get your act together right now, *signora*, your estate is going to be consumed by the starving Italian earth—and sooner rather than later.'

He took a long, slow drink of champagne while she registered his warning.

'Do you have any qualifications which allow you to be so certain about that?' She spoke slowly. Her mind was working on automatic. She was already fully aware of the qualifications he possessed for turning her mind and body into quivering jelly.

'Absolutely none—beyond my total honesty,' he said frankly. 'The point is, *signora*, I don't have to be a world authority on Ligurian farming to see that your place is going down the pan. Fences allowed to rot, the wilderness encroaching on your beautiful threadbare old villa as though it was Sleeping Beauty's palace—' He stopped.

Sienna immediately filled his pause with fantasy. He was Prince Charming, riding up on his white stallion to save her. If only…

After a long pause, she sighed. 'I suppose you must be right. There are times when I feel as if I am sleepwalking through life. The harder I try, the more difficult it is to please everybody.' She put a hand up to cover her face, desolate. The tiny sound of a glass being put down on the tray cut through her absorption. Before she could be alarmed, a firm hand was sliding around her shoulders.

'You are your own woman,' Garett said gently. 'It should never be a case of denying yourself a chance of happiness just because of what others might think.'

Wordlessly, she looked up into his face. His jaw was as resolute as ever, but when those unfathomable eyes looked at her now there was a glitter of something recognisable deep within them. She had first seen that look last night, when she'd walked into the Bradleys' dining room.

With a shiver, she tried to withdraw from his touch. Garett was having none of it. He might be determined not to seduce her, but he had never been able to resist playing with fire.

'Let's put that theory to the test, shall we?' His fingers ran around the gentle curve of her chin. His fantasies were calling for some real fuel. Suddenly hot and hard, he closed in on her body. 'You are as vital a creature as I am, Sienna di Imperia. Why do you try and hide it?' he breathed, soft and low.

'I—I don't know what you are talking about…'

'Innocence isn't the real reason your eyes refuse to meet mine, is it? No—it is quite the opposite. The reason for your rigid refusal to loosen up and enjoy the party last night is because you and I both know the truth. You want me. It is as simple as that. I'm guessing that for the first time in your life you have identified something you want so much that it might make you turn and swim against the tide of public opinion. Well, here's something that will convince you that your life shouldn't begin and end with other people.'

His hands slipped around her narrow waist. Sienna was transfixed. She knew she ought to call for help—scream, or make a scene—anything to contrast her decency with his lust. That would be the right and proper thing to do. But Garett's fingers were pressing against the thin cotton of her sundress. She could feel their warmth. Humanity was something that had been missing from her life for so long, and she could not bear to deny herself any longer.

'Someone might see.' Her words drifted between them as though through a dream, and Sienna realised she must have spoken them.

'Who? You've already told me you don't have any staff.'

She felt his words rise up from deep within his chest to chuckle into her hair.

'No, but Signora Mortari comes to help with the cooking on Fridays, and there's Ermanno and his wife, who run the home farm—'

'Today isn't Friday. And farming business doesn't include looking through your drawing room windows, does it?'

Within the circle of his arms, Sienna trembled.

'I could go straight over to that door and escape.' She tried to convince herself.

'Of course you could—if you thought anything bad was going to happen.'

His expression was that of a leopard appreciating his prey. He had not moved since laying claim to her with his hands, but now the smile that had been playing over his lips faded.

'But it isn't, is it?' Sienna said, and then cursed herself silently. She had meant it as a statement. What if he heard it as a challenge? She leaned back slightly against his grip, still trying to keep a decent distance between them.

'That rather depends how you define the word "bad".'

His voice was as smooth as silk. When he let her go, Sienna almost regretted it. Picking up her glass of champagne again, he poured into it another cascade of foam before handing it over. Then he raised his own glass, scrutinising the lines of tiny bubbles fizzing up to the golden surface. His dark, intelligent eyes watched her over the rim of his glass as he took a long, slow draught of the fine wine.

'I'm a man who always gets what he wants. And the one thing that connects all the things I want is success.'

Sienna trembled. In an effort to hide her nervousness, she gripped the slender cylinder of her glass. His eyes darted to the tiny movement, and he smiled. Too late, she realised her knuckles must have bleached with the pressure, betraying her fear.

Garett was in no hurry. There was absolutely no point. He could have her—at any time and in any place. It had been obvious from the look in her eyes on that first day, down in the marketplace, but taking her was the *last* thing he wanted. Her fragile state combined with this wreck of a house made Sienna di Imperia a challenge too far.

But he needed to silence Molly's nagging—and his own conscience. It had taken some thought, but he had worked out how to do it. The satisfaction of knowing broadened his smile.

'I can see that you are desperate to know what I am talking about, *signora*.'

'I suppose…' Sienna swallowed hard, trying to keep the sad inevitability out of her voice. 'I suppose you are going to suggest something indecent?'

CHAPTER SIX

HE LAUGHED softly. The echo reflected around the shabby surfaces of the gold and crystal salon.

'Well, that rather depends on how you interpret the word, Signora di Imperia. Kane and Molly ought to have more sense, but I believe they expect me to succumb to your pretty face and make everything all right. Though, let's face it, I'm more likely to make you a straight offer to buy your wreck of an estate than I am to fall in love with you.'

He laughed. Sienna joined in, but only because she was desperate to appear polite. In reality she felt crushed and confused.

'Let me put it to you straight: Kane and Molly suspect your life is in chaos. If you carry on firefighting as you have been doing—patching here, recycling there—any money you currently have will trickle away completely. What this place needs is one massive, carefully planned overhaul to give it an independent future. You are already being run ragged by your stepmother, or so I'm told. Unless you come up with the goods, *signora*, she won't rest until she sees you safely married again. If you won't take my advice and get out while you still can, the obvious solution to all these challenges is simple. Get your estate and buildings up and running properly, so they can support you. Then you can thumb your nose at them all and live the way *you* want to. It will take money—a lot of it. But if you are willing to do as I want, then I'll finance everything until this old place can fund a mortgage to repay me. Then you can grab your dream—whatever it may be.' He stopped, and his smile broadened.

Here it comes, thought Sienna bleakly.

He took a long slow drink of his champagne. Sienna watched him with an awful feeling of inevitability. He looked like a tiger quaffing cream.

She sighed. He might as well not have bothered with the champagne, the smiles, and the artful pauses. All her adult life her body had been sold—she knew nothing else. First it had been Aldo, now it was the horrible prospect of marriage to grisly cousin Claudio.

'You mean…you and I…' Her voice faltered and died. Garett's flirtation, her fantasies, the brush of his fingers against her skin—sex would ruin all that, dragging it through the mire and rubbing all the nap off her dreams. She swallowed hard. 'You…and…I…'

However often she repeated it, she could not get any further. The words lodged in her throat. She could not bear to put into words the hideous reality that it must become.

His voice broke over her misery. '*Signora*—I offer all my skills. But I will want something in return.'

Sienna could not move. She was staring at the floor, knowing that Imelda would scream at her to look him straight in the face and thank her good fortune. This was, after all, a man who had all the good-looks and charm any woman could ever want. According to her friend Molly, he had the money too. Everything about Garett Lazlo should have been so right. In her dreams last night Sienna had fallen into his arms a thousand times. But in the full glare of daylight life was turning out to be as hard and cruel and painful as always. Aldo's death had dropped a heavy burden on her. Now she was being offered paradise—but at an enormous cost.

Not that she should have expected anything better. Shouldn't Garett's opening statement have trampled all her fantasies about a white knight riding to her rescue? *I'm more likely to make you a straight offer to buy your wreck of an estate than I am to fall in love with you!* he had said. There had been more feeling in that statement than in any other. It was a trait Sienna recognised. And the easy way he spoke about her wanting him. She shut her eyes and thought back to her late husband, Aldo.

Hadn't her marriage to him been arranged on exactly the same lines? The old man had been invited to dine by Imelda, who had been playing the part of lonely widow at the time. She'd been looking for advice about what to do with the Basso property in the village, she'd said.

Aldo di Imperia had been quick to spot an opportunity to expand his small empire. And then Sienna had opened the front door of the home she shared with her stepmother. She had seen a stooped husk of a man, bearing roses. He had seen an opportunity.

The Widow Basso had got his advice, but Sienna had been given the flowers. And so it had begun...

She needed time to think.

'As I see it, Signor Lazlo, I can either economise still further, or get a job,' she said slowly. 'On the one hand, I can't believe it's possible to cut any more corners. I've scrimped and scraped for so long I don't think I know how to spend any longer. On the other hand there are no jobs in Piccia beyond the co-operative. The few euros that my work brings in could never support Imelda and me.'

'Then dump her and save yourself.'

'No. I can never do that, *signor*. I made a promise to my father that I would care for her. I shall have to manage.'

'I am offering you an escape route,' he repeated, as though either of them needed a reminder. 'Why go on starving in a ruin, heckled by the original wicked stepmother?'

'Please don't insult my family, *signor*,' Sienna said in a small voice. She had to be polite, but that did not mean she had to let him get away with murder—just something worse.

'Imelda Basso is not your family. She is merely a woman with an eye for the main chance.'

Sienna heard him tap his glass, and then he began pacing to and fro in front of her. She could see the gloss on his handmade leather shoes, but she could not and would not raise her head to see his expression.

'Molly says you own a little place in the centre of the village. Is that right?'

'It's the place where I was born, yes,' Sienna said miserably. If only she could be there now, safe and sound. But Imelda insisted she stayed at the villa, to keep her company. Sienna never had time to visit her old family home at the bakery now. She was always so busy—running around doing farm work, cooking, working for the co-operative or beating back the undergrowth around the villa.

'If you are so determined not to sell up, perhaps you could renovate your old home first? When that's finished, you can move back in, leaving Imelda here. Once everything is up and running, operating this estate according to my guidelines will free you financially. If you're determined, there's profit to be made here—with plenty left over to pay someone to run around after your stepmother. That will please her, and rescue you into the bargain. Better that than waiting around like a parcel to be haggled over by any interested party.'

'When I married Aldo I became a part of his family's history. It is my duty to keep his house and his memory free from scandal.'

'But you won't be able to do any of that without a secure investment base.'

Suddenly his feet disappeared from Sienna's field of vision.

'Oh, *damn* your stubbornness!'

Sienna jumped, and looked up at him in alarm. The only person who ever spoke to her like that was Imelda. For seconds on end she stared at Garett's broad back. 'When do you want me?' Her words whispered out, with hardly the strength to cross the space between them.

The moment she spoke he caught her eye and held it, exactly as he had done in the market. But this time it was different. This time she was scared. She had looked up expecting to find that his face was cold and calculating— except that it wasn't. She blinked. For a split second she thought she saw confusion there, but no—when she looked again his expression was totally unreadable.

'What did you say?'

She wavered. Speaking the words had been hard enough. Repeating them would be torture. She tried to make the awful task easier. Garett was young and gorgeous—but to sleep with a man for gain was still nothing short of prostitution. Yet her situation was desperate—no money, no hope, no future—so didn't she owe it to herself to grab this one chance? She knew better than to expect any happiness from her life. The fact that Garett Lazlo could make such a suggestion must mean he was no better than any other man, but she would have to close her mind to that. She had managed to shut out a lot of pain and disappointment over the years in that way. Her experience with Garett would be familiar in that respect. But, despite his lack of heart, surely he possessed all the other qualifications she needed? Sienna knew that from the way his every movement fired such unusual sensations in her body. Garett was a towering monument to fantasy. His clear skin, the direct dark brown stare, and those strong, square hands…

'All right, then. I'll sleep with you,' she said quietly.

'What?'

The beginnings of the smile on his face froze into a fixed stare. He seemed to be having difficulty in understanding her reply. Sienna was not surprised. Her throat was so constricted the words had hardly been able to struggle out.

'Yes,' she managed, with more conviction this time. 'I accept. If you can rescue my future, then I will spend one night with you.'

He did not answer for a long time. His mind was too full. He had never in his life met a woman like Sienna di Imperia. First she ran away from him in a five-star restaurant. Now she invited herself into his bed. But, being the girl she was, Sienna was not coiling herself around him like a career courtesan. Oh, no. She was approaching him like an appointment with danger.

Looking into her eyes—when she actually managed to meet his gaze—banished any feelings of anger or offence he might have had. It didn't take a financial wizard to realise that her marriage of convenience had taken a heavy toll. For once in his life he was lost for words. There really did not seem to be anything he could say without sounding patronising. If he did that, she might cry. Then he would have to put his arms around her, and all hell would probably break loose.

Perplexed, Garett stuck one hand in his pocket. There he felt the cold kiss of coins, and it gave him an idea. Money really could talk—so it was lucky he was such a good conversationalist. He had spent years thinking on his feet. With relief, he found he could still do it, despite all the circumstances.

'Well, well, well—you're a dark horse and no mistake, aren't you, *signora*?' he breathed.

He was playing for time, but she showed no signs of realising that. She was gorgeous, and twenty-four hours before he would have seduced her like a shot if it hadn't been for his mad idea of taking a holiday from life. Now she was offering herself to him like a sacrifice. He grimaced. Her attitude was turning something he had always treated as an amusement into a dark, hole-and-corner obscenity. That was not his style at all.

He knew she must be afraid of what he might say now. She was certainly far too nervous to look at him. Their relationship had changed—and not in a good way. She had been a fantasy. He didn't want to force her to live his dream. Why had he got into this mess, and what in the hell had persuaded her to agree? He had never paid a woman to sleep with him before—and wasn't that what this amounted to? The stark reality of it hit him hard. Even after decent champagne, she clearly had no stomach for sex. She was as rigid as ever—and now there was genuine fear in her eyes. Garett had never backed down on a deal in his life. Nor had he ever refused to rise to a challenge. And he was not about to start now.

'My undertaking is to put in place a complete and thorough restoration of your house and estate,' he announced. 'In return for one night together when the work has been done.'

That gave him an automatic get-out clause, but with luck she would not realise it. Garett had exacting standards. The international business world was bound to track him down and reclaim him before he was satisfied that her project was finished. He would leave without taking Sienna up on her offer. With a sigh of relief he would be out of her life for ever, with no loss of face on either side. She would never need to present herself like a trembling lamb on his altar. He had no idea where she had picked up the notion that his fee was her body, but now that she had suggested it he was going to make the best of the situation. Neither of them could retreat now without a total loss of dignity and self-esteem. And Sienna doesn't have much of either, Garett thought with a strange pang. That must be why she came up with the notion—she has absolutely nothing to lose. If it had not been so tragic he might have laughed. Unlike her, he was supposed to possess all the chips in life's poker game. Yet right now he felt as miserable as she looked.

'*Signora*, let's have a toast!'

His voice was as light and teasing as ever. Warily, Sienna looked him up and down. She was considering all her fantasies, every word they had shared over the past twenty-four hours. Garett was totally irresistible—in the same way that a spring avalanche carried all before it. I can always claim I'm being picked up and bundled along by events beyond my control as usual, she thought tentatively. At least this time it will be with a truly desirable man. But one who has secrets, she reminded herself with a shiver.

Slowly, hesitantly, she raised her glass and let him kiss it with his own. The fine lead crystal chimed, and it was over. Her fate was sealed.

'You can rely on me, *signora*,' Garett was saying. 'I will not lay a single finger on you until work here is finished to our complete satisfaction. My self-restraint is about to become legendary.'

He took the champagne bottle over to the French doors. Forcing open the rusted catch, he gave one last lingering look at its label. Then he watered the overgrown flower-erbed with the remaining contents. Sienna watched in silent acceptance of the waste. Garett shut out the fragrance of wine-soaked rosemary. Then he gestured towards the silver tray and its abandoned glasses. 'You take care of those while I dispose of the evidence. I delayed your cooking. You had better get back to it.'

He strode out of the room. By the time Sienna reached the kitchen sink he was returning from the yard empty-handed.

All her previous spirit had evaporated, he noticed with a twist of distaste.

'Don't look like that, *signora*. Many women find sleeping in my bed a pleasure.'

'I'm not too grand to starve in a wreck like this.' Sienna's reply was heavy. 'And it isn't the sleeping that worries me.'

He exhaled sharply and planted his hands on his hips. 'Look, *signora*, forget about all that for the moment. I've got much more important things than sex on my mind right now. I should be making a start on managing your project!'

Sienna eyed him cautiously. The restless air about him was constant, but it was no longer directed at her. He clearly had other targets in his sights. It made her feel less like a hunting trophy and more like an abandoned parcel—something to be worked around, or tripped over and cursed at at regular intervals. It was a role Sienna was used to. Sex might be a physical torment for her, but pandering to others was something she could manage *very* well.

'Of course.' She said meekly. 'What do you want me to do first?'

He glanced around, a hawk on the lookout.

'Er…you can finish your baking, and then get cleared up in here. That's all.'

'I could help you outside,' she ventured uncertainly.

'No. Your place is here in the house—at least for the moment. I make better headway when I work alone.'

He was watching her as though his mind was operating at a much deeper level than his words. He saw Sienna's shoulder muscles begin to soften. There was the slightest slowing in her movements as she tied on her apron again. His plan was taking effect—for the moment at least. She no longer saw him as an immediate threat. That suited him. With a crooked smile, he seasoned his story with some diffidence.

'The truth is I can't wait to get back to my office job. And I'd *really* hate to have all the other billionaires laughing at me because I had to abandon my holiday project,' he joked, in an attempt to make light of the situation. 'I can hardly set myself up to advise clients if I leave my own work half finished, can I?'

She looked up, and this time she gave him a sad smile.

He knew then that there was hope for her. There was still a spark of something left. All it needed was encouragement. She stopped assaulting the dough she was working with, and began patting it instead.

'You've beaten that *pandolce* into a pulp, then?'

She shook her head. As she moved across the room to dampen a clean towel at the sink sunlight danced over her copper hair, making it shine like the array of pots and pans hanging from their rack above the kitchen table.

'This is pasta dough, *signor*. The cake is rising in a tin under that cloth over there on the dresser.'

'Pasta? I thought that came in tubs from Marshall's Deli, smothered in mayo.'

Sienna frowned, grazing her lower lip with her teeth as she covered the freshly finished dough to stop it drying out. 'Mayo?'

'Mayonnaise,' he translated helpfully.

'I must try that,' she murmured.

Garett laughed his tantalising laugh.

'Don't worry—you don't need to humour me, Signora di Imperia.'

'No—really—I like trying out new recipes. Aldo—

my late husband—knew what he liked, and unfortunately that didn't include many things. I cook all sorts of things now that I would never have dreamed of making a few months ago.'

'Imagine that—I've never had home-made pasta.' Garett shook his head slowly.

'Then you've never really tasted the best.' Sienna turned back one corner of the red and white checked cloth she had used to cover the dough and pulled off a handful of smooth, silky pasta in the raw. 'This is how it begins. Spaghetti, fusilli, manilli—it all starts out the same,' she went on, relaxing still further.

He was watching with genuine interest. The threat had receded for a little while, and Sienna was glad.

She warmed the dough for a moment, by rolling it between her hands, and then went back to the kitchen table. A pasta machine was clamped to one of its edges.

'Do you make pasta every day, *signora*?'

'I don't do all *this* every day, no. I prepare it in bulk once a week or so. We eat some fresh that day, and I dry the rest. It's easy enough, but it takes a long time to do it properly. And the trouble is, of course, that as the sheets of dough get thinner, they get longer, and end up draped all along the length of the table. That's why I like to make it early, when there is no one else around.'

'Would it be any easier with two?'

She looked at him quickly, but when her answer was not immediate he went over to the sink and washed his hands.

Sienna was impressed. After all these years, she *still* had to remind Signora Mortari to do that before handling food.

'You must do a lot of cooking, Mr Lazlo.'

'No—French toast is about my limit. But when I was a kid, they parked me in front of a television showing too many public information films. It put me off salmonella for life. Oh—and go back to calling me Garett.'

'Yes—Garett.'

He was ready for a towel. Before he could reach for the one draped over Sienna's shoulder, she flipped it across at him. As an attempt to keep him at arm's length, it failed miserably. Once he had dried his hands, he folded the towel in half lengthwise and dropped it onto her shoulder again. Sienna half turned her head, but stopped when it became obvious this was not some flirtatious gesture on his part. Although he took his time, it was only to drape the folds carefully.

'There.'

'Thank you,' Sienna muttered, edging away. She could not escape for long.

'What next?'

'Oh…'

Sienna knew she should act quickly, and brush off his offer of help, but it was impossible. The nearness of him was bringing back all the strange feelings of guilty pleasure she had experienced at Il Pettirosso.

'Well, Garett…if you stand next to me…' she said, keeping her head down. 'I have to feed the dough between these rollers…'

'It's like a mangle, squeezing the water out of wet washing.'

Sienna stopped and looked up at him uncertainly. 'Are you making fun of me?' she ventured. 'Are you going to say you've seen a mangle just like ours in a museum?'

'Not at all.' He frowned. 'We had one at home. When I was four years old I tried feeding a dead rat through it. Thirty years later I can still remember the noise my mother made when she saw it.'

Sienna exploded with laughter, then instantly clapped a hand to her mouth.

'You aren't telling me they have rats in America?'

'They do where I come from. Great big ones!' he added with relish when she gasped.

'I suppose it was left to your father to clear up the mess?' she giggled.

'No. He only ever came home when he wanted something.'

His reply silenced her. Sienna knew all about that sort of a relationship. Her stomach began to churn, so she moved quickly to fill the awkward silence between them. Setting the rollers of the pasta machine to their widest setting, she lodged one end of the dough between them. As she began feeding it through, Garett bent over her, intrigued by what was going on.

'So, although this looks like a complicated device, its design is actually quite simple?'

'Yes—you just keep feeding dough through it over and over again, each time narrowing the gap between the rollers so that the sheets become thinner and thinner.'

'And longer and longer—I can see why this job will be easier with two,' he mused, as the dough zigzagged into a neat stack beneath the bottom roller. 'How do you make it fold like that?'

Sienna glowed. She had actually managed to impress

somebody for once. She gave him an impish smile. 'It takes years of practice.'

He returned her look with equal mischief, and she had to confess.

'Not really—it just comes out like that automatically.'

'You don't say?'

He was already moving to take the handle from her, expecting her to stand back as if it was his divine right. Although his arrogance annoyed her, something stopped Sienna putting her feelings into words and she retreated in silence.

'There—look. I'm a natural.' He nodded towards the river of pasta that was falling in graceful folds onto the worktop.

'Careful—if you don't keep the underside of the machine clear the individual leaves stick together, and then there is no prising them apart.'

Sienna reached under the pasta machine exactly as Garett swept the handle around again. His knuckles struck the back of her hand and she leapt back in alarm.

He winced on her behalf. 'That must have hurt. Sorry. There wasn't much clearance between the table and my fist. Are you all right?'

'Yes—yes—it was just the shock that made me jump—'

'Let me see.'

He reached out and caught her wrist. His touch was light but firm. Sienna watched as he drew her hand towards him. It lay motionless in his grasp. She knew by now that there was no earthly point in trying to resist him. She tried to summon up all the fear she should feel at the prospect of paying him back for saving her home, but it was hopeless.

CHAPTER SEVEN

HE MUST have known what was going through her mind, because he levelled a dark stare straight at her.

'You are afraid I'm going to call in my debt early. Don't be. I've told you I'm not looking to do that.'

'If you say so,' Sienna said, sounding more confident than she felt.

'This is how it is going to be, Sienna. Until your house and estate are completely together again. I give you my word—and I never go back on that.'

His fingers were warm and confident on her skin as he gently turned her hand over in his.

'It was the back of my hand—not there.' Sienna felt bound to say it, but secretly she was glad when he took no notice and continued to study her pale, smooth palm.

'Ah, yes, but this is the point where I tell you about the glowing future I can see for the Entroterra estate, outlined here in your hand.'

'The pasta will dry up.'

'And that's exactly what I see here.'

Flirting with beautiful girls was a difficult habit for him

to break, he thought wryly. He scraped a tiny flake of desiccated dough from her skin.

'Lucky in love, unlucky in lunch.'

Sienna pulled her hand away sharply. 'There won't *be* any lunch if I don't get on with this,' she said hurriedly, desperate to turn away from his provocative gaze. 'I'll turn the handle this time, and you can support the dough when it comes out from between the rollers. If you don't mind,' she added shyly.

They worked in silence as the mobile creamy pasta was cranked through, centimetre by centimetre. After the first run Sienna adjusted the rollers and sent the sheet through a second time. As the process was repeated over and again the dough grew longer and thinner, forced through a narrower and narrower gap in the machine.

'This is making me feel hungry,' Garett said, when the dough began to emerge through the narrowest setting. The pasta was so thin now that it would have been possible to read newsprint through it. He held part of it up to the light, marvelling at its texture. 'It makes me wish I hadn't skipped breakfast.'

Sienna looked at him incredulously. 'How can anyone manage to leave the house without food?'

'Eating first thing in the morning slows me up. Missing breakfast means I can be on the spot and busy before anyone else. It makes extra time to fit in more work. But…if you're so concerned, maybe you'd like to try and find me something?'

It was the sort of order Sienna was only too happy to follow. She went over to where the *pandolce* was rising. Lifting one corner of the brightly coloured teatowel covering it, she frowned. 'This will take some time, but I could make you some stracchi with pesto instead.'

'Whatever it is, if it plugs a gap fast, I'll try it.'

She had been starting to come out of her shell again, but with that remark he saw her contract slightly.

'I'm sure it'll be delicious, Sienna. What is it, by the way?'

'Stracchi are thin sheets of pasta. Pesto is made from toasted pinenuts ground with basil, olive oil and Parmesan or peccorino cheese—whichever I have to hand. It takes longer to talk about than it takes to make,' she explained, reaching up to unhook a large copper saucepan from the rack above the table.

Garett would have done it for her, but admiring the graceful movements of her body as she stretched up meant he was a fraction too slow. Instead he offered to fill the pot with water, and put it on the range.

She was already tossing pinenuts in a frittata pan.

'Now I must fetch a big bunch of basil from Ermanno's greenhouse. That is what takes the time, but I can chop it while these are cooling.'

He stepped in and took the skillet from her, putting up a finger to silence any complaints. 'You could clearly do with a hand. I'll do this while you go out in the garden.'

'Keep those kernels on the move—you only want them toasted, not too dark. There's a knack to tossing them—you might be better off stirring them with this wooden spoon—'

'I'll be fine.' he said firmly. And he was. By the time Sienna dashed back into the kitchen with a fragrant bouquet of *Genovese dolce*, he was flipping the pinenuts like a professional.

'Garett! I am impressed!'

'That's nothing compared to the reaction I shall get when I recreate this for Kane and Molly.'

'They won't want to eat *povera* food like this.' Sienna giggled.

'Ah, you never know. This might be a dish that travels well. Without you throwing it at my head, that is.'

She stopped laughing. 'I wouldn't do that.'

You might if you knew the promise you made so painfully might all be for nothing, Garett thought, but he returned her smile.

She washed the basil and shook it dry in a cloth. A head of garlic hanging by the fireplace was raided for fat cloves, which she pounded in a basin with the pinenuts he tipped in from the pan. Grated cheese and the basil leaves were added at the last moment, to retain all their fragrance.

'The water is boiling. I'll put the pasta in for you.' Garett was halfway to the range before he had finished speaking.

Sienna dithered. He had been a fast learner with the skillet, but fresh pasta was so easily overcooked.

'Don't worry—if you could slice some extra Parmesan, I'll start the stracchi. In the time it takes them to cook we will have finished the sauce.'

'Co-operation, eh?' He chuckled, and Sienna felt again the lurch of desire that had tumbled her emotions before she had made her promise.

She went to fetch a new can of olive oil from the larder, expecting to be glad of any excuse to move away from him. Instead, she returned faster than she'd left. While he shaved paper-thin slices from a slab of Parmesan, Sienna tore the pasta into thin sheets. Slipping a few stracchi into the boiling water, she checked her watch. There was just time

to thin the pesto with a stream of delicate gold-green oil
and bring down a plate from the cupboard beside the range.
Placing it on the table, she took cutlery out from a drawer
and began looking around for a tray. With a sigh she
realised her stepmother must have forgotten to bring the
breakfast things down from her suite. Again.

'I'm afraid it looks as though you'll have to carry your
own lunch through to the drawing room, Mr Lazlo.'

'We'll eat right here. Why make extra work and give the
food a chance to go cold?' He said, straightening up and
pushing both hands through his hair. The cut was so good
that its midnight darkness fell straight back into place. 'It
is hot in here, though—I never know how people survive
without air-con.'

'The kitchen should cool down a bit when I've closed the
range. If you could open all the windows a bit wider while I
finish the pasta, that would make more of a through-draught.'

If the heat troubled him, he was hiding it well. As he
passed close behind her to reach the windows, Sienna
could not resist taking in an extra deep breath. Warmth was
enlivening the discreet resinous tang of his aftershave. It
was an intimate fragrance that made her think of woodland
glades and dark, mysterious forests.

'Are you all right, Sienna?'

She looked up at him—and suddenly 'all right' hardly
covered the feelings that flooded through her body. Garett
in the flesh was even better than her fantasies. He was
absolutely lovely—and in the not-too-distant future she
would be sleeping with him. Right at this moment he was
within touching distance. Surely if she made a move he
would respond in kind? For long seconds Sienna could not

speak. She was torn between getting the awful business over and done with and the dancing possibility that it might be somehow *different* with Garett...

Then bubbling water erupted over the side of the pasta pan, and she had to tear herself away.

'I'm fine, Garett—and luckily so is the stracchi!' She kept her laughter light, and hoped he had not picked up on her nervousness. After draining the pasta, she carried the pan to the table while he took a seat. Giving him all the stracchi, she picked up the bowl of freshly prepared pesto and offered that to him, too.

'Aren't you having any?' He cast a faintly disapproving look at her.

'Not at the moment—I had a proper breakfast,' she said virtuously as he spooned pesto over his lunch. Taking the dish when he had finished, she handed him the bowl of Parmesan shavings. 'Have as much as you like.'

He did. The surge of passion Sienna felt whenever she looked at him was almost outdone by her happiness at the sight of his healthy appetite. She loved it when people enjoyed her cooking. It was the one thing in her life about which she felt secure. From billionaires to farm workers— everyone needed to eat. Sienna had discovered a talent for feeding them—and a pleasure in seeing their pleasure, too.

With her eyes on her guest's plate, Sienna moved to take the basin of pesto from him. It was slick with oil, and her fingers slipped. Although she did not drop the dish, she knocked the spoon and sent a splash of pesto onto her hand. Without thinking, she raised her hand to her mouth and licked off the spilled sauce. She was so used to eating alone that it was the most natural thing in the world. She closed her eyes, revelling in every last drop of the unctuous liquor. Then a tiny noise reminded her that she had company. Her lids flew open—and she found herself gazing straight into Garett's eyes. He had put down his fork and was watching her.

His scrutiny was too intense. Sienna felt his attention trapping her like an embrace. Suddenly she was conscious of each and every breath sighing in and out of her body as desire laid siege to her respectability.

Garett swallowed, and realized his throat had gone dry. She had that effect on him. 'Aren't you going to offer me anything to drink?'

His words snapped her back into life and she emerged from her trance. There was nothing for it now but to look at him directly and ask what he would like. When she raised her head, she saw with a pang that he was still observing her, even as he ate.

'Coffee, if you have any.' Then he saw her expression and smiled. *'Please.'*

Garett watched her take the kettle to fill it at the sink.

He thought about the way her eyes had locked with his, only a moment before. Despite her obvious terror about what might be in store for her, for a second or two they had been full of smouldering promise. It was as though the universe had consisted of him and him alone.

Garett knew from past experience that he could have taken her then and there, as he had taken a hundred other women.

With a start, he rounded on himself savagely. What sort of thinking is that? The girl is clearly put upon, isolated and lonely. She's still in mourning, and missing her husband. I'm unaccustomed to that sort of frailty in women. I've merely mistaken it for attraction, that's all, his analytical mind told him.

But Garett Lazlo's body was purely primitive. It was accustomed to working on instinct, not analysis. As Sienna moved about the kitchen making coffee, her every movement aroused him. She was irresistible, but after seeing the fear in her eyes he had sworn not to taste her temptation. Now her body had become an instrument of torture for him. It was fascinating.

He was silent over coffee, struggling with his impulses. If he seduced her now he would break the spell she had cast over his body. The trouble was that would torment her—and break the promise he had made to himself. Nothing would persuade him to do either, he told himself.

But it was the look of terror in Sienna's eyes that haunted him more than any fanciful ideas about honour.

'Where would you like to start?' Sienna asked Garett later, as she led him out into the yard. The sooner she could demonstrate to the outside world—and to herself—that this was nothing more than a professional visit, the better. It didn't matter that no one was about: Sienna knew the locals watched the movements of every stranger in Piccia. Garett's arrival would have been noticed, if not his departure.

'I'll begin by working around the boundary,' he announced. 'Give me an idea of where it runs.'

'Ermanno will have finished in the dairy by now—I'll give him a call and he can escort you—'

'You don't need to do that. My everyday life is so noisy with people jostling for attention it will be a pleasure to explore such a beautiful place on my own. I can get much more done, and at a faster pace. Besides, I prefer working alone.'

'Oh, so do I!' Sienna said with real feeling. 'But it would be as well if Ermanno and his wife knew what you were doing. I wouldn't want them to think you were an intruder. And at this time of year you will need to watch out for vipers coming out to warm up in the sun.'

'Isn't it me that you consider to be the snake?' he murmured, then gave himself a virtual kick as he watched Sienna's eyes widen at the smoky meaning behind his words.

Although it was a dangerous situation, delight fizzed through Sienna's veins like Asti. Then she flinched. She desperately needed his expertise in checking over her estate, but it would be at the expense of her good name. If Imelda looked out and saw her talking alone to a man like Garett, her respectable disguise would be no protection any more. She would be married off to hideous cousin Claudio in a flash—before Garett could act.

Oh, *damn* respectability! Sienna suddenly thought to herself, with a violence that alarmed her. If only she could let Garett pull her bodily and mentally into his world. Relationships for a man like him must be free and fun, not handcuffed by other people's expectations. I'll bet Garett never insists meals are taken in silence in case his staff gossip, she thought bitterly.

After that one, distant night he might even bring me breakfast in bed, with flowers, and champagne…

'I hope you aren't trying to tempt me before time, Garett?' Sienna's heart gave a double thump. She had intended the words to be a crisp, businesslike warning, but something unexpected had happened. They'd come out sounding husky and provocative instead.

He raised his eyebrows, looking down at her with such sensual amusement in his dark eyes that she knew at once what was going through his mind. She blossomed despite herself as warmth ran through her veins like sunlight. It pushed back her shadows—for all of ten seconds.

'Would I do a thing like that?' He arched one dark eyebrow. 'Although...perhaps you *had* better call for your man Ermanno, Sienna.'

'Who? Oh, yes. Of course.'

I've made her blush, Garett realised with an unusual pang. Then she passed the tip of her tongue over her lips and he found himself holding his breath. He was so used to women coming on to him and flirting that he barely noticed them any more. So why did Sienna's tiny, involuntary action feel like such a triumph? Conflicting urges powered through his body. He wanted to protect her, but at the same time he felt as hot for her as any teenager. There was no way he could risk putting a comforting arm around her shoulders. The way he felt, it wouldn't stop there. Shifting uncomfortably, he looked away. This wasn't supposed to be happening. Business came first, and he had a lot to achieve here. That should be his first consideration, beyond keeping his physical responses under complete control. It was all part of not letting anyone get too close to the real Garett Lazlo.

Sienna was in trouble with her feelings as well. I must keep this on a purely business footing, she thought. Taking a step back, she called out for Ermanno. She sensed that

Garett was on the brink of making something happen. Something that would fulfil all her fantasies—and her fears.

Distraction came just in time. When Ermanno sprang into view, she was torn between relief and disappointment. As she gave him instructions to show their visitor around, Sienna's mind was in a whirl. Garett promised all sorts of things with his eyes. But her experiences with Aldo had taught her never to expect anything good from a man.

A name on a marriage certificate is enough, Imelda had told her. You don't need anything more.

But I did, Sienna yearned to herself. And I *do*…

This sudden independence of thought alarmed her. But in some exciting, illicit way it was fun.

'Ermanno will show you the extent of my land, and the things we do here.' She took off her apron and shook it, sending a cloud of flour into the air. Tying the strings around her narrow waist again gave her one good excuse not to look at Garett. 'I must go back inside and finish my baking.'

'Do you speak English, Ermanno?' she heard him say as the farm manager walked towards them across the yard. It made her smile.

'He knows enough to be able to give you a tour, Garett.'

But not enough to reveal anything about me, she thought, brushing the last streaks of flour from her apron.

'I'm sorry you won't be seeing things at their best. It's been a bad winter, and I haven't really been able to get back on top of things since Aldo died.' Her spirits sank with every hesitant word. Why on earth had she agreed to all this? The man Molly called the world's greatest trouble-shooter was bound to come up with winning ideas—but it was going be at such a heavy price.

Garett watched her head droop. It looked as though the ghost of her old husband would always be on hand, manning the barrier she kept raising. He smiled, put out a hand as though to cup her shoulder, but stopped before making contact. Withdrawing it, he murmured, 'I understand what you must be going through, Sienna. You will never be able to forget your husband, but with each passing day his memory will be encouraging you to carry on living your life in the way he would have liked.'

Her head went up at that, but when their eyes met he watched the words die on her lips. Instead she stayed silent, gazing at him with an expression he could not fathom.

It must be love. That's why I don't recognise it, he thought with cynical amusement. A long apprenticeship in the school of hard knocks had given him immunity.

'I tell you what, Sienna. Why don't you come around the grounds with us? Ermanno can act as chaperon.'

He expected her to back away rapidly at the idea, mindful of her reputation as always. Instead, she looked down to where she was idly drawing a line in the dust between them with the toe of her sandal.

Desperate that Ermanno should not see her disappointment, she shook her head. 'Thank you for your kind offer, Mr Lazlo, but I must get back to the kitchen. When my stepmother learns about you, I am sure you will gain a proper invitation into the house.'

'I'll look forward to that,' he assured her, trying to sound believable.

To Sienna's amazement, Imelda Basso was not remotely impressed by the idea of a foreigner entering her territory—even if he *was* a top-flight businessman. The second Sienna mentioned he was a friend of the Bradleys, Garett Lazlo received the social kiss of death. Imelda would not believe Kane and Molly had money. She considered that they lived too quietly, and that any acquaintance of theirs was likely to be telling equally tall tales about wealth and status. Imelda always needed to see money being spent, not just hear about it.

Sienna retreated to her room. Later, she watched from her window as her visitor strolled up through the over-grown terraces of olive trees at the end of his tour. Ermanno must have found something else to do, because Garett was sauntering towards the house alone. One hand in his pocket, he looked around him with the air of a man who could make himself at home anywhere. But not here, Sienna thought, springing out of her trance. She ran down-stairs, desperate to get to him before he could reach the heavy iron doorknocker.

'You certainly have a beautiful place here.' He laughed. The light breeze had tousled his hair and the warm sun had undone several of his buttons. 'When I was up on that far ridge I could see sunlight glittering on the sea, right in the distance.'

'I know. It is one of the compensations of living here.'

He put his head on one side, frowning.

'That's a strange thing to say.'

Sienna clasped her hands. They were damp. She felt nervous, having revealed her true feelings. 'Er…that is…it is one of the *delights* of living here. I'm sorry—my English sometimes lets me down…'

He did not look convinced.

'It would be a pity to lose it.' He was looking at her acutely. 'I'll be perfectly honest with you, Sienna. I need to get working right away. In fact, it would be better if I came in now and made a start. You can sort me out space for a site office—'

'No!'

He was already heading for the kitchen door, but Sienna moved to block him. 'I mean…my stepmother has forbidden it.'

He nipped at his lower lip.

'The time for listening to her has gone, *signora*. You are going to have to start putting yourself first—and fast.'

There was a strange echo of Molly's words in what Garett was telling her now. Sienna might ignore her own needs, but within the past day two different people—Garett and the old *nonna* at the market—had told her to follow her instincts. And that was without Molly and Kane's constant nagging about Imelda's treatment of her.

Sienna hesitated—but only for a second.

'Very well—but I can't possibly let you into the house now that my stepmother has refused.'

'Excuse me—whose house is this?'

'Mine.' Sienna missed the irony in his tone. She was distracted, casting around the outbuildings and trying to decide where they might talk in private, yet without causing a scandal. 'You can work in the lemon shelter. It is an open-fronted shed where the potted orchard used to be kept during the winter—'

His mind was too busy for explanations. He was already walking away.

'I'm off to set up the headquarters of the Entroterra project in a corner of Kane and Molly's villa. The moment you can convince yourself you can get away, come over and see me.'

And with that he was gone.

Garett's first conclusions about Sienna's estate were gloomy. Her future seemed bleak. Leaving his hire-car outside her kitchen, he decided to walk back to the Bradleys' villa. It would give him plenty of time to think.

Cruising around the Mediterranean had seemed an ideal way to avoid the pressures and stress of New York City life. He had thought he could escape by throwing money at his problems, paying in cash to remain anonymous and evading all calls from his office. He had accepted the Bradleys' invitation to stay in the hope of finding an answer to the dissatisfaction that tormented him. Instead he found himself adrift on a whole new raft of puzzles.

As an intensely private person, he had thought the novelty of company might help. He was accustomed to having staff on hand every hour of the day and night, but that was not quite the same as having a friendship. Garett caught himself shying away from the word 'relationship'. It conjured up all sorts of bad memories. His only meaningful one to date had ended when he was six years old. That was when he had watched his father kill his mother. From that moment on Garett had vowed never to put any woman in such a vulnerable position. That was why he did not stay too long in one place. Lingering made people—especially women—start thinking about commitment. Garett made a point of committing only to work. It proved a harsh mistress, but his loyalty had paid off a billion times over.

He was concentrating on that achievement when a

sound stirred his unquiet conscience. He turned to locate the source and saw, twenty yards away, Ermanno approaching the open door of a small house adjoining the yard. A woman stood there, a flour-streaked apron covering her sensible black skirt and blouse. She had a mixing bowl in her hand, and as Garett watched she held the spoon out to Ermanno to taste. Existing on a diet of split-second timing and vending machine coffee, Garett was touched. The scene reminded him of the false intimacy he had shared with Sienna over her pasta-making. What *was* it about home cooking? It always looked such fun. Perhaps women felt a deep-seated urge to create something, and as a man he was genetically programmed to appreciate it. Or were they naturally more generous than men, and liked to share?

He wanted to go on watching Ermanno and his wife, but found he had to look away. The moment was too intimate. Garett regularly dined with princes, and probably earned more in one minute than a farm worker saw in a year, but in those sixty seconds Garett sensed that Ermanno possessed something that he had never owned—peace of mind.

CHAPTER EIGHT

Sienna presented herself at the Bradleys' front door within the hour. A maid showed her into a small room leading off the main lobby. Sienna had been in there many times before, but it was unrecognisable now. Every horizontal surface was covered with spreadsheets, and computer hardware and software. Garett sat in the middle of this organised chaos. Phone clamped to his ear, he was rocking back in his chair as he made some complicated arrangements for sub-contracting labour.

'What have you done to Molly's craft room?' Sienna gasped, the moment he finished his call.

'She won't mind. Kane's taken her off on a shopping trip to Portofino.'

'That is a long way to go on a whim, at this time of day,' Sienna said suspiciously.

'Oh? And I thought you Europeans enjoyed stretching each day to the max,' he teased. 'I've already hired back all the builders who worked on this house. The proof of their good work is all around me. But now I need you and your beautiful native tongue to put some more complicated concepts to the firms on this list—' He pulled a sheet of paper out of the computer's printer tray and flourished it at her.

'Oh—no—I couldn't possibly—I haven't come here to work!' Sienna held up her hands and started backing away. 'What will people say? The whole village will be alight with gossip—'

Broken sentences tumbled over one another as she gabbled her way towards the door. She was as anxious to escape as her words, but Garett put a stop to it all. He beat her to the exit in half a dozen long strides. Putting out his hand to the doorframe, he barred her way.

'Oh, no, you don't! If you're genuine about wanting to save Aldo's villa, then you are going to have to give me a hand. I achieve miracles every day of my working life. I will do it for you, too. But to pull off a near-impossible project like this one I will need your help.'

It was that honey voice of his—the one that always threatened to turn her self-control into a memory. Sienna gulped. He was within centimetres of her, so close that she could feel the warmth radiating from him.

'I can do this, but not without your help.'

His voice breathed through her confusion. Without knowing why, she raised her hands in an almost childlike gesture. She was about to apologise, but he gave her no time. Impulse overtook him at that moment, and he kissed her.

It was supposed to be a gesture of reassurance. Simple, unthreatening proof that he would go only so far, but no further. It did not turn out like that.

The moment his lips touched hers, he felt all the tension leave her body. She melted like marshmallow in chocolate fondue. The effect transformed him in a heartbeat. Her perfume felt like balm. She was all fresh air and flowers, mingled with simple human warmth. It aroused such a yearning in him that his kiss went on, and on. He kissed her until her mouth opened—not in fear or complaint, but in invitation. Garett had heard that the mind went blank while kissing. It had never yet happened to him. He prided himself on keeping his wits about him at all times. That was what made him such a success. So this kiss was something he fully intended to enjoy to the full. Gradually, he allowed the tip of his tongue to test her, to tease her, flickering over the plump cushions of her lips but venturing no further.

Let other men have their virgins—once a woman discovers sex there is no holding her, he thought, rejoicing in the supple warmth of her body. She swayed, and leaned against him heavily. Is it just for support, or to test me? he wondered. Then all of a sudden his mind dissolved. Her body was pressing against him. In that moment, all his other experiences counted for nothing. This was the only one that mattered. Yet he wanted gratification, nothing more. That was what he kept telling himself. Sienna di Imperia could mean nothing to him. Although she had such passivity and inner beauty… He had never encountered things like this in any other woman. He had to have her—here, now—

Sienna began to want him. The air escaped from her lungs in a little gasp of pleasure. Closing her eyes, she touched her lips to his again. It was a hesitant gesture that he was only too quick to capitalise upon. Cupping her head with his hands, he kissed her once more, with a passion that burned like fire. The suddenness was too much. It lashed Sienna out of her trance and she leapt back as though burned.

No—this was all wrong. She wanted him, but she

did not want the emotionless sex of this bargain. There had been too much of that in her recent past. That was why she had to put a distance between her and Garett. She was too physically frail to resist him. She was used to losing her dignity beneath the crushing weight of male authority—but that was nothing like this. What happened when Garett kissed her was far more frightening than that. In those first few seconds of unbridled passion she had almost lost her mind.

She braced her hands against his shoulders and shook her head.

'No. I cannot. It is too soon—'

Garett was breathing fast. Restraint was not in his sexual nature. Waiting—plans—challenges—they could all go to hell. He had sampled her kisses, and now he wanted more. That was the only thing that mattered.

'Would you do this to save Aldo's inheritance?' His breath whispered past her cheek.

Sienna's fingers tightened on his arms. She closed her eyes. If only it was as easy to shut out her problems by retreating behind the small, well-loved front door she had left behind so regretfully, so long ago.

'For the villa?' She could not confess, and looked away. 'If I thought I could go back to my own little house in the village and never be bothered with anyone or anything ever again then, yes—yes, I would sell my very soul…'

Her voice had been steady, but her legs were shaking as she pulled herself out of his grasp. Walking out of the room, she slammed the door behind her with a report that thundered through the whole house.

* * *

Sienna walked away from the Bradleys' villa with her head held high. It was only when she was out of sight of the house that her eyes began to fill. She blundered off the gritty track and into the hazel grove that bordered her route home. Standing in a clearing, she cried furious tears of disappointment and frustration.

In an instant she had gone from ecstasy to terror. Once again Garett had ignited sparks within her body—and then stifled the curling, smoky tendrils of her passion by moving in on her straight away. He was going to break his side of the bargain. She knew it, and there was nothing she could do about it. His body was too much of a temptation. But if she gave in, he would have no incentive to work on her house. And if she refused him, there was nothing to stop him walking away. Both options had the power to drive her insane. She desperately wanted to run—to escape. But there *was* no escape. All she wanted was to retreat to the little cottage where she had grown up. But Imelda would never stoop to moving there, and with no hope of saving the building anyway without Garett's help she was cursed. She would have to stay here, on this land and in Aldo's villa, which was crammed with so many bad memories.

She was trapped. Her father must have found something in Imelda to love, so Sienna knew it was her duty to care for the woman. It didn't matter about her own feelings. She had to keep in mind what her father would have wanted. Caring for Imelda meant staying at Entroterra—and that needed money. Imelda's plan was to move old Claudio into the property with them, but it was a price Sienna did not want to pay. Her refusal had kept the atmosphere simmering at home since Aldo's funeral. It boiled over into open warfare whenever Imelda brought the subject up.

Now Garett was offering her an escape from that. All she had to do was sit tight and endure for just a short while longer. Then her problems would be over—but only as long as he kept his side of the bargain. Garett had explained he would be providing finance to restore her properties and land. Then, once everything was under way, it would all be mortgaged in Sienna's sole name. That meant he must make a start right now, pouring his own money directly into the Entroterra estate. He would be in full control of all the finances at all times, and Imelda would be unable to bully her way into spending any of it.

Sienna tried to console herself with the idea that sacrificing her body would save Aldo's house and the good name of his ancient family. And giving Garett an excuse to stay in the area would be sure to delight her friends Molly and Kane too. Also, wonder of wonders, living in a clean, warm, light house might even keep Imelda quiet—at least for a while.

But it meant that Sienna would have to give her body to a man who treated sex like a hobby. Otherwise, how could he think of using it as a bargaining tool?

Sienna had never forgiven herself for agreeing to marry Aldo. She had made the best of it then, because it had safeguarded all her father's property. Now she would have to desert her principles a second time. Desperate circumstances had pushed her at Aldo. This time she was faced with selling herself to Garett. But was that really any worse than marrying Claudio, simply in the hope that

Aldo's rich cousin could silence Imelda's continual demands for cash?

Garett was everything Sienna could ever want in a man—he was gorgeous, he was clever, he even admired her knitting. Best of all, he liked her cooking. Sienna knew there would never be any other man for her.

But now her dream was turning into a nightmare. In reality, he was proving to be no different from Aldo. He wanted the one thing Sienna was afraid to give him.

But something had to be done to safeguard Aldo's property and the other little home she loved. And surely Garett Lazlo was the man to do it? But he had blown into her life so suddenly. He could vanish with equal ease. He was brisk and efficient, certainly, but that was now—when he still had her in his sights. Who was to say he really had the determination and patience to do his best for places that had existed for hundreds of years?

He was the most incredible man she had ever met. But Sienna knew she could not let that blind her to his dangers. She only had one thing in her favour. He really did want her. She had seen it in his eyes and felt it under the keen pressure of his fingertips. There was no faking the physical reaction she ignited in him, and Sienna's mind flickered with sudden hope.

She would have to keep a tighter curb on her own body. If she was careful, she might turn the one thing he wanted more than anything else into a weapon. She would hold it against him—but nothing more—until his work on the estate was completed. Only when she was satisfied would he get his own satisfaction.

* * *

Garett made no move to follow Sienna when she left. To do so would be counter-productive—and anyway, he knew he did not need to. She would be back. Sooner or later.

Head down, he worked on without a break until it was time to go up and change for dinner. His suite was as welcoming as ever, but he was not in a mood to appreciate it. The computer-controlled shower in his marble and silver wet room was the last word in luxury. One touch provided a deliciously warm tropical downpour. But that was not what Garett needed right now. Stripping off his clothes, he adjusted the thermostat and dived in. Freezing needles of ice assaulted his hard, toned muscles.

He tried to organise his thoughts. All he could see was Sienna's face. People tended to smile at him only when they wanted something. Garett had taught himself not to trust any of them. But Sienna was an unknown quantity.

He worked hard, he worked alone, and he worked incessantly. Recent events had shocked him into realising that there must be another way. The flashpoint had come when he'd erupted at a street kid who'd happened to follow him for a couple of blocks, hoping for quarters. Garett had found himself looming over the terrified boy like a playground bully, and hating himself for doing it. Hell— not so long ago, *he* had been that little guy! The thought that success was turning him into one of the loveless, paranoid monsters who had wrecked his own childhood had horrified Garett. That last day in Manhattan had been a wake-up call for his conscience. He had escaped, turned his back on everything he knew.

This unexpected stay with the Bradleys was good for him. They were decent people, who usually kept him in touch with reality. But he couldn't help thinking that they had confronted him with a dream. Sienna was everything he could ever want in a woman—beautiful, and infinitely charming. Not that it meant much, in the final reckoning. Garett knew women, and, however shy and retiring Sienna di Imperia might appear at the moment, in the end she would turn out to be just like all the rest. Once she fell fully for his charms those long, lovely lashes would start to flutter like a flurry of euros. Women wanted pleasure and they wanted money. Garett knew he was the man to supply both in an endless supply—until he got bored.

He shook himself, momentarily startled. He was supposed to be on holiday. Revelling in thoughts of pleasure was one thing. Acting on them was quite another. And it was out of the question for now. He had isolated himself from his business to give himself a holiday from all things stressful—including women. Working for the Entroterra estate was nothing special—it was simply a matter of keeping his hand in. He was certain that doing nothing but laze about on his new yacht or here in the Bradleys' villa would have killed him off within hours. Keeping his mind active with Sienna's project would be much more pleasurable. His body was being kept nicely alert by the power of his mind, and he could delight in playing Sienna like a beautiful silver salmon, bending her to his will without the slightest danger to his heart…

Deep down in her own heart, Sienna knew Garett could take her body as easily as he overwhelmed her mind. All it would take was one touch, one glance, and she would be lost. He had never needed to put his bargain into words.

For her, it was a natural progression. She had been attracted to him from the moment he strode into Portofino market. In those first few moments catching the eye of a man like him had seemed an impossible dream. And then he had talked to her—Sienna! The sound of his voice had stolen her heart and the firm mastery of his touch had secured it for ever. Her emotions were all his—but unfortunately her mind was still her own. It kept reminding her that this was a man who saw her body as a prize. Someone who could do that must be capable of anything.

Sienna was in an impossible position. It was either submit to Garett or succumb to Aldo's cousin Claudio—a straight choice between a smooth deceiver and a devious runt.

And that, as she already knew, was no choice at all.

Sienna was desperate—desperate enough to swallow her pride. Garett was right, of course. She needed to make her property work for itself if she was to catch her dream of moving back to the little village house of her childhood. The glimmer of independence was beginning to tempt her, but Imelda's eyes were glittering brighter with thoughts of tying rich old Claudio to their bank account. That was the easiest way, her stepmother argued. It did not involve foreigners, work or expense.

Sienna stood her ground. At least Garett's solution was honestly dishonest. It did not involve selling herself publicly, through a golden wedding ring.

Next day, she put on the black linen jacket and gored skirt she had bought for Aldo's funeral. Wrapping her velvet stilettos in a plastic bag, she walked over to the Bradleys' house. While still out of sight, in the hazel grove, she changed into the impractically beautiful sandals. If she was going to work for a man like Garett, she was going to look the part. Hiding her sensible-but-dull loafers among the coppiced hazel stumps, she smoothed down her skirt and neatened her collar, then made her way gingerly up the final slope.

As this was a formal visit, she went straight to the high-gloss black front door. A uniformed maid opened it, and told her that the master and mistress were out for the day. Sienna had spent her walk rehearsing how she would avoid breaking down and telling Molly about Garett's designs on her honour. Now she did not know what to do. All her good intentions evaporated and she dithered on the doorstep.

'Signora di Imperia!'

Before Sienna could move, or hide, or do anything at all, Garett's impressive figure swaggered down the wide marble staircase. He was turning back the cuffs of his white shirt, adding to the casual air about him. His open collar displayed a hint of body hair, and his smile widened as he saw her notice it.

'You nearly missed me,' he said, dismissing the maid with a nod. 'I've got everything well underway with regard to your estate, so I thought I'd factor in a little R and R. Kane says I can borrow his plane to slide over to Nice for a few hours. What do you reckon? You certainly look dressed for a day on the town.'

Sienna thought of the irresistible Mediterranean, lined with jostling sightseers and petulant rich people.

'I think you will enjoy yourself, Garett. I'm sorry to have disturbed you.' She was already turning away, but he reached out and placed a hand on her shoulder.

'But you haven't. Why don't you come with me?'

She could not argue with the hold he had over her, but she could make a stand.

'No, thank you—I came here to work this morning, Mr Lazlo.'

'It's good to hear that. Not a problem. We can do it in Nice, out of everybody's earshot.' He tipped his head in the direction of the retreating maid. As he spoke, his fingers glided down the length of Sienna's arm and grasped her hand. He was already out of the door, but she refused to be dragged along in his wake. Sensing that this was a serious moment, he stopped and looked down at her expectantly.

Sienna hoped he could not hear her knees trembling. 'I said that I came here to work, and I meant it, Mr Lazlo.'

'I didn't doubt you for a moment, *signora*.' He smiled lazily.

Sienna tried her hardest to maintain the formal air between them, even though she could sense he was mocking her. 'I'm glad you feel that way, Mr Lazlo, because I have a proposition to put to you—a decent one, before you revive any ideas about what happened yesterday. I desperately need help with my house, but I hardly slept last night for thinking about—well, for trying to reconcile my longing to reclaim my past with the fact that I must live in the present. I've decided that I cannot sacrifice my body to you. I would rather you sold my father's properties in the village to fund work on the Entroterra estate. Then I won't owe you anything—money, or…any other sort of obligation,' she finished with difficulty.

He regarded her with narrowed eyes. Gradually, his hold on her hand loosened.

'So...you won't be included in the deal?'

'No.'

He dropped her hand altogether.

'But you've told me how much that house means to you, Sienna.

'It means the world to me.' She held his gaze.

He dug his hands deep into his pockets and shrugged. 'Fine. I'll make arrangements for an agent to value your father's properties, and we can see how far that will get us with work on the villa.'

Sienna looked at him quizzically. 'You don't mind?'

'Why should I? If you've thought this through and come to a decision without any prompting from me, then I respect that. That's all there is to it. We'll forget all about the other...arrangement.' He looked away from her across the courtyard, as though the sparrows squabbling on the cobbles meant more to him than she did.

This was not the reaction Sienna had expected. She had needed all her courage to come out with this new idea, and had been expecting him to refuse. Instead, he was treating the whole thing as just another meeting in his busy schedule.

'Is that it?' she said eventually, when the suspense of his silence became too much for her.

'What do you mean? You surely weren't expecting me to beg? I'm not that sort of man. You've made your decision, and that's all there is to it. You've made a stand—possibly for the first time in your life—and I respect that,' he said, nonchalantly.

His nonchalance felt worse to Sienna than his fury would have done. If she had ever tried refusing sex in the past, it had always increased Aldo's annoyance rather than defusing it.

'Thank you,' Sienna said brightly, but her heart was dark. She was supposed to feel relieved. Yet she felt empty, let down, and—to her disbelief—disappointed.

Garett nodded, wondering why he felt neither thankful nor released.

He decided against driving his hire car to the airfield where Kane kept his plane. Instead, he called into the Bradleys' garage block.

'If we're going to be borrowing the plane, we might as well borrow a Mercedes too,' he said, holding open the rear door of a silver blue saloon for Sienna to step in.

She took a while to come to terms with such luxury. Aldo had owned a large top-of-the-range Fiat but it had been as old as Ermanno's donkey. This beautiful car was sleek, new, and softly upholstered. She spread her hands over the seats, marvelling at how anyone could keep cream upholstery so clean.

'All it takes is enough money to keep a fleet of staff.' Garett read her thoughts as he settled himself in the seat beside her. 'Now, just in case your properties don't provide enough funds to complete the Entroterra project, I wonder if you have any contingency plans to save yourself from my clutches?' he mused.

'Shh!' Sienna's eyes darted guiltily toward the back of the driver's head.

'Kane's staff are as discreet as they are hardworking.' Garett smiled, but all the same he raised the glass partition separating them from the chauffeur. Sitting back, he fastened his seat belt and gestured for her to do the same.

Sienna squirmed. She was having difficulty in getting comfortable. Unused to the sleek lines of her closely fitted skirt, she needed freedom to move. Unaware that one of his passengers was not yet secure, the chauffeur pulled away from the parking bay. The Mercedes surged forward with the smooth expense of power. Without the security of her seat belt Sienna was thrown across the car.

Garett acted purely on instinct. As she was jolted against him he grabbed her, and held her tight.

'And I thought you'd reconsidered!' He chuckled.

Sienna's face was pressed against the fine material of his white shirt. She could feel his heart beating, slow and rhythmically, against the broad expanse of his chest. It should have been reassuring. Instead it accelerated her own pulse to fever-pitch. Knowing that one more second would destroy all her good intentions, Sienna pushed herself upright. Her hair swung across her face, hiding her confusion as she made a great show of fastening her seat belt.

'I'm sorry about that. It should never have happened,' she said stiffly. The heat from his body had transferred to her, and the thin blouse she was wearing beneath her formal jacket suddenly felt painfully restricting. The nearness of him always had such an effect on her. Feeling his body so close to hers whipped her hormones into a frenzy of expectation. She could feel the delicate points of her nipples teasing against the lace of her bra, and hoped their arousal was not visible through her clothes.

'Accidents can happen,' he said mildly.

If he was showing any interest in her body, Sienna was too embarrassed to notice. She pressed herself into the corner of the car, unwilling to give him any inkling of the physical attraction his body had for hers.

'Not to me they don't. Not any more,' Sienna decided aloud.

'Then why don't you outline your back-up scheme for the Entroterra estate's salvation?'

Sienna looked down at her hands. Her fingers were trembling. She clasped them, hoping that was something else he would not notice.

'Well…as you seem to like it in this area, *signor*, you could always help me and do yourself a favour at the same time— without involving…you know…' She hesitated.

He gave a knowing half-smile, and nodded for her to continue.

'I haven't quite worked out the details, but I thought if you bought into the Entroterra estate, you could have all the benefits of living here while I gain from your expertise at no cost to myself,' she said simply.

'Well, you're coming along the path to independence in leaps and bounds, aren't you?' He smiled, but then shook his head with regret. 'Thanks, but no thanks, *signora*. I've got all the houses I need, I'm afraid. The gypsy in my soul means I'd rather stay with Molly and Kane for a while, or holiday on my yacht. I don't need to buy in to property here.' The expression in his eyes spoke of far more than mere bricks and mortar.

Sienna looked out across the sun-dried countryside speeding past the car windows. This was her land. It was the place where she had run and played as a child. The only thing worse than forsaking it for a cramped city flat would be to marry Cousin Claudio and for him to start lording it here. She swallowed hard, forcing down the bitter taste of compromise.

'I can't possibly offer you anything more.' She raised

her hand, ready to clap her palm to the car seat between them and emphasise the point.

'And that is your final word?'

'Yes,' she said with emphasis, and lowered her hand. A new confidence surged through her veins. It might be that straight talking would work better with Garett than dramatic gestures.

Her confidence was misplaced. When he finally nodded, a strange look flickered across his face. Sienna was too busy congratulating herself to notice.

In your own quiet way you're becoming quite a force to be reckoned with, Signora di Imperia, he thought to himself. *So let's see how you respond to being given a little bit more licence to live…*

CHAPTER NINE

SIENNA stood in the sunshine, trying to keep her mind on the task in hand. Raising her sunglasses, she used them to push the thick glossy mane of hair back from her face. Two hours had passed since she had got the better of Garett Lazlo.

She smiled, remembering his watchful silence for the rest of their journey. The moment they'd touched down in Nice he had disappeared, leaving her with a gleaming and expensive new hire-car. He wanted to go his own way for a while, he had told her. She should see this as a taste of the new freedom his temporary investment in the Entroterra estate gave her, he'd said. It would also be a perfect opportunity for her to enjoy the sights and sounds of Nice.

It was only after he'd walked off and left her alone that Sienna had realised he was giving her a chance to stand on her own two feet for once. Imelda and Aldo had always driven and manipulated her. Garett was not like that. Instead, he played up the advantages that his methods could bring, and never mentioned the twin pillars of duty and obedience.

Go to the market and buy yourself some flowers, he had said. They will raise your spirits. Live as though you have ten thousand a year more to spend than you actually do. Act the part, and people will respect you as though your fantasy is real.

So now she stood in the florist's, checking off her purchases as they were packed into the car Garett had picked up at the airport. This was the sort of 'work' she liked, and she took a lot of pleasure from the fresh fragrance and greenery. Bewitched by the scent of the potted gardenias lining the florist's shop, Sienna asked on impulse for one to be included in her order. She had never done such a reckless thing before, but tried to convince herself it could be written off as a proper business expense. The flower would sit in the hall and overpower the faint smell of mushrooms that always hung about the old place.

With a sudden sense of wonder Sienna realised that only a short time ago she would never have dreamed of making such a purchase. The idea that Garett's motivation was already bringing her some pleasure washed over her like a warm sea. Then a hand slipped under her elbow, and she found herself awash with guilt instead.

It was Garett. He gave a silent whistle.

'You've really taken my suggestion to heart, haven't you?'

'Mr Lazlo—Garett—I hope I haven't been too extravagant—'

'I told you to spend what you like.' He smiled. 'Leave me to worry about the cost. Believe me, that's not a problem.' He looked around the shop with a confidence that announced he could have bought the whole place a dozen times over.

'And—talking about extravagance—I've booked us into a restaurant for lunch. You'd better finish here so we can set off.'

Sienna checked her watch. 'It's far too early. Did you come out without breakfast again?' She levelled a look at him, but he shook his head.

'After the way you reacted the last time? No. I want to pick up a few things on the way, that's all, so by the time we eventually get there our table should be waiting.'

Sienna was only too happy to agree. The shops in Nice were every bit as stylish and imposing as those in Portofino. Alone, she would never have had the nerve to do anything but window-shop in such a grand setting. With Garett, she could walk straight into places she would never have dreamed of entering. As they approached the first designer outlet, she tried to look as though she shopped like this every day. In reality, she was secretly sizing up all the crystal-encrusted cocktail dresses and svelte evening gowns with the expertise of a commercial spy.

Her excitement soon turned to alarm when she was whisked away into a fitting room and poured into a selection of outfits. Each one was more beautiful than the last. Sienna's task, her pencil-thin personal shopper told her, was to choose which ones she liked best.

'I can't see any price tags,' Sienna managed uncomfortably as she was paraded out for Garett's inspection wearing a Chanel suit in silk, with matching bag. He was leaning against a marble pillar, chatting with the impressively fashionable manageress.

'Oh, don't worry about that. Just make sure you choose something that will impress the agents and bank managers you are going to be meeting this week. And me,' he added, with rather more of a smile than Sienna liked. 'If you want to persuade me you've got the spirit to fend for yourself once I've gone home to Manhattan, you can start by looking the part.'

The manageress gazed at him indulgently.

The staff were all so anxious to please that Sienna could not disappoint them. She smiled her practised smile—but she was uneasy. Standing in front of the full-length mirror while dressmakers flitted around her, Sienna interrogated her reflection. How could she let this perfect stranger buy her clothes and order her about?

The reason for that was only too obvious. Sienna needed clothes. The neatly folded pile of garments lying on the changing room vanity unit were the only new things she had bought in years. They had been purchased in a moment of dire necessity, for Aldo's funeral. Her late husband had hated spending money. He had considered that indestructible man-made fibres were the greatest discovery in the history of mankind. In order to keep Imelda dressed like the mother-in-law of a millionaire, Sienna had been forced to beg for a clothing allowance. The old man had been so reluctant that Sienna had never risked asking for anything for herself. Instead, she had repaired and restyled her existing clothes. The only time she got anything different to wear was when Imelda tired of a particular outfit. Then it would be passed down to her. Sienna would use panels of fabric removed from the width to lengthen Imelda's cast-offs, which led to some interesting results.

Now, today, the world's most desirable billionaire had flown her to Nice. He was driving her around in an electric blue cabriolet and buying her dresses from top designers. It wasn't right.

But it *was* nice.

She looked at all the window-shoppers jostling along on the pavements outside the shop. Any one of them would swap places with her in an instant. She had no right to be ungrateful. If money was what Garett understood, and he didn't want to buy into her property, then there was only one thing to do if she wanted to keep her integrity. She would have to sell something and pay him back. She could not allow herself to be in debt to him in any way.

While he settled up, Sienna tried to find out how much her new clothes had cost. Nobody in the shop would discuss money with her. She was left to guess. The idea of selling off something useless to settle her account with Garett began to appeal to her more and more. There was one particularly hideous oil painting leering down over a chimneybreast in the great hall back at home. It was the only thing that Sienna and her stepmother agreed about. Its dark depiction of contorted young men in various states of undress was, in Imelda's words, 'not quite nice'.

Perhaps Garett would take it away in settlement?

When she mentioned it, he was delighted that she was starting to think for herself, and knew instantly which picture she meant. He had spotted it on the first day, when he'd roamed around the ground floor of the villa on his own.

The moment they got home from Nice, he swung into action and rang someone to arrange for the picture to be checked out. The news was good—and from then on Garett felt completely reassured when he paid out on architects and builders. Without going into details before the picture was officially authenticated, he hinted to Sienna that Imelda would be better off not knowing anything about the investigations, and with a smile assured her that there would be enough security in the picture to satisfy him.

This turn of events finally convinced Garett that working on the Entroterra project was a good idea. He arranged for Sienna to visit banks and financial institutions on the strength of it. Insurance cover and bridging loans were put in place so that one day she would be able to pay back the money he was pouring into the refurbishments around her home and grounds.

Sleep had been difficult enough for Sienna when Garett was an untouchable fantasy. Now she was slipping further and further into his debt it was almost impossible. She not only worried about her own finances now, she grew increasingly suspicious about his apparently inexhaustible wealth. Several times during the dinner party at Kane and Molly's house the Bradleys had tried to get Garett to open up about the size of his fortune. Sienna had been quietly embarrassed at the time. Now she wished she had spoken up and encouraged him to explain his circumstances—although she hated herself for being so wrapped up in the subject of money.

Experience told her that Imelda was right, and that rich men offered security, but something deep within Sienna wanted to rebel. There must be more to life than lunging desperately from one financial lifebelt to another. Love…that is the thing I crave, she thought sadly. Piccia was full of families held together by bonds much stronger than paper and coins. They were poor, but honest and happy at the same time. Allegedly Garett Lazlo had everything they lacked, yet he always seemed so edgy and unsatisfied. Sienna was beginning to wonder if his conscience was troubling him. She decided to do some investigating.

The village co-operative was always glad of extra help, so one day, when her house was full of workmen and her garden full of machinery, Sienna offered to put in an extra day's work on the market stall. It would keep her out of everyone's way at home, and give her the perfect excuse to visit Portofino.

The minute her shift on the stall was over, she walked down to the harbour. The whole place was busy with summer, and everything smelled of new paint and money. Brightly coloured flags moved lazily in a light breeze, like pennons at a medieval tournament, and loving teams of polishers and engineers tended each luxury yacht as it waited on the gently breathing water. It was a whole new world—but Sienna did not have time for sightseeing. She was looking for one vessel in particular.

The Bradleys had been unable to get much information out of Garett about his new purchase, but Sienna was determined. She had started to see his silence about the yacht as slightly odd. From what Kane and Molly had told her about its size, and the number of crew, Sienna foresaw no problem in tracking it down. All she would need to do was ask around. Something that size would be noticeable, even in Portofino. Especially when a man like Garett Lazlo owned it, Sienna thought. It was rumoured that the crews employed by some rich people were only too happy to let visitors drool over the yachts at close quarters—for a price. Taking the last of her ready cash, she went off to find out.

She had expected it to be easy. Instead, nothing could have been more difficult. Nobody had heard of Garett Lazlo. She even screwed up her courage and spoke to some of the aristocratic blonde teenagers who draped themselves about the sundecks like trophies. They were hired by the season to provide cordon bleu cooking for image-conscious billionaires. That was exactly the type of thing Garett would invest in, Sienna thought—but, no. Despite cooing over her description, none of the girls knew anything about him.

Sienna returned to the market, deep in thought. The only thing that stopped her racing home to confront him immediately was her friendship with the Bradleys. If Molly and Kane liked him enough to let him stay in their luxury villa, then Garett couldn't possibly be the liar he seemed to be. Could he? She puzzled over the differences between the fantasy that was Garett Lazlo and his reality for the rest of the day.

'You're quiet, Sienna?' The co-operative's secretary probed as she drove them both back home from Portofino that afternoon.

'I'm always quiet, Anna Maria.' Sienna tried a smile.

'Yes, but this is a different sort of silence.' Her friend laughed, then stopped. 'Look over there—what's that plume of smoke?'

Sienna sat bolt upright in the passenger seat, straining forward to see through the branches of some roadside poplars.

'It's a fire—a fire at my place!'

Instantly Sienna forgot all her ideas about cornering Garett over his fictional boat. Anna Maria slammed her foot down on the accelerator. As the co-operative's tiny van reached Entroterra land, dancing flakes of ash added to the smell and crackle of burning that filled the air. Sienna's senses were overwhelmed, leaving no room for anything but panic.

'Wait—look—it's only a builder's bonfire.' Anna Maria

sighed with relief. Then suddenly her voice took on a smoky quality. 'And look who's in charge!'

'That's Garett.' Sienna felt herself blushing. He was stripped to the waist, muscles rippling, as he directed workman around the forecourt and buildings. Wreathed in smoke from the fire, it was some time before he looked around to see who was driving up.

'No wonder you've been quiet. A guy like that must give you a whole lot to think about!' Anna Maria was raking Garett's half-naked body with looks of unmistakable longing. He returned her gaze with a casual smile as he opened the van door to let Sienna out.

'Right…well, if there's no emergency here I'll be off, and leave you two to get on with…whatever it is you're going to be getting on with!' Anna Maria winked at Sienna, who was too furious to notice. She stood beside Garett, rigid with anger, until the co-operative's van careered off down the drive. Then she rounded on him.

'There is a great plume of smoke rising up from here! I was frightened to death! I expected to see this whole place burned to the ground. What the *hell* do you think you're doing?'

'I thought you wanted me to help save your future?'

'Yes, but at what cost?'

He treated her to a lopsided grin, and then looked away, across the scene of builders toiling away at every part of the building.

'Keep talking like that, Sienna, and I might start to think you're ready to manage without me.'

With his attention elsewhere, Sienna let her eyes be drawn to the sparkles of sweat beading his smooth, clear skin. As she watched, a trickle ran down over the taut muscles and disappeared into the dense mass of dark hair covering his pectorals. Without acknowledging her gaze, he turned aside and strolled over to a mechanical digger parked on the cobblestones. Pulling a cotton shirt from its cab, he dragged it on over his head. Unrolling the sleeves, he threw a few seemingly unimportant words over his shoulder.

'Is that better?' It was obvious he had caught her watching him.

Sienna flushed a deep red. 'If you take your shirt on and off like that without undoing its buttons, they'll all work loose and be lost.'

Garett had been presenting his broad back to her as he surveyed the work in progress. At her words he turned. Heavy, deliberate steps brought him almost too close. Then he bent his head until it was within centimetres of hers, and she could do nothing but stare straight back at him.

'Then I shall simply buy another shirt.' He grinned.

That was enough for Sienna. She had discovered he must be lying to Kane and Molly with his talk of a fictitious yacht, and she was not going to let him charm her out of her anger.

'What with?' she countered.

'Oh, I expect I'll be able to find a few spare coins down behind the cushions of my furniture somewhere.'

He was still highly amused. Sienna blinked, and with an effort remembered Portofino.

'I don't believe you *have* any money, Mr Lazlo,' she said, in a voice like distant thunder. 'You certainly don't have a yacht. I know, because I've been down to Portofino harbour today, and I did some asking around.'

'Ah, well, there's a reason for that.' He was unworried. 'If you were feeling in a curious mood, *signora*, then perhaps you should have started closer to home? For example with that picture of yours hanging over the fireplace.'

'That hideous black thing?'

'Indeed—though now the preliminary results are back, you might try calling it "that previously unknown masterpiece" to see if it helps you to like it better.'

'You're joking!'

Garett moved his head slowly and deliberately from side to side. 'The news came through today, while you were out. That picture could very well solve all your problems and more besides. Congratulations.'

Sienna had come so far she could not allow herself to back down now. With a careless flick of her hand she tried to laugh it off.

'Oh? So I suppose you're an international art expert now, as well as a hotshot businessman and fantasy yacht owner?'

'I'm smart enough to know a good thing when I see it, Sienna.'

She got the feeling he was not only talking about the picture. Suddenly her anger was adrift on a restless sea. This man might be an impetuous, arrogant liar—but he was plausible. And quite amazing to look at…

'Then I shall arrange to get a second opinion right away,' she announced.

He closed in on her instantly. 'Are you mad? With all these strangers about, any news like that will travel like lightning. I've been extremely discreet so far. It can stay where it is for the moment—the preliminary identification has been made through photographs. Detailed analysis can wait until the builders get to that room—then the picture will only need to be moved once. It can be taken straight to a secure place for a full assessment.'

'By a *friend* of yours?' Sienna narrowed her eyes.

'By the New York house that deals with all my fine art acquisitions,' he replied smoothly.

'I hope that doesn't mean my picture will be heading off on your fictitious yacht, for some equally remote horizon.'

'Fictitious, eh?' He took her hand in his and led her over to his hire car. Pausing only to wipe a thin layer of bonfire ash from its door handle with a corner of his shirt, he bundled her into the passenger seat. 'Then let me cordially invite you to come and have a taste of my fantasy.'

'Wait! I have to get Imelda's supper ready!' Sienna protested, but without much conviction.

'Let her get it herself for once.' Garett wound the car into a tight turn and roared off down the drive in squeal of tyres. 'It's time you started living for yourself.'

CHAPTER TEN

THEY reached the coast and he jammed the car into a parking space. By the time he opened the passenger door to help Sienna out he was already speaking rapidly into his mobile.

Snapping the phone shut, he pointed out across the harbour. A speedboat was approaching in a froth of sea foam. 'In under two minutes you will be guest of honour on the *Spinifex*. I hope you'll be able to manage a smile when I introduce you to my crew.'

'I still don't believe you,' Sienna persisted, though her hands were damp with uncertainty. 'The *Spinifex* is the biggest yacht in the area, and it is owned by a Canadian billionaire called O'Rourke. I know that because I checked with one of his off-duty deck hands this afternoon.'

Garett laughed, the sound instantly making Sienna feel foolish and silly for jumping to conclusions. 'And how many Europeans can tell the difference between a Canadian and an American accent?'

If Sienna had any doubts about him left, they were whipped away by the launch which collected them a few seconds later.

'I left Manhattan under quite a cloud,' Garett said as they

streaked towards the spectacular ocean-going yacht that was moored not far offshore. 'I had to get away—put some distance between that lifestyle and this. Paying in cash ensures that the only people in Italy who know my real identity are you, Kane, Molly, a couple of businesses and the people who checked my passport.'

'Have you done something illegal in America?' Sienna swallowed nervously.

'No, but perhaps it should be.'

'Immoral?'

'No, although I'm beginning to realise it was hardly moral.'

Sienna could not imagine what he might have done. She looked him up and down cautiously. He was intent on the horizon. The sight of his new ship hardly moved him at all. Sienna could not imagine why it didn't. It was so beautiful, and from the moment Garett helped her aboard she was treated like fine bone china.

After the dusty decrepitude of Aldo's house, the yacht was heaven. It had a sundeck the size of Sienna's kitchen garden, and a staff who could not do enough for her. They treated her as a guest of honour, plying her with canapés and champagne, and as she stood with Garett at the ship's rail, high above the azure waves, she felt like a princess. Standing beside her was the man who was every inch her prince. He was so close she could notice the way his thick dark hair curled at the nape of his neck, and the lighter tone of his skin where his open collar revealed that he did not always work without his shirt. She jumped guiltily the instant he moved to speak, and looked back at the sea to hide her confusion.

'I hope you've got a good appetite for dinner, Sienna.'

'Dinner? But I'm not dressed for it—I've come straight from work.'

'So have I.'

Sienna fingered the lead-crystal glass she was holding. *Now* what was she supposed to do? He had filled her wardrobe with expensive clothes, but she had dressed for a day at the market this morning—not dinner on an ocean-going yacht.

'Oh, dear—I didn't expect this. I would have dressed up for the occasion—'

His dark eyes smiled at her kindly. 'You look all right to me.'

'Are you sure?' Sienna said doubtfully.

'Signora di Imperia, please give me the honour of taking dinner with me this evening—dress entirely optional.' He held out his hand as a gesture of invitation.

Sienna bit her lip. And then she placed her hand in his. She was silent as he escorted her down to the state dining room.

Garett lightened the atmosphere by explaining to her that his unexpected arrival on board had thrown the catering staff into confusion. Sienna would never have guessed. His crew were professional to their fingertips.

Nerves did not ruin her first taste of lobster, and champagne sorbet took away the bitter taste of her shame.

'I'm sorry I ever doubted that you owned the *Spinifex*, Garett,' she murmured after dinner, as he led her away from the dining table on a tour of his new toy.

'Don't worry about it.' He shrugged off her apology, and when he saw the look of unease in her eyes changed the subject to more neutral conversation. 'The workforce at the

Entroterra estate is doing spectacularly well, but I keep my eye on things to make sure everything goes to plan. It makes a terrific change to be on the spot and working in the open air, rather than being cooped up somewhere like this all the time.'

He smiled as he pushed open a russet cherrywood door to show her the sleek interior of an office suite. His comment was tinged with regret, and there was a fleeting bittersweet expression in his eyes.

'You sound as though you aren't looking forward to the end of your holiday project,' she remarked casually.

'There's nothing much left in it for me, is there? Not since you decided to pull back on our arrangement.' There was a devilish glint in his eye.

Sienna darted a look at him. 'So…you really aren't going to keep me to my original promise?'

'No.' He leaned back against the office wall with a heavy sigh. 'There's no pleasure for me in an unwilling partner.'

Sienna wondered how she would have reacted if he'd said he had only suggested the deal on sufferance. 'I have to admit I was nervous.' She looked up at him with worried eyes. 'It is not my sort of thing at all, you see…'

Garett was mystified. How could anyone be nervous when faced with the most pleasurable experience in the world? She had practically signed up for it by herself, in any case— Garett didn't remember giving her any sort of ultimatum. He would certainly never have expected such a shy, retiring girl to agree. When she had taken it on herself to do so, he had known there could be no question of carrying it out. One look into those beautiful, tormented eyes had told him that. How strange it should be that something he looked forward to like paradise filled her with fear. It was unimaginable that any woman should have to force herself to enjoy a night of passion. What must she have been through to make her feel like that?

'Ah, well, it's your choice. But you've denied yourself what would have been a breathtaking experience, Sienna.' He gave her a smile that promised everything but threatened nothing.

Sienna was not so easily persuaded.

'No, I haven't. Sex is nothing but pistons and valves.'

She looked up at him again, and he recognised the pain of memory in her eyes. He recognised it because it stared back at him each morning from his own bathroom mirror.

'Not with me it isn't,' he said softly. 'I could have promised you that, Sienna, believe me.'

'Why should I? Sex has meant nothing but trouble for me in the past. I'm better off without it,' she said in a flat, defeated voice.

'Now, why in the world should you think that?' He had intended the words to sound as dispassionate as hers, but he was unable to hide his annoyance at the man who had spoiled her life.

'All it does is make men angry.'

'No, Sienna, it does not.' He looked deep into her eyes.

'It does. It provokes anger. Anger is what killed Aldo.'

'Your husband died because he got mad at you?'

She nodded. 'I left the telephone flex twisted after making a call. *Again.* What made it worse was the fact that I was ringing the wool shop. Aldo hated me knitting when I should have been running errands. My wilfulness finally sent him over the edge, so the doctor said.'

'The doctor said that? Or was it Imelda?' Garett said slowly. A picture was beginning to form in his mind, and it was not a happy one.

'Imelda told me. Aldo's death certificate gave the cause of his death as a stroke, but Imelda said the doctors were fools, trying to spare my feelings.'

'So…you think you killed your husband?' he probed, watching intently for her reaction to his words.

She nodded. Then shifted in her seat. 'Although some-times…I think…the doctors are probably more likely to be right than…Imelda.' With each hesitation she glanced up at him nervously from beneath her lashes, as though looking for permission to carry on with her awful admission.

'Ahh. I see.'

Garett put the tips of his fingers together and leaned forward in the same way he had faced her at Il Pettirosso.

'I wonder if you would have told me all that before you started standing on your own two feet, organising builders and shopping in Nice, Sienna? And does your hidden streak of rebellion explain why every telephone flex at Entroterra is hopelessly tangled to this day?'

Sienna's head went up. She stared at him for some time. And then she spoke, very slowly and deliberately.

'Yes. I'm very careful to make sure I add a twist to each one every time I use it.'

He held her gaze for a long time. And then he smiled.

'Good. Then there's hope for you yet.'

'What do you mean?'

He answered her question with one of his own.

'Tell me—what exactly do you think would have happened if you and I had gone to bed together, Sienna?'

Her head drooped again. 'You would have lost your temper with me.'

'Never, Sienna. Never in a million years,' he said softly. Seduction was one of the great delights of his life, and he could not stand by and watch anyone throw their life away in celibacy. 'It's the best thing in the world, Sienna.'

He smiled, watching her consider this. It was like seeing a non-swimmer trying to convince themselves they would like to drown. Nothing short of a truly mad impulse was going to save this situation. Garett could not bear to think of such a lovely girl being lost to love. 'Look, why don't you give yourself the luxury of drafting yourself a new agreement, Sienna?'

She shook her head miserably. But as she looked up at him he could see that his words had tempted her. There was intrigue as well as hesitancy in her eyes.

'The work on your villa will be finished within a few weeks. Then perhaps the two of us can have a celebratory toast. On that night you can decide if you want to take things further—to find out what delights life can hold. Does that sound good to you?'

Sienna nodded, but did not move.

'And now you can forget all about it until and unless you fancy taking advantage of that offer. It's your choice, Sienna.' He looked down at her and tucked a wayward strand of hair behind her ear. Sienna shivered, but she wasn't cold at all.

When she refused to meet his eyes it was because of guilt rather than fear. She had been a willing partner in every touch and every kiss they had shared. A more than willing partner, if she was to be truthful. Now, the power lay in her own hands to cross that invisible line dividing irresistible Garett from terrifying Aldo. Garett was giving her that choice.

She shook her head slowly. 'Why should a man like you, with all your advantages in life, be bothered about somebody like me? You could have anyone you want, whenever you want them.' Sienna sighed, finally putting her chronic lack of self-esteem into words.

He strolled around to the front of his desk and sat down on it, one leg swinging. 'Sienna, something happened to me a short time ago which made me want to outgrow that lifestyle. The more I look about me now, the more I think I should enjoy what I have and not worry about amassing more and more "stuff". I'd lost sight of what was important in life. I only began to realise my mistake when I found myself sounding off at a little urchin who was a mirror image of me at the same age. Like him, I lost my mother early in life and had to live on the streets. I had no right to consider myself any better than he was. I simply escaped by making my own luck. That's the only difference between us.'

'Oh, Garett...' Sienna gasped, staring at him wide-eyed. Suddenly she lost all her fear. It was all she could do to resist throwing herself into his arms. The emotion scared her. She had never felt like that before about anyone or anything— particularly not a man. 'What happened to you?'

'My drunken father beat my mother to death because she couldn't stop me crying.'

Sienna looked him straight in the eyes. The expression there warned her that any offer of sympathy would be quickly brushed aside.

He stood a little straighter, and his voice held a note of shock when he spoke again. 'Do you know, I've never told anyone that before?'

The way he discounted his tragedy with an easy laugh did not fool Sienna for a second.

'What on earth became of you?'

'I was very quiet after that.'

He stood up and walked over to a cupboard. There, he took out a bottle of champagne and some glasses. Silently, he poured them each a small measure and handed one to her.

'And yet you still drink?'

'Champagne doesn't have the kick of homemade liquor. And I am always careful to pace myself. Social drinking is fine. I don't need to get drunk to have fun. I've got all the entertainment any man could ever need right here on board the *Spinifex*. Computers, cinema, top-quality sound systems everywhere—even in there...' He gestured to one of the smoke-coloured walls of his office. At the flick of a switch the glass cleared, and she was looking into a fully-fitted executive gym. He saluted her with his champagne flute. 'In fact I could up-anchor right now and live the rest of my life without ever setting foot on shore again. I could become a water-gypsy, travelling the Seven Seas.'

'And will you?'

'Don't worry. I'm not going anywhere before I've completed the Entroterra project. And then who knows? It might be the Southern Ocean—although to be perfectly honest it won't be long before I start hankering for the offices of Lazlo, Manhattan, again. I'm expecting my console fingers to start twitching at any moment.'

'You have all this, and yet you still want to go back to the city?' Sienna shook her head, amazed.

'Not yet—although, as I say, it can't be long before I get the urge. The longest I've been away from the office in the past was when my appendix got tired of being ignored and I developed peritonitis. Even then I had my staff smuggle work into my hospital suite as soon as I was fit to hold a pen.'

Sienna gazed at him. 'But you tell *me* to slow down and chill out!'

'You know what they say: "those who can, do—those who can't, teach". I've had dozens of health professionals of one sort or another on my case for years. The aquarium, the relaxing recordings, the ambient lighting, the exercise regimes—they've tried all those techniques and it's all been a total waste of time. I'm completely immune. Nothing works on me. I like to work.' He shrugged, leaving his words hanging in the air.

Sienna's brow wrinkled in thought, but only for an instant. 'There must be something that could help you to unwind,' she said slowly—then caught sight of the clock. 'Look at the time! I must go—I need to get back for Imelda.' She jumped up.

'I keep telling you—let her look after herself,' Garett said, but he made no real attempt to stop her. Instead he turned away.

He reached for his jacket, when Sienna might have expected him to criticise her desperate need to run according to someone else's timetable. The only comment he made was when he dropped her off outside the villa.

He came around and opened the car door for her, and

she darted out immediately. 'Don't be in such a hurry. Anyone would think you were trying to escape from me!' He observed dryly as he closed her door.

Sienna *was* keen to get inside—but not to get away from Garett. In fact the opposite was true. She almost found the nerve to give him a peck on the cheek as she thanked him for the spontaneous evening they had shared, but backed away at the last moment and ducked inside the house. There, she raced upstairs to watch the lights of Garett's car disappearing down the drive. She had discovered the secret of his past. Now an idea was forming in her mind. It *was* true that she needed to attend to Imelda—but her stepmother was not the main reason Sienna had wanted to get home. She intended that tomorrow would be a busy day. Her alarm clock was going to be waking her before first light. She needed to get some sleep.

Garett arrived on foot next morning. Now that the fences were all repaired and painted gleaming white, he enjoyed the walk. Dressed in his working clothes of casual shirt and jeans, he swung along the lane between the Bradleys' house and Sienna's villa. The summer was being kind. Dry, clear days allowed the workmen to get on at speed.

Swallows were skimming over the hazel grove as he walked between the coppiced stumps. He stopped and watched them for a few minutes. Sienna had shown him their nests in the hayloft, where the birds returned each spring. It would be well into the autumn before their final chicks were fledged. He had postponed renovating the building where they nested without telling Sienna he would probably have left Italy before the work started. Like the swallows, he would be on the move soon enough.

For once in his life the idea made him feel uncomfortable. Garett was in no hurry to see this project come to an end. He was growing more reluctant with each passing day, and it was the only time he could remember being in such a situation. The problem is Sienna, he thought. At first she had been nothing but a beautiful distraction. Then gradually he had learned of the sadness hiding behind her beautiful eyes. Until his arrival, everyone had bullied her. Now, she was discovering confidence in her own abilities. Within the past couple of days she had even suggested making a start on some of the redundant farm buildings outside of the first phase of redevelopment. She wanted to turn them into holiday homes. Tourism would help the whole area, not just the Entroterra estate.

Garett hoped he could put some of her plans into place for her before he got the urge to leave. At least then he would have the satisfaction of leaving her a potential business with firm foundations, which she could develop after he was gone. He gritted his teeth and faced a grim reality. She might struggle to survive without him. He would certainly worry about her—or at least spare her a thought now and then, he corrected himself. She was finding more and more determination by the day, but she would need it. He wondered how he would eventually find the words to tell her his work was finished and he was leaving. His fists clenched at the thought, and he was surprised to find how uncomfortable and unnatural the action felt to him now. If he was a two-legged rat he would just up-anchor one day and disappear over the horizon.

That would be the quick, clean way to go. But it would also be the act of a coward. And he could never be accused of being one of those.

Despite the depth of his concentration, Garett became aware of irregular sounds bouncing across the valley towards him. Someone was using a sledgehammer. The sound echoed through the peaceful hazel grove like the mating racket of a trainee woodpecker. It was too early for any of the men to be at work yet. As he reached the villa, everything fell still and silent. He strode around to the kitchen, looking for Sienna, but he could not find her. She was not anywhere on the ground floor of the villa. He went back out into the yard just as the inexpert thumping started up again. It was coming from the range of sheds Sienna wanted to turn into holiday homes. She must have got her man Ermanno on the job, he thought grimly. Why couldn't everyone wait for him to arrive and take control?

A fine cloud of dust rose lazily through the still air, glowing in the early-morning sunlight. He wrenched open the cowshed doors, ready to give the hired help a piece of his mind.

Instead of meeting Ermanno, he came face to face with Sienna. She was alone in the byre, all wide-eyed innocence and streaked with dust. Seeing him, she dropped the enormous sledgehammer she was holding with a great gasp of relief. Garett strode forward.

'What in the world are you doing, Sienna?'

She scuffed one toe across the plaster-dusted cobblestones. 'Well…you are all so busy with everything else, but the idea of doing something for myself really appealed to me. Restoring this range of buildings must be right down at the bottom of your list of priorities, so thought I'd make a start alone.'

'What on? Killing yourself? How do you know you aren't going to bring the whole place down on your head by attacking it like this?'

'Because your notes have all the supporting walls marked in red, and this one is drawn in blue,' she said simply, holding out a copy of his own document towards him as proof. 'See?'

'Perhaps I'd better take charge of that.' Garett's expression was almost as dark as the barn. 'Where is your man Ermanno? Has he gone out of his mind, letting you run riot like this?'

'Ermanno has a bad back. I sent him out to bring the goats in, instead. He can manage that.'

'I'd rather you didn't take on heavy work like this.' Garett put down the toolbox he had brought with him. After a moment's consideration he took the hammer from her. 'This job needs strength.'

He tightened his fingers on the shaft of the hammer, feeling its weight and substance. This was real man's work. He flexed all his muscles, ripples of power coursing through his body. If only he could have had an outlet like this the day of his crime on Wall Street. That little boy's face haunted him still. All he'd done was beg for quarters, and Garett had rounded on him in fury. It had been the last straw at the end of a frantic day full of deadlines, a busy week packed with demands, and the never-ending pressure of business with no hope of a break—

His outburst had been so loud, so terrible, that hard-faced pedestrians had almost stopped to stare. The crowds had parted around them, leaving Garett's towering rage pinning the tiny boy beneath his tirade. That was the moment, the second, the heartbeat, when Garett had realised he had to get away. He had turned and marched straight to the airport, hardly caring where he went so long as it was completely outside the orbit of Planet Business.

And now here he was, working again. The difference was that he had left all the traffic, burger fumes and bustle far behind. Here, birdsong, warm breezes, and the perfume of roses from the garden surrounded him. Best of all, the most beautiful woman in the world was looking on. This was the sort of work he liked.

CHAPTER ELEVEN

'STAND well back, Sienna.'

Always obedient, she did as she was told. Sliding one hand down the wooden shaft to test its weight again, Garett considered. Hefting the weapon once, twice, and then a third time, he took an almighty swing at the wall. The hammer's head smashed into the plaster. Garett's arms absorbed the shockwaves effortlessly, and he blew a cloud of dust out of his face. Sienna's face was a study. She was impressed, and he responded.

'How's that?' He raised a brow nonchalantly in mock arrogance. She laughed.

'You've done more with one blow than I managed with all my pecking.'

'Shall I carry on?'

They both knew the answer to that.

Garett took a deep breath, and attacked the wall again. Wielding the hammer produced a lot of dust—and the realisation that he had wasted God knew how many years sitting behind a desk when he might have been doing something useful like this. Inspired, he threw three more massive blows at the masonry. It began to crumble.

Within minutes his shirt was wet with sweat, and both he and Sienna were breathless with laughter. Stopping to strip off, he laid bare the body that Sienna had been dreaming about.

'This is tremendous therapy.'

His glistening chest rose and fell in a way that stirred Sienna as surely as feeling his hands working over her body had done.

'That's what I thought. I know exactly how you feel.'

'No.' He shook his head, laughing as droplets of perspiration flew from his tousled hair. 'You can't begin to imagine. It's giving me such satisfaction to throw all my energy into a violent act like this. I'm working out frustrations I didn't know I had.'

'I knew.' Sienna's lips parted. It was only a small smile, but there was no mistaking the major triumph she was trying to hide.

'No.' He dropped the head of the sledgehammer on the cobblestone floor with a hollow thud. 'How could a quiet, retiring girl like you ever know what demons were hiding inside me?'

'You didn't see what this wall looked like before I started work.' She laughed. Crouching down in the wreckage, she began pulling the smashed spars and lumps of plaster around, fitting them back together. There were chalk marks scrawled on them, he noticed. Then, as he watched, Sienna's jigsaw began to make sense. Soon it revealed two inexpert portraits in white chalk.

'There! Imelda and Aldo.'

'Not very flattering likenesses.' He leaned on the hammer and smiled. 'Now, why don't you go inside and fetch us some drinks? You don't want to get involved in dirty work like this.'

But *I* do, Garett thought, enjoying the benefits of physical labour for the first time.

He lifted the hammer again, testing the shaft as though testing himself against its weight. Sienna revelled in the sight of all that power contained within his muscular torso. It deserved far more than the soft drinks and fast food her other workmen enjoyed. While he went back to demolishing the partition, Sienna returned to her kitchen— as soon as she could tear her eyes away from his body.

Garett eventually delegated the job to workmen—but only when he had burned off a lot of stress. It powered him with a new enthusiasm for the rest of the project. At midday, Sienna brought a picnic out from the house for him. Before eating, he washed in a bucket of ice-cold water at the well.

Sienna spread out a blanket beneath the lemon shelter, but her mind was not on her work. She was distracted by the backlit image of Garett, showering drops of glittering sunshine. As he strolled back across the courtyard, he ran his work-shirt over his chest, then around and beneath his arms. Sienna jumped to her feet.

'I'll fetch you a towel—'

'There's no need. There. It's done.' Pulling the shirt on again, he dropped down to sit opposite her. The airy conservatory held only the faintest tang of new paint, but this was quickly masked when she cut into the pie she had brought.

'That smells good,' he murmured appreciatively. Leaning forward to inspect the filling, he showered both the calzone and Sienna with droplets of water.

'Your hair is soaking!' She laughed, flapping her hand at him.

Immediately he leaned back. What surprised her was that he did it with a laugh. It was a reaction Sienna never normally experienced when she asked someone to do something, so she giggled, too.

'You should do that more often, Sienna. Smiling suits you.'

She blinked at him. It was a compliment, but this time it had nothing to do with trying to get her into bed. Garett was not even bothering to check on the result of his words. Instead, he was attacking her cooking as though there was a danger someone might take it away from him. He was *not* complaining that she had saved time and effort by making one large calzone instead of several smaller ones. Unlike Aldo, Garett never once mentioned dyspepsia, acid reflux, indigestion, oxalic acid levels or dairy and wheat intolerance.

While Sienna marvelled at this busily contented silence, Garett picked up the knife she had put down and carved himself a second man-sized chunk of pie. She gasped.

More than half of it was gone already, and his appetite showed no signs of slowing down.

'What's the matter?'

'N-nothing.' Sienna tried not to look too hungry as she eyed the remaining calzone.

'Aren't you having any?'

'Only when you are sure you've finished.'

He stopped eating and looked at her strangely. Then he jammed the knife through the portion he was about to start eating. Scraping half onto the second plate she had brought, he pushed it towards her.

'You don't honestly think I'd only let you eat when I've finished?' He was shocked, and his reaction surprised Sienna.

'It's what I'm used to.'

He let out his breath in a thin stream.

'That is *not* the way I do things.'

This time Sienna smiled at him in a way he had never seen anyone smile before—man, woman or business associate. In the time it took him to recognise gratitude, she had picked up the pitcher of lemonade she'd carried out from the kitchen. Garett guessed what was coming next. Before she could pour him a glass, his hand closed over hers.

'I'll do it.'

Putting down his plate, he reached for a tumbler and filled it to the brim. Then he handed it to her.

'Go on—take it.'

Sienna accepted it with another welcome smile. Garett did not return to his meal immediately. He waited until she started to eat. Only when he was sure she was catering for herself as well as for him did he pick up his fork again. A warm glow of satisfaction brought genuine expression to his lips. He had been so busy with the Entroterra estate that there had been no time to dwell on his own feelings before now. Now he felt fit and fulfilled in a way he had never known, and in a better state to put everyone else's world to rights, too.

It must be the weather—and the enforced absence of a computer link with his international offices.

'I'm sorry you didn't believe I owned the *Spinifex,* Sienna,' he said eventually, when the edges had been knocked off his hunger. 'But I had my reasons for arriving here undercover. I wanted to get away—to put some distance between the office and me. My staff would have tracked me down in seconds if I'd been entirely truthful everywhere. Do you believe in me now?'

They looked at each other. Garett usually hid his true feelings, but today he could only hope Sienna's expression was not mirroring his own. She looked as amazed as he felt. As her features became troubled, he risked another question.

'You don't look very sure?'

She put down her cutlery. One finger rubbed absently across her brow. 'Well…if you want the truth…I'm still a bit worried about things. Whether it is quite right to sell that big painting, for a start…'

'What's the worst that can happen? Some dusty old museum buys it for a healthy sum and you never have to worry about money again. Where's the harm in that? You're *minus* one monstrosity, and *plus* one small fortune.' He gave her a quick smile, but as he glanced at her it dissolved into a frown. 'What's the matter? Have you got a headache, Sienna?'

'Yes. How did you know?'

'Something about the way you're currently rubbing a hole in your forehead gave it away. Here.' He reached into the pocket of his jeans and pulled out a small plastic case. He handed it to her. Opening it, she found sealed blisters of painkillers. Garett was already pouring her a glass of mineral water.

'I'm an expert in stress headaches—though it's been weeks since I've needed any of these tablets myself. A couple of them and you'll improve quite soon. Although to speed things up…'

He moved around until he was kneeling behind her on the picnic rug. Placing his hands lightly on her shoulders, he began easing her taut muscles, untying all the knots that Aldo and Imelda and shyness and worry and debt had tied.

Sienna allowed herself to do the impossible. She leaned against his hands and sighed.

Garett had expected her to resist. Her willing consent gave him something to think about. Did she realise how he ached for her body? How he had been purposely denying himself for his own selfish reasons? Because he wanted a break from women as much as he needed one from work? Watching her grimace as she took the painkillers, he wondered which of them was suffering most. He certainly wasn't. It had been ages since he'd last checked into the office computer system to see how things were going. Until recently an enforced break like this would have had him climbing the walls. But Garett was beginning to realise he did not need work as much as it needed him.

'Now you've finished your medicine, lean back against the wall and relax,' he murmured, leaning forward to take her glass.

'I can't really get comfortable, sitting here.'

'Close your eyes, and try.'

Alert to every sound, Sienna heard him moving around in front of her. Then she felt him catch up her wrist. The next moment he was working magic. He started to massage the back of her hand with slow, sure movements. Millimetre by millimetre the pressure of his thumbs worked in concert over her thin, delicate skin. Tiny circling movements worked at the tension, smoothing and kneading it all away. For minutes on end she sat transfixed by the feel of his touch, hypnotised by the distant sound of a robin's song fluting over from the hazel coppice. She could not move, but she did not want to. Garett was in charge. Reaching her fingers, he manipulated each one, working over them to warm and free the frozen muscles. It was the first time in her adult life that anyone had ever done anything so personal, just for her. When he finally finished working over her little finger and his touch fell away, she sighed.

'Your fingers were as inflexible as a fistful of birch twigs. You must learn to let go, Sienna.' His voice drifted through the warm, rose-perfumed air.

'Oh, it would be nice.'

There was real longing in her voice. She felt him move around in front of her again. If only this pampering could go on for ever…

With a gasp, she felt him lift her other hand. Her eyes flew open and met with his. For long moments they gazed at each other. Sienna could feel the embers of her desire stirring beneath his steady gaze, but she did not dare make any move or sound which might make him reconsider, change his mind and stop.

'Do you want me to carry on, or not?' His voice was husky, almost challenging. Obediently she lowered her lashes again. This time, though, she did not entirely close her eyes. She made sure she could see enough to watch him continue the massage. The sight of his long, strong fingers at work was almost as much of a distraction as the warmth of his nearness.

'This is wonderful,' she breathed at last.

'Of course it is. Every woman deserves pampering, and you more than most, Sienna.'

'Molly was right. You really do have a silver tongue.'

He smiled, straight into her eyes. Sienna's lips parted. Already her body was warming in response to the closeness of him. His touch on her wrist made her painfully aware of a thudding pulse, but to whom it belonged—him, her, either or both—Sienna was powerless to know. She trembled, and in response his hands slid up her arms, moulding her body to his will as he drew her gently towards his body.

'I can read the mind of every woman I meet,' he breathed, resting his face lightly against the sleek luxuriance of her hair. 'Every woman loves pleasure—and I am the man to give it to you, Sienna.'

Her heart rose. Breathless and dizzy, she could not resist when his mouth closed on hers, kissing away all her doubts.

'Please…no. We shouldn't. This isn't decent…' she gasped, with a total lack of credibility. The waterfall of desire that was powering through her body was washing away any will-power she might possess. Garett had fascinated her from the moment they first met. Tortured by guilt then, Sienna had read lust in his every smile. Whenever they'd made physical contact by accident—the brush of fingers over that spilled glass of wine, their creation of the stracchi—she had thought it was the ultimate high. But this…this was so right, so unlike anything she had experienced before, that nothing could stop her now.

'Oh, it can get a lot more indecent than this, believe me,' he breathed, his lips parted in a smile that was at once triumphant and expectant. 'It will become as indecent as you want it, Sienna. No more and no less. When you are ready, I am going to pleasure you in a way that you will never forget.'

He stood up, drawing her to her feet as well. Then he allowed his fingers to trail down her arm until he could enclose her hand with his.

'Come with me… Have you seen the Entroterra's master suite now that the interior designers have finished?' He threw a smile over his shoulder.

'Garett…I can't…'

'Why not?'

She did not know. Every touch of his hand, each look, drew her closer to Garett and widened the yawning chasm between her experiences with him and with Aldo. She could barely remember the dead days of her marriage. All that existed was the warm anticipation of Garett's body.

She was almost delirious with expectation as he led her through the house that he had transformed into a home for her. When they reached the polished oak door of the master suite, he took a key from his pocket and unlocked it. The door swung open silently, revealing a reception room with thick, soft carpet and opulent furnishings. The suite was so muffled with fine damasks and silks that Sienna knew they would be completely cocooned in luxurious privacy. Garett stepped forward.

She hesitated one last time on the threshold, leaning back against the steady pressure of his hand.

'I can't. Not here…'

'It is the ideal place. We are behind locked doors…' He clicked the catch and his milk chocolate eyes smiled their slow, seductive smile.

'It isn't that.'

He let go of her hand.

'Garett…' She swallowed hard, moistening her lips with

the tip of her tongue. It was an action he clearly found fascinating, which didn't make it any easier for Sienna to continue. 'Is it true that you really do have—what did Molly call it?—a girl in every port?'

He laughed, touched by her innocence. 'Molly does me a disservice.' He smiled roguishly. 'In my time I've had girls in practically every port, city, prairie and valley throughout the civilised world. And parts of the uncivilised world too,' he added with a wink. 'It would be cruel to disappoint any of the lovely ladies of my acquaintance.'

'Do you remember them all?'

'But of course.'

He watched her for a moment, seeing the first flush of lust fade from her skin. It looked as though he was losing her.

'It all depends what a woman wants from a relationship,' he said.

Sienna's face worked through several emotions, until she could manage to put her fear into words.

'I couldn't bear to fall in love with a man like you,' she said carefully.

Ah. Garett allowed himself a small, playful smile. 'Who said anything about love?'

He saw her shoulders soften with relief. He had been right. That was it.

'You mean, Sienna, that you might like to try a taste of afternoon delight without any strings attached?'

'I wouldn't put it quite like that. It's just that…I want to know what I've been missing, but I can't bear being hurt.'

There spoke a woman after his own heart—though not the business about being hurt, of course. Garett had developed armour plating at the age of six. There wasn't a woman alive who could get through that, he was sure. His mother was dead, and he had seen it happen. That was why he was determined to treat women in the way they deserved, with generosity, expertise and fun—because Gilda Lazlo had never known anything like that in her short, miserable life. Her son had spent his own life trying to make up for that. It was a challenge to which he was perfectly suited, in body, mind and spirit.

'So…if we were to…' She looked away, embarrassed. 'You wouldn't tell anyone about it, Garett? Not Kane, or Molly, or anyone at all?'

'No, of course not. That is not the action of a gentleman.'

They looked at each other for long moments. Then Sienna made a tiny movement toward him. Before she could change her mind he was there, taking her in his arms again.

'What will everyone say if they find out?'

'They aren't going to find out. Nobody will ever know. And if they did, they'd all wonder what took you so long.'

'Even Imelda?'

'Imelda will be green with envy.'

Sienna put her hands on his shoulders and levered herself out of his grasp long enough to give him a look of amused astonishment.

'You really think a lot of yourself, don't you, Mr Garett Lazlo?'

'I have to, or nobody else will,' he said succinctly, his eyes on her lips. 'Now, let's have no more talking.'

He kissed her, pushing his fingers through the tangle of her hair to draw her near, cupping her shoulders. His every movement urged her to snuggle closer. Marriage had taught Sienna to see sex in terms of duty, not lust. When Garett responded to her tentative hands it was with a speed that took her breath away. She felt his taut muscles glide under the smooth golden skin, with well-practised economical movements. His touch was already moving over her top, pulling it down to expose the thin flesh-coloured bra beneath. Those actions gave her such a rush of adrenaline that her own fingers went to the buttons of his shirt, desperate to expose his warm, perfect skin. Peeling the white cotton away from his shoulders, she was entranced once again by the dusting of dark hair across the taut perfection of his chest.

'Two can play at that game.' He leaned forward, simultaneously removing her top and burying his face against the fluid curve of her shoulder. Sexual electricity crackled through her, as brutal as the rasp of his cheek against her delicate skin.

'I need a shave.' He looked down with wicked amusement. Her creamy white shoulder was pink with the pressure from his slightly roughened chin. It was a physical manifestation of his masculinity, and it gave her an extra tingle of pleasure.

'It doesn't matter,' Sienna breathed, closing her eyes. She was being transported to a totally different world. This was all so different from her previous experiences of sex. She wanted everything to be new and exciting, to touch and be touched in ways that would have been unthinkable during her life with Aldo. Her *half*-life, she realised, as Garett's hands swept over her back and dived into the waistband of her skirt.

They were still standing up, and this was broad daylight. Intimacy for Garett was clearly not some brief embarrassment, to be hidden away in the darkness of night. He was relishing every moment. She could see it in the clear, untroubled planes of his face, and in his eyes, half closed, but still watching her from beneath those long dark, lashes. He intended her to enjoy the sensation, too.

With practised movements he removed her skirt. His long, strong fingers were massaging her bottom through the thin fabric of her silk panties. Slowly, dreamily, she began moving in response to his touch: pushing herself against the resistance of his hands. As he drew his teeth across her throat, sending shiver after shiver of pleasure streaming through her body, his thumbs hooked into the flimsy ties at the sides of her briefs. When she realised what he was doing, Sienna wriggled with pleasure. The movement helped him to release the ribbons. With a gasp she felt the insubstantial triangles of lace fall away. Before she could pull back in alarm his hands returned to her shoulders, pulling her into a kiss that made the world fall away.

'Garett…' she breathed, as his lips moved across her cheek to taste the outline of her ear.

'I know.'

Lifting her off her feet, he strode across the salon. Kicking open the bedroom door, he took her inside. But the force he had used to enter frightened her. Feeling her go rigid in his arms, he stopped and looked at her sharply.

'If you are having second thoughts, Sienna, now is the time to call a halt.'

'You would do that for me?'

'I would do it for any woman.'

She watched his face minutely. 'Despite the way you opened that door?'

'What? Oh, Sienna.' He laughed. "To put you down and use my hand on the latch would have ruined the moment. Rather like conversation,' he finished pointedly.

Tentatively, Sienna lifted a hand to his hair. Savouring the feel of the fine, dense darkness, she moved her fingers upward until her palm was close to his ear.

'And has it?'

In response he moved his head to lean gently against her hand. 'No, Sienna. No, it has not…' His voice was low and rough, as though he was not used to whispering. 'Tell me how much you want me.'

She closed her eyes. There was no time for speech. Her lips parted as a small moan of anticipation escaped. He did not need any more encouragement. Tossing her lightly onto the bed, he followed her with the predatory grace of a panther. She felt herself quail beneath the towering masculinity of his need—but only for an instant. As he took her mouth with an urgent kiss of possession she felt a shockwave of desire sear through her whole body. Engulfing her with his arms, he pulled her into a savage embrace. He was an irresistible force. She absorbed it with a frisson of fear tipped with excitement. She was powerless to resist. He assaulted all her senses at once. The warm, sweet fragrance of his masculinity, the pressure of his body against hers, the sound of her name on his lips… She was a petal, tumbled and teased and overwhelmed by the hurricane of his desire.

The shadow of him moved over her like a cloud. She closed her eyes, blinded by pleasure as his mouth sought hers. His tongue was a dagger of desire, thrusting into her mouth as he kissed, kissed and kissed again. Roving over her body with his hands, he was eager to sample delight. She felt the tiny abrasions as his work-hardened hands slid over her silky skin to cup the fullness of her breasts. His thumbs moved in circles, tantalising her nipples into rigid peaks. Her whole body began to rise, synchronised with his rhythmic movements. The friction of his arousal excited her still more, until uncontrollable cries of longing stole all the breath from her body. Over and over she pleaded for a release from the temptation that had burned within her since their first meeting.

'Wait…I want to make this last—for both of us.'

He held his body taut against the soft appeal of hers. Desire for her had almost robbed him of control, but he never allowed anything to spoil his pleasure.

'Garett…' she called to him softly, pleading with her eyes. They were large and dark with unspoken promise. 'I've waited so long for this moment… Oh, Garett, I want you so badly…'

'You can have everything you want. Just reach out. There are no limits…'

His breath escaped in a low throb of desire. She would never know how tight a curb he had been keeping on his own libido since he had first seen her, first imagined her here in bed, in his arms and in his power… The reality was even better than his wildest fantasies. There was nothing to compare with the sweet softness of Sienna's skin beneath his fingers, the texture of her nipples against his tongue and the undiluted tang of rosewater on her skin. The pleasure was so intense it was all he could do to stop himself plunging into her straight away, sinking to the hilt in the warm, welcoming depth he had imagined so vividly.

His heart was racing. Any moment now he was going to gain the ultimate prize.

Sienna's hands clenched on his shoulders. She could hear her breath sighing. As long as she could take him with her—all the way—she was ready to plunge off this precipice of desire...

'I've never felt like this before,' she gasped. 'Oh, Garett...love me...'

They coupled and tumbled all afternoon and long into the night. Garett filled her body, mind and senses with absolute rapture. All memory of her cold, lonely marriage evaporated like frost in sunlight. They moved through dreams of cotton sheets and flickering firelight. Sienna could not remember falling asleep. Only the lightness of his fingers as they traced over the smooth, soft skin of her thigh...

She drifted into the next day through a haze of warmth and perfume. For long moments she lay still and silent, hoping not to disturb him. It had been a hot, heady night. Lying on her side like this, she could see straight out of the open French doors leading onto the master bedroom's balcony. The sun was a ripe peach, hanging over the pine ridge. It was just waiting to be enjoyed to the full.

Sienna relished the silence for a few moments more, wondering what they might get up to with a whole summer day stretching ahead of them. The builders were practically finished on the estate. Garett would not be needed for work. She could keep him trapped within her arms for as long as she liked. The idea of his long, strong limbs tangling with hers again began to arouse her fully from sleep. Lazily, she stretched out in the bed, intending to stroke him with her instep. She reached, and then rolled over to find him in their enormous playground—but he was not there. The bed was empty. She ran her hands over the tumbled sheets. They were as cold as only cotton could be.

Sitting up, she listened for any sounds coming through from the adjoining bathroom. There was absolute silence.

'Garett?'

Sliding out of bed, she grabbed her negligee and, barefoot, started off across the bedroom. Billowing silk and lace around her shoulders, she pushed open the *en suite* bathroom door and went in. The marble floor was cool and welcoming, but the room was empty. She went through the door leading directly from the wet-room into the dressing room beyond. That was empty, too.

'Garett?'

The windows on this side of the house were closed. Looking down onto the courtyard, she saw that his ice-blue hire-car was gone.

Don't panic, she told herself. That's the first thing the old Sienna would have done. There are a million reasons why he is not here. He might have gone out to fetch a newspaper, or a surprise breakfast from the village.

Then she thought of the internet news he accessed in his site office each morning. He had no need to visit the shops. And his instructions to Sienna about spending freely but wisely had extended to grocery deliveries. To save her time and stress, everything was brought right to the door. She knew that fresh orange juice and pastries would be waiting downstairs for her right now.

Where was Garett? What could he possibly need?

It would have been the act of a desperate woman to rush

outside and interrogate the first builder she met. Sienna was desperate, but discretion was ingrained in her. She forced herself to shower and dress before going downstairs. She was still pulling a brush through her hair as she dashed into the small salon leading from the villa's great hall. Garett had transferred his site office from the Bradleys' villa the moment there had been a decent space on site.

She walked around the desk to see if it held any clues to his disappearance. A screensaver of the *Spinifex* cut across the blank screen. She hit a key at random and found herself staring at his computer's calendar. Garett was meticulous in all things. Every delivery, each appointment for the Entroterra project was logged by date and time. He never left anything to chance. She could track everything—right through to the projected completion date. Sienna studied each day, but there was nothing to suggest any problem or appointment that would drag him away from her bed.

With growing panic she thought back over those past few frantic hours. Two memories—one bitter, one sweet— collided in her mind. She remembered the remark he had made, as light as air, that he could leave at any minute, ready to take up the carefree life of a water gypsy. And as his voice echoed across the emptiness, she heard herself calling out to him through the shadows of night: *'Love me, Garett, I love you so much…'*

She had felt him draw back at the time—only minutely, but the movement had definitely been there.

Sienna covered her face with her hands. What had she done? Of all the things to say to a free spirit like Garett, whose life was so different from her own that she could not begin to understand him. A declaration like that must have been poison to him. He had obviously waited until she'd fallen asleep and then left her.

Ice water ran through her veins. She thought desperately of where he might go. Perhaps he had stopped by to pick up his things from the Bradleys'. Before she could think of ringing them, a warning message flashed up on the computer screen in front of her. It was a list of meetings based in New York. The first was to happen in fewer than eighteen hours, and after that the calendar was divided up into time slots and notes, all referring to Garett.

Her words of love must have been too much, and he had thrown himself back into work. She was sure of it. As she watched, the screen refreshed itself again. This time it was with confirmation that a single first-class flight to New York had been booked in Garett's name.

It was a one-way ticket.

CHAPTER TWELVE

IT WAS a long time before Sienna got up from the computer screen. She was red-eyed and resigned. There was no point in chasing after him. Instinctively she had always known this would happen, but now she was faced with the agonising reality. Garett was a free agent. He had never made any secret about that. Now he had made the decision to go. But he had torn out her heart and taken it with him. She walked slowly out into the kitchen, trying to come to terms with what had happened.

When she opened her brand-new maximum efficiency fridge, the flood of cold air brought her to her senses. Her whole life had been spent living in the past—until Garett arrived. He had taught her to look forward to the future, not back. She had made a monumental mistake in opening up to him, and he had acted completely in character. He had taken action, and moved on. Sienna realised that was what *she* must do now. There were final arrangements to be made with the builders and landscapers working around her estate. It was nothing she could not handle, fired by the confidence Garett had inspired in her.

But Sienna did not feel inspired. She felt small,

abandoned and alone. She poured herself a long, cold glass of fresh orange juice. Then she put two croissants to warm and went to look for the organic chocolate spread.

She moved around her sparkling new kitchen in a daze. Plates were rattled and cutlery was dropped instead of being placed. She hardly knew what she was doing. The warm bouquet of hot, buttery pastry and freshly ground coffee only added to her misery. They were all things that Garett had brought her. Now she had ruined everything by saying the one thing a man like that never wanted to hear. Abandonment was no more than she should have expected. His awful childhood must have damaged him, planted something wayward in his nature. After all, he had told her about those legions of girls in his past. And it was no more than Molly had joked about.

Working on automatic, Sienna loaded her croissants with chocolate spread.

Yes, she realised slowly, Garett brought all this into my life. But he never *bought* it, she reminded herself. She had kept her integrity right to the end. She had only slept with him when she wanted to—not because it had been part of some bargain. The authenticated painting meant she would be able to hold on to her honour independently, too.

Piling her tray with the pastries, the glass of juice and a foaming cappuccino, she headed back to Garett's office to call up the Lazlo, Manhattan, website.

What she read there confirmed all her worst fears. A newsflash announced that the boss was back in command after his unscheduled break.

That was all it had ever been, Sienna told herself: a beautiful, temporary dream. She closed her eyes, reliving

every touch, every kiss, each burning moment of searing
passion they had shared. Then a call from somewhere far
away, from Imelda's suite, reminded her that she was on her
own again. Or at least she would be—if she could find that
inner strength Garett had always talked about. She opened
her eyes and stared down at her abandoned breakfast. Then
she came to a decision. She picked up the telephone.

Garett Lazlo had certainly made things happen on the
Entroterra estate. But Sienna had started to realise she
could do that, too. The changes around this place had only
just begun. She would see to that.

Garett began regretting his action the instant he eased his
way from beneath Sienna's sleeping body. His pride kept
telling him it was for the best. She had told him she loved
him, and any woman who made that sort of claim meant
nothing but trouble. He knew that from bitter experience.
Work was the only worthwhile mistress, his inner voice
repeated, over and over again.

Now, he strode through airports and subway stations,
oblivious to the packs of photographers and journalists
who hunted him all the way back to his office. The racket
was phenomenal. It crushed in on him like a pain. He had
forgotten just how loud New York City was. It was as
different from the peace and beauty of Entroterra as
Sienna's *latte* was from instant coffee.

That thought worked like aversion therapy as a secretary greeted him with a cup of double-decaffeinated, as
prescribed by his healthcare team. He grimaced, and
handed it straight over to the girl who introduced herself
as his new PA. Within thirty seconds Garett was yearning

for Sienna's soft lilt, and the prospect of her home cooking. But he soon confined those longings to memory. This was his future—where he belonged.

Three weeks went by. Garett's face was never off the TV screen and the front pages of the newspapers. The novelty of a billionaire strolling back into work after disappearing like a high-school drop-out fascinated everyone—everyone except Sienna, it seemed. Garett had almost expected her to call, and when he hadn't heard from her he'd felt an unfamiliar twist of disappointment. Renewed publicity about his wealth had brought conquests old and new flocking around him, but not Sienna. Now he was beginning to realise he had underestimated her. She was different. He knew that now. She had never once asked him directly for money. Quite the opposite, he thought—and realised that for the first time since he'd left Entroterra he was smiling. His expression broadened still further when he remembered what she *had* begged him for, on that final night. And how often…

He leaned back in his chair. That was another new sensation. Work no longer filled his every waking moment. Sienna had cured him of that, by showing him how bad things could be for a woman married to an obsessive man. Aldo di Imperia had worshipped money. Garett's own father had been a slave to the bottle. Determined to avoid that particular fate, Garett had been married to his work and it had ruined his life, he realised. But meeting Sienna had changed all that. It had given him a wider perspective. Now he could see how life should be.

Happiness did not rely on how much money you had.

It came from within. And the greatest happiness came with the sort of love he had never imagined could exist for him: pure and simple. Meeting Sienna had allowed him to make that connection. It completed the circuit. The final piece in the jigsaw of his life had dropped into place. How could he have been so blind for so long? All these years he had been searching in a haphazard quest for fulfilment. Nothing had come close to providing him with a solution, because finding Sienna had been the answer to all the emptiness he had been trying to fill for the past thirty years. He realised now what he had been searching for all this time. There had been a hole in his life—and Sienna fitted it perfectly.

Now all he had to do was find out how to make everything right for her.

Sienna tried to blot out the memory of Garett, but it was hopeless. Visions of him and the ghostly touch of his fingers taunted her at every turn. The way he had walked out on her was seared into her mind for ever—but so were thoughts of his kindness, his body, and the night of love they had shared.

It was beyond all sense.

And that was what made Garett so unforgettable. He had shown her just how good life could be, and she loved him for it.

She loved him. That was the unbelievable truth.

You can have everything you want. Just reach out. There are no limits…

The last words Garett had said to her haunted Sienna's every waking moment. His voice echoed through her daydreams. He had brought her so much: self-esteem, and a sense of purpose. And Sienna's villa had been awakened from years of neglect. Garett's expertise had brought it back to life and given her a home to be proud of. Now she could walk through its grand halls and high passageways, marvelling at the gleam of gold leaf and the sheen of polished marble.

The house had changed out of all recognition, and so had Sienna. She had been a mousy, downtrodden little thing when Garett had first blown into her life. Now she felt…different. If it hadn't been physically impossible, Sienna would have sworn she was several inches taller. She was certainly lighter. Lately, she had lost her appetite. Garett was the cause of that, too. Thoughts of him left no time in her life for picking treats from the larder. Now the waistband of her jeans seemed roomier, somehow. Losing him had changed her—both physically and mentally. She was no longer afraid to look anyone in the eye. Garett had started by teaching her that everyone had a right to make the best of their life. He had given her the confidence to believe it.

Then he'd pulled the rug out from under her feet by abandoning her.

The only way Sienna could cope was by telling herself the whole affair had been a one-sided holiday romance. She could only deal with it by trying to make a completely fresh start. Her mind was made up. But her heart was empty.

Imelda was the first casualty of her broken dreams. Sienna's stepmother was moved into one of the newly refurbished estate cottages, next to Ermanno and his wife. Her rage counted for nothing, because Sienna was determined. She was going to sell the villa, and that meant losing its sitting tenant. The sale went through almost immediately, much to Sienna's relief. She could not wait to get back to the little village house where she had been born. It was her intention to open it as a bakery again, following the age-old tradition of her family.

Putting the worries and heartbreak associated with Entroterra and its estate behind her should have been a tremendous relief, but Sienna could not appreciate it. On her last day as owner of the villa, she took a final walk around the beautiful old house. Strolling into any of the grand salons, the ballroom or the drawing room, she could dazzle every newly restored corner with the flick of a light switch—but her life remained dark. Garett had left her a bed of roses, but she was alone in it. The single person who had made all this possible was lost to her for ever. His monument was in the perfect plasterwork and glowing gold leaf, the clean lines and classic beauty of a house ready to be filled and loved, as it deserved.

Leaning over the banisters, she gazed down into the airy entrance hall. From this vantage point she only half heard a car draw up outside, but there was no doubt somebody had arrived. She heard the vehicle's door slam, and the rattle of keys. Checking her watch, she pinned on her practised smile. The new owner was early.

She started along the landing, and down the wide, sweeping staircase. Her steps were slower and slower and she tried to put off the evil moment when she became a stranger in her own house. The villa had felt like a prison when Aldo was alive, but now it was showing its true potential, and she realised she was quite attached to the old place. It was all thanks to Garett. The irony was, her change of heart had come too late.

At the exact moment her foot touched the marble tiles of the ground floor, the great oak doors of the villa swung open. Sienna made a tremendous effort to raise her head and smile. Then she stopped.

'Garett? What are you doing here?'

'I might well ask you the same thing.'

His tone of voice gave nothing away. His expression was hidden from her too, as he entered the building and closed the door behind him. Then he turned and leaned back against the thick wood of the door, holding up the huge iron key that he had used to get in. 'I was told I would have vacant possession of my new home.'

'*You're* the buyer? But how?'

'The same way anyone buys a house anywhere.' His dark eyes were as watchful as ever. 'I told my agents where I wanted to live, and they found me an ideal place a few miles beyond Genoa. Then, as my pen was hovering over the dotted line, I got news that Entroterra was up for sale. The money you got for the painting wasn't enough for you, I take it?'

'Memories made me sell. Not money,' Sienna replied, flexing the spine of steel he had discovered for her.

Garett's lips moved, but they did not make it as far as a smile. When he spoke again it was with slow deliberation.

'Good ones, I hope?'

She shook her head.

'That's my fault, I suppose?'

She did not deny it.

He was dressed immaculately, in a dark suit and tie, white shirt, and black shoes polished to such a high gloss they reflected the chandelier in stars. Sienna remembered the times she had stared at his feet in the past, too nervous to look him in the eye. Now she could trap his gaze. She had to rely on hearing the squeak of his leather soles against the tiles to tell her that he was uneasy. There was certainly no sign of it in his steady, level stare.

'Sienna, when I left you here, I never expected to come back—but I could not stop myself. I've been a fool for thirty years. All it took was a few weeks with you to show me how life should be. I thought I could shrug off the experience and go back refreshed, but basically the same. It didn't work. I need the peace and tranquillity of this place, and, more importantly, I've discovered that I can't live without you.' His gaze held hers.

Sienna did not say anything for some moments. Dealing with agents and Imelda and every other trouble that had been forced onto her had taken an enormous toll. Faced with his confession, it all became too much. For a few seconds she forgot everything he had taught her. Lowering her head, she shook it slowly.

'What do you want me to say?'

He took half a dozen steps towards her across the echoing hall.

'I might have been attracted to a mouse, Sienna, but I fell in love with a girl who has more spirit than that.'

'Love?' She sprang back to life. 'You took me to bed, then you abandoned me!'

Sienna watched his reaction to her accusation. He looked as honest and apologetic as she felt, but she still had to know for certain.

'How do I know you won't leave me again, Garett?'

'Because I've come back to marry you.'

In one movement he covered the distance that still separated them and silenced her cry of astonishment with a long, lingering kiss. He kissed her until she could barely remember her own name, much less why she had been angry with him.

'You are mine, and you have been the only woman for me since the moment I first set eyes on you in the market,' he breathed, his voice dark with seduction. 'Marry me. I need you—now and for ever.'

There should have been no argument left. Garett had made up his mind, so there was no more to be said. It was one of the things about him that Sienna had known from the start. But she had to be sure.

'I don't want to be hurt again, Garett.'

'You won't be. I promise you that.'

'But you left me,' she persisted. 'You walked off and abandoned me while I was asleep in bed.'

'That was nothing but my stupid pride. It took a lot to keep me heading back to New York. I let work suck me into its vortex again—but nothing was ever the same. It couldn't be. My heart was no longer in it, so my team has taken control of the business, and I'm determined to take a back seat. I told the Bradleys I was coming back for you, but Molly says you've shut them out. I'm sorry, Sienna.' He threw up his hands and let them fall to his sides. 'I should never have left you. No amount of words can put that right. So will you let my actions speak for me?' he said slowly, a cautious smile playing around his lips.

For seconds on end they were held in a universe made for two. Then her lips parted in a slow smile.

She nodded, and immediately he took her in his arms.

Their kiss became a slow exploration of their new relationship.

'I just can't help acting on impulse where you are concerned,' he murmured softly, as his kisses moved from her lips to her earlobe.

'I don't mind that at all,' Sienna breathed, safe again in the security of his arms. 'All that matters is that you will never leave me again.'

'You can be quite sure of that, my love,' he murmured, sipping another kiss.

WHEN ONLY DIAMONDS WILL DO

BY
LINDSAY ARMSTRONG

Lindsay Armstrong was born in South Africa, but now lives in Australia with her New Zealand-born husband and their five children. They have lived in nearly every state of Australia and have tried their hand at some unusual occupations, such as farming and horse-training—all grist to the mill for a writer! Lindsay started writing romances when their youngest child began school and she was left feeling at a loose end. She is still doing it and loving it.

In 2011, Lindsay's book THE SOCIALITE AND THE CATTLE KING won a R*BY award in the "Short Sexy" category.

PROLOGUE

REITH RICHARDSON slammed his phone down and swore beneath his breath.

His secretary, Alice Hawthorn, grey-haired and in her fifties, raised her eyebrows. 'Francis Theron, I gather?'

'You gather right,' Reith agreed. 'He doesn't believe I'm a suitable person to be—' he paused and grimaced '—within a hundred miles of his beloved winery, no doubt. Despite the fact he's in dire straits, despite the fact my offer is the only one he's got and he could end up bankrupt in the near future.'

'Hmm…' Alice mused. 'A very socially prominent family, the Therons of Balthazar and Saldanha. Very proud.'

'You know what they say about pride and the proverbial fall,' Reith murmured. 'OK, Alice, I'm withdrawing the offer I made. I'll leave the Therons to their fate.' He bundled the papers before him into a stack and handed them over to her.

'There's a daughter, you know,' Alice said, as she

packed the papers into a folder. 'An absolute stunner, I believe. About twenty-two.'

Reith shrugged. 'Maybe they need to find her a rich husband who can save them all.'

'There's also a son.'

'I know, I've met him—all the right schools, top polo player, seriously into horses, in fact, but singularly unblessed with any business sense,' Reith replied dryly then he smiled a crooked grin. 'Maybe they need to find *him* a horsy but rich wife.'

Alice laughed and got up. 'Will you be in Perth or Bunbury for the next few days?'

'Bunbury, probably, there's a stud down that way I'm interested in. Alice,' Reith said with a frown as he looked around his office, one of his new luxury suite of offices in Perth that overlooked the Swan River, 'I don't like the artwork the interior decorator's supplied. I don't know why, it just doesn't do anything for me.'

Alice looked around at the Impressionist landscapes and marine life on the walls. 'Well, perhaps you ought to choose it yourself?' she suggested.

Reith got up and strolled over to the windows. 'All right, when I get the time,' he said wryly. 'Thanks, Alice.'

She took the hint but when she got back to her desk she sat deep in thought for a while. It wasn't often her boss backed a wrong hunch—made an offer that was knocked back, in other words. In fact his timing was usually impeccable and he was little short of a genius when it came to buying businesses in trouble and turning them around. It was how he'd consolidated a small fortune made from a mining venture into a very large fortune, but this was obviously different. This was something that involved pride and history; the Therons went back a long way to their Huguenot ancestors in South Africa and viticulture ran in their veins.

Whereas Reith Richardson went back to a cattle station beyond the black stump...

Alice shrugged and patted the folder she was about to file away for the last time. Concerning her boss, there were times when she fervently wished herself twenty years younger, and other times when she felt rather motherly. This was one of those motherly times, she decided. A time when she wished he would be a little more understanding, a little less the steel-hard businessman.

What he really needed, she mused, was a softening influence in his life, like a wife. And heaven knew there were plenty of women who found his tall, dark looks fascinating but of course his disinclination to marry any of them could be due to the fact that he had lost his first wife.

Alice stopped her thoughts at this point as her phone rang and she was completely unaware that, at the same time, her boss was staring at a framed photo on his desk and thinking about his lost wife.

It wasn't a photo of his wife but a boy, a freckled, fair boy who went by the name of Darcy Richardson. His only son, his only child. Born of a girl who had been little more than a child herself except in years. She'd been nineteen when they'd married because she was pregnant, twenty when she'd given birth to Darcy and died from unforeseen complications.

And he very much doubted he'd ever get over the guilt he felt. Guilt because it had all happened so quickly. He'd never expected a pregnancy but he should have sensed that she was being naïve when she claimed she was protected; a country girl who'd stopped taking the Pill when it made her sick. But most of all guilt over her dying—as if he'd caused it.

And now the guilt over Darcy, his son, who'd been mostly brought up by his maternal grandmother until six months ago when she'd died. Darcy, who wore a polite protective shell around him that he, his father, could not get through.

Darcy, who was coming soon from his boarding school, not only to remind his father of his mother, who he looked a lot like—not that he knew it—but also to be the perfect guest in his own home.

Reith Richardson dug his hands into his pockets and breathed savagely. Give him sterile business relationships rather than complicated, tense, still-waters-run-deep, personal relationships any day.

And thinking of that led him to think of Frank Theron and what he'd said on the phone… *Not only have I got my family to think of but I've got my pride…*

You'd be better to concentrate on your family and forget about your pride, Mr Theron, he reflected, much better. And his expression hardened as he thought of Francis Theron and his son Damien…

CHAPTER ONE

'LADY—are you *mad*?'

A complete stranger said this as he got out of his car. He was breathing heavily.

There was dust swirling around them, dust raised when the stranger, in response to her signal for help, had almost driven his car into a large tree. He'd only corrected the situation at the last moment. The car was a late model gun-metal luxury four-wheel drive.

'I'm sorry,' she said hastily. 'My name is Kimberley Theron and I'm in a dreadful hurry but the thing is I appear to have run out of petrol. Would you be able to help?'

'Kimberley Theron?' the man she was addressing repeated.

'You may have heard of...well, not me so much but the name?' She looked at him searchingly, and her eyes suddenly widened.

Talk about tall, dark and handsome—no, not handsome; that was too bland a way to put it—rugged and interesting said it much better, she decided. He looked to be in his middle thirties. He was tanned with wide shoulders and an admirable physique beneath cargo pants and a grey sweatshirt. He had dark eyes and short dark hair.

'Kimberley Theron,' he repeated and studied her comprehensively from top to toe, then her silver convertible, its cream leather upholstery now coated with dust. 'Well, Miss Theron, has no one—' he folded his arms across his chest '—ever told you that dancing into the road pulling up your skirt and exposing your legs could cause…chaos?'

'Actually—' she paused for a moment and screwed up her forehead '—no one ever thought to mention that!' She looked down at her legs, now demurely clothed beneath her denim skirt. She looked up and her sapphire-blue eyes were laughing. 'I am sorry,' she said contritely, however. 'But I guess there is a funny side to it. I really couldn't think of any other way to make *sure* you stopped.'

He didn't look amused. He swore beneath his breath instead and looked around. It was a country road with lion-coloured paddocks running along either side of it. There was no sign of any habitation in either direction; there was absolutely no sign of any traffic. The sun was beating down.

He said, 'I can't siphon off any fuel for you because I run on diesel; you don't. Where are you going?'

'Bunbury. Are you— You *are* going in the right direction. Is there any chance I could get a lift with you?'

The stranger looked Kimberley Theron up and down again. Early twenties, he guessed, and she *was* stunning, with red-gold hair, those sapphire eyes, a good figure, not to mention, he thought dryly, sensational legs.

There was also an innate liveliness to her you couldn't mistake, even if she had just about caused you to collide with a very big tree.

There was more, though. Behind the liveliness and whimsical humour lurked a...what was it?...an unshakeable conviction that she was no mere mortal—she was a Theron! And, consequently, begging a lift from a complete stranger posed no hazards.

He grimaced. 'All right, but are you just going to leave it here?' He gestured to her car.

'No.' She hesitated. 'Here's the other thing, my phone has run out of battery. Would you have a mobile on you? And, if so, could I borrow it to call home and get them to come and pick the car up? I would pay for the call, naturally. And, naturally, I would pay for the petrol to get to Bunbury.'

'You don't have to—'

'I insist,' she told him with an imperious little toss of her head.

He looked at her then shrugged and pulled his phone out of his pocket and handed it to her. Moments later he was treated to a one-sided Theron to Theron conversation.

'Hello, Mum, it's Kim. Darling, be an angel...'

And there followed all the details of Kim Theron's predicament, plus the indication that she wasn't completely impractical as she gave a short but accurate description of his car, including the registration number. Then she ended the call and handed his phone back to him with a rueful expression.

'Sorry, I hope you didn't mind me giving my mother some details about you, but she's a worrier.'

He looked at her ironically.

'And that explains that, so I don't have to feel completely stupid!' she went on. 'My mother borrowed my car and neglected to replace the petrol she used. I didn't even think to check the gauge because I was in such a rush.'

'Why are you in such a rush?' he enquired.

'Can I tell you as we go along?'

He hesitated briefly, then gestured for her to get in.

'My friend Penny,' she said, settling herself into the passenger seat and doing up her seat belt, 'one of my best friends, is pregnant and the baby is—*was* due in a fortnight but she's gone into labour this morning. Her mother's in Melbourne—other side of the continent—her husband's driving a barge out from Port Hedland. She has no one else and it's her first baby.'

'I see,' he said. 'Did it cross your mind, once you'd phoned home, to wait for one of your family to come and rescue you?'

She shook her head. 'Saldanha, where I live, I mean, is half an hour's drive the *other* way and by the time they'd organized things—' she gestured expressively '—I could have lost hours.' She turned to him. 'Do you *mind* doing this?'

He changed gear to negotiate a sharp bend and wondered what she'd say if he told her that the last person he'd wanted to meet was a member of the Theron family of Saldanha and Balthazar...

'I was going to Bunbury anyway,' he said.

Kim watched him for a long moment, then, 'What's your name?'

'Reith.'

'That's unusual. What is it? Welsh?'

'No idea.' He shrugged.

'How strange,' Kim murmured.

He flicked her another ironic little glance. 'I suppose you know exactly where your name comes from?'

'As a matter of fact, I do,' she said gravely, although her eyes were sparkling. 'I was named after a diamond mine.'

'That's—' he paused '—curiously appropriate.'

'What does that mean?' Kim queried.

'You look like a diamond kind of girl.'

'I'm so glad you didn't say I look like the kind of girl whose best *friends* are diamonds,' she responded and tossed her red-gold hair. But she went on, apparently not seriously offended, 'Want to know which diamond mine?'

'Let me guess. The Kimberley mine in South Africa.'

'Got it in one! You are clever…er…Reith. Not a lot of people—in Australia—know about Kimberley in South Africa although, of course, a lot of them know about the Kimberley area up north, also associated with diamonds.'

He said nothing.

'May I borrow your phone again?' she requested then. 'I could ring the hospital and find out how things are going.'

* * *

Things were going apace at the hospital and Kim was blinking rapidly as she ended the call. 'I'll be lucky to get there in time!'

'Hold on,' he recommended.

She held on and the next ten minutes were breathless until they hit the outskirts of Bunbury and finally made the hospital.

'Thanks so much,' she panted. 'I—'

'Just go.' He gestured.

'Wait here, though,' she ordered, 'I'll get the news. At least you deserve to know if everything's all right. Besides I owe you some money.' And she flung herself out of the car and up the hospital stairs.

Reith Richardson grimaced, hesitated for a moment then put his car into gear and was about to drive off when Kim reappeared and danced down the steps.

'Seven pounds, ten minutes ago, a boy, mother and son are both fine—' she beamed through the window '—and I can't thank you enough. However, here's the thing, I can't *pay* you because I forgot to bring any money!'

'I never expected to be paid for a couple of lousy phone calls, so forget it, Miss Theron.'

'Well, I wish I could but I didn't bring anything, actually.'

He stared at her. 'You mean—no credit cards, no cash card?'

'Nothing,' she said ruefully. 'Not that it'll be a problem when my car arrives—but I just would love to take some flowers with me when I'm allowed in to see Penny. They have a florist here but—'

She stopped as Reith reached into his pocket and pulled out a hundred dollars.

'Oh, thank you so much! But look, I need your address so I can repay you.' She fished in her pocket and brought out a scrap of paper and a pen.

Reith Richardson opened his mouth to tell her to forget it again, but he changed his mind as he put the money into her hand. 'Have dinner with me, only if you feel like it.' He named a restaurant and a time and, as she stepped back looking thoroughly surprised, he drove off.

At ten to seven that evening he was sitting at a table for two in a luxury restaurant that overlooked the bay. It was a blue and tinsel evening, deep blue sky and water through the wide windows, silver-white patterned moon looming in the sky.

Rather than the moon, he was contemplating the beer he'd ordered and a few other things. Would Kimberley Theron take up his invitation? Why had he issued it in the first place? Was there something about her that intrigued him—obviously, he thought impatiently—but what was it?

Her looks, her body, her legs? Had to be more than that...

'Penny for them?' the object of his thoughts murmured as she pulled out the chair opposite.

He stood up and had to smile in admiration.

She'd changed from her denim skirt and cotton blouse into a dusty-pink linen dress, sleeveless and round-necked, which she wore with a string of bauble-sized glass beads and emerald cork-soled platform sandals. Her hair was loose and casual and a pair of diamond earrings nestled in the red-gold strands.

She looked sensational but she also looked different, a more mature—no, that was the wrong word, he decided—a more sophisticated version of Kimberley Theron.

She slid into her chair with a sigh of relief, looked appreciatively at the moisture-dappled bottle of champagne in an ice bucket and said, 'How nice. Nice to sit down, nice to think of a deliciously cool glass of bubbly. Today,' she added as he sat down, 'has been one of my wackier days.'

He poured her champagne. 'Wacky? How are mother and son, by the way?'

'They really are fine, despite his early arrival. And despite me arriving too late—not your fault,' she hastened to assure him. 'Wacky? Yes. When I got Penny's call, she sounded so lost and scared I just dropped everything and...well—' she smiled at him '—you know the rest of it. Incidentally—' she reached into her purse and withdrew a hundred-dollar note, which she slid across the table towards him '—thank you so much.'

He let it lie on the table.

'I gather you've got your resources back?'

She nodded. 'Yes, my car got delivered to the hospital so I was able to go home and change, et cetera.' She sipped her champagne. 'Mmm... Delicious. Tell me something, Reith—what do you do?'

'This and that.'

She looked comically askance at him but she was

frowning. He'd changed his cargo pants and sweatshirt for jeans, a navy shirt open at the throat and a beautifully cut finest tweed sports jacket. And he wore a sports watch that would have cost a small fortune. All in all, he looked right at home in this very expensive restaurant, not to mention darkly attractive.

'That sounds rather evasive.' She traced the rim of her glass with one slender finger as she withdrew her senses from the masculine onslaught of the man and thought of his answer to her question.

'It's also true.' He shrugged. 'I specialize in buying and rescuing companies in trouble.'

Kim frowned. 'What's the appeal in that?'

He studied her for a long moment. 'What do you mean?'

'Well, usually one has a vocation; you're drawn to medicine or law or farming or something.'

'It's the challenge,' he said. 'It's always a learning curve but some business principles, supply and demand, for example, always stand whether you're dealing with fashion or minerals or sheep. What do you do?'

She took another sip of champagne and looked thoughtful. 'I teach. English,' she said and smiled at his expression. 'Thought that might surprise you,' she murmured.

He grimaced. 'Why?'

'Why did I think it would surprise you? I get the feeling you don't approve of me, Mr...um...Reith.' She eyed him with a glimmer of wry humour in her blue eyes. 'It's quite a strong feeling,' she added gently.

'You did nearly cause me to wipe myself out,' he reminded her.

She laughed. 'Yes, well, I've already confessed to having a...an unusual kind of day. I'm generally a much more organized person.'

His lips twitched and he shrugged.

Kim planted her elbows on the table and rested her chin in her hands. 'You couldn't have said it more eloquently if you'd actually spoken the words.'

He raised his eyebrows. 'What?'

'You find that hard to believe?'

'I...'

Kim sat back and interrupted. 'Not that I mind. We're a bit like ships in the night, aren't we?'

He didn't answer, merely studied her.

'Would you mind if we ordered dinner?'

'Not at all.'

'That's the other thing I messed up today,' she confided. 'I haven't had a thing to eat since breakfast. And do you mind if I order lobster? I always have lobster here; I can thoroughly recommend it.'

'Be my guest,' he murmured.

'Oh, I wouldn't dream of it. It's not cheap so I insist on paying for my dinner. Actually, I'd like to pay for yours too!'

As a way of cutting me down to size? Reith wondered. As a way of being a Theron and making others aware that they're not quite in the same class?

'As a way of saying thank-you for the lift today and for lending me money for flowers and suggesting dinner,' Kim murmured.

Their gazes clashed.

Had she read his mind? he wondered, then became aware of a resolve forming within him that he didn't think he'd be able to ignore—he wanted this girl in his bed; he wanted to find out how she liked being made love to, whether she was still a Theron to her fingertips when she was hot and excited and writhing beneath him.

'Do you surf?'

They were out in the cooling night air, strolling towards the car park, when Reith asked the question.

'Of course,' Kim said without hesitation.

'Of course?' he queried, glancing down at her with some irony.

She paused and looked up. She wasn't short, five feet six, plus her wedges tonight, which meant he had to be well over six feet, and a little frisson ran through her because he was not only tall but beautifully proportioned...

But why that look of irony? she wondered.

'Have I said something wrong?'

He took her hand and swung it. 'No, I suppose not.'

'Now come on, tell me,' she insisted.

He stopped walking and turned her to face him but it was a long moment before he replied. In fact as his gaze roamed up and down her figure then lingered ruefully on her legs, Kim experienced another frisson but this one seemed to sizzle between them.

Then he shrugged and said, 'It's just that I get the feeling you do everything well—ride, swim, surf, play

tennis, play the piano, draw or paint, speak fluent—
something or other and—'

'Stop!' She held up her free hand. 'You're having a
go at me, aren't you? You still think I'm rich and idle,
despite the fact that I work.'

He rubbed his jaw reflectively. 'Not idle, no, but for
the rest of it, you have the sort of assurance that leads
one to suspect you of attending a good finishing school.
Do you do any of those things?'

'I…' Kim closed her mouth and shrugged resign-
edly. 'I do swim and surf. I ride. I don't play the piano
but I do play the harp, I do play tennis, I do speak fluent Spanish—but I do not draw or paint!' she finished
triumphantly. 'Mind you, I have a good eye for art,'
she confessed. 'But, tell me this, what's it all got to do
with surfing?'

'Should we go down to Margaret River for a surf
tomorrow?' He paused. 'The weather forecast is good
and the swell is up.'

Kim's lips parted and her eyes lit up. 'I can think of
nothing nicer, Mr—what *is* your name?'

His eyes narrowed for no reason she could detect.
'Richardson,' he said and waited a moment. 'Reith
Richardson.'

'Well, Mr Richardson, I'd love to! I haven't surfed
for a while.'

'And you can just take off from your teaching job
when and wherever?' he queried.

'Oh, no, but I have time off at the moment. I did
some overtime in the boarding house.' She raised her
eyebrows. 'Where shall we meet?'

'Would you mind driving down to Busselton?'

'No-o,' Kim said slowly.

He swung her hand. 'I have a very early appointment down there—it would save me driving back. We can go on in one car.'

'Sure,' she said easily.

He lifted her hand and kissed her knuckles.

Kim swallowed as a tremor of pure physical attraction towards this tall, dark, rugged stranger ran through her. But he didn't feel like a stranger any more, although she didn't know much more about him than she'd known earlier in the day.

Well, she knew he preferred steak to lobster, beer to champagne, that his hands were clean and scrubbed but scarred and callused as if he'd done plenty of physical work at some time or another. Yet he sounded educated and well-read.

He released her hand as they reached her car. 'Try not to lure any more men to their doom against large, immovable objects, Miss Theron,' he advised as she unlocked the driver's door.

She laughed, 'I won't!'

'Oh, and this.' He took her purse from her and tucked her hundred-dollar note into it.

'But—'

'I'd like to pay for the flowers, that's all. Goodnight.'

'You know—' Kim stared up at him '—I've got the feeling you're quite addicted to getting your own way.'

'I have been accused of that, yes,' he agreed gravely. 'It's nonsense, of course.' He paused. 'On the other hand, we could be two of a kind.'

'Do you think so?' Kim asked wryly. 'That could make for some uncomfortable times between us, assuming we last any kind of distance. Goodnight.'

His lips twitched. 'It could. Yes, it could. Goodnight.'

Kim drove home in a thoughtful mood.

The moon was silvering the familiar landscape, so it wasn't familiar any more but an exotic surround with secretive dark patches.

Of course, she knew it off by heart but, thinking of how secretive and unknown in the moonlight it looked now, her thoughts took off down another path. Was she entering an unknown period of her life?

How could she be as affected as she was by a man she'd only just met? There was no doubt he sent shivers down her spine—shivers of pleasure. One light kiss on her knuckles had not only raised goose bumps for her but it had caused her to warm to him as if they could be friends who cared for each other.

Or was that being extremely fanciful? she asked herself as she swung into the driveway of the estate called Saldanha, the place she had always called home.

Set against the background of the Darling Range foothills, Saldanha was special. The Harvey and Margaret River districts south of Perth in Western Australia were beautiful and diverse, with their white beaches, jarrah forests, sleek cattle and the sheer fertility that produced glorious gardens. And adjacent to Saldanha was the Balthazar Winery, also owned by her parents—the other, and probably most famous, export of the area that grew premium grapes was wine.

Both Saldanha and Balthazar—a Balthazar was a

twelve-litre wine bottle—were the names brought by the Theron family, of Huguenot descent, from South Africa to the similar conditions and climate around Perth. The Theron family had also brought their viticulture skills and the Balthazar Winery had flourished. At the same time Saldanha, named after a sheltered bay north of Cape Town, had flourished and the Cape Dutch–style architecture of the house, white gables and a thatched roof, had become distinctive in the district.

So had the classic dry white that Balthazar was famous for as well as its Cellar Door, run on the estate and visited by wine-lovers from all over the world.

It was none of this Kim Theron was thinking of as she parked her car, greeted her dog, a devoted blue heeler that went by the name of Sunny Bob, and let herself into the darkened house.

Her parents were out and her brother no longer lived at home, although he kept his horses there, and the housekeeper had taken the opportunity to visit family.

But, as she switched on some lamps and kicked off her shoes, Kim's thoughts were still firmly centred on Reith Richardson.

Was it unusual to suggest they go surfing? she wondered. Perhaps, but a great idea nonetheless.

She paused at the foot of the stairs as she tried to analyse her emotions. She was intrigued, without a doubt. But, of course, as the saying went: look before you leap…

She had no idea, as she stood with her hand on the banister, how that phrase was going to come back to haunt her.

* * *

Margaret River was beautiful.

The peaceful river gave its name to a district that stretched between two capes—Cape Naturaliste and Cape Leeuwin—and ran inland as well. The town of Margaret River was not the only one in the area; there were quite a few, from Busselton to Yallingup and Cowaramup and more. There were some magnificent kauri forests as well as some fascinating limestone caves. The whole district was renowned not only for its wine but also its cuisine.

It was straight to the beach that Reith Richardson steered his four-wheel vehicle, though, after he'd collected Kim from their appointed meeting place in Busselton, along with her surfboard—and her dog.

'Hope you don't mind,' Kim said as she introduced them. 'Reith, this is Sunny Bob, and this, Sunny Bob,' she said to the blue heeler sitting politely at her feet, 'is Reith. He's a friend.'

'How do you do,' Reith said gravely but with his lips twitching as he patted the dog. 'Is he for protection—or what?'

'Oh, no!' Kim denied. 'Well, if the need ever arose—' She gestured and shrugged. 'But no, he loves the sea and he loves going out with me.'

Reith studied her for a moment. She wore colourful knee-length board shorts and a shocking pink bikini top under a string vest. Her hair was tied back and her beautiful designer sunglasses alone would have cost a small fortune.

'You look the part,' he commented as he transferred

her board across, then looked at what was left in her boot. 'What's all this?'

'I thought as much,' Kim replied with a mischievous grin. 'You're a typical iron-man surfer with no thought of creature comforts. You can put it all in your car,' she directed.

'But—'

'There's only a sun umbrella, a couple of folding chairs and a cooler with food and beverages. What's wrong with that?' she asked, with her hands planted on her hips.

He grimaced, then grinned. 'Nothing, I guess. I was going to drive us somewhere for lunch.'

'Perish the thought,' she said and looked around. 'On a perfect day like this, who wants to leave the beach?'

Several hours later, Reith, with a beer in one hand and a chicken drumstick in the other, said, 'You're a genius. How did you know cold roast chicken, beer—or, in your case, wine—go down perfectly after a surf?'

Kim giggled. 'Anyone knows that.' She lay back in her folding chair and sipped her wine. Sunny Bob lay contentedly beside her, having had an energetic few hours chasing waves whilst Kim and Reith had had a magnificent surf. He had his own bowl of cool fresh water.

She'd wrapped a pink sarong around her before she'd set out lunch. The sun was just starting to slide down from its zenith and there were a few wispy clouds trailing across the sky. The tide was out now so the roar of the surf was muted but you could still taste the salt in the air and feel the prickle of it on your skin. And it was hot and still, apart from some cicadas in the bush behind the beach.

'Why did you suggest this?' Kim's question seemed to pop out of nowhere.

'Why not?'

She hesitated. 'It just seems unusual for a businessman—look, I'm not complaining,' she said with a grin, 'but think barristers, stockbrokers, CEOs, medical men and you tend to spend a lot of time going out to dinner or cocktail parties or nightclubs or the theatre. Occasionally you may get a day out on a yacht or a day at the races but they're often too busy making money even to do that.'

'I spend a lot of time working behind a desk these days. Whereas I used to—' He paused.

'Go on. Used to—?' she prompted.

'Work on cattle stations, then I was a miner.'

'I wondered about that.'

He looked at her. 'Is it so obvious?'

'No,' she said slowly. 'It was your hands.'

He looked at his hands and grimaced. 'Anyway, I love the sea—most people who don't get to see it until their teens do—and it's good exercise.'

'So you grew up inland?'

'Yep.' He stared out over the ocean and for a moment there was an intensity to his dark gaze that made her frown and believe that he did love it. 'And beyond the black stump, speaking metaphorically,' he added.

Kim smiled. 'Are you married?'

He stirred. 'What makes you think that?'

'All the best ones are, according to Penny.' She pushed herself up against the back of her chair, bent her knees and smoothed her sarong over them. 'What kind of answer is that—are you or aren't you?'

'I'm not. I once was but she passed away.'

Kim sat up, looking appalled. 'You mean she died? What from?'

He nodded. 'A rare complication in childbirth.'

'Is… Did the baby survive?'

'Yes. His name's Darcy and he's ten now.'

Kim lay back. 'I'm sorry—very sorry.'

'Thanks,' he said briefly, then smiled slightly. 'What will Penny make of that?'

Kim shrugged. 'Put you in a special category, I guess.'

'How did I come up, anyway?'

Kim looked a touch embarrassed. 'I went to see her this morning before I drove down to Busselton. Naturally, I told her why I was dressed for the beach,' she said.

'Naturally.'

'Oh, look—' Kim closed her eyes '—ever since Penny got married she's been trying to sell me the state of matrimony as if it's the only state of bliss on the planet. Mind you, that doesn't stop her from warning me of the folly of falling for married men.'

'I think I get the drift,' he replied seriously.

Kim tossed him an annoyed little glance. 'Somehow you've made me feel about twelve,' she said crossly. Then her lips twitched. 'Penny and I have known each other since we were six so we're pretty close. And I suppose pretty girlish at times. But it's not girlish to want to know... Look, it doesn't matter.' She got up suddenly, stripped off her sarong and ran out from beneath the shade of the umbrella and across the hot sand to where the tide was tracing silvery crescents of foam on the damp sand.

And, barking joyfully, Sunny Bob streaked along beside her. The last to join her as she splashed in the shallows was Reith Richardson.

'You know,' he said, 'I would actually like to meet your Penny.'

'Why?' Kim stood still and stared at him.

'If it hadn't been for her I wouldn't have met you. Besides, maybe I could put her mind at rest.'

She eyed him but if he was laughing at her, he was hiding it well. There was no hiding, however, the streamlined strength of his body. He was lightly tanned and beautifully proportioned and she had to turn away suddenly as her breath caught in her throat at the thought of being in his arms.

She felt his hand on her and she looked over her shoulder and up at him.

It was a long, sober look they exchanged but it sent tremors of excitement and danger coursing through Kim's body because, in no uncertain terms, it told her that this man wanted her. She could see it in the way his gaze lingered on her breasts, her slim bare waist, her legs. Then he looked back into her eyes.

She licked her lips and curled her hands into fists because she desperately wanted to touch and be touched intimately, but Sunny Bob chose that moment to break the 'moment'. He raced up and threaded his way between them, and stayed there.

'Saved by the bell,' Reith murmured as he removed his hand.

Her eyes widened. 'Sunny Bob?'

'I get the feeling I'm on notice. Behave or else.'

Kim had to smile. 'Well—obviously,' she hastened to assure him, 'I wouldn't allow him to attack you.'

'Thank you,' he said formally, 'but having narrowly escaped death on the road because of you, I don't think I'll take any more risks. Do you dance?'

She turned round with a frown. 'Of course I dance! What's that got to do with anything?'

'Silly question,' he murmured. 'Do you take Sunny Bob out dancing with you?'

'Of course *not*,' Kim denied and had to stifle a chuckle at the mental image this conjured up. 'Why?'

'I thought if we went dancing it might be easier to get close to you without there being any misunderstandings with your dog.'

This time Kim didn't even try to stifle her laughter.

'It's not that funny,' he assured her.

'What exactly did you have in mind?'

'Sorry to fall into the category of your typical "businessmen" but I was wondering if you'd have dinner with me and then we could go on to a nightclub.'

'I am also sorry,' she said and directed a sparkling blue look up at him, 'for all the dangerous situations I've put you in, Mr Richardson. As for your suggestion, I like the sound of it very much and I will attempt to keep things safe for you.'

He grimaced.

'But I'll have to go home to get changed and then drive back into Bunbury—'

'I'll send a car for you,' he said, interrupting her.

Kim looked at him with a faint frown in her eyes as she wondered why he didn't pick her up himself.

He gestured. 'I have a heap of stuff to deal with—the penalty for taking a day off.'

'Well, OK. Thanks.'

'Seven-thirty suit you?' He raised an eyebrow at her.

'Fine, but really, I could drive in.'

'No.' He said it lightly but quite definitely.

'If that isn't an example of how you like to get your own way, I don't know what is,' she commented a little dryly.

'Not at all,' he denied. 'It's concern for your welfare, that's all.'

Several expressions chased across Kim's face, exasperation being foremost. Then her lips twisted and she looked rueful. 'Hoist by my own petard. All right.'

He laughed.

CHAPTER TWO

THERE was no one home when Kim got back to Saldanha from Margaret River.

There was nothing unusual in this. Her parents travelled frequently as well as socializing often and they were currently in Perth.

Kim taught at a boarding school down the coast at Esperance so she'd moved down there for term time but she spent the school holidays at home.

Fortunately, most of her formal clothes still resided in her bedroom at home and she was able to have a choice of what to wear for dinner and a nightclub with Reith Richardson.

Her bedroom was always a comfort to her. Her mother had given her carte blanche to redecorate it when she left school and she'd created a blue room, saying, 'If you can have a green room, why not a blue one?' And it was not only where she stored her clothes and slept, it was where she read, dreamed, played her harp and wondered sometimes what kind of a wife and mother she would be.

She showered and washed her hair while she thought

what she would wear, then, decision made, thought back over the day. And she was a little startled to feel a tremor run through her just at the thought of Reith Richardson…

I'm falling, she thought. In love or prey to a massive physical attraction? Strange, he didn't lay a hand on me today, other than just before… 'You made your intentions clear,' she said to Sunny Bob, who was lying on the carpet beside her.

The dog lifted his head and thumped his tail, then went back to sleep.

Kim grimaced and pictured what would have happened but for Sunny Bob. She would have revelled in Reith's arms, she knew. Just the thought of it now made her blush and she picked up her perfume bottle and touched the cool glass to her cheeks.

Whoa, she thought then. Take it slowly, Kim. Don't let this get out of hand. You need to know a lot more about this man…

She put the bottle down and picked up her brush, turning it slowly over and over in her hand as she thought of some of her actions today. Such as, for example, her precipitous dash from the cool and shade of the umbrella down the beach to the water earlier.

What had prompted that had been embarrassment. Yes, she wanted to know more about him but, in hindsight, asking him if he was married *had* sounded juvenile, and then intrusive, especially in the light of learning he had lost his wife.

So what was it about him that threw her off her usually even keel? she wondered. That underlying disapproval she'd sensed in him from the start? But why would he disapprove of her? Unless he thought she was completely wacky. But, if so, why would he want to keep on seeing her…?

Perhaps that was part of her enjoyment in his company, however—the light-hearted sparring she, at least, undertook, to challenge his perception of her?

She shook her head and stood up and got dressed. Her choice was a pair of dark grey palazzo pants and a silvery-grey halter top with wide lapels at the front and a low back. She wore no jewellery and no bra. Her shoes were high black sandals, her hair was sleek and smoothed back in a chignon.

Not over-dressed, not under-dressed, just right, she thought as she studied her reflection. The sun and the surf had given her a glow but there was still a frown in her eyes, indicating some inner unease.

She wandered over to her harp and plucked the strings. Romance, she conceded, had been a slightly bumpy road for her until she'd learnt to sort the wheat from the chaff—sort the men who were on the make and drawn by her wealthy parents and background more than by her soul, she thought with a dry little twist of her lips.

And, sadly, there had been more of the 'on the make' kind than the other with the result that she was very wary these days and on the lookout for fortune-hunters. Wary, somewhat hardened and definitely cynical. But did Reith Richardson fall into that class?

On the surface, it appeared not. He didn't seem to be at all interested in her background, but of course they'd only known each other for a short time. Yet there was something—her brow creased—a sort of stamp of authority about him that was impressive. There was also a reserve she sensed.

She sighed and picked up her purse at the sound of a car on the drive. 'Just—take it very slowly with this man,' she advised herself and went downstairs to be driven into town.

A few hours later, she stirred in his arms and said in a low husky voice, 'Do you ever take your own advice?'

He swung her round on the small, darkened, crowded floor with its coloured spotlights above, and they came together again. They'd danced for hours. It was the height of sophistication, the nightclub, on the second floor of a beautifully restored old building in Bunbury, and the music had been sensational.

'Sometimes.' He looked down at her rather wryly. 'How about you?'

'Not always.' She laid her head on his shoulder as, rather than dancing, they swayed to the music and, as she'd suspected, she revelled in being in his arms.

In fact, when she'd first laid eyes on him, when she'd walked into the restaurant and he'd stood up in a dark suit, the jacket of which had moulded his broad shoulders, she'd missed a step because he'd been so darkly attractive. From that moment on she'd been physically conscious of him in a way that had taken her by storm because she'd never felt this way before, never had her senses so stirred up by a man.

At the same time as a river of rhythm had flowed

through her veins, so had a river of sensuality. His hands on her hips had ignited a swathe of sensation up and down her body. And to rest her body against his, to feel the hard strength of him, the power, had made her feel as light as a feather and giddy with pleasure.

'Not always, which is very stupid of me. I——'

The music stopped, the band announced they were having a break and some recorded music took over.

Kim didn't finish what she was saying and sighed as they drew apart, then she led the way back to their table.

'More champagne?' he queried.

She shook her head. 'Just some iced water, thanks.'

'Not a bad idea,' he agreed. 'Why stupid? Now? At this moment in time?' he queried.

Kim put her elbows on the table and rested her chin on her clasped hands. 'I was going to take things very, very slowly with you, Mr Richardson,' she said. 'That was not supposed to include dancing the night away.' Kim smiled austerely. 'Do you have the same problem I have?'

He raised his eyebrows. 'The disinclination to keep my hands off you?'

'Something like that,' she said ruefully and thanked the waiter who brought them two glasses of iced water with slices of lemon. 'But perhaps we should——' She paused.

'We should look before we leap?' he suggested with some irony.

Kim narrowed her eyes as she caught the irony and said tartly, despite it being not what she wanted to do at all, 'My sentiments entirely.'

He put his head on one side and studied her. 'That annoyed you?'

'Not at all.'

'That I should feel we need to stop and think?' he persisted.

'Well…no, we should! But—' she paused '—you didn't sound entirely genuine. More, in fact, as if you were paraphrasing, with sarcasm, what you thought I would say.'

'It was the awful euphemism I used that offended me,' he said.

Kim stared at him. 'Look before we leap?' she murmured, then her lips curved and she started to laugh.

He put his hand over hers on the table and laughed with her, his dark eyes glinting with amusement.

Then he looked at his watch. 'Your car will be here shortly. I ordered it for midnight.'

Kim removed her hand. 'That solves that. I can go home feeling like Cinderella.'

He ignored that. 'Do you have any more time off?'

Kim blinked at the change of subject. 'Two more days.'

'Tomorrow, would you like to help me select some classy artwork?'

Her lips parted.

'You did say you had a good eye for art.'

'What's it for?'

'Some offices—some new offices in Perth. I'm not that keen on what the interior decorators have come up with.'

She thought for a moment then she shrugged. 'All

right. Yes, I'd like to. I have a couple of favourite galleries. You know—' she looked at him consideringly '—you're clever.'

He looked surprised. 'Why?'

'You've defused us. There we were, a pretty hot item on the dance floor, but now we're talking art and I'm about to be shipped off home.' She put her elbows on the table and rested her chin on her hands and narrowed her eyes. 'I'm just not sure why you're taking this course but you're right,' she said mischievously, 'you should *always* look before you leap.'

'Kim—' he pushed back his chair and stood up '—come with me.'

She raised her eyebrows but shrugged when she got no response and rose to follow him. He led her out of the main room, along a passage and onto a secluded balcony overlooking the street.

There Reith paused and looked up and down the street. Whatever he saw—nothing—must have gained his approval because he turned back to Kim, took her in his arms and kissed her swiftly but at the same time comprehensively.

So comprehensively she clutched him when their lips parted and she could only say his name on a note of stunned amazement as tremors of desire ran through her body.

'Kim?'

'You… I…I mean,' she stammered, 'why did you do that?'

His dark eyes rested on her lips, then the lovely line

of her throat and the curves of her breasts beneath the silvery-grey silk of her halter top.

'Why?' he repeated and smiled suddenly, a wicked little smile full of masculine arrogance. 'I wanted to.'

Kim gasped. 'That's… But I thought… *You* were the one who…hosed us down!'

He shrugged. 'You were the one who thought she was being shipped home like Cinderella.'

Kim touched her lips and opened her mouth to speak as a long black limousine pulled into the kerb down below.

She eyed it, then turned back to him. 'So?'

'I just wanted to make it clear that, while I believe we should exercise some caution, I'd much rather not be shipping you home.'

Kim stared up into his eyes and saw they were amused, wicked, but also just a shade rueful.

'You… You're serious,' she said incredulously.

'Uh-huh.'

'That…that makes me feel a bit better,' she conceded. 'OK—time and place for tomorrow?' she added huskily.

'You name it.'

She thought for a moment, then did so.

'Fine.' He bent his head and kissed her lightly. 'Goodnight. Sleep well.'

Kim donned black silk pyjamas and sat down at her dressing table when she arrived back at Saldanha.

'It's just you and me,' she murmured to Sunny Bob, who'd accorded her an enthusiastic but slightly puzzled welcome because of the strange black car.

'Puzzling days, you're right,' she said now as she smoothed cleanser onto her face and wiped it off with a tissue. 'For example, Sunny Bob,' she continued her conversation with the dog, 'I thought I felt better when he said he'd kissed me because he wanted to, and he wasn't that keen on shipping me home. Now I'm not so sure.'

She moistened a cotton pad with toner and patted it onto her skin, enjoying the cool feel of it.

Because the thing is—I do feel shipped home, she continued her monologue internally. What's more, I feel as if I'm the one making all the running, so to speak—how dare he do that to me?

Am I? she asked herself next, as she massaged a night cream into her skin. Making all the running?

No, look here, he keeps suggesting things, *he's* the one who keeps pushing us onwards and upwards.

She grimaced at her choice of words, then she thought, with a frown, yes, he does, but he's also the one who holds back. Why? Is there a sort of no-go zone around him or is it only my imagination? Why would that be, though, if it was so? Am I still a rather ridiculous little rich girl to him?

Am I being observed like some sort of scientific phenomenon he hasn't experienced before? Or is this stop/ start approach meant to entice me on?

She put the tub of night cream with its gold top down with a little thump as a flash of annoyance at the thought claimed her, and she got up and roamed around the room.

Finally she got into bed and turned the light off but

her thoughts took another direction, one not greatly removed, however.

Should she call it off?

Should she pull a really arrogant, if not necessarily rich, stunt and simply not turn up tomorrow?

Or, even better, have a message delivered to him as he waited for her, to the effect that she'd decided she had better things to do…

She sat up suddenly as it struck her—forcibly—that it had only been two days—she'd only known Reith Richardson for two days! How could she be going through this level of turmoil for a man she barely knew?

She lay back and commanded herself to breathe slowly and calmly but it didn't work in helping her to fall asleep.

CHAPTER THREE

'SLEEP well?'

'No,' Kim said flatly.

'Neither did I, if it's any help,' Reith Richardson offered.

Kim switched her attention from the painting she was studying and looked up at him. She wore a fitted leather miniskirt in peach with a loose scarlet top in a filmy material. Her shoes were high cork wedges, her hair was looped back in a roll, she had big diamond-studded gold hoops in her ears and there were the faintest blue shadows beneath her eyes.

She looked, he thought wryly, gorgeous, from her red-gold hair down to those sensational legs, but moody. And he was presented with a sudden mental picture of her waking up in his bed with that same moody expression. Could she maintain it, though, if he cupped her breasts, then drew his hands down her body and made love to her slowly, very slowly, until they were both on fire? Careful, he warned himself, remember who this is…

She said, 'Why should it be any help?' then gestured as if to erase the words. 'It doesn't matter. Look, it's very difficult to choose art when you have no idea where it's going to end up.'

'I've got some sketches.'

'You've also got to be in the mood,' she added.

He paused and narrowed his eyes. 'I'm getting some pretty distressed vibes here so, starting at the top, is it that time of the month?'

'No,' she snapped.

'Is it the lack of really good sex then?' He shrugged. 'Can give you the blues.'

Kim beamed a glance of the opposite—pure blue fire—his way but at the same time a mental image of her lying naked in his arms and as aroused as he was streaked through her mind. And she couldn't for the life of her decide what annoyed her more—the tingle that went through her, lovely though it was, or the fact that he could do this to her after shipping her home last night.

'No,' she said through her teeth and was about to add a pithy comment, although she hadn't actually thought of one, but he interrupted.

'Have you had breakfast?'

She closed her mouth, then opened it again. 'What makes you think I didn't?' she answered.

'Did you?'

She looked mutinous. 'No.'

'Why not?'

She shrugged. 'I went for a ride, then I was running late.'

'Another wacky day in the making,' he commented, and put his arm through hers. 'Come.'

'Where? We haven't picked a thing yet.'

'You'll see.'

She shrugged again, as if to say she didn't give a damn one way or the other, and walked out with him.

An hour and a delicious mushroom omelette later, Kim looked around at the rustic restaurant he'd brought her to and said ruefully, 'You were right. Sorry. I feel much better.'

'Good. Is that all it was? A lack of food.'

'Don't start that again,' she warned, then grimaced as she recalled her turmoil of the night before. 'Not entirely, but I do find it hard to be miserable for long.'

'Miserable?' He frowned.

'Confused. Not one hundred per cent sure what game you're playing, Mr Richardson, put it that way.'

He raised an eyebrow and waited. When she offered no more, he said questioningly, 'Game?'

'I can't work out whether you're trying to seduce me or not.'

Their gazes clashed.

'There's a certain—' she moved her hands around each other '—stop/start approach you employ that I find a bit strange.'

'Are you suggesting we should jump into bed?'

Kim smiled but there was a touch of frost to it. 'No. But perhaps I should let you know that the disapproval and reserve is not all on your side.'

'That's what you think it is—disapproval?'

'Yes. Besides which, I have the feeling you're a loner at heart!' She said it almost jauntily.

'Would you prefer it if you had to fight me off?' he asked.

'Naturally not. Look, I've had enough of this conversation—you'll have me all gloom and doom again if we're not careful. Show me your sketches,' she commanded.

He pulled some papers out of his jacket pocket and handed them over to her.

She smoothed them out. 'Hmm...' she said eventually. 'Not bad. Do you have any preferences?' She opened her hands. 'Do you like your art conventional, for example, or could you live with a bit of—' she broke off and smiled suddenly '—wackiness?'

He stirred his coffee thoughtfully. 'I don't mind a bit of wackiness.'

'Good,' she approved briskly. 'Do you have any pet hates? For example, I don't like—sorry, I know you love it—but I don't like seascapes. With a passion.'

He looked amused. 'Why not?'

'I'm not sure. Perhaps you just can't capture the movement of the sea in paint. Any of those dislikes— or anything you particularly *like*?'

He rubbed his jaw. 'I've seen some Aboriginal art that has a sort of mysterious power that draws you in— it's hard to describe but it makes you feel it's alive.'

Kim put her cup down and sat up, her expression heavy with frustration. 'Why on earth didn't you tell me this sooner?'

'You have access to it?'

She nodded. 'I have friends who get right to the source, painters who still live in their traditional areas and are able to transfer the sheer magic—' she clenched a hand and her face glowed '—of their culture onto canvas.' She opened her purse and pulled out her phone. 'Hold thumbs they're not out in the desert.'

They weren't out in the desert so Kim took Reith to their gallery and they spent nearly the whole of the rest of the day going through canvases, making choices and deciding on frames.

Finally, he suggested dinner.

Kim agreed but told him she'd like to shower and change. 'And don't worry about sending me around in great big black limousines,' she told him. 'It doesn't do much for my mood. Anyway, I'm used to driving in and out of Bunbury.'

He looked at her, smiling. 'OK. What do you suggest restaurant-wise?'

She thought for a moment, then she told him with a toss of her head that she had a craving for pasta and nothing else would do. She also named a restaurant.

'So be it,' he said gravely.

Kim suffered a moment's disquiet. 'Do you like pasta? If you don't I suppose we could—'

'It would not be game to dislike pasta,' he broke in to say.

She looked disconcerted for a moment, then pulled a face at him and retreated to her car.

* * *

A couple of hours later, she parked her car in Bunbury and walked towards the restaurant.

She'd changed into a long, floaty flame-coloured dress streaked with white, and nude platform shoes. She'd left her hair loose and she carried a boxy little gold bag.

Reith was waiting for her and she walked towards him with her long free stride and her dress billowing around her, only to slow down then come to a stop a couple of feet away from him.

She shivered suddenly as his dark gaze roamed up and down her. Because there was something completely riveted about him and the way he was examining her body. In fact, she got the feeling she was naked beneath that compelling gaze, that he'd mentally undressed her, even dispensing with her underwear, and it was tense, yet, at the same time, incredibly erotic. It sent her pulses racing and tremors of desire running through her.

Then he moved and reached out to take her hand. 'You look sensational, Kim. Shall we go in?'

But she hesitated. 'You shouldn't do that to me. Not in public, Reith.'

'Sorry.' He didn't pretend to misunderstand. 'I couldn't help myself.'

She hesitated a moment longer.

He raised her hand and kissed her knuckles. 'I'm probably better off if I can see your legs,' he added.

Kim blinked, then said bewilderedly, 'The first time you saw them you nearly crashed!'

'Well, I could be over that now. But to be totally deprived makes me try to imagine them, you see.'

'Reith Richardson,' she said severely, 'you're talking utter claptrap. It's something men do all the time. Mind you—' she paused '—I have to confess you're pretty good at it.'

'Uh-huh?' He frowned. 'In what way?'

'When you get your face slapped, you'll know you're doing it wrong,' she advised. 'And now—may I eat? I'm starving!'

He laughed down at her and she turned a little pink because she knew he knew how affected she'd been by his mental undressing.

'I am starving,' she said a little lamely.

'All right. After you.'

'That turned out to be a much better day than I expected,' Kim said later. The Italian restaurant had candles in wine bottles and a folksy atmosphere and the pasta came highly recommended. 'Artwork-wise,' she added.

His lips twitched. 'You wouldn't be on commission, by any chance?'

She wrinkled her nose. 'No. But I wouldn't be surprised to get a bottle of French champagne and some Belgian chocolates for Christmas.' She smiled as a waiter poured her a glass of wine and she raised it in a toast to Reith. 'I hope you get a lot of pleasure out of your paintings, Mr Richardson!'

'Thank you, Miss Theron. Shall we order?'

She nodded, told him what she'd like and sat back. And they only spoke desultorily until their meals were served.

Then he said, 'Can we go back to our earlier discussion?'

'Which one was that?'

'The one,' he said, 'where you accused me of disapproving of you and failing to make my intentions clear.'

'Clear?'

He smiled dryly. 'Was I out to seduce you or not.'

'Oh, that one.' Kim sampled some fettuccine marinara, then raised a napkin to her lips. 'Mmm! OK. Are you?'

He narrowed his eyes. 'Would it be a problem?'

'Certainly,' Kim replied promptly.

'I might have thought otherwise last night on the dance floor.'

'Well, I might have too.' She gestured expansively. 'But that was last night. Today is a different matter.' Her eyes glinted very blue as she glanced at him then turned her attention back to her dinner.

'What about tomorrow?' he asked.

'I'm having a day off tomorrow.'

'I know, you told me. It's your last day off so—'

'What I mean is—' she interrupted '—I'm having a day off from *you*.'

He didn't miss a beat. He said, 'That's a pity, I was hoping you'd come to Clover Hill with me. I'm going over to look at some yearlings.'

Kim put her fork down. 'Horses?'

His lips twitched. 'So far as I know, that's all they breed at Clover.'

She clicked her tongue with some exasperation. 'I know that. Do you race horses?'

'Yes.'

'Is this an open day?'

He shook his head. 'A private viewing.'

Kim's eyes widened. 'You're getting a *private* viewing?'

He shrugged.

Kim simply stared at him. Clover Hill Stud was renowned throughout Australia in horse-breeding circles. Renowned for the stallions they stood and the percentage of winners amongst their progeny. It was also a showplace with a beautiful old homestead, magnificent gardens and paddocks. And if Reith Richardson had gone out of his way to pick an outing Kim Theron would not be able to resist he couldn't have chosen better. But, of course, he couldn't have gone out of his way; this would probably have been arranged well beforehand…

'Kim?'

She blinked, then shook her head. 'I don't know how you do it but you're a master tactician. Thank you, I cannot tell a lie, I've never been to Clover Hill and I would love to see it.'

'You obviously know a bit about horses.' It was a statement rather than a question.

'I know a bit,' Kim agreed. 'I've ridden since I was six and my parents raced them. But, hang on, Penny is going home tomorrow—not that she needs me, her mum and hubby are both here now—but I'd like to spend a couple of hours with her when she gets back. So I'll probably be tied up until after lunch.'

He sat back and pushed his plate away. 'You take good care of your friends, don't you?'

She lifted her shoulders. 'Who doesn't? So—'

'It's not a problem if you could meet me there at two o'clock.'

Kim smiled with noticeable radiance. 'Done!'

Her parents were home but in bed when she got back that night.

She took care not to wake them but was surprised when her father stayed in bed the next morning.

'He's not feeling well,' her mother confided, closing his bedroom door—they had separate bedrooms.

'Has he seen a doctor?'

'No.' Fiona Theron tightened the sash of her beautiful silk dressing gown. 'But I'll keep an eye on him. So, what have you been doing with yourself, darling?' She led the way downstairs to the breakfast room.

'This and that,' Kim heard herself say and grimaced as she thought how evasive the phrase had sounded to her when uttered by Reith Richardson. So she made an effort to elaborate but something kept her from mentioning Reith and she waxed lyrical instead on the subject of Penny's baby.

The housekeeper, Mary Hiddens, came in with a coffee pot.

'Hi, Mary! How's the family?' Kim enquired as she helped herself to some bacon and French toast from a silver warmer, and poured herself a cup of coffee.

'All well, thank you, Kim,' Mary replied, then turned to Fiona, who had taken nothing from the warmer but reached now for the coffee pot.

'Ma'am, please have some breakfast,' Mary said.

'Just now, Mary. You know how I always have to whet my whistle first!'

Mary hesitated, then withdrew and Kim looked at her mother curiously. 'You're not dieting, are you, Mum? You don't need to; you look marvellous!' She studied her mother's slim waistline.

'No, no,' Fiona said hastily. 'So you're back to Esperance tomorrow?'

'Uh-huh.' Kim fed some bacon to Sunny Bob, who placed his head lovingly in her lap. 'But it's not that long to the school holidays, then I'll be home for a month.'

'Lovely,' Fiona said, but with a curious lack of conviction.

Kim frowned and opened her mouth, but her father could be heard calling for her mother.

'Do you want me to call the doctor, Mum?' she asked.

'No. No,' her mother repeated with her hand on the door handle. 'He'll be fine. Have a nice day, sweetheart!'

Clover Hill exceeded Kim's expectations.

The rose gardens alone were worth the visit but she loved the parade of yearlings, still flighty, still to partake in their first official yearling sale, still, some of them, with short bushy tails and frizzy manes.

The stud-master sat with them on a stand in the parade ring and gave them a run-down on the horses' breeding as the little ones pranced around the ring.

'Will you buy today?' Kim asked Reith.

He shook his head. 'Some of them are barely broken in to lead, some aren't, but it's interesting to be able to keep track of them from an earlier age, before they hit the sales ring.'

'Do you have your own trainer?'

'No. I spread them around: Perth, Melbourne, Sydney.'

Kim frowned. 'How many horses do you have in training?'

He rubbed his jaw. 'About twenty.'

Kim swallowed. She had a very good idea how much that would cost. 'Many winners?'

'Not yet.' He looked down at her amusedly. 'Haven't been in the game that long.'

'Rescuing businesses in trouble must be profitable,' she commented.

He said nothing and they walked in silence for a while. They were on their own now; the stud-master had left them after inviting them to have a wander around.

It was a cool, overcast day, unusual for the time of year. Kim wore jeans, boots and a navy leather bomber jacket, whereas Reith had a lined anorak over his shirt and jeans and suede desert boots.

Kim remembered him handling the horses when they'd visited the foals still with their mums in the paddock. It was obvious he knew his horses—a man after my own heart, she thought with a fleeting smile.

Now, as they strolled along a swept path, a sharp little breeze got up and she moved closer to him.

'Feels as if it's come up from the Antarctic, that breeze,' she said with a shiver.

He put an arm around her and drew her towards a creeper-covered shelter with a bench inside. Inside, as they sank down onto the bench, they found themselves protected from the breeze but he pulled her closer.

She breathed deeply and nestled against him but at the same time she had no idea what was coming next between them.

'So, back to work tomorrow,' he murmured.

'Mmm...'

'Looking forward to it?'

Kim hesitated and, rather than answering, asked a question herself. 'What will you be doing?'

'I'm off to points north for a few weeks.'

A little of the Antarctic chill seemed to enter her soul, let in, she thought, by the casualness of his words but, not only that, by the lack of detail.

The thought transferred to a larger issue between them—the lack of *all* she knew about him. And refused to ask now, yes, she acknowledged, despite how close she felt to him. She couldn't think of anywhere she'd rather be than sitting close to him, breathing in his essence, conscious of his bulk and strength, but there was a huge mental divide between them.

She moistened her lips and asked another question. 'Reith, how did we come to this?'

'You don't think we should have come to "this"?' he queried.

'I'm just a bit surprised, but that's not what I meant,' Kim confessed. 'To begin with I saw us more as adversaries...well, maybe not that so much, but enjoying fencing, verbally, with each other. Now—'

'You tend to forget—' he interrupted '—that one glimpse of your legs nearly drove me into a tree.'

Kim laughed softly. 'You were furious with me at the time, though,' she reminded him and deepened her voice. *'Lady—are you mad?'*

He grimaced.

'But this is what I still don't know—are you trying to seduce me or not?' She leant her head on his shoulder.

He loosened one hand and slipped some strands of her hair under her cheek. 'I can't tell a lie,' he conceded. 'Well, the thought of going to bed with you, Kimberley Theron, is, paradoxically, keeping me awake at night.'

She moved her cheek on the fabric of his jacket. 'I must say I've also thought about it.' She looked up into his eyes. 'You must know that. Not—' she pulled herself out of his arms and sat up '—that I'm going to do it.'

His lips twisted and he looked down at her quizzically. 'No?'

She shook her head. 'Not yet, anyway.'

'Does that mean to say I'm on a promise?'

She chuckled and leant back against him, growing serious. 'What I mean is, I think we need to know each other better.' She paused. And suddenly realized that she meant it. This uncertainty about what he felt for her and vice versa—about what would become of them—had become like an emotional roller coaster for her and she had to find a way to get off.

'What would you like me to know about you?' he queried.

'I would like,' she said somewhat darkly, 'not to be classified as a spoilt socialite, a ditsy redhead or—at least you can't accuse me of being a dumb blonde—'

He interrupted her by the simple expedient of putting a finger to her lips. Then he bent his head and started to kiss her.

Kim was lost. Lost beneath the finesse of his touch as he cupped her face and his fingers slid down the side of her neck, causing her to shiver in delight and anticipation.

'You do that so well,' she whispered when their lips parted.

'Thank you,' he murmured, but added, 'You expected me to do it like the local yokel or a country hick, Miss Theron?'

She wrinkled her nose. 'Not at all. I just didn't expect you to do it better than anyone else I've ever known.'

He lifted his head and looked down at her with a glimmer of humour in his dark eyes. 'Either you haven't been kissed a lot or—' He stopped.

'Or what? I've made lousy choices in men?'

'You said it,' he returned ruefully.

'You thought it.' Kim leant back against him. 'But it could be true. I'd hate to think what you could do to me if you really tried. But—' she hesitated as some sanity returned and she recalled her conviction that she had to get off the roundabout '—Reith, we don't need to rush into anything, do we?'

She felt him move against her.

She took a breath. 'Do we?' she queried, at the same time conscious of an alarm bell going off inside her.

He hesitated. 'Has something gone wrong?'

'No.' As she said it, it occurred to her that it wasn't quite true but how to explain her reservations accurately? Or should she lighten up a bit until she could be more articulate?

'Tell me a bit more about you, though. Where do you actually live, for example?' she asked teasingly.

He laughed. 'I spend so much time on the move it's hard to say. But I have an apartment in Perth where my offices are and it's where Darcy comes home to for the school holidays.'

'Darcy,' Kim said on an unexpected breath. 'So… he's at boarding school? But he's only ten.'

'And he's not the only ten-year-old boarder.'

'True,' Kim conceded slowly, 'although we have very few that young in the school where I teach.'

'He's only been there for six months since his grandmother died.'

'Your wife's mother?'

He nodded. 'She more or less brought him up. But he seems to have settled down well.'

'I hope you spend a lot of time with him,' Kim said severely.

'As much as I can.'

'Talking of time,' she added, 'I need to spend a bit of time at home.' She frowned as it occurred to her that something had felt different about 'home' lately but she hadn't been able to put her finger on it.

'You don't live at home?'

'For the last year I've been living in Esperance, that's where I teach, so I've been out of the home "loop", so to speak,' she said slowly, then shrugged. 'But it's school holidays in a week or so.'

He paused, then picked up her hand. 'I can't visualize you as a teacher.'

'Neither could I, at first.' She shrugged. 'Then I found I had a knack for it. I really like kids.'

'I thought something entrepreneurial would be more in your line.'

'Oh, a friend and I have opened a gallery in Esperance. Not paintings but metalwork, pottery, papier mâché, really creative knitting, et cetera.' Her eyes glinted. 'Satisfied?'

He took her chin in his hand and dropped a light kiss on her lips. 'Yes.' Then he looked narrowly into her eyes. 'We're not parting on bad terms, are we?'

She looked up at him, completely sober now, and knew that this man, this mystery man, could be the one to lure her onto the rocks. The rocks of loving him without being loved in return.

She had no idea how she knew this; it was an instinct that somehow told her he was a loner... Yes, there was no doubt he was quite cagey about his life—for that matter, so was she. Apart from one mention of Saldanha, she'd told him nothing about her family, nothing about Balthazar.

Come to that, she thought with a blink, he hadn't asked her a single question about her background.

She grimaced and returned to this loner she sensed in him, this *something* that told her he maintained an emotional exclusion zone around him...

And yet they were always good together; they seemed to have a rapport, a similar sense of humour, a similar sense of what was fine, even a similar taste in music. And now it even seemed as if he could read her mind. As if he could sense her uncertainty beneath her attempts to make light of it. So *where* did this feeling come from?

'Kim?'

She came back from her thoughts. 'No. Not on bad terms. Guess what?'

He looked at her.

'Penny's settled on a name for their baby. Reith.'

His eyebrows shot up. 'Because I gave you a lift?'

'No. Because it's unusual and she likes it. When are you going?'

'Tomorrow afternoon.'

'Then I won't see you until you come back.'

He grimaced but said, 'I'll look forward to it. Kim?'

'No, Reith,' she said quietly. 'That's how we should leave it.'

'Or…like this.' He gathered her in his arms and kissed her deeply.

Then he surprised her. He rubbed his chin on the top of her head and said, 'What do you think of this place?'

'Clover Hill?' She looked around the paddocks and their horses, at the roses and the creeper-covered homestead, at the Darling Hills in the background, and she breathed deeply and smiled. 'It's special. Why?'

He shrugged. 'Just asking. OK, time to go.'

But after he'd watched her drive off, Reith didn't leave immediately. He leant back against the car and attempted to think things through.

Such as being accused of a stop/start approach in his attempts to seduce Kimberley Theron.

He shoved his hands in his pockets and chewed his lip. She was right, of course. Every now and then his conscience pricked him. And every now and then he felt guilt associated with Sylvia, his wife, the guilt he'd felt at wanting her but not being able to love her. As for Kim, he'd even once asked himself why he hadn't rung for roadside assistance for her that first day and simply driven off when he well knew her family would hate him having anything to do with her.

For that matter, why hadn't he just told her? He'd been on the brink of it several times. But, despite his growing respect for her, he knew well enough that that could lose her to him. The more you got to know Kim Theron, the more evidence there was that loyalty to friends was paramount with her. It made sense that loyalty to her family would be the same. But she was no fool, so...?

He left the question hanging in the air, but one thing he did know was that he wasn't prepared to lose her.

Not yet.

He grimaced and got into his car. But, instead of driving away from Clover Hill, he drove from the stables round to the house...

Two weeks later, Kim made a discovery that horrified her.

She'd been preoccupied since her parting from Reith. Up in the air and down in the dumps described her alternating state of mind accurately. Would she ever see him again? Why did life seem dull and sepia because he wasn't around? Could you fall deeply in love in four days?

Should she have got some contact details at least, instead of allowing her mobile number to be the only link between them? Although he did know where to find her.

Then school had broken up and she'd come home for the holidays. A couple of days later, she came home one evening to find her father slumped on the floor in the lounge, apparently unconscious.

She checked his pulse and flew upstairs to get her mother, gabbling at the same time about how he must have tripped on the rug or…

'No, darling, he's drunk,' Fiona Theron said sadly as she twisted her thin hands and stared down at her comatose husband.

'Drunk?' Kim echoed incredulously.

Fiona nodded. 'It happens a lot these days.'

'Why?'

'We're going under, sweetheart. I begged him to tell you but he keeps…well…hoping for a miracle.'

'I don't believe this,' Kim whispered. 'Why didn't Damien tell me?' Damien was her older brother and her father's second in command.

'Damien…' Fiona gestured helplessly. 'But anyway…'

'No! Tell me about Damien,' Kim insisted.

'Damien—' her mother swallowed painfully '—oh, look, Damien is not a businessman, Kim. You must know that. Horses are his life.' Fiona paused and burst into tears.

* * *

The next morning at ten, Kim held an emergency family meeting. She looked so pale, and still so confused, her father and brother, both of whom would have preferred to be a million miles away, thought twice about it and attended.

'Tell me, Dad,' she begged. 'Tell me what's happened.'

Frank Theron was a big man, silver-haired now but still good-looking, although he had a livid bruise on his cheek from his collapse last night, and other signs Kim hadn't noticed that all was not well—red veins in his cheeks, prominent pouches beneath his eyes.

'Kim,' he said on a heavy sigh, 'the last five years have been very difficult. We've had several outbreaks of powdery mildew and you know how that can affect not only the grapes but wine quality. We've had a drought, then floods, then a fire. We've had a global financial downturn.' He stopped to sigh again. 'And we live quite an extravagant lifestyle.'

Damien, her brother, looked down. He maintained a stable of polo ponies. Kim looked at the lovely designer dress she wore and thought of her sports car, her twenty-first birthday present...

'So?' she queried.

'So we put the winery on the market,' Frank continued, looking animated for the first time, although angrily so, 'and attracted the attention of a complete upstart!'

'I wouldn't call him that,' Fiona murmured.

'You mightn't but I would,' her husband insisted.

'What does he know about wine, about grapes? He was born in a boundary rider's hut on some godforsaken cattle station. And he had the nerve to offer me a pittance. For Balthazar!'

'Upstart or not,' Damien Theron said moodily, 'he's made a fortune.' Damien had inherited their mother's dark eyes and hair and their father's height but not his bulk. He was whip-thin but that was deceptive—when you saw him on a headstrong horse, you couldn't doubt he was strong. 'You have to admit that, Dad,' he added.

Frank turned angrily on his son but Kim intervened.

'Just a minute. If he was born in a boundary rider's hut, how can he be offering... Even a pittance for Balthazar has got to be quite a sum!'

'Mining,' Frank said succinctly. 'He bought a mine no one else wanted and the rest—i.e., a fortune when he sold it—is history. Now he specializes in buying run-down companies. He waits until they're on their knees, then comes in like a scavenger.'

Kim's lips parted and a shiver ran down her spine as a dreadful premonition took her in its grip...

'What's his name?' she asked with a dry throat.

Her father waved a hand. 'Doesn't matter. Don't concern yourself, Kimmie.'

'I must.' She swivelled her gaze to her brother. 'S-so...so you rejected his offer?' Her voice shook.

Damien sighed and nodded. 'Not only that, he's bought Clover Hill. I heard the news yesterday. I don't suppose he'll be interested in another property in the same area.'

Kim dropped the papers she was holding. 'Bought Clover Hill?' she whispered. 'What's his *name*?'

'Richardson,' her father answered shortly.

'Reith Richardson,' Fiona contributed. 'Rather unusual... Kim, dear, you look dreadful. Is there anything the matter? Anything else, I mean?'

CHAPTER FOUR

IT WAS two weeks after she'd learnt the true state of affairs at home before Kim saw Reith again.

Which turned out to be plenty of time to find herself in even greater turmoil than she'd been in before he'd taken off for 'points north'.

She couldn't forgive herself for not sensing that things were badly wrong at home a lot sooner than she had. It made her flinch to think that Mary, the housekeeper, had been concerned for her mother, who was eating poorly, whereas she herself had not even noticed it.

It hurt her to think she'd not interpreted her father's pent-up rage correctly or even taken much notice of it. And she could have kicked herself for not realizing Damien's heart wasn't in the winery. True, she and Damien had never been that close—there were five years between them—but all the same...

Then Reith rang and suggested dinner.

She suggested lunch instead.

They met at a country pub, also her suggestion, not far from Saldanha. She drove there in an estate station wagon; she'd sold her convertible. The money had been like a drop in the ocean but it had made her feel she was contributing something to the mountain of debt facing the family.

She walked into the pub, wearing jeans and a check shirt and with her hair fish-plaited. Her heart banged once at the sight of him, also in jeans and a black T-shirt, but she ignored it and pulled out a chair...

'Kim.' He stood up and studied her closely. Somehow the dimensions of her face were different, the changes wrought by stress, blue shadows beneath her eyes, but the whole beautiful although in a new way, and he went still. 'You know,' he said then.

She sat down. 'I know,' she repeated. 'When, as a matter of interest, were you thinking of telling me?'

'Today,' he said laconically and signalled to the barman, who brought over a bottle of wine and poured her a glass. Reith had a tankard of beer. The pub, adorned with ancient saddles, bridles and other horse memorabilia, was empty apart from them.

'Oh, that's easy enough to say, Reith,' she taunted.

'It's true.'

She stared at him with her lips working, then took a sip of wine to steady herself. 'Why? Why didn't you tell me who you were?'

He sat back and rested his arm along the back of the chair beside him. 'I...' He paused and narrowed his eyes. 'Did it matter if you knew who I was or not?'

'Of course it did! My father regards you as public enemy number one. He feels you've offered him a pittance for Balthazar, but not only that, you don't have the…the expertise to do justice to what is a famous name.' She stopped, frustrated. Because, at the back of her mind, although she was employing her father's arguments, she wasn't a hundred per cent convinced they were correct. 'Look,' she said, 'my father—'

'Thinks I'm an upstart from beyond the black stump? It's OK, I know; he told me,' Reith drawled. 'As for your brother, with his polo ponies and his old school tie—we might as well be on different planets.' He paused and narrowed his eyes. 'I was hoping you mightn't share their opinion.'

'Were you? Were you really, Reith? This is my family we're talking about. This isn't just a winery and an estate, not to me it isn't. It's something that goes way back…'

'Look, Kim—' he broke in '—that's all very well but sentiment is no match for cold hard facts. It doesn't pay the bills.'

She glared at him, then closed her eyes briefly. 'Perhaps you're right,' she said tonelessly. 'But perhaps,' she added with more fire, 'you could never understand how we feel unless you've been in a similar position. Not only that, I always suspected you were impossible to get through to.'

He frowned. 'What do you mean?'

She paused, then said, 'That there's an exclusion zone around you I would never have got through on a personal level and this is just an extension of that.'

Their gazes clashed.

'Did it not matter one way or another who I was?' she asked and her eyes widened. 'Or was it precisely because I was a Theron, a member of a family you had cause to despise, that you…that you… Oh! Of course!' She blinked. 'That explains it. Why I got the distinct impression you didn't approve of me even while you were…you were…' She stopped breathlessly but her eyes were accusing.

There was a brittle little pause, then he said dryly, 'How we came to meet was due to a wacky episode of *your* making, Kim. I would never have sought you out. Come to that, if I could have got out of giving you that lift I would have, but did you honestly expect me to leave you there?'

'You didn't have to ask me to dinner,' she reminded him bitterly.

He looked away as a party of men in khaki clothes and boots came in and threw their dusty hats down.

He looked back at last. 'Well, you see, Kim, by then I was wondering what it would be like to make love to you. Whether, like the rest of your family, you'd be an arrogant Theron—even in bed.'

She gasped. She did more. She picked up her wine glass to dash the contents in his face but he caught her wrist and held it in an iron grip until she was forced to put the glass down.

'No violence, Kim,' he warned softly.

She subsided and he released her wrist. But he could see the blue fire in her eyes and the *hauteur* in the set of her mouth, both clear indications that he was now persona non grata in her estimation, and he discovered he had a devil riding in him with regard to Kimberley Theron.

He still wanted her. In fact he wanted her more than ever...

He was also reminded of something he'd said to his secretary on the subject of Francis Theron's apparently stunning daughter—*maybe they need to find her a rich husband...* How ironic, he thought to himself.

'Besides, I've got a proposition to put to you,' he said to her.

'Obviously not a business one,' she retorted.

He shrugged. 'You could say so.'

Her eyes widened. 'But I thought you'd withdrawn your offer. I believe you've bought Clover Hill instead!' Her eyes challenged him. 'Something else you didn't see fit to tell me.'

He grimaced. 'I hadn't entirely made up my mind then but, yes, I did buy Clover Hill.'

'So?' she queried impatiently.

He took his time and allowed his dark gaze to roam over her. 'Marry me,' he said slowly. 'If you do, I'll save your parents from bankruptcy.'

Three weeks later, they stood side by side at a register office and were pronounced man and wife.

Kimberley Maria Richardson née Theron wore a filmy dress splashed with oversized blooms in cream and rose-pink on a pale grey background. The dress had a blouson bodice with a dropped waistline and a three-quarter skirt and carried a very famous designer label. It lived up to its label in every way so she looked marvellous, although she was a little pale.

Reith Richardson—no middle name, Kim thought; is

that significant?—then chastised herself for being ridiculous, but the fact of the matter was her mind was turning crazy circles. It had been since the day she'd agreed to marry Reith because she couldn't bear to think of her parents ending up in the poor house, so to speak.

They had no one to witness their union so the magistrate obliged, then they were seated side by side in his car and speeding towards Saldanha for the next momentous encounter—breaking the news to her parents.

She'd insisted on doing things this way, although now she was beginning to regret the decision. Beginning to regret not taking his offer to break the news himself.

'What can *you* say?' she'd taunted. 'In exchange for your daughter I'll get you out of hock?'

'No,' he'd replied. 'I could say that an intense attraction has sprung up between us and—'

She'd turned on him. 'Believe me, it's died an instant death!'

He'd watched her impassively for a long moment then he'd shot her last hopes down in flames. 'Kim, I don't know about you but the alternative for your parents would be disastrous. Both Balthazar and Saldanha would go into receivership. This way, my offer for them will clear the debts, your father'll have a place on the Balthazar board in an advisory capacity and *you* will get to play lady of the manor at Saldanha.' His eyes had mocked her.

She'd gone white. 'If you think insulting me is going to help, you're wrong. Why can't Mum and Dad stay on at Saldanha?'

'It would never work.'

'I don't think they've got anywhere else to go,' she'd objected. Then she'd bitten her lip and said painfully, 'They may be able to clear their debts if they sell to you but I don't think there'll be anything left over.' She'd pressed her hands into fists at the thought of the absolute mess she'd found her parents' personal finances to be in; at the thought of them honourably solvent rather than bankrupted, but only just, only a hair's breadth from being out on the street.

He'd noticed the gesture. 'Your brother,' he'd suggested.

Kim had shaken her head. 'Damien has no more resources than I have.'

She'd taken a deep breath then and risked saying, 'I don't think you're rating me highly enough, Reith, to be honest.'

'Oh?' He'd raised an eyebrow.

'No. As a wife, especially for a billionaire, I'll be superb.'

They'd stared at each other and it became a prickly-tense, heart-stopping moment.

'Do you mean in bed?' he'd queried at last, with a significant scan up and down her figure that effectively stripped her naked but not in a humorous way at all.

'Now, that,' she'd said, inwardly threatening to shoot herself if she blushed but in fact she was way too angry to blush, 'might depend on you so I'll suspend judgement until it happens...*if* it happens. What I meant was that I would run your homes beautifully, I'd handle the entertaining a billionaire might find appropriate with ease, I'd look the part and—' she'd paused '—I'm good with kids.'

Reith had said slowly, 'I've got an apartment in Bunbury; I'll lease it to your parents rent-free and I'll set up an allowance for them—for as long as you stay with me, Kim.'

She'd drawn a breath. 'You drive a hard bargain.'

'You're not exactly playing softball yourself,' he'd said derisively.

She'd opened her mouth to protest that it was no such thing but said instead, 'Why shouldn't it be a game two can play?'

'Indeed. Why not?' he'd responded with a flash of humour that had infuriated her. She hadn't been mollified when he'd added, 'But you certainly deserve full marks for standing behind your nearest and dearest, Kim Theron.'

Now, as the miles got chewed up, as the roads became country ones and they got closer, she became less and less certain she was doing this the right way round. Less certain that she shouldn't have warned her parents first...

'Stop,' she said suddenly. 'Please stop. I feel sick.'

He pulled up on the side of the road. There was a fairly broad grassy verge, then a fence and a line of bushes beyond, indicating a water course of some kind.

Kim swallowed frantically several times, then pushed her door open precipitously and stumbled out, and there followed a painful little interlude for her, during which she lost what little she'd eaten that day.

Eventually she staggered back to the car and sat down on the seat sideways.

'Here.'

She squinted upwards to see Reith minus his suit jacket and with his tie loosened and his shirtsleeves pushed up, offering her a wet towel.

'Where… How?' she stammered.

'The towel's been in the back since we went surfing. And—' he gestured behind him '—there's a creek over the fence. The water is flowing and clean.'

'Oh, thank you.' She took the towel gratefully and held it to her face and neck. 'Sorry but—'

'Don't be,' he said, interrupting her, and took the towel from her. 'I'll wet it again. There's also a bottle of drinking water in the console.' He leant past her and pushed a button, revealing a plastic bottle of spring water.

Half an hour later they were on their way again.

Reith had tossed his jacket in the back seat and Kim had done what she could to restore herself.

'Don't worry about it,' he advised after glancing at her. They were proceeding, she noticed, at a much slower pace. 'You look fine,' he said. He added very quietly, 'You always do.'

She turned her head to look at him and their gazes clashed briefly before she looked away.

What does that *mean*? she wondered.

Should I be complimented? Complimented enough to forgive him for forcing me to marry him? Does he honestly think that's all it's going to take? Still, he was kind just now, and helpful—if *only* I knew exactly what I was dealing with.

'What are you going to say to your parents, Kim?'

She tensed as his question broke the silence, and pleated the silk chiffon of her skirt. 'I don't know.'

'That doesn't sound particularly like you,' he observed with a tinge of sarcasm.

She bridled but forced herself to simmer down. 'I was just going to…to present it as a fait accompli, but I don't think that's going to work, now that I come to think of it,' she said. Then she took a breath. 'Perhaps,' she said slowly, 'what you had in mind to say is…the best way to go.'

'At least it's honest.'

'No, it's not honest, Reith, from the point of view of getting married because of it but—' she hesitated '—all right; I'll go along with it.'

'We don't have to make such heavy weather of this, Kim. Not that long ago, we were good together,' he said as he changed gear and swung into Saldanha's driveway.

She took a very deep breath. 'You're right,' she agreed, and took some more deep breaths as she prepared to face her parents.

In the event, however, the encounter proved to be catastrophic.

Kim groaned as they pulled under the rear portico. 'Damien's here.' She pointed towards the parked racing-green sports car. She frowned.

'We might as well get it all over and done with.' Reith switched the engine off and got out of the car.

He retrieved his jacket from the back seat, fixed his shirtsleeves, fiddled with his tie and came round to open her door.

Kim didn't move for a moment as she stared down at the shiny gold band now on the ring finger of her left hand—she'd refused an engagement ring. As she did so, she thought of her parents, thought of all they'd done for her, and she found the strength to slip out of the car without his assistance.

But what greeted them as she led the way inside, stopping only to pat a delighted Sunny Bob, was a scene of trauma. Her father was slumped on the settee in the main lounge, her mother was kneeling beside him crying. Mary Hiddens was hovering, wringing her hands, and Damien was savagely punching numbers into his phone.

'Kim…Kim…' Her mother caught sight of her. 'Oh, Kim!' Her gaze fell on Reith and she gasped. 'So it's true!'

'What's true?' Kim ran forward to kneel down beside her mother.

'Some journalist just rang your father and asked him if it was true that you'd married Reith Richardson. He hadn't been feeling well, your father, but that…at that… he just collapsed.'

'You've probably killed him,' Damien said darkly to Reith.

Thanks to Reith's best efforts—he'd taken command— Frank survived the attack.

Reith had told Damien not to worry about calling an

ambulance and instead he'd summoned a medical emergency helicopter. He'd made Frank as comfortable as possible until it had arrived, and administered some of the emergency medicine Frank had been prescribed but no one had thought to give him in their panic.

And he'd been with Kim when the specialist told her that her father had a heart condition that had been ticking away like a time bomb, a condition that might or might not respond to open-heart bypass surgery—something her father dreaded.

The specialist had also told her that the attack could have happened at any time.

'How did anyone find out? About us?'

She asked the question in a vague, distracted way when they were alone at Saldanha. Her mother had been persuaded to be admitted to the hospital and sedated, Damien was still at the hospital and arrangements were being made for bypass surgery on Frank as soon as possible. The subject of her marriage to Reith Richardson had apparently sunk from sight beneath the weight of the medical emergency, for both Damien and her mother.

Once again, Reith had discarded his jacket and loosened his tie. He'd poured them both a brandy.

'Someone must have recognized—you, most probably. Kim—' he paused '—what do you want to do?'

She sipped some brandy and laid her head back. 'What do you mean? Now? In a week's time? When?'

'Now, for starters,' he said dryly.

'Look, I don't know,' she replied frustratedly. 'I can't

think straight.' She looked around the lovely room with a frown and it occurred to her that Reith looked, if not exactly at home, almost as if he knew his way around it.

But, of course, she thought then, he's been here before, hasn't he? My father or Damien probably offered him a drink out of the cocktail cabinet, so that was how he knew where to find the brandy. Of course they wouldn't have been offering him drinks after he made his first paltry offer for Balthazar... She paused her thoughts.

'Tell me something,' she said with another frown. 'Were Saldanha and Balthazar just business propositions to you? Not any desire to live here and be involved in the wine industry or...' She trailed off, then gathered steam again. 'Or put down roots that have more substance than the boundary rider's hut on some godforsaken cattle station—' She stopped abruptly and put a horrified hand to her mouth.

He watched her for a long moment, narrowly, but otherwise curiously without expression. Then he said, 'It wasn't a boundary rider's hut—but I suppose you could call it a godforsaken cattle station. It was out from Karratha.' He grimaced. 'No, in answer to your question. I'm not interested in roots or substance, so I'm never going to appeal to your father or brother, Kim. I'm never going to be good enough for you in their estimation. If that's what you're wondering.'

Kim sat up abruptly. 'Why *do* they... Why are they *so* against you, though, Reith?'

He rolled his balloon glass between his hands and

stared down at the cognac. 'They consider me a country hick who had a bit of luck with a patch of dirt.'

'But you're not a country hick. I mean—'

'You mean I don't uncap beer bottles with my teeth? No, I don't. I do lack an old school tie, though.'

'That's rubbish.'

He shrugged.

'There's got to be more to it,' Kim persisted, although she wasn't sure why. It was just that she was so tired, so shocked by the events of the day, yet this was the one topic her mind seemed to want to pursue, as if it had an extraordinary significance.

Reith took a long sip of his brandy, then put the glass down and pushed it away from him. 'It's probably because I was able to expose all the mistakes they made over the past few years, the misjudgements—'

'But I thought it was flood, fire, drought, global financial crises—' she interrupted '—powdery mildew! And so on. Things you couldn't prevent, in other words.'

'They didn't help, but there were no contingency plans in place, for one thing. Kim, look—' he rubbed his jaw '—it's how I operate. It's by digging beneath the surface that I can accurately evaluate what I'm getting into, but it doesn't necessarily endear me to the people on the other end of it.'

He got up abruptly and came to stand in front of her with his hands shoved into his pockets. 'Look,' he said, 'I'm sorry about your father but, little though he knows it, you'll be better off with me than—'

'How can you *say* that?' Kim stumbled to her feet.

'You make me feel like a…a commodity! And there's no way you can know what my welfare depends on.'

'Kim, I know exactly what ensures your welfare. I only have to kiss you to—'

She raised her hand to slap him but he caught her wrist and pulled her into his arms.

'Don't,' he warned softly.

'Let me go,' she said through her teeth.

'No. Not until we've sorted something out.'

'Well, sort away!' she commanded. 'Just don't you dare kiss me.' But, despite the command, tears ran down her cheeks.

He grinned fleetingly. 'That's more like the girl I know. No, listen.' He tightened his grip on her as she wriggled. 'I'm not expecting you to leap into the marital bed in these circumstances—' he gestured '—your father, I mean—unless you'd like to?'

Kim refused to look at him but he didn't let her go. 'Take that as a definite no, Richardson,' he murmured to himself. 'Then it'll have to be a moratorium.'

Kim stilled and turned towards him. 'What do you mean?'

He lifted a sardonic eyebrow. 'A freeze on all contentious matters. For a period of time.'

'Why don't we just separate and get a divorce?'

'No, Kim.'

She stared up at him. 'Just—no, Kim?'

'Uh-huh.'

She sagged against him. 'I can't believe this,' she said, distraught.

'Life does hand out some brickbats,' he agreed.

She opened her mouth on a sharp retort, then closed it, nearly biting her tongue in the process because, of course, it was true.

'But for the time being,' he went on, 'while your father is so sick, we won't make any lifestyle decisions or major changes.'

Kim straightened and looked into his eyes. 'Where will you stay? Bunbury? Perth?'

He shook his head. 'Clover Hill.'

She gasped. 'Have you taken possession?' But she immediately fired another question. 'What's wrong with Clover—what did you have to ferret out about it before you bought it?'

His eyes glinted and a nerve flickered in his jaw at the implied insult, but he answered evenly enough. 'Nothing's wrong with Clover. It was on the market because its owners are getting on and have no family to leave it to.'

'So why did you buy it? Doesn't sound like your usual modus operandi,' she taunted.

He let her go and smiled, a cool chiselled movement of his lips. 'I bought Clover because you thought it was special, Kim. Goodnight.'

He retrieved his jacket, slung it over his shoulder and strode out.

CHAPTER FIVE

REITH RICHARDSON regarded his wife and took his time about it.

She was fairly tall, she was slim with a good figure and she was stunningly beautiful, with red-gold hair and sapphire-blue eyes. Her smooth skin was complemented by a pair of sparkling diamond earrings he had given her but was surprised to see her wearing. She usually made a point of refusing to wear any of the jewellery that came with the position of being his wife.

Of course, as a Theron of Saldanha and the Balthazar winery, the position of being his wife was a bit of a comedown for her, other than in monetary terms.

Her dress was cream and silky and long. It looked sleek when she stood still but when she moved it revealed yards of material in the skirt. With it she wore high nude platform shoes. But, beautiful as the dress was, as well as fashionable, it provoked one regret in him—it hid her legs and that was a pity; she had sensational legs.

In fact there was no doubt, so far as looks and an innate sort of classiness went, that she would be an asset to any man. In lots of ways she was to him but there was one downside—she hated him.

She blamed him for profiting from her family's misfortunes, she considered that she'd been manipulated into marrying him to stem some of the worst of those misfortunes. She despised his occupation, she'd accused him of having a questionable modus operandi—but in all other respects, bar one, she was a superb wife as, indeed, she'd promised to be.

She ran their homes perfectly, although she'd refused point-blank to live at Clover Hill. Out of necessity, he had moved in to Saldanha, though he was rarely there. She was an accomplished hostess so their social lives ran like clockwork and she was good with his motherless son.

And they all lived, like the old lady in the shoe, he thought with a wry twist of his lips, in Western Australia, south of Perth and towards the Margaret River district.

None of the Theron family, however, had approved of the Balthazar winery or the Saldanha estate straying out of the family, least of all his wife.

However, as he had once pointed out to her, she'd come with it and she *was* family. He'd also pointed out to her that, without his intervention, her parents—her father had recovered well from a heart bypass operation—would not now be settled in a fashionable unit overlooking the beach and bay, with its iconic dolphins, at Bunbury, enjoying a leisurely retirement. In fact they would have been much closer to a bedsit and Meals on Wheels. Nor would they have been able to afford the luxury cruise he had paid for, which had contributed significantly to Frank Theron's recovery from open-heart surgery.

She'd tossed her red-gold hair at him and her eyes had glinted sapphire fire but as he'd waited politely she'd clamped her mouth shut and stalked off.

Strangely, he'd taken himself to task for that encounter. How galling must it be to have things like that thrown into your face on a regular basis? he'd asked himself. Not that he did it often because, truth be told, he admired her fiery resolve not to forgive him for the proposition he'd put to her—marry me and I'll save your parents from bankruptcy.

Well, he amended to himself, he had admired that fiery resolve but he was starting to lose patience. Two months had passed since he'd married her.

'What are you thinking, Reith?'

Kim's voice broke into his thoughts. He grimaced as he saw the puzzled frown in her eyes, and shoved his hands into his pockets. 'That you look lovely; that you've been an accomplished wife and it's just a pity that you hate me. Let's see.' He pulled a hand out of his pocket, rubbed his jaw and looked out over the gardens of Saldanha in the slanting rays of the setting sun. 'What else was I thinking? I do appreciate how you've coped with Darcy; I do actually admire your hostility—well, I did—I'm starting to lose patience with it now.'

'What…what do you mean?' She frowned.

They were standing on the front doorstep. There was a gleaming gun-metal four-wheel drive parked on the driveway below them and they were about to go to a neighbouring property for dinner. Sunny Bob sat beside the car, ever hopeful that he'd get taken for a ride.

'This was never meant to be a marriage in name only, Kim,' he said, bringing his dark gaze back to rest on her.

Fresh colour stained her cheeks. 'I thought... I thought...' She stopped.

'You thought?'

'You promised me time,' she said more composedly. 'And I thought...you might change your mind anyway. You might find someone who suited you better. Or someone you actually loved,' she said with irony.

A dry smile twisted his lips. 'Is that what you were hoping? If so, you shouldn't have made yourself almost indispensable.'

Kim looked at him. 'Any good housekeeper could have done—'

'Not quite,' he broke in. 'They wouldn't care about Saldanha and Balthazar as you do or have taken the time with Darcy that you have,' he said dryly. 'You know,' he added, 'when we come home, we could take a walk through the garden in the moonlight—it's a full moon tonight—then I could take you upstairs and make love to you. After all, Kim,' he said deliberately, 'we *were* once on kissing terms.'

She took a ragged breath. 'I didn't know who you were.'

'That didn't affect the chemistry between us.' He looked down at her with something like contempt.

Kim closed her eyes because he was right and her objection had been unworthy—she had once kissed Reith Richardson with wonderful abandon, with passion and with promise—before she'd found out who he was. All the same…

She made a frustrated little sound and went to turn away.

He put out his hand and stopped her. 'And there was a lot more to it, as you damn well know.'

'Reith—' she looked pointedly at his hand on her arm '—this isn't the time or place to be having this kind of discussion.'

He didn't release her. 'You pick a suitable time and place then.' He shrugged and looked at her cynically. 'Provided it's within the foreseeable future and not a year down the track—or ten.'

She flinched inwardly at the insult. 'What I meant was…we're already running late for dinner.'

He did release her arm then and stepped back. 'You know, I never thought you were a coward, Kim.'

'I'm not,' she said icily.

'Or an ostrich,' he went on imperturbably.

'I'm not that either,' she flashed, her iciness turning to anger.

He shrugged. 'You could have fooled me. After you.' He stood aside.

She hesitated under the influence of an almighty desire to run away. But, really, she was like a puppet on a string and there was no way she could run away without breaking those strings. And the consequences of that could be catastrophic for her proud, dysfunctional family, whom she loved nonetheless…

She walked down the steps and got into the car.

* * *

It was a superb dinner.

Twenty people sat around the dining table. The meal had been served on exquisite porcelain and the wine had flowed out of crystal glasses. The tablecloth alone was a work of art, hand-embroidered with birds of paradise on ecru linen.

They were dining with their neighbours, Molly and Bill Lawson. Kim had known them all her life. She'd grown up with their children, all boys, and had been looked upon as a de facto daughter. That was still the case, which meant that Reith had been accepted without question, she thought darkly at times.

Then again, Reith could charm the socks off anyone when he set his mind to it and it wasn't only his dark good looks, his height and physique that did it. He had a way of making you laugh with a few wry words and a crooked grin. Sometimes he had a way of making you feel like the only person on the planet for him.

Not that her husband spent a lot of his life charming people, she thought as she put down her wine glass and pushed away her plate with nothing left of what had been a mouth-watering Bombe Alaska. No, impressing people was his other forte.

There was no doubt Bill Lawson, an astute judge of character with a good grasp of the business world, admired Reith greatly. There was no doubt Molly thought he was divine.

Why, oh, why, she sometimes thought, couldn't her parents have accepted Reith as the Lawsons had? Of course the answer was obvious—money and reputation and so much more had come into it, hadn't it?

She picked up her glass and took another sip of wine.

And now Reith had laid down a gauntlet.

Why hadn't she seen it coming? Because she'd been too immersed in restoring Saldanha to its former glory? Too busy doing the same for Balthazar?

Or *was* she a coward and had she been burying her head in the sand?

What if she…acquiesced? she wondered. Or—what if she confessed to Reith that she was never sure whether she loved him to distraction or hated him like poison?

There were certainly times when just to look at him or hear his voice brought on a deluge of anger as she recalled how beholden she was to him.

Equally certainly, though, there were times when she couldn't deny the potent physical effect he had on her. The times when—out of the blue, usually—she'd look at his hands and suffer the acute desire to have them running up and down her body. Times when she wanted to laugh with him and go into his arms to be held in affection and companionship and love.

Times when she longed to be in his bed, being made love to until she was sated and exhausted and slippery with sweat and…

She broke off those thoughts with a snap as something alerted her to the fact Reith was staring at her with a question mark in his eyes.

Oh, God, don't let me blush, she prayed, and was saved by Molly rising and gesturing towards the lounge, where the coffee tray was awaiting them. She rose swiftly and followed their hostess into the lounge.

* * *

It was midnight when the car turned into the long Saldanha driveway.

'Pleasant evening,' Reith murmured.

'Y...yes,' Kim agreed and could have shot herself for the slight quiver of nerves her voice betrayed.

He glanced at her and grimaced. 'You don't sound too sure.'

'I... What did you think of Chilli George?' she countered.

Reith pulled the car up opposite the back door and shrugged. 'Exotic—like her name, but then I suppose fashion designers need to be.' He paused, then he went on, 'Is that to be the extent of our conversation tonight, Kim? A dissection of Molly's guest list?'

Kim clasped her hands, then unclasped them as she struggled to find something to say, something that wasn't inane, that wasn't designed to ignore the situation between them, but no inspiration came. 'It's late,' she said. 'I... And...' She trailed off.

'Not the right time or place?' he suggested, his voice hardening.

She stayed silent.

'All right. Out you get,' he ordered.

'You could leave the car here, under the portico,' she said without thinking.

'I'm not taking it to the garage, I'm taking it to Perth.'

Kim jumped. 'At this time of night? Why?' She stared at him, wide-eyed.

Their gazes clashed. 'You're not really that naïve, are you?' he said with soft but patently lethal sarcasm.

'I...I... When will you be back?'

'No idea.' He drummed his fingers on the steering wheel.

'Reith!'

'Kimberley?' he replied politely, but with a world of contempt in his dark eyes.

She bit her lip, then got angry although she tried to rein it in. 'Suit yourself,' she told him coolly and got out but anger got the better of her and she slammed the car door.

It didn't help her state of mind to hear him laugh softly before he gunned the motor and drove off, sputtering gravel beneath his tyres.

The next morning, after what had felt like a sleepless night, Kim saddled her mare Matilda, affectionately known as Mattie, and went for a ride. Sunny Bob went with them and they headed for Balthazar and its Cellar Door, run on the estate and visited by wine-lovers from all over the world.

It was one thing she had always taken a special interest in, the Balthazar Cellar Door. Most wineries offered wine-tastings and sold their wines from their 'Cellar Doors' and many had restaurants as well as offering conducted tours through the winery itself. The Balthazar Cellar Door was housed in a stone and thatch building set in surroundings that were magical—gardens full of blooms, flowering creepers and trees, especially jacarandas, a stream that wound under wooden bridges, a thatched wishing well. And there was a natural amphitheatre backed by tall cypress-pines.

Inside, as well as the wine-tasting area, was the restaurant and a souvenir shop where she now worked several days a week, having given up her teaching job.

And as she cantered Mattie, then galloped her with their breath steaming in the early morning air as the pale colours of dawn smudged the horizon, it was Balthazar she was forcing herself to concentrate on.

Some wineries hosted art shows, some were famous for their music festivals. Balthazar held an annual fashion parade that was due in a couple of days. This year Kim had offered the opportunity to debut her spring collection to a new but dynamic Perth designer—the unfortunate Chilli George.

She grimaced as Mattie's hooves thudded over the turf. Not that Chilli was unfortunate in any context other than featuring unwittingly in the ongoing battle between Reith and Kimberley Richardson. She was in fact a petite, exquisitely chic blonde in her thirties. Perhaps she was a touch exotic but she certainly designed gorgeous clothes.

Kim owned some Chilli George clothes and they were fresh and exciting.

Was there something about Chilli that went beyond being a touch exotic, something she couldn't put her finger on that bothered her, though? she wondered, then shrugged.

Really, the designer was the least of her problems, she reminded herself, as she slowed Mattie to a walk as they did a quick tour of the Cellar Door and the winery itself as well as the gardens. Then she turned back towards Saldanha.

And as they got closer, as always, these days anyway,

it pulled at her heart-strings to see her home. Until a few months ago she'd taken Saldanha pretty much for granted. True, she'd always been appreciative of the lovely Cape Dutch architecture, brought from South Africa by a great-great-grandfather.

But although the sight of Saldanha pulled at her heart-strings, it was the carte blanche Reith had given her to renovate the estate that had saved her sanity in the early days of her loveless marriage. Not only that, it had brought to light skills she hadn't known she possessed, such as gardening. She was taken by surprise when the head gardener had approached her for instructions but, once the idea that she was in charge settled in, she took to it like the proverbial duck to water.

She supervised everything that went into the garden and everything that came out of it. She cherished her mother's and grandmother's beloved roses. She'd built a Japanese water garden with lilies and carp in the pond and stone benches under a jasmine creeper-covered lattice canopy. In the heat of mid-summer just the sound of water trickling down into the pond would be cooling.

Then she'd turned her attention to the house and looked around with new eyes. Saldanha homestead was still beautiful, it was still filled with furniture brought from South Africa in different woods—kiaat or teak, stinkwood, yellowwood—but it had got shabby and her parents hadn't been in the position to remedy that.

The first thing she did was have the house painted inside and out. She used some of her favourite colours, like chalk and lagoon-blue, mocha, raspberry, mango, mushroom and heritage green and some beautiful wallpapers, although she maintained white for the exterior. Then she'd pulled up all the fitted carpets and replaced them. Fortunately this was restricted to the second floor, as the ground floor and the main rooms had wooden parquet floors that were almost an artwork on their own. And she'd had all the bathrooms upgraded.

After this major upheaval, her efforts had been less disruptive—she and Mary Hiddens had had a great time modernizing the kitchen as well as replenishing the linen.

And after all the work and cherishing she'd lavished on it, on top of coming so close to losing it, Saldanha meant even more to her than ever.

But there were other things that weighed on her and filled her with a feeling of guilt at times—how lightly she'd taken everything that had made up her old life. Expensive schooling, then a gap year backpacking around Africa and Asia. University, all the right clothes, all the right friends, her horses, her parents' wealth.

She'd heard it said that Damien and Kimberley Theron went around as if they owned the district. She'd ignored the jibe at the time but now she was forced to look back and acknowledge that she may have, at times, behaved like a spoilt socialite.

If so, it sometimes helped to remind herself that at the grand old age of twenty-two she'd come to earth with an almighty bump. And she would never forgive herself for not noticing the dire straits her parents had got themselves into sooner.

Thinking of her parents led her to wondering—yet again—if Reith had sent them on a luxury cruise to relieve the pressure of their shock and disapproval about their daughter's marriage.

That's me, she reminded herself. And she had to confess it made things much easier because, since they'd got back, the sting and impossibility of it all seemed to have subsided.

Yes, her mother had several times tried to dig below the surface Kim presented of a busy, capable if not deliriously happy wife, until Kim had sat her down one day, taken Fiona's hands in hers and said, 'Mum, I'm fine. Please don't ask me to explain things between me and Reith...they're complicated but he's no monster and...I am fine.'

Fiona had grimaced, then said tremulously, 'I just wish we were a happy family again. I hardly see anything of Damien these days.'

'You're lucky to see him at all,' Kim had replied, then bitten her tongue. 'But you've got me,' she'd teased then.

And her mother had hugged her mightily.

One of the other aspects of her new life that was more rewarding than contemplating how things had changed for her, was dealing with Reith's motherless son.

For the most part, Darcy Richardson appeared to be a perfectly normal ten-year-old. Unlike his father, he was fair with hazel eyes and freckles, but it had struck Kim early on that he was just too perfect. He was polite, he had beautiful manners, he ate everything that was put in front of him and he came and went from his boarding school every second weekend with no sign of any regrets, no evidence of homesickness, no elation at being home either. In fact she got the feeling he was happier at school.

Once, Kim had involuntarily said to Reith as they'd dropped Darcy back at school, 'Is he a bit traumatized?'

Reith had stared at the image of his son diminishing in his rear-view mirror and, as she'd watched him, Kim had taken an unexpected breath.

There was not much she cared to admit she admired about Reith Richardson, but for one moment she'd seen a sort of suffering in his eyes she hadn't expected him to be capable of feeling.

'He…he can be a little hard to get through to sometimes,' he'd said.

'Because he lost his mother? And now his grandmother?'

Reith had accelerated the car down the school drive. 'He never knew his mother, but that's obviously a cross to bear for any child. Unfortunately, I haven't been able to spend as much time with him as I'd like to have.'

'That's not unusual for a father, a breadwinner,' Kimberley had said slowly. 'Perhaps especially without a wife. What about your parents? Did they help out?'

He'd cast her a look of such irony, she'd been jolted. 'My parents?' he'd said. 'My mother left home when I was ten and my father never recovered. He died before Darcy was born.'

'I'm sorry,' she'd murmured and one glance beneath her lashes at his harsh features had not encouraged her to pursue the subject.

It hadn't left her, though, and she might not have mentioned it or discussed it with Reith but from then on she'd taken a special interest in Darcy. From her interest in and experience with kids, she knew not to crowd the boy so she bided her time and watched what he did and how he reacted to life at Saldanha. It wasn't long before she noticed something that appeared to break through that excruciatingly polite, almost touch-me-not exterior Darcy Richardson presented to the world—a horse.

Mattie's half-brother, to be precise, a chestnut two-year-old Kim had often despaired of raising because of a throat deformity. But an operation had finally cured the problem and, although the colt was small and would only ever be a children's pony, he was now sound and just the right size for Darcy. What was more, she could see that Darcy was drawn to the chestnut.

'What's his name?' he'd asked Kim one day as he was scratching his forehead.

Kim grimaced. 'Rusty. Not very original but we didn't think he was going to survive.'

'Can he be ridden?'

'Sure—do you ride, Darcy?'

The boy had nodded. 'I get lessons at school. But they're all old hacks.'

'Would you like to ride Rusty?'

'Yes, if it's OK.'

'No problem, but we'll have to find a saddle and a hat for you. We'll go out together because he hasn't been ridden for a while and Mattie will be a good influence on him. And, just for safety's sake, we'll use a leading rein. But only until you've got to know him.'

So that was what they did, and got into the habit of doing it whenever Darcy was home.

Then one day Darcy had said to her, 'Kim?'

She'd looked across at him in some surprise as they jogged through the paddock, because it was the first time he'd called her by name. 'Yep?'

'Can I give Rusty a new name?'

Kim blinked. 'What did you have in mind?'

'Rimfire!'

She'd scanned the two of them, the under-sized chestnut horse and his freckle-faced, enthusiastic rider and smiled to herself as she wondered what flights of fancy Darcy was indulging in with his horse. 'Wow! Sounds super.'

'Really? Do you really, really think so?'

'Yes, I really, really do.'

The other thing she noticed was how Reith went out of his way to establish a rapport with his son, not entirely successfully, however.

Coming back to the present, the morning after Reith had driven to Perth in the middle of the night, she slid off Mattie and took some time to wash her down, dry her and mix her feed. Time, she understood, she was using to delay her return to the house, where it was much more difficult to ignore her problems…

'Thanks, Mary,' she said as the housekeeper delivered a laden trolley to the breakfast room.

Kim loved the breakfast room, with its view out over the herb garden. It had a stone fireplace, her mother's desk, which she'd inherited, and some comfortable armchairs as well as the walnut dining table and chairs. The décor was beige walls, white woodwork and splashes of peppermint-green and rose-pink. Despite being labelled the breakfast room, they took all their meals there when they were alone.

Mary had been part of the Saldanha establishment for as long as Kim could remember and she was the soul of discretion. However, possibly because she'd known Kim since she was a baby, Mary also took a stance at times that advised Kim she liked to be kept up to date with 'movement on the station' and not only physical movement, a stance she demonstrated as she returned with the silver coffee pot.

'Mr Richardson didn't mention he was going away,' she said as she placed the pot carefully on a trivet.

'No,' Kim agreed. 'It…uh…came up out of the blue.'

'When will he be back?'

'I don't know,' Kim replied and grimaced at the sharp look she received. 'That is to say *he* didn't seem to know.'

Mary tidied the table unnecessarily. 'He didn't take any clothes.'

'Well, you know, Mary, we keep things in the apartment so we don't have to pack and so on.'

'The apartment in Perth? So that's where he's gone?'

'That's what he said,' Kimberley replied with a lilt, meant to convey complete unconcern, although, of course, Reith had said nothing of the kind.

But the housekeeper shrugged and went on her way looking reassured, although leaving Kim wondering whether she ever fooled Mary Hiddens.

She stared at her breakfast, bacon and eggs, then poured herself a glass of orange juice.

Fortunately, considering the state of her marriage, she mused, her parents had always had separate bedrooms.

Could they have any idea how handy that had been to their only daughter when she'd embarked on her marriage of convenience to Reith Richardson? she often wondered.

Mind you, she reminded herself, the other thing that helped conceal the true state of their marriage was the fact that Reith spent very little time at home. He'd had a helicopter pad installed behind the house and his royal-blue chopper was a common sight coming and going. He often left home ridiculously early or late, so it made sense for Kim to have her own bedroom. Well, she grimaced, more or less.

She thought about Reith's secretary, Alice Hawthorn, who was devoted to him. Alice was in her fifties, a widow, and secretly in love with Reith but a model of efficiency. She lived in Perth and worked in the office Reith maintained in the city.

If she had any doubts about her employer's marriage being made in heaven she never gave the slightest indication of it. But surely she must wonder, Kim sometimes thought. *She* has to brief me about all his movements, all the engagements we need to attend together—surely she must wonder if we ever pass the time of day with each other?

She shook her head and turned her attention to her breakfast, feeding most of her bacon to Sunny Bob, who grinned widely at her. Then she poured herself some coffee and found she was unable to tear her thoughts away from Reith and his dramatic departure last night, not to mention the gauntlet he'd laid down.

And with the memory of that came a cold little bubbling sense of fear brought on by the thought that if she didn't hold up her side of the bargain she would lose Saldanha and Balthazar. Not only that, but her parents could lose their pleasant lifestyle and her father could lose his position on the board of the winery, which seemed crucial to his self-respect.

Would he do that to her?

She sighed, a sound of pure frustration, because trying to read Reith was like trying to break a particularly difficult code.

Yes, the last few months had revealed that he was a tough businessman who invariably got his own way, but then she'd guessed that although she'd not known the full extent of it.

What had surprised her, as well as her father, who was nevertheless loath to admit it, was the depth and breadth of his vision in the cattle and wine business. It should have been new to him, she'd reasoned, the wine business anyway. But, new to him or not, what many saw as risks, he saw as challenges and some of his lightning decisions had taken her breath away.

She sometimes thought back to their first dinner, when she'd asked him what the appeal was in rescuing and buying ailing businesses. When she'd been, she thought with a private little grimace, a touch superior about vocations, and he'd answered that it was the challenge and the learning curve, or words to that effect. She now saw a powerful intellect at work as he absorbed knowledge like blotting paper.

She'd seen Balthazar pick up and only in seeing it did she realize she hadn't noticed its decline. She'd seen the Saldanha estate and the cattle it ran go through the same transformation.

She'd not known what to make of it when he'd complimented her on having a commercial instinct herself.

'What do you mean?' she'd asked rather sharply.

He'd grimaced and leant his wide shoulders against her bedroom door frame. She'd been sitting at her dressing table, brushing her hair as her final step towards getting ready for a luncheon they were hosting at home.

'It appears,' he'd said, 'that you could sell ice to Eskimos.'

Kim had been watching him in her mirror but she twisted on the stool and frowned at him. 'I don't understand. It sounds a bit fishy…'

He'd grinned. 'I shouldn't be surprised.'

'Why? What about?'

'That anything to do with commercialism has vulgar connotations for you.'

Kim had blinked several times. 'I said no such thing,' she objected.

'You didn't, but you didn't have to, you looked it. Or—' he'd shrugged and pushed his hands into the pockets of his trousers '—maybe it was just being compared to me in any way that you objected to.'

Kim had set her teeth as she rolled her brush in her

hands. 'Will you please tell me what you're talking about, Reith?'

'On the days you work in the Cellar Door shop, the takings increase by nearly thirty per cent.'

Kim's lips had parted.

'Which led me to believe you have a flair for parting people from their hard-earned dosh,' he added, 'to put it mildly.' He smiled.

She'd sucked in a breath. 'I don't do that. It sounds awful. All I do is—' she gestured '—make some suggestions.'

'Good ones, obviously. But if you have that kind of sales flair, you may have been wasted as a teacher, my dear.'

Kim had turned back on the stool. 'I enjoyed teaching,' she said, and lifted her brush, determined not to engage in any more infuriating conversation with her infuriating husband.

But her eyes had widened as he stepped up behind her and calmly removed the brush from her hand.

'Oh, much more genteel, teaching, I agree,' he'd said and threw the brush onto the bed, then ran his hands through her hair.

They'd stared at each other in the mirror, Kim wide-eyed and frozen. 'Looks much better a bit mussed up,' he drawled. 'Mmm—I could almost imagine that you've just got out of bed.'

He'd glanced significantly at her bed, she'd followed his glance and, to her horror, an image came to mind of the two of them writhing against each other, of her being wild and wanton in her love-making, electric but silken at the same time, and he wielding the strength of his beautiful body lightly at first and then more powerfully until…

She'd felt the breath rasp in her throat and a rush of sensation fizzed through her so that a pulse beat rapidly and she felt hot all over.

'Then again,' he'd drawled, 'I'd need a very vivid imagination, wouldn't I, Kim?'

He'd turned on his heel and walked out before she could think of a thing to say.

But when she'd calmed down, she had retaliated.

She'd appeared on the terrace where they were to eat, just as the first guests had arrived—with her hair tied back severely into a bun.

Only to see him looking stunned for a bare second, before his dark eyes had flooded with laughter.

She came back to the present and clicked her tongue because the whole incident still had the power to make her feel foolish.

There were other things that made her feel not so much foolish as—well, yes, she had to concede—like an ostrich intent on burying its head in the sand, but not in the way Reith had meant it. More to do with the questions she hadn't asked, about Darcy's mother, for example.

Where and how had he met her? How old had she been? He would have been about twenty-four. Had it been love at first sight? Was she the love of his life? Was that how he'd been able to propose a marriage of convenience to her? Because he knew he'd never be able to put another woman in Darcy's mother's place in his heart?

She finished her coffee and went upstairs to shower and change but her internal monologue refused to subside.

They were questions she *should* have asked, she told herself as she finished washing and turned the needle-sharp spray of the shower to cold so her skin tingled.

Yes—she stepped out of the shower and started to dry herself—instead of being as haughty about it all as only she could be, instead of being scared to the core of her being, but determined to put a brave but angry face on it, she should have asked some pertinent questions.

She rubbed her hair, then dropped the towel and reached for her underwear, matching bra and tiny panties in apple-green silk. She paused for a moment to consider her day—morning in the garden, afternoon at the Cellar Door, getting ready for the fashion parade—she donned jeans with a fresh pink cotton shirt and sat down at her dressing table.

These days, it often seemed like one of life's little ironies that she should, as a married woman, still be using the bedroom she'd used as a girl and one that was several doors away from the master bedroom. But in the early days of her marriage it had seemed like an excellent idea to stay put.

Anyway, in the early days, Reith had stayed at Clover Hill. And it was only when she'd explained to him, in casual tones but with her eyes an arctic blue, that if he thought he could bribe her into his bed by allowing her to believe he'd bought Clover Hill specially for her, he should have another think coming, that he'd retaliated by moving into Saldanha. This had caused her some frustration. Life had been easier the other way around.

But it was no longer a blue room, her bedroom.

Now she had ivory walls and white French colonial furniture on a thyme-green carpet. On one wall hung an intricate silk tapestry of a garden and a beautifully carved sandalwood chest stood at the end of the bed.

All of it couldn't have been further from her mind, however, as she rested her chin on her hands and voiced the thought she'd been fighting to avoid ever since she'd stepped out of the car the night before under the portico…

'Who's he with?'

Was it realistic to imagine that Reith was living like a monk while she held onto her pride? Or, as he himself had said, was that being naïve? But was there one mistress, or several?

What did she look like, if it was one? Did he prefer blondes or brunettes? Redheads weren't that easy to come by— Oh, stop it! she commanded herself. It's insane to be thinking these thoughts. It's crazy to be jealous of some faceless woman, or a dozen of them, for that matter, when for ninety-nine per cent of the time you hate the man.

CHAPTER SIX

THERE was no sign of Reith and the fashion parade was upon them.

Kim dressed in some of her Chilli George clothes, a gorgeous taupe silk tunic with long sleeves and a ruffled neckline and slim ivory trousers, but she kept her eye on the window as she dressed because it was apparent from the moment she'd woken that the sun wasn't shining for her...

It was raining, but not gently—it poured. It literally teemed so that just getting people into the Cellar Door from the flooded car park became an exercise in logistics.

Then there was a power failure and candles had to be lit before the backup generator kicked in.

'Keep the champagne flowing,' Kim's mother advised.

Kim grinned but agreed and it was a strategy that worked. The crowd remained good-humoured, despite all the delays and inconveniences.

Good humour was hard to come by behind the scenes, however.

There'd certainly been nothing in any of their meetings that had suggested to Kim that Chilli George would work herself into a state of near hysteria over the weather, the delay in getting the generator going and the non-appearance of her wardrobe co-ordinator and assistant, who'd both been caught on the wrong side of a flooded creek.

'Look, it doesn't really matter,' Kim said soothingly. 'The girls must know roughly what they have to wear.'

But suddenly she wasn't so sure as she looked around the colourful behind-the-scenes chaos of the dressing room. There were armfuls of clothes everywhere. There were cosmetics strewn across every flat surface. It was hot, despite the rain. There was a hairdresser torturing, by the look of it, one of the model's hair into ringlets with a hot hair iron.

'It matters,' Chilli stated through her teeth. 'The models need someone behind the scenes. You must do it, Kimberley!'

Kim opened her eyes. 'Do what?'

'Co-ordinate the clothes.'

'Don't be ridiculous. I don't know the ins and outs of the outfits, how they do up, what shoes— I've got no more idea of what goes with what than...than the man in the moon!'

'Then we must cancel.' Chilli flapped her arms, then buried her face in her hands.

'Don't be silly,' Kim remonstrated this time. 'I've got a hundred people sitting out there dying to see your clothes! They've paid a small fortune and some of them nearly *drowned* getting here. Look, I know you were going to compère and you probably know it off by heart, but if you've got some notes, I'll do that and you can stay behind the scenes and sort things out here.'

'Won't like that, but here,' one of the models murmured in an aside to Kim and put a sheaf of printed notes into her hand, a numbered description of all the outfits.

'No!' Chilli said dramatically. 'You couldn't possibly handle the compèring.'

''Specially not with the most gorgeous, sexy man I've seen for years sitting in the front row!' came another aside, beamed Kim's way.

Kim frowned and peered through a crack in the makeshift wall. There was only one man sitting in the front row to date—Reith, sitting with Molly Lawson, chatting away comfortably.

Kim stared at him through the crack and discovered she could have killed him. He was wearing jeans and a navy leather jacket. His hair looked damp but he was entirely at ease as he and Molly chatted. Not only at ease but, with his tall body squashed into a folding chair, he still managed to look formidably attractive, dark and exciting and enough to take your breath away...

Then they laughed, he and Molly, and she thought furiously—how dare you, Reith Richardson? How dare you carry on as if there's nothing amiss? How dare you not be here for *me* when I needed help with generators and all sorts of things earlier?

How dare you turn up now and steal the show so they're even talking about you backstage?

Then she froze because he looked up and seemed to

be looking straight at her. A tremor ran through her and she was rooted to the spot for a long moment until she turned away and made a decision—no hysterical fashion designer was going to dictate anything to her, let alone be offered the chance to drool over her husband.

She grimaced immediately as the irony of this hit her but it also hit her at the same time that that was what she'd been unable to put her finger on in Chilli George at Molly and Bill's dinner party—a very subtle but nonetheless perceptible interest in Reith. And she didn't care if it made no sane, rational sense but that annoyed her all the more.

She turned back. 'That's my last offer, Chilli,' she said coolly. 'But I'll help you pack up if you like, if that's what you really want to do. We'll have to refund—'

Chilli came to a hasty decision. 'No. But, for heaven's sake, get me a glass of…something and I don't mean a soft drink.'

Kim smiled more warmly at her. 'What a great idea! I'll have one too.'

Hours later, Kim drove back to Saldanha.

It had stopped raining but the night air was misty and cool.

She threw her car keys down onto the hall table, stretched, kicked her shoes off and hesitated.

She could see partly into the lounge, with its lovely lamps that Mary would have lit. With its beautiful rugs on the shining parquet floor, the linen settee covers and the bowl of magnificent roses on a drum table. And she smiled as she thought how well wine, grapes anyway, and roses went together.

But did she want to go straight upstairs to bed or did she want a nightcap to round off a difficult day? A nightcap to perhaps dull the sting of not knowing where Reith was. She'd seen him walk out of the Cellar Door after the parade and that was the last she'd seen of him.

She shrugged and wandered into the lounge, and stopped dead.

Reith looked up from the paper he was reading. There was a brandy in a balloon glass on the occasional table beside him.

He said nothing.

Kim came to life. 'That's where you are,' she murmured and walked over to the bar to pour herself a brandy.

'So we're talking? I wasn't sure,' he said dryly.

She merely looked at him and sat down in an armchair.

'OK, let's try this—you thought I should have stayed and helped? That's what you're mad about?' he queried.

She shrugged. 'It would have been a help, but no.'

'No? You don't think I should have stayed or—you're not mad?'

Kim tensed inwardly, bitterly regretting getting herself into this but she felt exhausted and didn't have the will to go away—where to, anyway? So she took refuge in her drink. She took a sip and stared into her glass.

'Next minute you'll be telling me there's nothing wrong,' he said softly. 'One of the all time favourite lies women employ when they're hiding huge grievances.'

She looked up, her eyes glittering like sapphires in the sudden pallor of her face. 'Of course you know this from your extensive experience of women, I presume?'

He laughed. 'Thought that might flush you out, my dear Kim. So, why don't you go on and spill the beans?'

'There's—' She closed her mouth, nearly biting her lip, and took another sip of her brandy.

'Nothing,' he said flatly. 'Is that why you didn't look at me? Not once while you were doing your stint on the microphone. Then or later. I might have been non-existent—'

'Why should I acknowledge you?' she broke in. 'I don't even know where you are half the time. I had no idea you'd be back for the parade. I had no idea where you went the two nights you were away but, no, I'm not so naïve as to imagine you're living like a monk.'

'I spent the first night, what was left of it, in the apartment, alone,' he said harshly. 'And the second night, last night, I got permission to take Darcy and some of his mates to a rugby game and they slept over.'

'That's—' her voice shook '—not what you intimated when you drove off.'

'No?' He stared at her with his mouth set. 'Then our lines must have crossed. I was intimating that spending another chaste night in this damn house with you was not going to work for me. That's *all*.'

Kim took several distressed breaths. 'I...I'm sorry if I got it wrong but—'

'Why would it bother you if I *was* sleeping around?' he cut in to ask with a frown. 'I thought you hated me.'

Kim stared at him. Then she got up and paced the

room. Finally she stopped in front of him with her arms crossed over her beautiful taupe silk top. 'Reith,' she said carefully, 'yes, there are times when I hate you quite…a lot.'

A nerve flickered in his jaw. 'I did save your family.'

'You could have done it differently.'

'No, Kim. I know what you're going to say. I could have given your father an active position—'

'Why not?' she broke in intensely.

'It wouldn't have worked,' he said flatly. 'You know as well as I do, he would have hated any innovation, he would hate anything I suggested. As for your brother,' he went on cynically, 'didn't any of you realize it's not wine and viticulture he lives and breathes, but horses?'

Kim flinched. 'Well…'

'Not only that—he's quite clueless when it comes to business.'

She walked back to her chair and took up her glass, turmoil clearly etched into her expression. 'I still can't—' She paused, then heaved a sigh. 'They're still my father and brother.'

Reith picked up his drink and looked sceptically into the tawny depths. Then he grimaced. 'It's hard to be objective about one's family, I guess. For example, I've gone the other way. I've never forgiven my parents, but—' he gestured '—be that as it may, what about the rest of the time?'

She blinked at him uncomprehendingly.

'You said there are times when you hate me quite a lot.' He looked sardonic. 'What about the other times?'

Kim hesitated, then sat down and finished her

brandy. She put the glass down precisely in the centre of the round occasional table. 'I...' She looked across at him and came to a sudden decision. 'Reith, I often feel I'm working without a script. You seem to know all my answers but I don't know yours. Tell me about your first wife.'

He raised an eyebrow. 'What do you want to know about her?' It wasn't said patiently.

Kim gestured. 'How you met. How long you knew each other, that kind of thing.'

'Kim, it's over ten years ago; it can't have any bearing on us.'

'Reith,' she said stubbornly, 'I want to know. I don't like being married to a stranger, which is what you are, to all intents and purposes. You always were.' Sudden tears blurred her vision. 'If you really want to know, I bitterly regret getting myself into this ridiculous position with you.'

'All right,' he said through his teeth, 'she was a country girl; she'd lived all her life on a cattle station. She would have been struck dumb in your company, but put her on a horse and she had her own kind of...class. Six months after we got married, though, we had nothing to talk about but she was pregnant and then...and then there was Darcy—but she was gone. She would have loved Darcy, but even more so because I think she knew—' He stopped.

'Knew you didn't love her any more?' Kim whispered, her eyes wide with horror.

He looked away. 'Yes, if ever. But she didn't even have that consolation.'

'And you don't think,' Kim said through her tears, 'that has left its mark on you?'

He stared at her with that nerve flickering in his jaw again. 'Of course. It has no bearing whatsoever on you, however.'

'You may not think so but,' she said tautly, 'I always knew there was an exclusion zone around you and now I know why.'

'That's nonsense,' he said roughly. 'I—'

'Believe me—' she interrupted '—if I'd had that kind of tragedy, or I'd caused that kind of tragedy in my love life, I'd have an exclusion zone.'

'Caused,' he repeated harshly and picked up his brandy glass and swirled it impatiently.

'Oh, not wittingly.' Kim gestured. 'Lots of people fall out of love or they were never really in love in the first place, or their nonsense is one-sided. But it's enough to make you—' she paused as she gathered her thoughts, then, still pale but more composed, she eyed him as if struck by a new thought '—enough to make you force someone to marry you for all the wrong reasons, though?'

She let the question dangle in the air as she stood up, tall and elegant, with her red-gold hair a little dishevelled—just as he liked it—but her eyes very blue and steady.

'No,' she said, 'not enough for that. Not in my book. So what's left? The way my arrogant family treated you? Was that enough for you to force me to marry you? No. You can hold your own anywhere, Reith, even if it involves an old school tie and a polo team, and you know it.'

'So what's left?' Reith said as he stood up and faced her.

'What's left?' Kim murmured and shrugged. 'It's up to you. All I'm telling you is I don't accept that I should be obliged to make this a real marriage unless you can come up with a vastly better reason for it.'

She turned on her heel and walked away.

'Kim.'

She hesitated mid-stride, then turned back to him, a frown and a question mark in her eyes.

He was standing with his hands pushed into the pockets of his jeans. His deep blue shirt was open at the throat. He was tall and dark and enough to make you catch your breath even when you were questioning his every motive, his every rationale. Even when your heart was aching for the wife who'd died knowing he'd fallen out of love with her, if he'd ever been in love.

'Yes?'

'You didn't have to do it,' he said.

She licked her lips. 'You mean…?'

'You didn't have to marry me.' He waited to see her reaction, which was to suck in an unsteady breath. He smiled unamusedly. 'You could have ridden off into the sunset, so to speak, with your parents and your brother. At least your pride would have been intact even if you'd all been penniless.'

A tide of colour rushed up her throat and into her cheeks because, of course, he was right. But how to explain she couldn't have done it to her parents? 'I never wanted any of your money or *anything* from you,' she said hotly, 'but I couldn't do it to my parents; I just *couldn't.*'

He ignored the last bit. 'You haven't seemed to mind spending my money,' he said dryly, with a significant little look around.

Kim tossed her head. 'Don't waste your time trying to make me feel guilty about that,' she said proudly. 'You'd have got someone else to do it if it hadn't been me, but no one,' she assured him, 'would have restored Saldanha as well as I could.'

'Spoken like a true Theron,' he drawled. 'It's just a pity you don't—you haven't to date—made it a happy home.'

She shrugged. 'If you ever thought I was going to—'

'Lie down in a bed of your own making?' he interrupted sardonically. 'All right, let's talk about that, Kim.' He closed the gap between them in a few steps.

She stood her ground. 'Not *my* making,' she denied through her teeth.

'*Our* making, then.' He stopped in front of her.

She shivered but she knew immediately that she should have run, she should not have allowed herself to be trapped by the fatal physical fascination he'd held for her almost from the start. How *could* she still feel like this about him? she wondered in fleeting despair. Her pulse started to race as he stared down at her mouth and then his hands circled her waist.

'You said something about a "vastly better reason" for us to be married.' He looked into her eyes and his hands moved on her waist. 'There is, there always has been—and it's this.' He drew her into his arms.

'Reith—'

It was a breath of sound but he ignored it. She thought

he was going to kiss her, but he said, barely audibly, 'Remember doing this?'

Her eyes widened in surprise. 'I… Yes. I mean— yes, of course, well…' She closed her eyes and bit her lip in some confusion.

He laughed softly. 'So do I. It went something like this, didn't it?' And this time he did kiss her.

Kim tensed but he took his hands from her waist and cupped her face and trailed his fingers down the side of her neck—and all the things he'd made her feel came back to haunt her. Things she hadn't even been able to document to herself but now the memories of them, which must have lain just below the surface, were aroused. All her appreciation of his hard, honed bulk, the feeling of protection his arms around her had brought, the shivery delight caused by his fingers on her skin, the way her nipples flowered in almost un- bearable expectation…

She was breathing raggedly as they drew apart and her legs felt unsteady. She was completely under his spell as she looked up into his eyes. There was not an ounce of fight left in her—she would have collapsed if he'd let her go, so great had been the impact of his kiss, so like a starving person brought to a feast had he made her feel.

Then, finally, a sound she knew well gained her at- tention. The familiar whirl of helicopter rotors as his company chopper settled onto the helipad outside.

'You… What… Where?' she stammered in disbelief. 'Is that for you?' She managed to sound more coherent.

He nodded. 'I'm off to Geraldton.'

'Did you know this?'

'Did I know I was leaving tonight? Yes. Kim—'

She pulled herself out of his arms. 'Don't let me detain you.'

'Kim—' a glint of amusement lit his eyes '—I'm sorry, I'd forgotten. You're not the only one somewhat... discomfited.'

'Oh, I'll be fine,' she assured him and shrugged. 'Just another of those ships in the night encounters we have from time to time.'

'Kim,' he said deliberately.

'No, Reith, I'm really tired anyway. Get Alice to let me know your movements if they affect mine. Goodnight.' She turned away as the helicopter pilot knocked on the back door.

But getting to sleep was another matter. She couldn't stop thinking about how she couldn't relinquish her opposition to the way Reith had married her but she couldn't stifle her attraction to him either... She couldn't quell her fears about the loner she sensed in him—and now knew it was not her imagination but a reality.

'I have to do something, though,' she whispered to herself as she dried her eyes and lay back. 'This is so... so unlike me.'

To make matters worse for her, when she did fall into a restless sleep it was to dream of Reith and a girl with Darcy's fair hair but with Reith always walking away from her...

* * *

She didn't come into contact with her husband for nearly a week and then more or less by accident.

It was five o'clock on a sunny afternoon and she was dressing to go to a neighbour's barbecue when she paused with her brush in her hand and a frown growing on her forehead. It wasn't the sound of the chopper she was hearing but in the clear afternoon air she could hear a vehicle coming up the driveway that sounded just like Reith's.

She walked over to the window and, sure enough, it was Reith—who was supposed to be in Adelaide.

She stood rooted to the spot, for some reason unable to move as she heard the car pull up, the front door open, then his footsteps on the stairs.

Thoughts raced through her mind: I don't know what to say to him—I haven't spoken to him since that evening!

'Kim? Are you home?'

She tried to say yes, but nothing came out. She cleared her throat. '...In here.'

He came in and her heart seemed to beat somewhere up in her throat just at the sight of him. She forced herself into speech to counteract that accelerated heartbeat.

'I thought you were in Adelaide.'

'I was supposed to be but—' he shrugged '—the meeting I had scheduled was cancelled.' He looked her up and down, her long ink-blue skirt, her chic hyacinth pink silk shirt, the wide turquoise belt emphasizing her narrow waist, her jewelled sandals. 'Going somewhere?' he asked with a lifted eyebrow.

Kim nodded. 'Pippa Longreach's barbecue. I did tell Alice about it but she told me you'd be in Adelaide.'

'I'd be in Adelaide,' he echoed. 'Just as well I'm not.'

'Oh?' she queried.

He smiled at her. 'I can keep you safe from Lachlan.'

Kim blinked. 'What do you mean?'

'You know very well what I mean, Kim. He may be Pippa's toy boy—' he grimaced '—but he's got a huge crush on you. Give me ten minutes; I need a shower.' And he disappeared into his bedroom.

Kim stared after him, prey to a host of conflicting emotions. She'd been dreading this encounter.

She was thoroughly conscious that on the night of the fashion parade what she'd set out to achieve—a fact-finding mission, in essence—had rebounded on her somewhat.

In other words, Reith's motivation for marrying her, other than physical attraction, was still unclear but her own motivation—her parents—had sounded, well, flimsy. Would it have been proudly foolhardy but somehow more—what was the right word—honourable?—to have turned his offer down?

She turned away, put her brush down and finished her make-up.

But of course—her hands stilled in the act of stroking mascara onto her lashes—her real fear about this meeting had been how she would react to him, how she would be able to defend herself against kissing him the way she had, if he called her to account over it, if he had that right.

She capped the mascara wand and picked up her

lipstick. But it had been quite normal, this first meeting after that night, she thought, as she painted her lips a soft luminous pink, then reached for a tissue to blot them. Would things stay that way between them, though, or was her moment of reckoning still to come?

CHAPTER SEVEN

PIPPA LONGREACH'S barbecues were usually a lot of fun.

Pippa was an artist of quite some repute. In her fifties she'd divorced her second husband and was currently maintaining a toy boy who went by the name of Lachlan. He was ridiculously good-looking and well-built, with not a lot to say, however.

Although Pippa was primarily a painter, she was also a talented potter and screen-printer. Her home and its large terrace and garden showed off her art in many ways. There were pottery urns and statues in the garden and Pippa didn't only paint on canvas, she painted on walls, ceilings and doors.

She was also a gourmet chef and she grew a lot of her own vegetables, fruit and herbs.

Not only were her barbecues delicious, but they were also visual feasts and you never knew who you were likely to meet—from the famous to the notorious.

It was a starry night above the lively throng of guests and there were fairy lights strung through the trees, beneath which long wooden tables and benches had been set up and laid with colourful crockery.

A pig spit-roasted over a bed of glowing coals was part of the first course, accompanied by delicious home-grown roasted beetroot and corn, new potatoes in their jackets drizzled with melted butter and parsley, and a divine ratatouille. Homemade cob breads and real butter were on the tables.

As if all that wasn't enough, after a suitable interval Pippa served desserts, in typical Pippa style. She wheeled a whole trolley of them out: pavlovas topped with cream and passion fruit or cream and strawberries, a mocha soufflé, a brandy pudding, a sticky date pudding, orange glacé iced cupcakes…

Kim stared at the trolley, then turned to Reith, only to find him looking at her with comical disbelief, dismay and the same *will I be able to resist this?* expression that she wore.

She had to laugh and so did he.

He'd changed into jeans and boots and a cream linen shirt with patch pockets. During dinner he'd been good company but unobtrusively so.

Now, her smile faded and she turned away.

He drew a bottle of wine out of a pottery cooler and filled up her glass, then reached into an ice-filled tub, pulled out a beer and poured it into his glass.

'Cheers,' he said, touching his glass to hers.

'Cheers,' she repeated, still not looking at him.

'Hasn't been so bad, has it?' He narrowed his eyes as he watched for her reaction.

Kim blinked. 'No. I mean…I'm not sure what you mean. It's been a lovely evening.' She paused and frowned. 'Do you really believe what you said about Lachlan?'

Reith allowed his dark gaze to drift over to where Lachlan was sitting alone, looking magnificently moody, although he had been helping Pippa earlier.

'Yep.' He grimaced.

'But he hasn't been near me tonight and he's never said a thing to me that could be construed as…as anything but…OK.'

'Sensible guy,' Reith commented dryly.

'What's that supposed to mean?' Kim stared at him with a frown in her eyes. 'Surely not what I think?'

'Surely yes.' He shrugged and a fleeting smile twisted his lips. 'You don't honestly think I'd stand by and allow some overgrown hunk to pay attention to my wife? I—'

'Reith—' she broke in '—are you sure you're not imagining it?'

'Kim, no,' he said impatiently. 'I've seen the way he looks at you.'

She stared at him with her lips parted. 'Well, he's wasting his time,' she said at last. 'I don't like him, I don't like the way he's sponging off Pippa.'

'Pippa's old enough to be able to work things out for herself,' he drawled, 'but I'm glad you don't like him. Maybe, one day, he'll even be on the receiving end of some of your famed Theron arrogance— No—' he put his hand on her arm as she went to jump up '—don't. I'm sorry, I shouldn't have said that. Anyway, I wasn't talking about Lachlan or the party in the first place.'

She subsided and looked confused. 'What were you talking about?'

He paused and stretched out a hand to touch the gold bracelet she wore on her right wrist, giving her goose bumps as his long fingers played with the little links. And he seemed content to concentrate on what he was doing until, at last, he raised his dark gaze to hers.

'Us,' he said. 'Our last meeting was traumatic, to say the least, but it hasn't been so bad being in each other's company tonight, has it?'

A slow tide of colour mounted in Kim's cheeks and she lowered her lashes to hide the confusion in her eyes.

'You were worried about it?' he hazarded.

She could only nod after a moment.

'Of course, it's always easier in the midst of a crowd,' he suggested rather quizzically.

Kim glanced around at the 'crowd' but no one seemed to be taking the least interest in them. Then she looked directly at him at last. 'I…I suppose so,' she agreed.

'So, despite the fact that we make good sparring partners, we're also good in crowds, you and I.'

'What are you getting at now, Reith?' she enquired with a frown.

He shrugged. 'Just putting together a base table of the things we *can* do together.'

Kim stared at him and her lips twitched in spite of herself. 'You can't go very far on… That's only two.'

'I left out the most notable one. We'd need to be alone, as we were the other night until fate intervened—' he looked heavenwards a shade dryly '—to go into that.' He watched with interest as another tide of colour rose in her cheeks.

Kim bit her lip. 'I thought I might have to account for that—talking of base tables and things,' she added with a touch of tartness. 'I presume that's what you're on about?'

He played with her bracelet in silence for a few moments, then, 'Any thoughts you'd like to contribute? At all?'

Kim hesitated, then she said slowly and painfully, 'There is a physical attraction, but how do you know what the real thing is?'

'Love?'

'Yes.'

'You don't. Perhaps only time can tell.' He stared into her eyes.

'What was her name?' Kim heard herself asking barely audibly. 'Darcy's mother.'

She flinched as she saw the hardening of his expression and was quite prepared for him not to answer, but he said after a little pause, 'Sylvia. Sylvie or even Syl for short.'

'Did she… No.' Something inside her made her draw the line at asking him any more about Darcy's mother but it had also prompted her to think about his life at the time and before. 'You told me you didn't really grow up in a boundary rider's hut.'

He grimaced. 'No. But I did grow up on a remote cattle station. All the same, I went to the station school and my mother was a teacher so I had that influence before she took off for parts unknown. I'm told I was reading the Bible when I was four.'

Kim blinked as she absorbed this and at the same time absorbed the flicker of something cold in his eyes as he'd mentioned his mother. And she remembered what he'd said once about not forgiving his parents.

'So…so your father was a cattleman?'

He shook his head. 'My father was a chartered accountant who got caught up in a scam that was not of his making. He got barred all the same and never recovered from the shame of it all. He wasn't even a boundary rider, which at least sounds a bit romantic; he was the station bookkeeper.'

Kim stared at him with her lips parted. 'That's… awful.'

He shrugged. 'He certainly made heavy weather of it. He was cynical and untrusting.' He paused. 'If there was ever any joy in him it all got leached out. What persuaded my mother to stay with him as long as she did I don't know but the one thing I found hard to forgive her for was not taking me with her when she decamped.'

Kim's eyes were huge now. 'That's worse. So your mother ran away? How could she have left you, though? What was she like?' she asked with a frown.

'She was bright and bouncy, she was fun and she always tried to make the best of things. I think she came to know it was never going to work but my father would never let me go. She may even have thought he'd "go easier" on me if she wasn't there.' He shrugged. 'All he said when he read the note she left was, "Good riddance".'

'Did he go "easier" on you?'

'It wasn't in him to go easily on anyone.' He smiled dryly. 'It's all water under the bridge now, although—' he paused and narrowed his eyes '—you said something once about an exclusion zone. I think it was something Sylvie found she couldn't get through, while I couldn't even put a name to it or understand it; I think that in hindsight, at least. What a pity,' he said with considerable irony, 'hindsight couldn't be foresight.'

'Are you… Are you doing enough for Darcy, Reith?' Kim heard herself asking urgently after she'd thought all this through. 'I mean—why does he have to go to boarding school?'

Reith finally stopped fiddling with her bracelet and took a draught of his beer. 'It's a very good boarding school.'

'I'm not saying it isn't,' she replied impatiently.

'He seems happy there.'

'He seems too happy there,' Kim observed. 'I mean—' she gestured '—I get the feeling he's relieved to go back, although not so much now he's got Rusty— incidentally, I meant to ask you about that. The local gymkhana is coming up. Can I enter them? It'll be during the school holidays.'

'If they're good enough. What? Jumping? Dressage?'

'I'll look at the programme. He's really come along amazingly well—Darcy, I mean.'

Reith looked amused. 'He should. It's in his blood on both sides.'

'You ride? You rode—of course you did!' Kim

marvelled at her own stupidity. 'Why don't you ride at Saldanha?' She stared at him questioningly.

'Never seem to have the time.'

There was a whoosh as a bonfire was lit and flames and glowing points of light flew skywards.

Kim blinked and watched for a while but she had something on her mind, brought there by his story and the loneliness he must have experienced. 'Reith, why don't you bring Darcy home?' she asked at last.

Reith took a draught of his beer and put his glass down. 'Kim—' He stopped abruptly, then said deliberately, 'I can't guarantee Saldanha as a happy home for him.'

Kim clicked her tongue in annoyance. 'I have never shown the slightest animosity towards you in front of Darcy—and don't you dare dispute that,' she warned him with her most haughty expression.

'I wouldn't dream of it,' he said with mock meekness. 'But living together all the time is different.'

'Is that one of the reasons you married me?' she asked out of the blue as the thought struck her. 'If so, why didn't you say so?'

'You mean you'd have married me happily because of my son?' He tilted his head to one side to look at her quizzically. 'Pity I didn't think of that. Incidentally, Kimberley Theron—' he pressed on as she made to speak '—I had no intention of asking you to marry me.'

'Blackmailing me into marrying you, don't you mean?'

He rubbed his jaw. 'Whatever—until you took your family's side that day in the pub.'

'You expected me to...to take your side?' she said raggedly and gestured helplessly as she couldn't go on, so extreme was her frustration.

'I expected at least one of you to take a sane, rational, businesslike view of the matter,' he said coolly. 'I even thought we, you and I,' he said deliberately, 'had got on well enough for you to assess the facts first before you gave me my marching orders.'

Kim opened her mouth to say something bitter and pithy but she was reminded suddenly of her feeling of discomfort at the time when she was using her father's arguments—discomfort because they hadn't sounded sane, rational and businesslike?

'I also found it hard to believe you didn't know who I was,' he said.

Kim blinked several times. 'Come again?'

He shrugged. 'It was hard to imagine how they'd been able to keep it from you.'

She swallowed and drank some of her wine. 'That was partly my fault. I should have realized something was wrong.' She shook her head. 'I must have been blind. If it's any comfort to you, Reith Richardson—' her eyes were sombre '—there's an awful lot I've taken myself to task for since you—' she grimaced '—came into my life.'

'Change was going to happen for you anyway, Kim. It would have been someone else changing your life if it hadn't been me,' he said quietly.

A sparkle of amusement lit her eyes for one brief moment. 'They might not have wanted to marry me, though.'

She propped her chin on her hand and looked into the firelight for a long moment. Until it slowly dawned on her that Reith had gone very still as he stared at her. She had no idea that her profile was exquisite in the firelight against the darkened sky, that her skin was rose on gold, her hair more gold than red in the same firelight and her eyes like sapphires.

She lifted an eyebrow at him. 'Penny for them?'

He seemed to come back from a long way away. He finished his beer and said, as he put his glass down and squared it with the edge of the table, 'We don't need to be married any more, Kim. Oh—' he gestured as her eyes widened and she paled '—don't worry about your parents.'

'I don't understand!'

They were back at Saldanha.

They'd taken a distracted leave of Pippa—at least Kim had been distracted. Reith had been perfectly normal. And on the short drive home she'd struggled to find words through the utter sense of shock she was experiencing, whilst he'd said nothing at all and hadn't appeared to be struggling with anything.

'Reith,' she implored, all but tripping over her skirt and Sunny Bob as she climbed out of the car.

'It's over, Kim,' he said as he unlocked the door and gestured for her to precede him into the house. 'I'll move out tomorrow. That's all there is to it.'

Kim stalked inside and waited for him to do the same. Then she stopped him with a hand on his arm. 'Reith Richardson,' she said precisely, 'I've spent all the time I've known you on one kind of a roller coaster or another. Equally, I've had to make do with the limited information you see fit to feed me and I'm sick to *death* of it. So hand over my car keys. They're on the table behind you.' She put out a hand imperiously.

'Where the hell do you think you're going at this time of night?' he queried harshly.

'No idea! Maybe Perth—it seems a popular spot for midnight flits—but if you're not going to explain, I'm off!'

'Kim—all right,' he said through his teeth. 'There's no bloody point in going on, is there?' His eyes blazed. 'You're never going to forgive or forget. We could go on for years setting each other alight physically and spending every other damn moment fighting each other.'

She simply stared at him.

'Look,' he went on in the same hard voice, 'you're entirely in the right, if it's any consolation. I should never have done it.'

Kim opened and closed her mouth several times. And what finally came out surprised her. 'Wh...what about Darcy?'

If she'd surprised herself, she could see that she'd shocked him.

He blinked several times. 'I...' But he didn't seem able to finish.

'I haven't told you this, but I'm finally getting through to him,' she went on. 'He's even decided on a new name for his horse—Rimfire. What are you going to tell him?'

'I don't know—I haven't thought about it.'

She opened her hands. 'Ah. Another lack-of-information exercise in the making.'

He swore audibly. 'Better for it to happen now rather than later.'

'No,' Kim whispered with sudden tears in her eyes.

He studied the tears for a moment and a nerve flickered in his jaw. 'So what are you suggesting?' he asked with a frown. 'The same kind of hell we're going through, only a more amicable version of it for Darcy's sake? It's not going to work, Kim. We've wanted each other for months now. I don't know about you, but it's starting to drive me crazy. My only option now is to... go.'

'Why did you do it, Reith?' she asked, tears now streaking her mascara. 'Why *did* you ask me to marry you like that?'

'Because, despite what you might like to think,' he said curtly, 'I have a chip on my shoulder a mile wide, I probably always will have. And your brother and father were able to expose it in all its glory. Particularly your brother.'

She gasped. 'How? Why?'

'I could have understood your father's reaction to a certain extent, an older man with old-fashioned notions, but Damien...' He stopped and shook his head. 'They were so bloody superior when they discovered my background. Not only that, they made me feel like a scavenger when I knew damn well they'd dug their own hole and were responsible for their own downfall.'

'They were... It's possible they were just desperate, isn't it?'

He shook his head again and smiled with no amusement at all. 'Then you came along and you were all fabulous, rich, classy, sassy *Theron*,' he went on, and stopped, breathing harshly. 'Although one thing I have to salute you for, Kimberley. I thought you'd be much easier to seduce than you were. In fact, if there was a man with any backbone in your family, it was you.' And with his mouth in a hard line, he sketched a mocking little salute.

Kim's lips parted and for a moment something very much like stunned heartbreak showed in her eyes. Then she turned and started to walk away.

'Kim…' He said her name hoarsely but, with a slight shake of her head, she kept on walking.

'Kim.' He came round in front of her and barred her way and he put his hands on her arms. 'I'm sorry,' he said. 'I should never have said that.' He scanned her pale face and darkened eyes. 'I'm *sorry*. It's the way I am, though, it's the way I've been since I was ten.' And he pulled her into his arms. 'I'm sorry,' he said barely audibly into her hair.

She trembled and went to pull away but he resisted easily, then he picked her up and carried her through to the lounge and sat down on a settee with her.

He didn't say anything for a long time, just stroked her hair as she lay with her head turned into his shoulder.

And gradually the trembling that had attacked her eased and she lay against him feeling a strange kind of peace come over her. A release, almost, that puzzled her and puckered her brow briefly, then she realized what it was. Despite everything and after the long months of holding herself aloof, there was no other feeling for her that came close to the magic of being in Reith Richardson's arms.

As it struck her, her eyes flew open and she looked up to see him staring down at her.

'Reith?' It came out as a husky little breath of sound.

'Kim?'

They stared into each other's eyes for a long moment, then he pulled her close and started to kiss her.

The master bedroom at Saldanha was a beautiful room. It had a white ceiling, greyish-blue carpeting, mushroom walls and ivory curtains. The ivory silk bedspread hung over the antique ottoman and, by the light of the Chinese porcelain bedside lamps, Kim lay still as Reith paid tribute to the whole silken, slim, curved length of her.

But stillness wasn't going to stay with her much longer, she knew. Indeed, how she'd survived the way he'd undressed her item by item she didn't know.

Nor did she know how she'd contained her delight and awe at the sight of him powerfully naked next to her. The contrast between them was breathtaking. She felt slight and as light as air and vulnerable, but in a way that was thrilling to her senses, against him. He was so tall and tanned, broad-shouldered, lean and strong, his body sprinkled with dark hairs, his hands...

His hands, she thought with a visible tremor, so wise on her body, so sure in the way they found her most erogenous spots—she'd never be able to look at his hands again without remembering this—this sheer delight he was inflicting on her.

Then he eased his leg between hers and bent his dark head to taste and tease her nipples.

'Oh, Reith,' she whispered as she felt a deep clenching within her body. 'Oh, Reith, I'm dying. I need you.'

And he was there for her, with a mounting rhythm that she began to echo; one that carried them on a wave of rapture that exploded for both of them.

'So.'

Kim stirred and repeated his one word very quietly. 'So.'

He pulled a cover over them, took her in his arms and buried his head in the curve of her shoulder and they lay in silence, completely absorbed in each other and the memory of the event that had just taken place.

Then he asked a question. 'How the hell did we manage to abstain for so long?'

She freed a hand and ran her fingers through his hair. 'Basically, we're lookers not leapers.'

He laughed and kissed her. 'I feel as if I've leapt up a mountain.'

'I feel...' She paused and he lifted his head and rested it on his elbow so he could look into her eyes. 'You've made me feel more wonderful than I've ever felt in my life.'

'Kim.' He put his palm on her cheek and his eyes softened. 'I've no right to hear you say that. Not after—'

He stopped as she put her fingers to his lips. 'Let's not go back,' she whispered.

'I need to explain.' He kissed her palm.

But this time she replaced her fingers with her lips and she effectively silenced him.

Some weeks later, she got an early morning call from Alice. Reith had been away for a couple of nights, the first time they'd been apart since the momentous night of Pippa's barbecue...

'Kim, dear—' she and Alice had been on first name terms for some time now '—Reith would like you to be in Perth today and he said please dress up because he wants to take you to the races at Ascot. He's got a runner.'

Kim blinked. 'He didn't say anything about it to me.'

'No, he forgot. Funny that, he's been quite forgetful lately, quite...I don't know...as if he has other things on his mind.'

Kim's lips twitched as she thought of her powerful, usually completely businesslike husband having her on his mind to the point of being forgetful, and decided she liked that very much. But her smile changed to a frown.

'Alice, I've got to get ready—I've been in the garden. And it will take me at least an hour and a half to drive to Perth.'

'The chopper is coming to pick you up. Should be there in an hour, so that will give you time to get ready, then it's only a quick little trip and at this end a limo will pick you up and deliver you to Burswood.'

'Burswood?' Kim repeated, sounding surprised.

'The hotel. He's booked, rather I've booked a suite

for the night so you can pack a bag and leave it there. He'll meet you there.'

Kim frowned. 'Why not the apartment?'

'Have you forgotten, Kim?' Alice clicked her tongue as if she couldn't believe how forgetful they were both being at the moment. 'It's being redecorated.'

'Oh. Yes, I had,' Kim said ruefully. 'Well, I guess I'd better get cracking. Thank you, Alice.'

Kim arrived at the Burswood Casino complex on the banks of the Swan River with plenty of time to spare, and checked into the luxury hotel.

She unpacked her overnight bag, then checked herself in the mirror. She had on a black linen dress with short cap sleeves and a tulip-layered knee-length skirt. She had an oyster mohair jacket to go with the outfit as autumn slid towards winter and brought with it cooler weather. Her hair was loose but sleek and sculptured and she wore a string of pearls and tear-drop pearl earrings. Her make-up was perfect, and she lifted a fascinator out of the hat box she'd brought with her. It was a froth of dotted black veil on a comb and she slid it carefully onto her head.

She was studying her reflection, twisting this way and that with her hands on her hips, when the outer door of the suite opened and Reith came in.

He paused, saw her through the bedroom door and walked towards her.

She stayed exactly as she was as he stopped, paces from her, and their gazes clashed.

'Hello,' she said barely audibly.

His gaze roamed over her, from the top of her fascinator to the tips of her high black heels. 'Hello.' He pulled his jacket off and threw it over the back of a chair, then he loosened his tie.

'You didn't mention the races to me,' she murmured, conscious of a prickle of tension between them.

'No. I forgot. As I'm about to do again.'

She raised her eyebrows. 'What do you mean?'

He pulled his tie off and consigned it to lie on his jacket. 'The next time I decide to go to the races it will have to be in different circumstances.'

'I still don't understand.' Kim frowned.

Reith moved and put his hands on her waist.

She trembled as an inkling of his intentions came to her.

'It won't be after I've spent two nights away from you—put it like that,' he drawled.

'I see,' Kim said very seriously. 'In other words, you mean to tell me, Reith Richardson, that I've gone to all this trouble—' she sketched the outline of her figure, then touched her fascinator delicately '—for nothing?'

His arms closed round her waist, but he eyed her with some irony. 'Depends what you classify as "nothing". But I have also to tell you that even if I'd made love to you a couple of hours ago I would still be subject to an irresistible urge.'

'Urge? To?' she queried, wide-eyed.

'Undress you, disrupt you, dispense with all this exquisite grooming and finery, take you to bed.'

Kim stared up at him. 'You're serious.'

'Yep,' he agreed.

'Reith—' her lips twitched but her pulse was starting to race '—that sounds a bit…caveman.'

He raised her hand and kissed her knuckles. 'Not
at all,' he said ruefully. 'Just some poor guy who can't
seem to get enough of you.'

Kim laughed softly and kissed him, and she didn't
object when he found the zip at the back of her dress
and slid it down.

In fact she stepped out of it regally. And she dis-
pensed with her black bra and suspender belt, her sheer
stockings, then she remembered the fascinator with a
little gurgle of laughter and took it off too.

He spanned her waist, then slid his hands up to cup
her breasts, causing her nipples to peak like tight buds.

'Down to my pearls,' she quipped breathlessly, then
promptly forgot about them as he looked down at her
in a heavy-lidded way and with a nerve beating in his
jaw that wreaked havoc with her senses.

She shivered with pleasure as he breathed harshly as
if he was going to say something, but instead he made
a growling little sound in his throat and swept her into
his arms.

Everything became urgent from then on—urgent
with desire. It was there in the way he got rid of his
own clothes, in the way his hands and lips moved on
her body. It was there in their breathing and their movements, the way she directed his hands, the way he directed hers. In the way they clung together as they
climaxed, both helpless beneath the physical force of
their union.

As they lay together, resting and relaxed, mentally

close as well as physically, it was perhaps half an hour before he said, 'Shall we do it?'

Her eyes widened. 'Again?'

'No—' he looked amused '—that might be a hard act to follow so soon. Shall we go back to Plan A?'

'You mean...' She sat up and blinked several times.

He nodded. 'Let's go to the races.'

They did just that, but while their undressing could not have been described as orderly, their dressing was much more leisurely.

Kim had the first shower in the en suite bathroom. He handed her a towel as she came out, kissed her on the lips in passing as he stepped in.

It was as he walked through to the bedroom, towelling his hair and with another towel slung around his hips, that he stopped and whistled.

Kim was wearing only a lacy black bra and a matching suspender belt and one sheer stocking. She was in the act of drawing the second stocking on and she completed the task but with a tinge of pink in her cheeks.

'Now that,' he murmured, 'is seriously sexy.'

She straightened. 'Think so?'

'Know so. It's also the first time I've seen you wear them. Do you wear them often?'

Kim shook her head. 'Not often, but some clothes just seem to cry out for you to be as elegant below as on the outer.'

'I see. Makes sense,' he murmured and raked his hand through his hair, then fingered his chin as if he was in two minds about something. 'Can I offer you some advice?'

She tilted her chin. 'If you like.'

He smiled slightly at the tinge of sheer Theron arrogance he saw in her expression. 'Put some clothes on—otherwise, despite what I said a few minutes ago, it could be back to Plan B.'

'Oh, dear.' Kim reached for her dress hastily and stepped into it. 'Is that better?' she asked innocently.

'No, it's not.' He took a step towards her.

'Hang on.' She tried to pull the zip up at the back but it jammed. 'Damn!' She looked over her shoulder as she tugged at it in vain.

'Here, let me help. You've got a bit of the lining caught in the teeth—there.' He pulled the zip up and slipped his arms around her waist from behind.

She leant back against him.

He said into her hair, 'OK. That was a close call but I think we could get this show on the road now.'

She turned around in his arms and laughed up at him, knowing that he caught his breath at the sheer animation of her expression, the wonderful colour of her eyes and hair, the lovely shape of her face, her smooth skin and tantalizing mouth.

Nor was she to know how close she had come to thawing the icy rock his emotions had become, how close to lightening the darkness that had invaded him a long time ago and grown within him.

But would he ever come to completely trust her? he wondered. And frowned suddenly. What did he mean by that? Was he always going to wonder if she would revert to her roots? In other words, decide or be persuaded he was not good enough for her? Would he ever entirely forget the encounter that had prompted him to force her to marry him?

'Reith?'

He came out of his reverie to see her looking questioningly up at him now. Questioningly and soberly.

'Nothing.' He kissed her and released her.

CHAPTER EIGHT

They had a fun afternoon at the races in the Members'
Enclosure. Reith's horse came second and Kim picked
two winners. They drank champagne. The fashions,
the glossy horses and the colourful jockey silks contributed to a gala feeling. Then there was the green
sweep of the track with the glint of the Swan River in
the background, the children playing on the grass, the
blue sky above—all of it gave Kim a feeling of being
on top of the world.

But the other reason for her feeling of well-being was
their closeness. They rarely left each other's side and,
once, she turned to him to find him looking down at
her intently and in a way that made her colour slightly.

He smiled and slid her hand into his and, although
they didn't say a word, their mental unity was complete.

The only thing that might have spoilt the day for Kim
was catching sight of her brother, Damien.

He was with a gorgeous, very expensive-looking
blonde in a party of six and if he saw her he gave no
sign of it. She half lifted her hand to wave to him as he
looked her way once but he looked away immediately.

She turned away with an inward shiver.

Whereas their father appeared to be reconciled to the idea of her marriage to Reith, Damien still hadn't forgiven her, much to their mother's ongoing distress. Kim couldn't understand why. Had he also hoped for some kind of a miracle to save them? Or was it the blow that had been administered to his pride by having his sister marry the man who'd exposed his lack of business acumen?

He'd moved his polo ponies out of the Saldanha stables and never came back to visit. He had, according to their mother, bought into a bloodstock agency.

It also struck her that Damien could rightly have expected to inherit Saldanha and seeing her in his place could be a thorn in his side. There was nothing she could do about it, though, and she deliberately pushed it from her mind.

In this she was aided by the fact that they picked Darcy up from school on their way home to Saldanha. It was a half-term holiday, and she was able to implement a plan she'd had in the making for some time.

Her first action some weeks ago had been to advise Alice that she needed Reith home for the three days of Darcy's half-term holiday. She had asked his secretary to make sure that Reith was appointment- and travel-free. Alice had been only too happy to comply.

Her next line of action had been to select a horse suitable for Reith and have it brought in from the paddock. She'd then groomed it and ridden it herself a couple of times.

The end result was that on the morning of the day

after they'd picked up Darcy, they loaded their horses onto a truck and took them down to the beach for a gallop.

It was a cool overcast day with showers etched like pencil lines over the ocean as it pounded against the shore.

They cantered side by side, rising rhythmically in the saddle on the hard sand left by the outgoing tide, with the balls of their feet planted firmly in the stirrups.

She and Darcy were bundled up in anoraks and tracksuits, while Reith wore a navy jumper and jeans. He looked completely at home on his horse, although he'd been a little taken aback on discovering what her plan was.

'I haven't ridden for years,' he'd said.

'It's not something you forget,' she'd replied.

He'd looked across the breakfast table at her with a faint frown. 'Something I wanted to ask you. You wouldn't by any chance be behind the fact that I have absolutely no appointments at the moment?'

'I?' She'd looked at him, wide-eyed.

'Yes, you.'

She was saved from answering by Darcy, who could barely contain his excitement at the prospect of a gallop along the beach. 'I'm sure Rimfire will love it. Has he ever seen the sea, Kim?'

'No,' she said, 'don't think so. So he may be a bit puzzled at first. Just take it slowly.'

'I will. I can't wait!' And he'd turned a glowing face on his father. 'Would you like Kim to take you on a leading rein for a while? She did that for me, just for the first couple of times until I was sure of myself. She's a really, really good rider,' he assured his father.

Kim had struggled not to laugh at the fleeting expression that crossed Reith's face before he brought it under control.

'I think I'll be OK,' he said gravely to his son.

Darcy shrugged. 'You did say you hadn't ridden for years.'

'True,' Reith agreed, 'but I still think I'll be OK.'

Back on the beach, Kim dropped behind after they'd had an exhilarating gallop through some light showers and she walked Mattie, patting her horse's steaming neck, while she watched Reith and Darcy splashing through the shallows.

Would this bring them together? she wondered. Would this common interest, assuming she could pin Reith down long enough to make it a common interest, be the bridge he needed to get through to his son?

Later that day, after Darcy had gone to bed and when they were getting ready for bed themselves, Reith, if not so much answering her question, acknowledged the thought behind it.

'You're clever, you know.'

She was sitting before her dressing table smoothing moisturizer into her skin. Her long nightgown was the finest pearl cotton, pintucked across the bodice and with frills at her wrists. It was also the height of modesty.

She turned on the stool and studied him. He was lying back in bed with his pillows pulled up behind him.

His pyjama jacket was unbuttoned, exposing his lean torso sprinkled with dark hair. He looked, in a word, she thought with an inward tremor, sexy.

'Clever? How so?'

'I never thought of horses as a means of getting through to Darcy. I've tried surfing, rugby, golf, athletics—' He broke off and grimaced.

She lifted her shoulders. 'That's probably only because you hadn't seen him exposed to them before.'

'Mmm...' He didn't sound convinced. 'I'm thinking of bringing him here now.'

'Oh, Reith!' She glinted him a radiant look. 'I'd love that and I think maybe he would too.'

He was silent for a long moment. 'Come to bed,' he suggested at last.

She did as requested, turning off the lights, except the bedside lamps.

'This is a very...old-fashioned item of nightwear,' he commented as she pulled the covers over her.

'Ah, but it cost a small fortune,' she replied. 'It's handmade, it's light but warm now the nights are getting chilly and it's comfortable. My mother has a lady who makes them and it's a pattern that came down from my great-great-grandmother.'

'So the history goes back even to what you wear to bed?' He paused, then said, 'If there's one thing I've come to understand through all this—' he took his fingers from her hair and fingered the material of her nightgown '—it's... I guess your nightgown encapsulates it.'

She frowned. 'What do you mean?'

'When there's as much history involved as there is here, there has to be a terrible, tearing sense of loss at the thought of losing it, however it happens.'

Again it was ages before Kim spoke and then it was with tears in her eyes. 'Thank you for that,' she said huskily, and she reached for his hand and kissed it.

'Of course,' he said, 'you do realize, history or none, that I'm going to take it off?'

She smiled and released his hand. 'My nightgown?'

He cupped the curve of her cheek. 'Uh-huh. I'm still a guy who can't get enough of you, I'm afraid.'

'Mr Richardson,' she replied seriously, 'which is how I would have addressed you in my great-great-grandmother's time, incidentally, be my guest.'

It was in the languorous aftermath of their love-making that he made another suggestion. 'Since you have me at your mercy for the next two days, will you come to Clover Hill?'

Kim stiffened slightly.

'Only to have a look around,' he said. 'I was thinking of taking Darcy. After all, it'll be his one day.'

Kim moved her head on his shoulder. 'All right,' she said slowly. 'Is anyone living there?'

'No. But it's being looked after.'

'All right,' she repeated, and relaxed as his arms went around her. What could it hurt? she thought, and fell asleep feeling loved and cherished.

* * *

That's what they did the next morning.

Sunny Bob went with them, and Darcy, in his new role of horse-lover, was visibly impressed.

Impressed by the three powerful stallions standing at Clover, by the mares and foals, the paddocks, the stables, all of which made the Saldanha horse presence look small.

Not only that, but he seemed to have a way, particularly with the foals, prompting Reith to say to him, 'You take after your mother.'

'Do I? How?'

'She was especially good with young horses. She...'

Kim found she had sudden tears in her eyes as she watched the two of them standing side by side and, as Reith went on to speak to Darcy about his mother, she melted away and took herself up to the house.

It was a two-storey creeper-clad house set on a slight rise which gave it a marvellous view, not only of the paddocks and surrounding countryside but the hills as well.

As Kim walked through the silent rooms, still partly furnished, not only the view impressed her but a strange feeling of peace came to her.

The reason it was partly furnished was because the previous owners had not been able to fit all their furniture into their new smaller home, but the lovely old pieces they'd left behind looked to be part of the house, part of its history. And although it didn't have the uniqueness of Saldanha with its distinctive Cape Dutch architecture, it was, as she'd sensed all those months ago, as special as the rest of the property.

She wandered upstairs and was charmed to find a nursery with a beautiful cherrywood cot and Mary Poppins flying round the walls.

There was a sewing room with a marvellous old treadle sewing machine, a linen press the size of a small room, an empty master bedroom that opened onto the veranda and just beyond it a huge jacaranda tree that would be a sight to behold in spring.

Downstairs, all the main rooms—library, lounge, dining room—opened onto the veranda, only a step above the formal gardens.

Kim strolled out into the garden and looked around. She was proud of her garden at Saldanha but even it couldn't rival the sweeps of lawn between beautiful old trees and the riot of colour in the vast beds of winter-flowering bulbs: daffodils, jonquils, hyacinth, narcissus, tulips, irises.

Nor could it rival the secret paths that led to separate areas with different plants: native plants, perennial beds, succulents, grevilleas.

And then there were the roses.

She was simply standing, drinking in the rose garden with the house behind it and wondering at the same time why the peace and tranquillity of Clover was so… so mesmerizing.

Did it have a more peaceful history than Saldanha?

That wouldn't be hard, not lately, anyway, she thought with a frown.

'There you are.' Reith and Darcy with Sunny Bob

came into view. 'What do you think of it?' Reith went on to ask.

'It's—' she paused and wondered how to do Clover justice '—beautiful.'

Reith looked at her intently for a long moment, but said nothing more on the subject and they strolled back to the car.

But Darcy was in good form. He didn't stop chatting all the way home about everything he'd seen, about how his dad thought he took after his mum, and Kim couldn't help marvelling at the difference in him. He'd changed from the quiet, self-contained child she'd first met to this eager, bubbling ten-year-old.

If nothing else good had come out of all the Saldanha strife, she caught herself thinking, Darcy had benefited so much.

Over dinner that night Reith enquired of her what she had planned for the next day.

Kim had cooked dinner—it was Mary's day off—and she'd served it in the breakfast room: steak, eggs, chips and a salad.

'Boy, oh, boy!' Darcy commented soulfully as he looked at his plate, 'you really, really know how to feed a kid, Kim.'

'Really? Thank you,' she replied, looking gratified.

That was when, with an amused grin, Reith asked his question.

'Nothing,' she replied. 'Well—'

'Thought you must have something planned,' Reith interrupted.

'I don't, but—'

'Highly unlikely for you not to have,' he broke in again.

Kim planted her fists on the table, with her knife and fork most inelegantly upright in them. 'Will you let me finish?'

'Yes, Dad,' Darcy said severely, 'it's rude to keep interrupting.'

'I stand corrected!' Reith looked rueful. 'You have the floor, Miss Theron.'

'I...'

But this time it was Darcy who interrupted. 'Why do you call her that?'

'He calls me that to annoy me, Darcy,' Kim said, shooting Reith a dark glance, 'but if you'll both desist, I thought that between you, you two, you could decide what you want to do tomorrow.'

'Ah,' Reith said.

'Wow!' Darcy said.

'So what'll it be?' She glanced from one to the other.

'How about,' Reith said thoughtfully, 'we take the chopper out to Rottnest?'

Rottnest Island, just eighteen kilometres off Perth in the Indian Ocean, with its secluded beaches and bays and its great surfing spots, was a tourist destination accessible by big ferries as well as helicopters and light planes. Darcy loved every minute of their time there.

Rotto, as it was affectionately known to the locals, was a car-free zone so they hired bicycles and explored some of the beaches, stopping to swim in the turquoise waters, as well as looking at some of its history, early buildings and the lighthouse.

They bought lunch from the famous local bakery and went quokka hunting, looking for the furry little marsupials for which the island was also famous.

Then, tired but exhilarated, they flew directly to Perth, where they dropped Darcy off at his boarding school and, for the first time, Kim detected a reluctance in Reith's son to go back.

He even hugged them both and extracted a promise from Kim to look after Rimfire, as well as thanking Reith for a really, really super day.

As the helicopter lifted off, Kim said to Reith, 'When will you bring him home?'

'At the end of the term. We'll have to decide what school to send him to in the district.'

She nodded. 'There are several.' And she found herself thinking out of the blue not so much of Darcy but, no doubt prompted by him, about being a mother herself, about starting a family. Probably a good idea not to leave it too long, from Darcy's point of view if nothing else.

She glanced at Reith. He was piloting the chopper himself on this occasion and concentrating on his flying.

'How do you feel about more children?' She put the question into words.

He glanced at her. 'I don't think we need to rush into it. What do you think?'

'Hmm,' she temporised, 'perhaps not.'

'We've only just got Darcy more or less sorted,' he added. 'We haven't even got him home yet.'

Kim stared straight ahead and wondered if she was imagining it, an undertone in his voice, a rather stark undertone that meant—what? That he wasn't that keen on having more children ever?

Then he was talking to an air-traffic controller through his mike and she was left thinking it was strange that they'd never discussed it before. Come to that there was quite a lot they'd never discussed. In fact, she mused, you could say their relationship was more like an affair from that point of view, couldn't you?

But she said no more and they flew home. And, despite the things they hadn't discussed, Kim found herself concentrating on the high points of the half-term weekend and feeling contented, with little inkling that it was to be short-lived.

The next morning Reith had an early appointment and would be away overnight. She gave him a quick kiss and told him to be back soon.

'No, you don't,' he told her. 'I need to be properly farewelled.'

She looked up at him, her blue eyes alight with laughter. 'You sound like some potentate.'

'Not at all,' he denied and put his arms around her.

'You're certainly well-dressed enough to be one.' She stood back a bit and studied his beautifully tailored navy blue suit with a navy waistcoat over a pale blue shirt and a lavender paisley tie and matching handkerchief in his breast pocket. Then she looked at him with a question mark in her eyes.

'A board meeting,' he supplied. 'Then lunch.'

'No women at either, I hope!'

He frowned. 'Probably. Why?'

'I don't think I should let you loose. They'll probably keel over in the aisles for you.'

'Kim—' he looked at her askance, as if not sure whether to take her seriously '—that's highly unlikely.'

'Oh, I don't know,' she said airily. 'I had it once on good—make that *very* good—authority that you were the most gorgeous, sexy man in the room—or words to that effect.'

He blinked. 'When?'

'The fashion parade.' She described the scene for him.

He started to laugh. 'Well, that explains it,' he said, still grinning.

'Explains what?' Kim raised her eyebrows.

'You were exceedingly angry with me that day. Remember?'

'Mmm…' She looked somewhat rueful. 'You're right. At the time, the fact that some exceedingly glamorous female thought you were God's gift to women did not appeal to me in the slightest.'

'You don't think it was a bit unfair to blame me?' he queried, his eyes wryly amused.

Her lips twitched. 'Not at all. OK—' she leant against him, put her hands on his shoulders and kissed him lingeringly '—off you go.'

He went but not before returning her kiss with extreme thoroughness so that she was both thrilled and shaken in roughly equal proportions, and quite distracted for the rest of the morning.

But part of her distraction, she felt, came from some curious mood swings. One moment she felt on top of the world, the next she could be deeply emotional. Only the day before, she'd discovered a dead bird in the garden, a colourful parrot that must have flown into a high wire and broken its neck. She'd wept as she'd buried it and been sad for hours.

Was it all to do with being deeply—and she couldn't doubt she was—in love? Was that why colours seemed brighter and small tragedies seemed darker?

Her mother came to morning tea that day.

Kim had never fully explained her marriage to Fiona. All the same, she'd assumed that her family understood there had been some sort of quid pro quo involved, although she'd subsequently refused to discuss it with any of them. How could you explain to your family that you'd been blackmailed into marriage on their behalf?

But now she could see that her mother was less troubled by it; in fact lately Kim had got the impression that she would like to give them her blessing.

It wasn't Reith that their discussion turned to, though, over Mary's special carrot cake and herb tea—it was Damien.

CHAPTER NINE

'I SEE so little of him,' Fiona said sadly.

Kim stirred her tea. 'He ignored me at the races. He was with a very exotic-looking blonde. Is he serious about her?'

Fiona shrugged. 'I don't know. He hasn't said and needless to say, I haven't met her.'

'At least bloodstock should suit him,' Kim murmured after a thoughtful pause between them, and was horrified to see her mother wiping away a tear. 'You're really upset about Damien—I wish there was something I could do.'

'In the end, all you really have is your family,' Fiona wept. 'I've learnt that lesson the hard way.'

Kim took herself for a ride after her mother had gone. It was a cool day, cloudy but with occasional patches of sunlight. The Darling foothills lay like sleeping behemoths on the western horizon beyond the dun winter paddocks.

As Mattie cantered towards a shallow creek, then splashed across, it seemed as if the birdsong, the thud of Mattie's hooves, the reins between her fingers and the creak of her saddle were the limits of her world.

She pulled up and dismounted alongside a huge gum tree with a water trough for stock beside it and a hitching post. There were also several tree stumps that made good seats.

She sat down on a stump after she'd let Mattie have a drink and tied her loosely to the hitching post. She stripped off her gloves and got up again to pull a slim plastic bottle of water in a padded container out of her saddle pocket. It had been iced water, it was now chilled water. She sipped as she sat back down on the tree stump and thought—*think, Kim!*

There's got to be something I can do to get Damien back. But how? And what would Reith think?

It struck her again that she still found Reith hard to read at times. Since the night they'd first made love there'd been no explanations—well, she herself had stopped him from explaining anything that night. But since then they'd said nothing about how they felt about each other, other than in a physical context. They hadn't discussed their life, they hadn't made any plans excepting his plans for Darcy, although now she did have the distinct impression he wasn't that keen on having more children.

But when he wasn't home, she went about her life much as she had ever since their marriage.

She spent the usual amount of time at Balthazar, in her garden, she entertained.

She had not, she realized suddenly as she watched Mattie switching her tail to discourage the flies, other than her quiet joy in their closeness, considered whether she would love Reith Richardson for ever, whether he loved her madly, as opposed to desiring her madly.

She'd lived from day to day, in other words, almost as if in a bubble, a bubble she shouldn't test or probe too much in case it burst on her…

But surely mending some fences with her brother couldn't burst the bubble? No, she wouldn't allow it to. She wouldn't allow Reith to dictate a stance to her on the subject of her brother. She would explain her mother's hurt, her own hurt, come to that. They may not have been that close but he was still her brother, he'd taught her to ride and, come to think of it, he'd vetted her boyfriends once she'd got to high school. Maybe it was a habit he hadn't got out of, she thought with a grimace.

In any event it saddened her, suddenly and tremendously, she realized, to think of Damien cut off from his family. And she was going to have to do something about it.

Later that day, dressed in a dark, warm but stylish trouser suit and with a small overnight bag, she got out her car. To his delight, Sunny Bob was invited to accompany her, and they set off for Perth.

The apartment was still being renovated, but that suited her. She didn't feel like encountering Reith until she'd laid her plans.

She booked into a handy motel, one that took dogs, then drove into the city centre, where Damien had an apartment.

She parked her car as close as she could get to the

building, which was not that close, but she decided a walk would help her crystallize her thoughts and decide what she was going to say to her brother.

A couple of hours later, she strolled back towards her car, marvelling at the revelations that had come from her meeting with Damien.

At first he'd been prickly and defensive and obviously not that happy to see her. Then, when she'd refused to take offence, he'd poured them both a drink and with a sudden harsh sigh, had told her that for most of his life he'd been trying to live up to their father's expectations of him as a wine-maker, when his heart wasn't in it. And then along had come Reith Richardson, who'd exposed not only his deficiencies as a wine-maker and a businessman but had married *her*.

'He made me feel so stupid,' he'd confessed.

'Deliberately?' Kim had enquired with a frown.

'No, not really,' Damien had conceded, 'but I could see the sheer acumen and the drive in him that I wouldn't ever have. Not unless it had to do with horses. And, on top of being about to lose Balthazar and Saldanha to him—well, I'm sorry, Kim—' he'd looked directly at her '—but there seemed to be only one way I could go and that was to hate him and try to belittle him through his background—or lack of it.'

She stopped walking and shook her head, still absolutely amazed at the complexities life threw up. She'd never imagined her suave, worldly brother—or that was how she'd seen him—could feel so inadequate. But at least she was several steps closer to reuniting the family. If only she could explain it all to Reith now...

She started to walk again and what she least expected to see was Reith coming out of a luxury hotel lobby with a woman beside him.

Not any woman, she saw, as she edged into the shadows along the inside of the pavement, but Chilli George.

A taxi was waiting at the kerb and Reith opened the door and gestured for Chilli to get in but she didn't, not immediately. She picked up Reith's free hand and placed it over her breast, and for a long moment both of them seemed to be etched in stone as they stared into each other's eyes. Then Reith took his hand away and Chilli got into the limo. Reith waited for it to draw away from the kerb before he turned and went back into the hotel.

Why didn't she just confront Reith? Kim wondered.

She'd gathered herself together after the little scene outside the hotel and she was back in her motel.

She'd brewed herself a cup of coffee but she wasn't sure why. Drinking coffee was the last thing she felt like doing. In fact the thought was thoroughly nauseating but what she really wanted to do—scream, shout, throw things, even smash things—was not permissible.

How *could* he?

When their marriage appeared to be going so well, when Darcy was coming to live with them, how could he be with another woman, but especially Chilli, she thought furiously, who had a reputation for chasing men?

And from fury she went to sorrow and found tears rolling down her cheeks.

Darcy—how would Darcy react? Would he go back

into his shell if she and Reith broke up? she wondered
as she tried to stem her tears with a tissue.

Would it come to that?

But how could she go on with him if she could never
trust him again?

She got up suddenly with a hand to her mouth, then
rushed to the bathroom where she was sick.

Emotion, she thought, as she rinsed her mouth and
studied her pale, mascara-streaked face in the mirror.

Or…?

She whirled on her heel and ran to find her purse.
She dragged her diary out of it and, with trembling fingers established, to her disbelief, that her period, which
usually came and went like clockwork, was two weeks
overdue. How could she have forgotten? Because she'd
been so over the moon and in love? But how could it
have happened?

She cast her mind back and it nearly broke her heart
to recall the one time she'd had unprotected sex with
Reith—a joyful coming together that had taken them
both by surprise and then, she'd reassured herself, it
wasn't the right time of the month for her to fall pregnant. So much for that theory, she thought. This was
the reality and the shock of it was huge.

So that was why she'd been so uneven lately, so
up, so down over nothing sometimes. Starving sometimes—she'd eaten two slices of Mary's carrot cake that
morning—then unable to face food.

She sank into an armchair, mentally reeling from
the impact of two huge revelations, then sat up precipitously. Was that why he didn't want any more children?

Did he view their marriage more as an affair, outside of which he could pursue another life?

Was it because of wretched Chilli George that he didn't want her, Kim, to have children? She covered her face with her hands and thought, distraught, that any woman other than Chilli George would not be quite so bad, but knew immediately she was kidding herself.

'Oh, Reith,' she whispered aloud, 'how could you do this to me? But don't think I'm going to take it lying down!' And she crossed to the phone.

'Ma'am, there's the red-eye flight,' the reservation clerk on the other end of the line told Kim. 'It leaves at midnight and gets into Brisbane at six thirty-five a.m. their time. You should be able to make it if you get to the airport shortly. We need a few extra minutes to process your dog.'

'I'll take it,' Kim responded.

The next day she sat on a veranda deck in Queensland, with an arm over Sunny Bob.

She was on the other side of the continent from Saldanha and Balthazar, from her parents, from Damien and, most especially, from Reith.

Most especially Reith because that hurt the most.

She'd hired a car and hunted around for accommodation that took pets, not that easy to find, so she'd kept driving. And, on a whim, she'd taken the car ferry across Moreton Bay, off Brisbane, to Russell Island, where, by chance, she'd found a house for rent where

Sunny Bob was welcome. It was also fully furnished and well-supplied with linen and everything she could need.

She'd paid the bond and a week's rent in advance and been invited to move right in with no further questions asked.

'You'll love it,' she'd been assured. 'Just watch out for the sandflies.'

Bearing that warning in mind, she'd stopped at the supermarket for some insect repellent as well as some essential supplies.

She'd been almost dead with tiredness by the time she'd let herself into the house and she hadn't taken much notice of it or the surroundings. She'd put the cold stuff in the fridge and collapsed on a sofa in the lounge.

She'd slept for hours.

Two days later, she was not only more alert, but she knew a bit more about her surroundings.

Her house was perched on a cliffside. The cliff ran down to what looked like a river but was called the Canaipa Passage and was the body of water that ran between Russell Island and North Stradbroke Island.

North Stradbroke rose across the water, uninhabited, opposite her house, and the birdlife was amazing. There were Brahminy kites with their deep bronze backs and wings, their snowy heads and their high free calls. There was a pair of White-breasted Sea Eagles that lived in the dark green jumble of foliage on a huge tree across the Canaipa. There were cormorants and shags, pelicans that paddled past, egrets and herons and black and white oyster catchers with their red beaks

and legs. Thanks to a coffee-table book about Moreton
Bay and a pair of binoculars, she was able to identify
most of them. She could also see fish jumping in the
water and wallabies foraging on the opposite shore.

She could identify the mangrove trees that lined the
shores on both sides of the passage. And, despite her
precautions, she'd received a couple of sandfly bites
and found them almost intolerably itchy.

Life on Russell Island was easy-going and laid-back.
A lot of the locals had boats and were keen fishermen.
And she'd walked as she tried to come to terms with
what she'd done. What she'd lost.

She'd sent a couple of text messages, one for her parents assuring them she was fine, one for Mary Hiddens
saying the same. Then her phone had died and she realized she didn't have the charger with her.

On the night of her second day, a full moon rose over
North Stradbroke Island and the colours of its great
blood-orange orb and then, as it got higher, the pearl-
pale radiance of the light it shed had been little short
of miraculous.

All the same, Kim had found herself sobbing suddenly because it was all so beautiful and she was so
alone and so devastated.

Sunny Bob put an anxious paw on her lap and she
wrapped her arms around his neck and wept into his fur.

'The thing is,' she told him as she sat up and fished
in her pocket for a tissue, 'I don't know if I did the right
thing. I came away because I just couldn't bear to go
back to the old hostilities that existed between me and
Reith. But is that cowardly? Am I hoping in my heart

of hearts that, despite all the precautions I took—and the fact that this is probably the last place he'd come looking for me—he will look?'

But why was he a womanizer anyway?

Her tearful thoughts slipped back to the night of Pippa Longreach's barbecue, the night she and Reith had first made love, but, before that, he'd told her why he was the way he was, then he'd demonstrated how implacable he could be.

How his mother's defection and his father's own brand of implacability and cynicism had shaped him. And through that confession she'd come to understand a little better the complex person who was Reith Richardson. It had to explain why it was hard for him to let anyone get too close. He'd even acknowledged that his first marriage had suffered from the exclusion zone without altogether acknowledging it.

Was this his way of maintaining that zone? By letting no one woman get too close to him?

She sat back and Sunny Bob settled at her feet.

'Anyway, lovely as it is, I can't sit around on Russell Island twiddling my thumbs for ever. What was I thinking?'

She answered her own question after a while. 'Not straight, just not able to face Reith.'

As for rushing into hasty decisions—was that what pregnancy did to you?

She got up and wandered out onto the deck.

Sunny Bob heaved a sigh but got up and followed her.

Not as cool as it was at home, nevertheless winter in Southern Queensland was chilly overnight and she drew her jumper more closely around her and folded her arms protectively over her belly at the same time as she thought—this should be such a joyous moment. I would love to have Reith's baby. Would he love to have our baby, though? And what about the 'other woman'?

'All the same, I think I'll have to go back.'

Her words seemed to echo as she stared out into the darkness.

There were ragged windy clouds partly obscuring the moon now and a south-easterly blowing up the passage. Twenty-five to thirty knots predicted for tomorrow, she recalled from watching the weather forecast on the TV news.

She shook her head, as if to say to herself, *concentrate!* and she repeated, 'I think we'll have to go back. I can't stay here for ever anyway and I need to sort things out, I need to make plans, I need to come back to earth…'

CHAPTER TEN

HER car was still parked in the long-term parking area at Perth Airport and not long after she'd landed she was driving down the Kwinana Freeway towards home, conducting a conversation with Sunny Bob.

'I've gone to a lot of trouble on your behalf,' she told him. 'It's not that easy to fly dogs around the country—actually it's easier to fly them than it is to do much else with them.'

Sunny Bob, curled up in the passenger seat, glanced at her reproachfully.

'Not that I'm holding anything against you,' she hastened to assure him. 'I don't know what I would have done without you. You've been a super friend.'

She patted him and grimaced because her nerves were jangling again. And concentrated on what she was going to say to Reith when she arrived at Saldanha.

Take hold, she advised herself. Don't, for heaven's sake, scream and shout at him. Don't get all emotional. Just tell him the truth. Tell him about the baby? Maybe. Maybe not yet...

But Reith wasn't there when she arrived home. Mary

was there and she gasped and burst into tears when she saw Kim.

'Oh, you shouldn't have, Kim,' she kept saying. 'We were so worried. Your parents...'

Kim comforted her as best she could and then asked the question that was burning on her brain. 'Where's Reith? Is he home? I believe he—'

'*Reith,*' Mary said with unmistakable venom. 'He's moved out and good riddance.'

Kim's mouth fell open at this absolutely uncharacteristic malice on the part of Mary.

'Where to?' she asked tonelessly.

'I don't know and I don't care,' Mary said militantly. 'Clover Hill, I believe. Oh, Kim...'

Kim hugged her again. 'Is he there now?'

'That I truly don't know. He could be but there've been all sorts of comings and goings. I believe he's here, there and everywhere.'

Kim went upstairs, where she showered and changed.

It was close to dusk and she put on a navy tracksuit and flat shoes. She left her hair loose with two wings pinned at the back. She put on no make-up other than lipgloss, but she sprayed a little perfume on. She noticed that her hands were shaking.

But, ready as she was, she still couldn't bring herself to go to Clover Hill. And she found herself wandering around the house, touching this and that, the old, old South African pieces, the silver- and copper-ware Mary kept so shiny. The lovely porcelain her grandmother had collected.

And she smiled at her renovations and how well she'd blended the new with the old. But the smile faded and a curious frown took its place. The old satisfaction she'd got from Saldanha and all its elegance, all its history seemed to have faded. In fact it seemed to have given way to a...what?

She looked around the lounge and realized what it was. A shivery little feeling woven in with the pleasure that told her the memories were mixed now; some were even memories she'd rather forget. It wasn't an entirely peaceful aura to Saldanha now.

She shook her head and wondered if she was being fanciful—and knew she could delay no longer.

Her car was in the garage but for once Sunny Bob looked less than enthusiastic about accompanying her.

She laughed. 'Have I taken all the wanderlust out of you, Sunny? OK, you can stay at home. I might be back soon myself, anyway.'

There were some lights on at Clover Hill but no one came to greet her when she parked opposite the front door.

There was a familiar gun-metal four-wheel drive parked on the gravel, though, and her nerves tightened.

But she forced herself to walk up to the front door and knock. There was no response, however.

Kim fought an almost overwhelming urge to run back to her car and drive away.

She tried the front door and it opened soundlessly under her hand. She took a very deep breath and walked in. There were lamps on in the lounge and one of the

French windows was open to the veranda. There was an untasted, by the look of it, glass of brandy on a side table.

'Anyone home?' she called softly.

There was no reply and something drew her to the open door to the terrace.

She stepped out into the darkness, made fragrant by the rose garden, and stopped dead as a tall figure loomed out of the twilight—Reith.

He stopped too and they simply stared at each other for an age. He wore jeans and a navy sweater. His hair was ruffled and his jaw was dark as if he hadn't shaved.

Then Kim made herself breathe normally and swallowed a couple of times. 'Reith,' she said huskily, 'I saw you with Chilli George in Perth a few nights ago. That's why I ran away. What was I doing in Perth? Not spying on you. I went up to see Damien, but that's another story.' She stopped abruptly as it struck her she'd forgotten about her brother in all the rest of it.

'I…' She put a hand up to her brow as she realized she felt a bit peculiar and wondered if her aversion to food was catching up with her. 'I…I mean you…well…' But she stopped again and this time her knees buckled and she would have fallen if he hadn't lunged forward and caught her.

The next few minutes were confused.

He picked her up in his arms and took her inside to lay her gently down on a settee. 'Stay there,' he warned.

She closed her eyes but it seemed like only moments later that he was back with a glass of brandy that he held to her lips.

She took a sip then pushed the glass away vehemently and sat up. 'No—'

'Kim,' he said quietly, 'it will help. Just—'

'No! No,' she said, 'you don't understand! I can't drink alcohol!'

'Why not?' He frowned.

'Because I'm…I'm…' She couldn't go on.

She saw the understanding that came to his eyes. 'Pregnant?'

'Yes.' Sudden tears streamed down her face. 'And on top of seeing you with another woman, a woman I *hate*, incidentally, I have no idea whether you want us to have children or if Darcy is the only family you want or if it's because of her you don't want more children—or what!' She couldn't go on as her throat started to hurt unbearably and she put her hand up to it.

He pulled up a chair and sat down facing her. 'Where were you?'

Her eyes widened. 'I… Queensland. A place called Russell Island.'

'Never heard of it.'

'Neither had I. It was…interesting and very peaceful. Reith,' she breathed, 'I—'

'I met Chilli,' he broke in and ran his hand gently over her hair, 'in the hotel lobby that evening. We bumped into each other, had a brief conversation—she asked after you, as a matter of fact. Then she said she had a taxi waiting for her and she invited me to have dinner with her. I declined and walked her out to the car. That's where she did something I was not ex-

pecting, an intimate gesture, I guess you could call it.'
He shrugged.

'Very intimate,' Kim said dryly.

'Very Chilli,' Reith responded, equally dryly. Then
he added levelly, 'But not me, Kim. Not me.'

She stared at him.

'I swear to you that's all there was to it.'

'You seemed…to be much struck,' she said raggedly.

A grim little smile twisted his lips. 'You could say
I got the surprise of my life. She's probably one of the
most predatory women I've ever met. She's certainly
not my type.'

Kim pushed herself upright. 'But, Reith, you don't
want more children, do you? You… I could tell in the
helicopter when I asked you, that you weren't keen and
it wasn't just a matter of taking our time.'

'Kim…' He picked up her hand and seemed to battle for words for a moment. Then he said simply, 'It
scares me.'

Kim blinked several times. 'Come again?'

'I've never quite forgiven myself for Sylvie's death. I
couldn't bear it if the same thing happened to you. But
tell me something, do *you* want this baby?'

There was a long pause as she searched his face,
then she said steadily, 'Reith, more than anything in
the world do I want your baby but—' she stopped and
gestured helplessly '—I sometimes feel as if we're having an affair rather than being married.'

'That could be because—' He paused, then went on,
'Because I can't help wondering whether you're going

to wake up one day and decide I'm not good enough for you.'

Her lips parted and her eyes were stunned. 'You... I don't believe it! Not you...' But, as she trailed off, thoughts of her brother Damien and his insecurities flashed across her mind.

'Really?' she said to Reith. 'Really, really?'

He took her hands in his. 'Really. In fact I thought that's what must have happened, that's why you'd run away.'

'No. Oh—' she grimaced '—I have to tell you, being pregnant does mysterious things to you. I've never made so many impetuous decisions in my entire life.'

He smiled but it faded and he rubbed the blue shadows on his jaw. 'I also wondered if you'd found out that I'd sold.'

'Sold?' she echoed.

He nodded.

'Sold what?'

He took a deep breath and his eyes never left her face. 'Saldanha and Balthazar.'

She gasped. 'What?' she whispered.

He nodded and saw the shock in her eyes. 'Kim,' he said intensely, 'there was never going to be any hope for us with those two thorny issues for ever between us. You were always going to be torn between me and your family.'

'I...I...' But she couldn't go on.

'If it's any consolation, they've gone to a South African consortium expanding their operations into

Western Australia. And they're happy to have your father on their board in an advisory capacity.'

Kim licked her lips. 'When did you do this?'

'It's been in the pipeline for a couple of months.'

'So you were thinking back then—even back then about me being torn?' she queried, her eyes huge with surprise.

'Yep.' He looked wry. 'You would have thought that might have alerted me to the way things stood for me regarding you.'

Kim stared at him. 'Mary,' she said agitatedly then. 'She's cross—she's *more* than cross with you! I don't understand. Why should she…?' She stopped.

He sighed. 'That's all my fault. When she told me you'd left with a bag and Sunny Bob but no hint of where you were going other than Perth, I told her, not pleasantly, that she should have stopped you. She then told *me* some home truths and—' he gestured '—we haven't got around to forgiving each other yet.'

Kim frowned. 'What home truths?'

'Along the lines of how I wasn't fit to kiss your feet, how she'd often wanted to strangle me because I was making you miserable.' He shrugged. 'That kind of thing.'

Kim put her glass down and the faintest shadow of a smile touched her mouth.

'You have no idea,' he continued gravely, but there was a little glint in his dark eyes that made her heart beat faster, 'the obstacles I've had to conquer for your fair hand, Kim Richardson.'

'Perhaps I can guess,' she said barely audibly. 'My

dog, my family and even my housekeeper. Oh, I forgot about causing you nearly to collide with a tree.'

'Kim.' His voice was unsteady and he stood up and this time there was a question in his eyes as he looked down at her.

Kim stood up slowly—and she flew into his arms. 'Oh, Reith, I love you! I've been so miserable, so…'

But he stopped her with his mouth on hers and he held her as if he'd never let her go.

'About Saldanha,' Reith said quite a bit later.

He'd lit a fire in the grate and closed the doors on the chill of the evening. He was sitting on the couch with her on his lap and he was slowly running his fingers through her hair.

'Mmm?' She looked up at him.

'Do you mind very much?'

Kim considered. 'No,' she said at last. 'I probably would have liked to think of a Theron always associated with Balthazar but you can't have everything.' She paused. 'Saldanha, though—I don't know how to describe it—but it doesn't seem to offer me peace any more, whereas this place does.' She looked around a little wonderingly.

'That's how I feel. As if we can leave all the trauma behind us and start afresh here.'

Hours later, she stirred in his arms.

The main bedroom had been furnished since she'd last seen it. It had a fireplace and there were glowing coals in the grate making flickering shadows on the walls. They lay beneath a light-as-air, warm-as-toast quilt.

'This Russell Island place,' he said, spanning her waist with his hands, 'must be well off the beaten track.'

'It is a bit.' She described it then said, 'Why?'

'It explains why I hadn't, to date, found you.'

'You looked?'

'Uh-huh.'

'Well, I ended up there mostly due to Sunny Bob—' She broke off and sat up. 'I told him I'd be back soon. Probably.'

The quilt slipped off her shoulders, revealing her to be naked to the waist. He removed his hands from her waist and cupped her breasts.

'He and Mary can console each other.'

Kim put a hand to her mouth. 'Her too! She'll be wondering.'

He plucked her nipples gently. 'Kim, they'll be fine.'

She took an unexpected breath. 'That's...not fair,' she breathed as she looked down at his strong hands on her breasts. She lay back and tremors of rapture and desire flowed down her body.

'I don't see what's unfair about it,' he replied.

'Well, we've already done this once tonight,' she reasoned.

'Who's counting?' he drawled and removed his hand from her breasts, only to start kissing them.

'Now that—' she had to take a very deep breath '—is very unfair. However, there's an old saying—what's sauce for the gander is sauce for the goose.'

He lifted his head and laughed down at her. 'It's the other way around.'

'Believe me, it can work both ways,' she advised as she trailed her fingertips down the hard wall of his chest, and lower.

It was his turn to suck in an unexpected breath and he swept her into his arms as they laughed together. Then he released her, but only to stare down at the sapphire-blue of her eyes, her red-gold hair, her lovely skin gilded in the firelight.

'Don't leave me again,' he growled.

'I won't,' she promised, and they made love for the second time.

CHAPTER ELEVEN

NEARLY eight months later, Darcy said, 'Wow, Kim, she's really, *really* tiny!' as he gingerly held a baby wrapped in a pink shawl.

'They usually are,' Reith murmured.

'Well, I knew that but—oh, she's going to cry. Here.' Darcy handed the little bundle hastily back to Kim, who was sitting propped up in bed in the same hospital where her friend Penny had had her baby—a baby that had, in a sense, thrown Kim Theron and Reith Richardson together.

Kim laughed as she took her newborn daughter back. 'No, she's not, she's just pulling a face. OK, guys! What are we going to call her?'

Reith looked down at her with his lips twitching. 'If I'm any judge, you've decided that yourself.'

Kim grimaced. 'I do have some ideas but I'm open to suggestions.'

Darcy looked at his father. Reith looked at his son.

Darcy said, 'We might as well let her decide. Saves time.'

'Yep,' Reith concurred.

Kim sat up, looking indignant. 'If you're suggesting that I always like to get my own way—'

'Always,' her husband and stepson broke in to agree.

Her expression defied description for a moment but the baby made a soft little gurgle and Kim looked down at her with a different expression entirely, one of such warmth and radiance that it nearly took Reith's breath away.

'Well,' she said, 'I suspect you'll attract a lot of names, sweetheart, *like* sweetheart, sweet pea, honey bunny, sugar bush, gorgeous—but to me you look like a Martha.'

Later, when they were alone, Kim said softly, 'You can relax now. There are no problems, no unforeseen complications.' But at the same time she blinked away some tears.

Reith looked a question at her.

'I was thinking of her.'

He sat on the bed and put his arms around her and they were quiet together in silent tribute to Darcy's mother.

Three months later, Martha Richardson was fast asleep, just, in her cot under the watchful eye of Mary Poppins, when her mother, dressed in a strapless sapphire gown that matched her eyes, descended the staircase at Clover Hill.

There was a spontaneous round of applause from the people grouped in the lounge. It was her birthday and her parents were there, Fiona in poppy-pink and look-

ing young and almost as elegant as her daughter; Frank
Theron looking distinguished in a dinner suit.

Damien was there with the same blonde, Lavinia,
Kim had seen him with at the races. They'd recently
married and Lavinia wore the most amazing silver
dress that moulded, and hid very little of, her figure.
Her hair was dyed platinum, her nails and lips were
painted black and she wore a quantity of rhinestones in
flamboyant jewellery. In spite of all this, she and Kim
had made friends and Kim had decided that she was a
shrewd, practical person and she certainly seemed to
have turned Damien round.

Reith and Damien could not be described as mates,
as Reith had predicted, but at least they mixed with
an apparent lack of hostility nowadays, and it was the
same with her father and Reith. Her mother, who'd always had plenty of respect for Reith, was now completely won over.

Pippa Longreach was there, in all shades of peacock-
blue. She'd ditched Lachlan and gone to the other extreme, a man thirty years older but with a lot—make
that a *lot*, she'd assured Kim—of money.

Bill and Molly Lawson were there.

Darcy was there, combed and ferociously clean.

And there was Reith, looking impossibly, darkly attractive in his dinner suit and snowy shirt, watching her
come down in a way that made her stumble slightly.

How does he do it? she wondered. How does he still
manage to make me feel sexy just by looking at me?

'Sorry,' she said lightly, 'I didn't mean to keep you
waiting but Miss Martha has only just decided to go to

sleep. Hello, Mum.' She walked up to her mother and hugged her. 'You look wonderful.'

'So do you, sweetheart, happy birthday!'

It was a happy dinner.

Mary Hiddens had forgiven Reith and moved over to Clover Hill, and she excelled herself on Kim's birthday dinner.

Then, just after the dessert had been cleared, Martha woke up, but not because she was cold, wet or hungry. So Kim brought her downstairs, where she put on, for a three-month-old, a bravura performance, smiling, gurgling and absolutely captivating all the guests.

'I'm not sure that this is such a good idea,' Kim said rather ruefully to Reith.

He looked down at her, 'Well, I've got the feeling she's going to be as much of a show-stopper as her mother.'

'I am not,' Kim denied.

'You are and I adore you for it,' he said quite casually, as if he was talking about the price of eggs. 'For example, if you hadn't danced into the middle of the road exposing your legs, I might never have met you.'

'You're never going to let me forget that, are you?'

He shrugged. 'Possibly not. Look at that,' he added with a smile in his voice as he gestured.

Kim looked in the direction he'd indicated and her eyes fell on Darcy, now holding his half-sister with a lot more confidence. If there was one person Martha loved above all, it was Darcy.

Kim felt a wonderful, warm glow flow through her

as she watched the baby and the boy. Now that's an achievement, she thought.

'What's this?' she said to Reith when all the guests had gone home, when Darcy was asleep and Martha was too, and Mary had closed herself into her own quarters.

'You may not have noticed but I didn't give you a birthday present,' he replied.

They were sitting on the veranda in the moonlight with the heady scent of the roses around them, having an Irish coffee. They had a candle in a glass on the table beside them.

'You've given me so much, Reith! I don't need a birthday present.'

'Yes, you do,' he contradicted. 'You need this, anyway.' And he put a velvet box tied with silver ribbon down on the table beside her.

Kim drew a careful breath, untied the ribbon and flicked open the box.

It was a ring, an exquisite square sapphire surrounded by diamonds on a gold band.

Reith got up and took the ring out of the box. Then he lifted her left hand and slipped it onto her ring finger on top of her wedding band.

She stared down at it, then looked up at him, and she didn't resist when he pulled her to her feet.

'Thank you,' she said huskily. 'It's beautiful.'

He drew her into his arms and said against her hair, 'I wish I could tell you how much I love you.'

'You have. You do.'

'So that you believe me, I mean. So that you never feel you have to run away because I don't love you.'

'Reith, I believe you,' she said, then smiled up at him. 'I really, *really* believe you.'

* * * * *

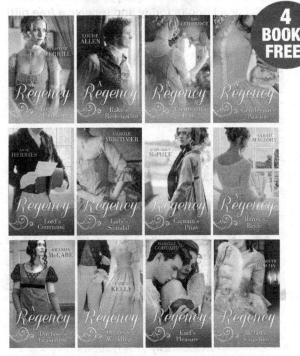
915_ST19

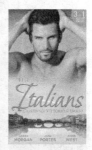

MILLS & BOON®
By Request

RELIVE THE ROMANCE WITH THE BEST OF THE BEST

A sneak peek at next month's titles...

In stores from 20th November 2015:

- **Scandal in the Spotlight** – Lucy King, Kimberly Lang & Anne Oliver

- **His Forbidden Conquest** – Kate Hardy, Aimee Carson & Kate Hoffmann

In stores from 4th December 2015:

- **Propositioned by the Prince** – Jennifer Lewis

- **A Diamond for Christmas** – Susan Meier, Scarlet Wilson & Patricia Thayer

Available at WHSmith, Tesco, Asda, Eason, Amazon and Apple

Just can't wait?
Buy our books online a month before they hit the shops!
visit www.millsandboon.co.uk

These books are also available in eBook format!